Colin Butler

DANGEROUS KNOWLEDGE

AUSTIN MACAULEY PUBLISHERS™
LONDON • CAMBRIDGE • NEW YORK • SHARJAH

A CIP catalogue record for this title is available from the British Library.

ISBN 978-1-78612-735-8 (Paperback)
ISBN 978-1-78612-736-5 (eBook)

www.austinmacauley.com

First Published (2017)
Austin Macauley Publishers Ltd.™
25 Canada Square
Canary Wharf
London
E14 5LQ

I

Long Shadows from the Past

Chapter 1

Control through Fear

It all began with an oil find off Sakhalin Island, a run-down Russian military outpost between Japan and the Arctic. The Russians couldn't raise the oil, so they asked in ExxonMobil, and Exxon were only too pleased to oblige, since the Cold War was supposed to be over and there was big money in it. They built an HQ, expanded the airfield, and a lot of the traffic came in from Moscow. Plenty of apparatchiks wanted a finger in the pie.

So, at 9.25 on a late June morning, a routine flight from the Russian capital touched down and taxied towards the terminal. Out came the steps, and three middle-aged functionaries in suits that weren't quite Western made their way down them with their overnight bags and their would-be wide-awake looks. They'd been in the plane for nearly nine hours, and their biological clocks were saying it was still only 2.25 am.

Behind them and keeping his distance came a fourth figure. He wouldn't see sixty again, his hair was close-cropped, and he had the jowly look of a strong man who had seen better days. Unlike the others, he wore his coat buttoned up, and he had a black leather document case under his arm. If he was short of sleep, it didn't show. He was listed as Industry and Trade like the rest; but as the others suspected, he was in the SVR, the Foreign Intelligence Service that succeeded the KGB. He had to be senior – he had the aura – and they got that right as well. He was a colonel, his name was Zembarov, and the Kremlin's dark places were his natural habitat.

In the Arrivals lounge, beneath an oversize photo of a stern-looking President Putin, a hostess from Exxon Hospitality did the greetings in Texas-accented Russian. Outside, two Ford SUVs were waiting; but when the gladhanding stopped, no one moved to the exit. Instead, a man in his early thirties who'd been hovering behind the Exxon hostess stepped forward through the pause and tensely shook hands with Zembarov as if there was no one else in the room. Everyone knew it was Oleg Dvorski, Industry and Trade's Johnny-on-the-Spot. Normally he'd be doing the greetings himself, but not this time. And when the first Ford headed off for Exxon HQ, he and Zembarov had the second one to themselves.

Their driver set off northwards without being told. There was plenty to take in, but Zembarov kept his eyes straight ahead, so Dvorski did the same. He kept his mouth shut as well. If he moved at all, it was to scratch his neck nervously or touch his right ear – its top part had been missing from birth. When they reached the Chayvo wellsite way up in the north-east, the driver halted in front of a quick-build office block and smartly opened their doors for them.

"I'll call you when we're ready," Dvorski told him. "Make sure you get here fast."

His office was one floor up. He made some tea while Zembarov settled in, then sat down opposite him and waited. He was in the SVR himself, and his career had been shaping up nicely, but the U-turn from liberal Boris Yeltsin to hard man Putin had left him seriously off-message. Worse yet, an Exxon oceanographer he'd turned was trying hard to dump him. If she managed it, he was finished.

Zembarov reached up and put his cup on Dvorski's desk. He'd been one of Dvorski's mentors once, but Dvorski had free-wheeled away from him, and he'd only contacted the aging hardliner because he had no one else to turn to. Kindred spirits didn't come into it. There weren't any.

"You were right to ask for help, Oleg Aleksandrovich," Zembarov said neutrally, pulling a thin sheaf of notes out of his document case. "This Dandy Torelli looks far too valuable to lose. Tell me what you know about her, I'll see if my briefing says the same. We don't want any crossed wires if you're planning a killing."

Dvorski's mouth was Sahara-dry from nerves. He poured more tea for both of them and got under way.

"Her first name's Amanda, but everyone calls her Dandy because she's smart to look at and very, very smart up top. She grew up in Florida and studied there as well. Her doctorate was on mapping the Caribbean seabed, and Exxon snapped her up when she was less than half way through, that was how much they wanted her. She's been top of the range here, she's had paid time to finish her doctorate, and Exxon want to hang on to her, but she's going to a British company called Klemmsley Oil and Gas. She says she needs North Sea experience, but what she really wants is to get away from us. She's told me that to my face more than once."

Zembarov shook his head in disbelief. Was she really so naïve?

"Betrayal's permanent," he mused. "She must know that. Tell me, how did you turn her?"

"Sakhalin was her big chance, but she needed a visa and a work permit to come here. So the deal was, if she leaked us Exxon know-how, she could have them on a plate. If not, she wouldn't get a look-in. She soon worked that one out, but now the shine's worn off."

"And you want to murder her father to keep her working for us. One moment ..." he ran his eye down his notes. "Ah, yes, here we are ... Jethro Torelli, Professor of Physics in the University of Florida. That's the same university his daughter went to. He's a camera specialist, I see."

"Cutting edge: Underwater cameras are one of his lines, and he spends his summers testing them in a place called Miranda Cove. That's at the Bahamas end of Florida on the Atlantic side. He's got a boat there and a cottage, so it's business and pleasure combined. Dandy says he's more in the water than out, and when I asked about sharks, she said tiger sharks for sure, but not in Miranda Cove, because the feeding was better further up. She should know, Florida's where she grew up; but I began to think at least one tiger shark might be persuaded in while her father's paddling about. What I need from you is help to make it happen."

"How will killing her father keep her with us?"

"I'll make it look like an accident, but I'll also get her to guess I set it up. That'll make her think, if I can do something as horrific as that, I've got no limits."

"And?"

"She'll be totally afraid of me. Every knock on the door, every creak of the stairs at night could be me. I'll control her through her fear."

"So you're expecting to go to England when she does. You must be. It follows from what you've just said."

Dvorski slammed on the brakes. This was dangerous. Where, when and how long he went for weren't for him even to think about.

"I can't expect anything, I know that very well," he grovelled. "But it'd make things work better if I did go."

"And are you also expecting to go to Miranda Cove? To make things work better, as you put it?"

He had been, he'd been wanting it to be all his own show. But not now, not in a thousand years.

"I was going to ask your advice about that," he mumbled, and chewed his lower lip.

Zembarov ran through his notes again, put them away and looked at his watch.

"Send for my car," he said as he got to his feet. "I have to get back to the terminal. You're not going to Miranda Cove, you'd be far too close if you did, but I can persuade someone I know into telling you what it's like there. Then you'll need someone to entice your shark in. I'll make enquiries. Now, my car, please."

Dvorski heard from Zembarov four days later. He said he'd be arriving the following day and Dvorski was to keep the morning clear. He'd made good progress.

Zembarov flew in once again on the 9.25 from Moscow, this time with some Americans who'd had time off, and Dvorski was just as tense this time round. Once they'd reached his office, Zembarov pulled an unlabelled video cassette out of his document case, said he'd checked the compatibility in Moscow, and asked for the blinds to be dropped.

"The man you're about to see," he said, speaking out of the shadow beyond Dvorski's desk lamp, "is a German named Peter Busch. He spent his working life in Bonn in the Ministry of Defence, and as long as Germany was divided, he worked for us as well. He was never found out. He still lives in Bonn, and I've contacted him through intermediaries I can trust. He's on video because it would be too dangerous for you and him to be seen meeting. I'll ask you to play it."

Apart from being bald, the years-long traitor didn't look much like a pensioner as he gazed straight into the camera and relaxedly said his piece. A plain curtain hung down to the floor behind him, a bed sheet hid the carpet, and he sat in a camping chair that could have come from anywhere. He spoke in not-quite English, since Dvorski didn't speak German. Zembarov spoke both languages, but he kept quiet about his English. He didn't want people thinking he was soft on the West.

"Good day," Busch began. "Please forgive me that I do not say your name, but it is best that it remain a secret between us.

"I am retired now and I go to Miranda Cove often. I went there for many years when my wife was living, but now I go alone. I get a temporary stay permit and I rent a cottage.

"Here is my advice to you.

"Russians never go to Miranda Cove, so do not send one. But some English sometimes go there because their *Angling Times* magazine carries little advertisements for it. You must therefore send an English person or better, an English pair, that can handle a boat and fish, because that is what most people do there. I am going again during July, and I am staying for one month. Your English pair must come for the first week in August, and they must not go home before the week is over. They will rent a cottage from Nancy's Bar on the quayside and a fishing boat from The Boat Hut, which is near. They can do that in advance. They will also eat from Nancy's Grill, which is part of Nancy's Bar. I sit outside it, and Professor Torelli also uses it. I must know what they look like, and they must recognise me, but they must not speak with me until I speak with them. Then I will tell them about Torelli and how to lure a tiger shark towards him. Torelli says a lot about what he is doing, and he also puts it on the internet. It is certain he will be there in the first week in August."

The picture shut off, leaving random flashes on the screen. Dvorski stopped the tape, wound it back, and handed the cassette to Zembarov, who packed it away.

"Did he have to know my name?" Dvorski asked nervously. "Isn't that dangerous?"

"I don't think so, and it got you a better response. He's completely trustworthy, we know that from all the years he worked for us, and in any case, we keep him under constant threat of exposure. So your name is safe with him, and his tape stays with me. Now, raise the blinds and make us some tea. I'm not leaving till tonight this time."

Dvorski toned down his unease, he felt the old man was on his side, and that had to make things right. He poured the tea and waited for Zembarov to speak again. When he did, he took Dvorski by surprise.

"You will be leaving with me tonight, and from Moscow you will fly to London. Your cover will be Ministry business. You will stay in safe accommodation near our embassy, where your contact is Andrey Ivanovich Valkov. He is on the Diplomatic List as a Principal Attaché, but he is SVR like us. He has identified a married couple who could be your assassins. He will help you all he can, but the face-to-face work is yours. If all goes well, you may yet get posted to England when Dandy Torelli goes. This afternoon you will need to pack only enough to travel with. Everything else is waiting for you in London, and your papers are ready in Moscow."

Zembarov finished his tea, and when the car came to take him on to Exxon HQ, he took his leave with something resembling a thaw on the way. Alone in his office, Dvorski was doing his best to control his glee when the phone rang. It was Dandy Torelli. Her voice was fresh and confident, like the photos on her files.

"Oleg, I want you to do me a favour," she said in English. His own was perfect, he'd been fully trained, but she wouldn't have learned Russian if she'd been stood against a wall. "My Daddy's sent me a brand new camera on the Exxon shuttle. He put a note in with it, and I'll read it to you so you'll know why I'm calling. Are you listening?"

"Of course. Go ahead."

"It says, 'A new toy for our clever little girl to try out. Have one picture only taken – I repeat, one picture only – of your pretty self, and send the camera back to me so I can take it apart and see what's happened inside. There's no film to wind. It's one of these new-fangled digital cameras, and I need to know how it works – Love, Daddy.' So, Oleg, can I ask you to take one picture only of my allegedly pretty self? It'll be like saying goodbye ahead of time."

Dvorski savoured the irony. If only she knew! Yes, of course he'd take the picture, he'd do it right now. Where was she?

"In the gym. I've just finished my work-out."

"Stay right there. I'll come over."

He put the phone down and went out, locking his door behind him. Outside, the air was still, and the Sea of Okhotsk smelled fresh. He'd suggest no grand background for the photo, just her face with a big smile on it. Maybe her Daddy would send her a print; he'd have plenty of time before August came round. She could hang memories on it after the shark had got him.

Chapter 2

Dvorski Pays a Visit

The Russian Embassy in London was a white-painted mansion in Kensington Palace Gardens. From the outside it looked sinister and watchful. On the inside it was sumptuous in a wanting-to-impress kind of way. Dvorski knew it from visits he'd made, but as he sat waiting for Valkov in the library, he didn't feel like an add-on any more, he felt he was almost part of the place. Valkov was one of the privileged few to have an apartment in the Embassy. Dvorski had never met him, but then that changed, and they took the lift to the third floor, where Valkov had his office. It was a plushly-furnished corner room with a heavily varnished door and thick gauzes over the windows that stayed firmly together.

Valkov was in his mid-fifties, and he'd been in London for thirty years. Impeccably dressed and as smooth as the skin of a snake, no one could have sounded more sincere as he asked Dvorski how he was finding his flat. Then, over fresh-brewed Colombian coffee, he got down to business.

"Colonel Zembarov asked me to find a killer for you by the time you arrived here. It had to be someone you had no connection with, and also someone who was either reliable or," he pulled a bulky beige folder from a drawer in his desk, "who could be made so. I've done that. In fact I've found two, which I gather is better still."

Dvorski was impressed and took care to show it.

"Come," Valkov responded languidly, "it wasn't so difficult. Part of our work here is to cultivate vermin who might one day be cleaners, canteen staff or whatever in places we want to know about. We've been tracking a back-street garage owner named Miller – Chris Miller. He and his wife, who shortens her name to Becky, live some ninety miles north of here in a place called Peterborough. He's been on the make for some time, but his last effort was a notch higher than bogus MOTs. He tried to break into a tyre depot, and he only got off because a key witness was afraid to testify. His accomplices – there were four of them – didn't inspire the same reluctance, so they're now gracing Her Majesty's prisons. Nothing like that would have happened if Miller had been in charge. He's not just ruthless, he's clever. That's why officially he's got a clean sheet."

"Was he armed, this Miller?"

"No. Two were, but he wasn't."

"Then he's no use, Andrey Ivanovich. I need a killer, not a tyre thief. What makes you think he's so good?"

"Take care," Valkov came back sharply. "You're speaking out of turn." Then, all charm again, "His psychogram makes me think he's so good. His wife's is positive too. We read him as a shrewd operator, and he'll kill on three conditions: if it's in his interest, if the reward is big enough, and if he thinks he can get away with it. He's highly confident, but he doesn't like people going behind his back."

"And his wife?"

"If he's for it, so is she; she's got an anxious streak, that's all. They're both tired of being hard up; they want to be rich like the people they see in the media. That's why they haven't got children. They don't want to share with anyone; they want it all for themselves."

"How do they feel about each other? That could matter when they come under pressure."

"Good question. He's deeply in love with her, but he's also male dominant, so he probably never tells her. She's never grown up. She thinks she's in love with him, but that's because he gives her what she wants. Plus the fact that, so far as we know, there's no one else on the horizon."

Valkov glanced at his watch. The coffee cups were empty, and he didn't offer any more.

"In my view, they're exactly what you need," he said with carefully measured insistence, "and you will take them without argument. Miller shuts his garage at five. At two o'clock this afternoon you will be waiting on the pavement outside your flat, and a dark blue Renault Mégane will pull up. The driver will be middle-aged, with thinning grey hair. He'll be called Mike and he'll take you to Peterborough. In the Renault will be a small suitcase containing 250 used £20 notes. They're the Millers' to keep if they accept your deal. If not, bring them back. But you must let them handle them first, that's important. There'll be a loaded Beretta in with the notes, a Cougar 8000. It's there to make an impression. We think it will."

"What's their pay-off?"

"£150,000 in cash and untraceable to us, plus expenses and the £5000 from the suitcase; it will seem big money to them. They'll want it a lot."

He glanced at his watch again, tapped the beige folder and reached towards a small console.

"When I press this button," he said, "one of my assistants will lock you in a room down the corridor and stay with you while you go through this folder. It contains all you need to know for this afternoon and includes some photos. When you've finished reading, you will give it back and be shown out of the building. You will brief me here tomorrow at 10.25. I shall expect good news."

Dvorski's heart sank as he combed through the surveillance reports, the hacking transcripts and the press cuttings the folder contained. But then came a section headed 'The Millers and Peterborough', and he'd have punched the air if Valkov's assistant hadn't been staring at him from three feet away. He'd found the leverage he needed. When he left the Embassy he felt everything had to go right, and he still felt that way when, at two o'clock sharp, Mike drew up in the Renault.

Mike stayed well within the speed limits up the A1, and when he spoke, which wasn't often, he sounded as if he came from Birmingham. It was eight minutes to five when he turned into Queen of Scots Lane and halted outside Millers' Repair Shop and Sales. Eight or nine used cars were standing on the forecourt, their selling points blazed out in multi-coloured felt-tip and stuck to the windscreens with Blu Tack. Behind them was the way in, and Dvorski could see Becky Miller sitting in what looked like a cinema box office. Its lights were on and she was typing something from a sheaf of A4 into a computer. Next to the sheaf was a half-read copy of *Bella*. Her hair was platinum, her lips and nails were crimson, and she wore large shell earrings. A nearby door in the wall must be the one she'd come through if she had to come into the foyer. Further along was another door. Dvorski guessed it led into the workshop.

"I'll park on the forecourt," Mike said, and without waiting for a reply, he pulled in next to a faded Rover 400. After he'd switched the engine off, he rootled around in the glove box.

"Here's the key to the suitcase," he went on, handing it over. "It's in the boot under a blanket, you can get it as you go. Take all the time you need, I'll stay right here."

Dvorski hesitated, the way Mike spoke struck him as out of order. He thought Mike was just a driver.

"You're not coming in then," he said uncertainly.

"I might have to testify against you one day. What I don't hear, I can't tell."

"Ah, yes, sorry. I can see that now."

Still rattled but determined not to show it, he got the case out, settled mentally into the role he'd decided on, and pushed the plate glass door open. Becky raised her head with a smile, but it froze as she took him in. She'd seen that look too often, it always meant trouble. Without appearing to move, she pressed a button in the floor with her foot.

"Can I help?" she asked, less confident than she sounded. "It'll have to be quick, we close at five."

As she spoke, the workshop door opened and Chris Miller came through, wiping his hands on a rag.

"Perhaps I can help instead," he said evenly. "Tell me what you want and I'll see."

"My name's Sanderson," Dvorski replied, pronouncing his English with an overlay of Slavic. The Millers thought in clichés, he knew that from their psychograms, and he wanted 'Russian mafia' to float up in their minds. "Shut your garage first, please. Then we'll talk in private. Just you, me, and Mrs Miller."

Chris glanced past him to the Renault outside. Dvorski saw him do it.

"No, I'm not alone," he said, into his part now. "I'm not so foolish. And I'm not used to waiting either."

When the front lights were out and the steel bars were all in place, he asked for all the CCTV images of himself and the Renault to be erased and watched while Becky did it.

"Now switch the whole thing off," he ordered, and she did that as well.

"The CCTV's my responsibility," she told him without being asked. "I can repair it as well. I put a new hard drive in three weeks ago. We save money if I do it."

She wanted to talk herself up, but all she did was sound scared.

Dvorski let Chris lead the way into the workshop. Built into a corner was a brick-and-glass office where Chris did his car deals. He unlocked the door and switched the lights on.

"I'll sit behind the desk," Dvorski said.

Chris cleared it by piling everything onto the floor, Dvorski occupied his swivel chair, and the Millers sat facing him. On the wall behind them was a trophy cabinet containing sea fishing cups, shields and photos. There were photos on the walls as well, and not only of fishing. Three recent-looking ones showed the Millers, gun in hand, on a pistol-shooting range. Dvorski filed them away in his memory. Then he unhurriedly unlocked the suitcase, put the Beretta where he could reach it, and laid the bundles of banknotes out.

"These are all twenties," he said, placing a hand on the Beretta. "I'll ask you to count them. Both of you."

It didn't take them long, and Dvorski saw their manner change as they felt the notes. They were touching real money, and their fingers were burning.

"You agree you're looking at £5000?" he asked, and they nodded. "Accept my offer and it's yours. If you say no, I'll take it away and make sure you tell no one what I've said."

He let his words sink in.

"What do you want us to do?" Chris asked, trying not to sound eager, and Dvorski knew he had him – and his greedy wife. Now he had to persuade them to commit murder.

He began with the fishing trip to Florida. No, they'd never been to Florida, but yes, their passports were valid, and yes again, they could close the garage for the first week in August. He told them about Peter Busch, and finally he came out with it: he wanted them to kill someone while they were over there. His name was Jethro Torelli.

"You'll get £150,000 in cash," he went on before they could speak. "That's on top of the £5000 in front of you. Your expenses will be covered as well. All of them."

He let them weigh up the trade-off. £150,000, that was serious money, but could they get away with it? It was as if they were thinking out loud.

"It's Torelli's life for the life you've dreamed of," he prompted. "And it's completely risk-free. Accidents with sharks happen all the while. No one will know this one was any different."

They were nearly there, but not quite, so Dvorski hardened his gaze, tapped the Beretta, and focused on what he'd read in the Embassy that had cheered him up so much.

"I know more about you than you think," he went on. "You're small crooks now, but you're on the way up – that's what our records say. Sadly, in small places like this, if someone goes up, someone else has to come down. That's why you've both got contracts out on you. A certain person's ordered one try on you both already. And it won't be the last one, will it?"

Becky grasped Chris's hand.

"But," Dvorski continued, "I can stop all that for good, if you make it worth my while. So, what do you say? Is it a deal or isn't it?"

Chris spoke for both of them. Dvorski had convinced him, but he didn't want to show it too soon.

"Tell us who you are first. Then tell us why we can trust you."

"Who I am is my business, and we'll leave it at that. As for trust, you can trust me step by step. First, there'll be no more threats on the phone and no one following you when you go out. Second, your expenses will be covered as they happen – I'll tell you how before I leave. Third, Peter Busch will be waiting for you in Florida. If he isn't, you get a free holiday on me. Check it all out and see for yourselves."

Chris felt his wife's hand relax.

"It sounds all right to me," she said. "I'm for it. What about you, Chris?"

"OK," he said, trying to sound cool. "It's a deal."

Dvorski took fifteen minutes more to get the Millers organised. That included fitting a small flat stud into their mobiles.

"They're your end of voiceprint neutralisers," he explained. "British authorities are like mine, they record people's phone calls. So I'll always speak in a roundabout way, I'll use different phones, and the neutraliser will make sure no one will know who's talking. That way we'll all be safe."

He locked the suitcase on the Beretta and came round the desk. Before he asked for the front door to be opened, he said,

"Don't restart the CCTV till I'm out of sight. And every time I come here in future, or anyone else comes in my place, make sure none of the images are kept."

"How will you know?" Becky asked.

"We'll check, and be warned – it's not in your interest to play games. I can say much more about you than you can about me, and I can also hurt you physically. Understood?"

She nodded, and as she stood up, he gripped her face.

"You've got a pretty wife, Miller," he said, remembering what Valkov had said about him. "Make sure she stays that way."

On the forecourt, Mike took the key and the case without getting out, and pointedly tested the case's weight before he reached it onto the back seat. Then, while Dvorski was putting on his seatbelt, he put a hand in the glove box and pulled out a radio microphone Dvorski didn't know was there. He clicked it on – the wavelength must have been pre-set – and switched to 'Encode'. Then, in fluent Russian, he said the deal was done and they were on their way back. As before, he drove mostly in silence.

The Millers made their bookings the same night, totted up the cost, and placed a pre-agreed car ad featuring the sum in the *Peterborough Telegraph*. It was covered in cash by courier the day it appeared. There were no more threatening phone calls either, and they were both in bucket-and-spade mood when, on the only flight they could get for the day Dvorski wanted, they took off from London Heathrow at 6.40 am. They had to wait three hours in Manchester to change planes, but they'd still be in Florida by 3.00 pm local time, and that was just fine. Any later, and they'd have felt they'd blown a whole day with someone else footing the bill.

Chapter 3

Murder in Plain Sight

Orlando was like an oven when the Millers got off the plane. The glare was lacerating and heat shimmered up from every hard surface. Not that they cared, they were in a place they'd only dreamed about till now. Once they'd cleared Immigration, they headed for the Hertz outlet, picked up a pre-booked Chevrolet, and set off for their motel. It was about 100 miles down the coast. Chris snapped the air conditioning on full, and Becky riffed through the radio stations. It didn't matter what was on them, just hearing them made her laugh and squeal. When she found one playing golden oldies, she stayed with it, and they belted out the bits they knew.

"All this for free!" Chris shouted, and he pounded the wheel with the flat of his hand. "And 150 big ones to come! Can you believe it, Becky?"

"I can now, Chris, but how're we going to spend it? You know what people are like. The first thing they'll ask is where it comes from."

He blew her a kiss.

"Leave it to me, Sweetie. I'll get a bank loan and mix Sanderson's money in with it. It's time we had a new garage. We'll call it Mafia Motors."

He threw his head back and laughed with his mouth wide open. Becky hooped and shrieked with him.

"Oh, Chris," she burbled, and went back to her mental wish list.

Their overnight stay took them into Friday, and Miranda Cove was only two and a half hours further on, so they'd have most of the day there. When they arrived, they parked by Nancy's Bar and picked up the keys to their cottage. Next came emptying their suitcases, sucking down two long cold drinks, and savouring a Nancy's Grill Special – all at a nice, slow pace. Then more sun cream and a leisurely stroll to The Boat Hut's marina. They soon spotted the boat they'd hired. It was a new-looking Albemarle 285 with 'Bluebell' in gold-edged blue caps on both sides of the prow. It had a range of rods sticking up from their holders, and it was theirs for the week. They relished the tingle as they took it all in, then they stepped into the Hut.

"She draws three feet, that's all, so you can go most places," the counter clerk told them. Her name tag said Gracie-Jane. "No worries about rocks, they're all marked with buoys. Keep your speed down, no one moves fast around here. And don't foul any lines."

"We can buy bait here, can we?" Chris asked as he signed the paperwork and took the keys.

"You name it, we have it. And diesel's on the quayside fifty yards down. You put your card in and help yourself."

Miranda Cove was a tapering inlet about three miles long. At the narrow end was a white sandy beach. The shallows off it were turquoise, and the air smelled relaxed and salty. One- and two-storey cottages dotted the northern side, and each one had its own jetty. The south side was mostly quayside where it was built up at all, and Nancy's Bar had a good piece of it. A notice on the lifeguards' boathouse ordered, 'No motorised craft in the swimming zone', and mooring buoys for fishing began where the seabed shelved away. Quite a few buoys were available, though some would get used over the weekend. Hard sell had yet to reach Miranda Cove. Its emblem – a pelican dozing on a post – got it right.

The sun was as hot as it had been in Orlando, so the Millers opted to get onto the water. Chris switched the twin Volvos on, Becky untied the ropes, and they moved slowly away from the quayside. Sunset was just after eight, so time wasn't a problem.

After he'd got the feel of the boat, Chris called Becky into the cabin from the open rear deck, where she was inspecting her hair in a hand-mirror. She'd dyed it ripe corn, her lips and nails were tangerine, and her earrings were miniature anchors. Chris had said they'd be all right.

"Don't stare," he said, turning his head very slightly to port as she came through the canvas flap, "but that's Torelli over there. He's fishing off the side of the Sea Ray."

Becky pulled her Polaroids down from her hair, followed Chris's gaze, and there he was, a rotund, grey-bearded man in baggy cotton shorts, a well stretched button-up shirt, and a floppy hat. He looked exactly like the picture Sanderson had got to them, along with one of Busch. Becky thought he was asleep, but then he waved casually, so they waved back. His boat was twenty years old and looked it. 'Dandy One' it said in peeling orange letters towards the stern.

"So he's the one," Becky murmured, the friendly smile fixed on her face.

She imagined a tiger shark closing in on him. Would it bite his side out or take off a limb? Or even crush his head? They crushed live turtles, she'd found that out on the internet. She stopped herself in mid-flow, she was scaring herself, but the thought of a gaping mouth lunging in from nowhere stayed with her. Chris didn't notice anything, he wasn't looking her way.

"He's the one, Becky. 150 grand's worth of blubber. I'm glad I've seen him. It's getting real now."

Becky stayed in the cabin for the rest of the ride round. She said it was too hot outside, but the truth was, she didn't want to be on her own any more. Chris pottered towards the Atlantic end of the cove, taking care not to create a wash. When he got there, he held his position so they could have a good long look. Behind them was the closed-in cove and ahead was the open sea. There were any number of craft out there, bright in the afternoon sunlight, but after a while the Millers didn't like it where they were, and they said so. They felt there was big danger about.

"Chris, let's go back, I'm not happy," Becky said, and Chris was glad to move into the cove again. When they were well in, Becky came back to how she'd felt.

"There must be hundreds of sharks out there," she said. "Big ones, too. It's just we can't see them, that's all."

Chris kissed her and gave her a protective squeeze.

"One's enough," he said. "The rest can do as they please."

"How are we going to get it in here though?"

"We'll find out soon enough. Maybe tonight, maybe tomorrow, it's up to Peter Busch. I'm going to moor up for a bit and go through the rods. What are you going to do?"

"Enjoy being here now we're back in the cove. I'll sit and watch."

It was close on four thirty when they re-passed Dandy One on their way to the marina. Torelli didn't see them this time; he was under water with his scuba gear on. The light was still bright, but because the sun was lower, there was the faintest hint night was on its way. They could sense it more than see it, but it was there. They tied up and walked back to their cottage for a shower and change of clothes. They'd be spending the evening outside Nancy's. The pictures on the menu looked good, and there were coloured lanterns in the trees for after nightfall. It was, they kept saying, the millionaire life.

The brief twilight had set in by the time they were ordering their food. Becky picked steamed oysters, clams and shrimp, while Chris had smoked mullet. He wanted to try one of the rum drinks, but Becky said better not, he might need a clear head. So he settled for beer, and Becky had a jug of chilled fruit juice. She'd put in hoop earrings and both her wrists had bangles on them. The place was close on full, so it looked routine when a bald senior citizen asked if he could share their table. They recognised him from his photo.

"My name's Peter Busch," he said as he sat down, glancing round to make sure no one could hear. "Welcome to Miranda Cove."

The sea was speckled with mooring lights, the tree lanterns were glowing, and Busch was keen to get talking. He said Torelli was stopping by later, so he wanted to say his piece now. He put his hessian shoulder bag on the spare seat to show it was taken.

"Someone has made a good choice," he began after he'd ordered. "When tiger sharks attack, they do it to eat, and that makes them deadly. They are stealthy, and normally they swim very slowly; then suddenly they go very fast, and their bite is immense. A single bite might be all they take, but that bite can be fatal."

He stopped when the meals were brought out, first the Millers', then his, and carried on when the service had gone.

"When the day fades, they come near to the surface to hunt, and they hunt on their own. They can be very long – fourteen feet is not unusual. They like inlets like this one, but they can get dolphin up the coast, so that is where they normally go."

"Fourteen feet? That's big," Chris said, mentally comparing it with a Mini. "So how do we get one in here?"

Busch picked up his shoulder bag. It had 'Cape Canaveral' stitched into it in red, and inside were some fliers about Miami which, if anyone asked, he just happened to have with him, he said. He put them upside down round his plate so they could see them properly.

"You will fish all day tomorrow, because fishing is what you are here for, or so people must think. You will try different places in the cove, but especially towards the open sea, and you will talk to Torelli and others when you can, but always as if by chance. You will fish and talk all Sunday as well, but you must say to everyone you are going sight-seeing in Miami on Monday."

He glanced round again and fetched out a small hand-drawn map.

"But you will not go to Miami, you will go to these four places instead. They are fishing centres, and they all have big supply stores. In each one you will buy for cash one 8lb block of frozen chum in a net bag. You will need a couple of cool boxes with you, but do not be seen loading them. You will read these fliers tonight so you can talk about Miami when you get back. You can also take my map to learn, but I want everything back tomorrow without anyone seeing."

"What's chum?" Becky asked Busch as he slipped the map under one of the fliers.

"It is fish that has been ground up and compressed. It is used as bait, but you can also lay a trail with it, because it is oily, and tiger sharks are known to respond to it. Seal it up in garbage bags and keep it in your freezer. Be careful, it will take up much room. On Tuesday you will fish again, and on Wednesday, starting at around ten past four in the afternoon, you will wait till Torelli gets into the water if he is not in it already and drop two blocks of chum in their net bags over the side on enough rope for them to hang below the surface. Do not let anyone see you do this. You must be near to Torelli and between him and the beach, and you will stay there for fifteen to twenty minutes passing the time of day. The tide will be going out. It will carry a trail of chum which no one will see under Torelli's boat and into the open sea. When your fifteen to twenty minutes are up, go towards the open sea yourselves and release all the rest of your chum into the water while you pause there for some reason or other – I leave that to you. When it is all gone, pull your ropes in and come back in past Torelli, but at a big distance from him. Let all the net bags drift out to sea, you must not have them on board."

As he finished speaking, someone called out, "Hi, Pete! Hi, everybody!" and came bustling over, carrying two large jugs of keg beer. It was Torelli. While he moved Busch's bag and fiddled with the tilt of his chair, Busch calmly gathered up the fliers plus the map underneath and told Becky to put them in her handbag so she wouldn't forget them. Then he did the introductions.

"You guys just carry on eating," Torelli said generally. "I had something already. I saw my friend Pete had company," he explained to the Millers, "so I brought some beer to share. When it runs out I'll get some more."

He poured for three, and Becky put more juice into her glass. He'd changed into clean clothes, but that still meant baggy shorts, and he had an easy way of speaking that helped Chris say he was a car mechanic without feeling inferior. Torelli told them he'd never been to Peterborough, but the UK was just great, and he'd go to London any time. Then, waving towards the north side of the cove, he pointed out the lights of the cottage he owned and said it was near the one Pete rented. Sometimes he brought Pete across in his runabout, but this evening he'd been busy, so Pete had had to drive round. That could happen when he was working on something.

"I hear you're a camera expert," Chris said.

He'd got it from Dvorski, but Busch put in to make it seem it came from him.

"Yes and no. I'm really an energy physicist, and my big thing is how light works. Water's different from air, so it makes light do strange things and that, plus the fishing, is why I spend my summers here."

When the eating was over, Torelli bought more beer, and they drifted down into friendly chatter. The air was warm, the sky was black, and in a space by the bar, a pianist was tinkling ballads on a pink-painted upright. "Play it again, Sam," Torelli chortled, and they all laughed. The Millers exchanged excited glances. Torelli had under five days to live. Then they'd be rich.

They stuck to Busch's instructions, and on Wednesday at ten past four, Chris reeled in his line, casually pootled from the south side of the cove towards the beach, and came round astern of Dandy One. Once his bow anchor was down, he turned the engines off and let the tide turn his rear deck towards the Sea Ray. Torelli was getting his scuba gear ready for another session. He never bothered with a wet suit, he'd said so outside Nancy's, so his skin, which hadn't tanned much, was good and bright.

Once more there was the faint sense night was on its way. Chris checked his watch, left the cabin for the rear deck, and closed the canvas flap behind him so that, out of sight of

Torelli, Becky could lower two bags of chum below the surface. She used a hand net with a pole handle, pivoting it on the Albemarle's side. That way no one got to see them.

Chris chatted with Torelli for the full twenty minutes, then said he hadn't caught much inshore lately, so he was going to try further out. Torelli, who was ready to make his dive, said if he saw anything down there he'd point it in his direction. And as soon as the Albemarle was clear of Dandy One, he rolled off the ledge at the back of his boat, clutching the camera he was working with. He came up once for a lighting bracket, and then he was gone. The Millers meanwhile were adding to the chum trail. They'd meant to fish near the mouth of the cove as cover, but once they were there, their fear came back, and the chum made it worse. They were sure a shark was on its way, they could imagine it relentlessly swimming towards them; so as soon as the chum was used up, they let the netting drift away and curved steadily back in, first towards the north side, then crossing to the south. If anyone asked why they'd hung about but not fished, Chris would say one of his engines had faltered and he'd given it a temporary fix. But it could always go again, so he'd come back in to take a proper look.

Time passed and everything seemed like any other day. The sun was still strong and Chris, who'd tied up opposite Nancy's and begun to cast there, could see Torelli sliding his lighting bracket on board with his legs trailing down. It looked as if he was going to survive, then out of nowhere there was a rise and fall in the water and he was gone. A friend moored up some space away let go his rod and shouted, "Shark! Shark!" while he ripped his flare gun from its holder and sent up three in a row. His wife scrabbled for her mobile and hit the buttons.

"It was a tiger!" he shouted to her. "Nearly full grown! I saw the spots and stripes!"

A siren on the lifeguards' boathouse wailed into life. Two guards raced down the beach to their rigid inflatable boat, two more – risking their own lives – began manhandling youngsters and anyone else who needed it towards the beach, while a fifth shouted, "Shark! Clear the water!" through a bullhorn. The RIB sped between the boats towards where the flares had gone up, at the same time calling, "Get your lines in, stay in your boats, and don't move them!" through the loud hailer. Torelli's friend waved his arms emergency-style till it got close. With his wife gripping his arm, he was shouting across what had happened, when two coastguard launches swung fast into the cove from the next bay north and slowed down to size things up.

"Over here, coastguards!" came through the loud hailer, followed by, "Have a care, there could be a body!"

One of the launches moved gingerly towards the RIB with a look-out on the prow. The other launch went onto standby. Police cars were reaching the beach in numbers, their sirens howling and their blue lights flashing, while three ambulances closed in behind them and a police helicopter began an aerial search. It didn't take long. The shark had bitten Torelli's right leg off at the hip. The water was bloodied where his corpse floated up. All the coastguards could do was retrieve his remains.

Outwardly the Millers were obeying instructions just like everyone else, but inside they were trying out their new situation and liking it a lot. Valkov's psychograms had been spot on. They'd killed, they'd be richer than they'd ever been before, and they just knew they'd get away with it. They felt no horror, no remorse, just surging satisfaction. But as they stood gleefully on Bluebell's rear deck, the helicopter must have radioed the second coastguard launch, because it suddenly came very slowly in their direction. They went tense. Had they slipped up somehow?

"Get down gently onto the deck and take hold of something solid!" came over the water towards them. "There's a tiger shark under your boat!"

Instinctively they glanced over the side and saw the broad head and forward part of the body protruding from underneath. In their witness statements later they said the spots and stripes were faded, while the helicopter gave its length as fifteen feet under a boat with a nine-and-a-half foot beam. At the time they felt blank terror, but before they could get down, it was gone.

It was well into the evening before they were finally allowed to return to their cottage. Most of the time had gone waiting to be interviewed on the beach. They'd told all they'd seen and been classed as witnesses not likely to be needed again. Yes, they could go back to England when their stay was up. If they were recalled, they'd have to come back, but no one could see it happening. Everyone was saying it was an NEF – a 'naturally evented fatality'.

"I can't believe it!" Becky sizzled as they switched the lights on and locked their cottage door. "We've done it and we're in the clear! They don't suspect a thing!"

Then came the rush. Their sex was frantic, they didn't even get all their clothes off. When they finished, they were still on highs, so Chris took himself over to the bar and bought a bottle of rum, a bottle of vodka and some orange juice. Food didn't matter, they just wanted to get stinking drunk. Busch was sitting outside as usual. Chris gave him a wave as he left the bar, but that was all. He'd committed the perfect crime – his words. He meant it to stay that way.

Chapter 4

Dinner with Dvorski

Dandy Torelli was ripped apart when she learned what had happened to her father, and Dvorski was overjoyed to see it. At the burial she stood helpless in the Florida sunshine, the tears streaming down her face. Afterwards, there was Irma, her mother, to attend to, plus the bank accounts, the will and the sell-offs, including Dandy One. They all took time – and, much worse, they kept the wound of her Daddy's loss open – so it was the third week in October before she finally got back. Her Exxon replacement was already on the island. All she had to do was talk him through the jobs, but she was in such poor shape, she kept breaking down, and he had to wait with good grace till she was with him again.

Dvorski watched her minutely, took his time, and on October 29th he asked her over for dinner. She didn't want to accept, she'd been doing her utmost to keep out of his way, but then she thought she might as well – it would help to keep the peace till she disappeared for good. It was close on seven when she backed into his drive. She didn't have to do that, there was plenty of room to turn, but all she could think about was getting away again. The sun had almost set, and she was wrapped up warm – temperatures were in the low forties now, and there'd already been some pre-winter storms. It wouldn't be long before the sea froze over.

As the Ministry's man on the island, Dvorski had the use of a refurbished dacha handily close to the airfield. It stemmed from when tsarist worthies liked to slaughter the local wildlife, but its updated function was to make Industry and Trade look as impressive as Exxon. In the Yeltsin years, the décor had tried to be upbeat, but with Putin had come ponderous tasselled furniture, densely patterned carpets and, on the ornately papered walls, massively framed portraits of nineteenth century moguls. Everything was Mother Russia. There wasn't a hammer and sickle in sight.

Dvorski smilingly waited while Torelli hung her outdoor clothes up, took off her boots, and slipped on the exercise sandals she liked to wear indoors; then he ushered her into the living room, which doubled as a dining room. At the far end was a Russian-style wood-burning stove, but its cladding tiles had all been replaced, and instead of dinky flowers, they now showed the moustachioed face of Tsar Nicholas I, one of the most aggressive and reactionary of the tsars. Dvorski invited Torelli to take a seat in a deep-stuffed easy chair, he made himself comfortable in another one, and while she was sipping sherry she didn't want, he took out what looked like a mobile, apologised for having to send one last text, and silently locked the living room door. Then, in the subdued light of the room's globular lamps, he tried to get her to talk. It wasn't easy. On top of her volcanic dislike of him, she was still grieving deeply, and she was all but exhausted as well. But he had an agenda and a script to go with it.

"I expect Klemmsley will be sending you to some weird and wonderful places," he led off with.

"How so?"

"Well, Klemmsley's fields are more off Scotland than England. And in oil and gas you go where the rigs are. You know that as well as I do."

She lost it right there.

"You know nothing, Oleg Dvorski," she spat out. "You're a stupid Russian, that's all. People like me have to be clever for stupid Russians like you, because you can't be clever for yourselves. For starters, Klemmsley takes in one half of the English coast before it even gets to Scotland. You hear that? One half. And I won't be in Scotland, I'll be in Essex. That's a county outside London in case you don't know even that, and there isn't a rig in sight there. Companies like Klemmsley use data streams these days, and Klemmsley's flow into Essex because that's where Klemmsley wants them to flow. Get real, Oleg. You Russians can't even make rubber bands. All you can make is guns and trouble."

The rings under her eyes had gone from purpley to black and her hands had the tremors, so she stood what was left of her sherry next to an engraved bronze samovar and stared fixedly at her feet. This wasn't keeping the peace, she scolded herself, it was kicking sand in his face. Well, she'd just have to start again, and this time try a bit harder.

"I'm sorry," she said meekly, and in a way it was true. "I take it all back."

That was the last thing Dvorski wanted, she had to blow up completely. He could see she hated Russia because it wouldn't let go of her. He could also see her hatred gave her strength to resist. But if he could use her hatred to break her open, he could sow his grains of fear in her, and with that fear would come what he wanted: submission. With that in view he'd turned the room into a trap. He'd made it even more Russian than it normally was and arranged the dining table so it would rile her constantly. The table cloth had troikas on snow woven into it, as did the serviettes. Every cup, saucer and plate carried scenes from Russian folklore, and the cutlery had the beaming face of a Russian peasant woman embossed on every handle. Only the food and wines were American. He'd bought them in the Exxon supermarket. His thinking was, if he could remind her of home as well, he could damage her even more.

"Don't apologise, I beg you," he said soothingly. "You're worn out, that's all, and I'm not surprised, not after what you've been through. So why don't we cheer ourselves up with some good old American cooking? I've got sliced turkey with trimmings and blueberry flan with double cream, all from your very own USA. If you'll move to the table, I'll see how the first course is doing. If it's ready, I'll serve it straight from the kitchen."

Dvorski enjoyed his meal but Torelli, who sat near the stove because she couldn't get warm, ate like a zombie. Fragments of conversation languished and died in the silence, then nothing got said till Dvorski kicked a new topic off. When the eating was done, he moved the plates and dishes to one end of the table instead of clearing them away. But he still went into the kitchen, once for some single cream and once more for the coffee.

"It's not Russian," he joked as he set the percolator down. "It's Brazilian."

She managed a half-laugh and left it at that.

The wines had seeped under Torelli's guard, the coffee was rich, and the two together, like a fifth column, helped Dvorski make the atmosphere confiding. When he thought he'd got it right, he said,

"You haven't let me tell you before, but I'll tell you now, if I may. I'm sorry about your father, really I am."

She stiffened, and her fingers and thumb clamped tight on her cup handle.

"Please," she said, "not that. You don't know how much it hurts."

But, not suspecting anything, she was the smallest bit glad he'd said it, because it gave her the chance to get something off her mind. She drained her cup, put it down with a clink of bone china, and forced herself to keep going.

"You know, it doesn't add up, Oleg, and I don't see how it can. There's never been any sharks in Miranda Cove, and then two tigers come in at once. That's way, way out of line. You'd think someone'd whistled them in or something."

It was a throw-away line or close to it, but there are ways of looking at someone who's speaking that say it all. So when Dvorski held her gaze with a hazily mocking smile, the unattached doubt she'd been carrying around hardened into certainty. Her fists clenched tight, she banged them on the tablecloth, and her voice started to rise.

"So someone *did* get them in there when my Daddy was in the water. I know they did now, I can see it in your face! It was you, wasn't it?"

"I was here on the island, Dandy, don't you remember? You saw me yourself. You even spoke to me."

"You wouldn't be there, not in person, you're too clever for that. But you were behind it all right, I'm one hundred percent sure of it now." She spaced her last words out to emphasise them, her voice rose to a scream, and she hammered frantically on the table. "My Daddy bled to death, Oleg! He had half his body bitten out, and he bled to death! And you fixed it to happen, Russian crap! Why don't you deny it instead of sitting there grinning? You can't, that's why, and you know it!"

"You could be right, Dandy," he answered, all relaxed, and still with his ghastly smile. "I'm not saying you are, but you could be."

He got exactly what he wanted. She didn't say anything, she looked straight at him and, white with rage, she picked up her coffee cup and hurled it at him. It bounced off his forearm as he raised it and shattered behind him. The saucer spun off his shoulder and shattered as well. Breathing hard through her nose, she got to her feet and looked all round. Next to the stove was an iron poker. She picked it up and held it like a cudgel.

"Don't you dare move," she panted, her anguish and her anger boiling hot. "I'll show you what I think of your asshole country. Then I'll show you what I think of you."

Piece by piece she smashed everything that was on the table, including the dinner and dessert plates Dvorski had purposely left there. Any large shards she thrashed into fragments, and if they carried even part of a design, she pulverised them. Then she grabbed hold of the table cloth, yanked everything onto the carpet with a crash, and stamped on it hard with her wooden-soled sandals. But still it wasn't enough, so she moved round the room, leaving a trail of shattered glassware, smashed pottery, fractured clocks and bent and dented metal. Finally she attacked the stove, deafeningly flailing at the tiles till the cement floor round it was covered in them and dust, while those that stayed put were crazed and fragmented. Dvorski kept where he was and didn't say a word. But when she came round the table for him, he jumped up fast, grabbed her wrist before she could hit him, and forced her onto the carpet. She writhed and squirmed manically, but he squeezed her wrist till the pain got through, and banged her hand down till she let the poker go. Then, changing hands but keeping hold of her wrist, he stood up and dragged her up after him, crashing his chair over as he did so. She was drained beyond measure, but she was still fighting all out, so he hauled her right away from the table, forced her down onto a thickly-cushioned settee, and with the flat of his hand struck the side of her head as hard as he could. He did it a second time and a third, each time hitting her where it wouldn't show. The shock made her stop fighting, and when he asked her whether she wanted him to hit her again, she said no. He dropped her hand, her body sagged, and her head drooped. He was still standing over her when she finally raised her gaze and looked him full in the face. That was the moment it really sunk in: she was looking at her Daddy's murderer. Her hatred and anguish flared up again, but this time real fear was in there as well. The seeds had been sown.

"Why did you do it, Oleg?" she asked plaintively. "You didn't even know him."

Dvorski saw he was almost there.

"Why don't we have some more coffee?" he countered. "Then we can talk things through."

She nodded dully, and he headed off into the kitchen, crunching bits of china under his shoes. As soon as he was gone, she shot to her feet and made for the living room door. She was glad she'd parked the way she had; she'd scoop up her outdoor things and get away fast. But the door was locked, and as she was pumping the handle, Dvorski came back in. He saw what she was doing, but he didn't seem surprised. It was as if he'd been expecting it.

"Good to see you moving about," he said amiably. "I came back to ask you, would you mind if we used decorated cups and saucers? I haven't got any plain ones, and the ones on the table seemed to upset you."

She let her hands drop to her sides.

"OK, Oleg, you win. Use whatever cups you like, say your piece, and let me get out of here. That's all I ask, and if you want me to say please, I'll say that as well."

They cleared some debris off the two deep-stuffed chairs they'd sat on when the evening began and drank their coffee in silence. When they finished, Dvorski spoke first. His tone was suddenly firm.

"When you go to Klemmsley, Dandy, I shall go to London which, as you say, is handily close to Essex, and I shall continue to be in charge of you. It's no good looking like that," he added, as horror filled her face. "You've belonged to us since you've been here, and that's the way you'll stay. Klemmsley's lining you up for a top job, but one word from us and you're out. Exxon wouldn't like you either. In fact, with your track record, you'd finish up in gaol. And if you try to hide anywhere, it'll be my shadow on the blind and my footfall on the stairs when you put your light out. Do you see these hands?" he asked, raising them palm outwards. "They're deadly when they close. Don't let them close on you."

She rammed her knuckles against her mouth and her eyes were staring wide, but he took no notice.

"On the other hand," he continued, "if you keep us informed about what's in these data streams, we'll make sure you enjoy a long and successful career. Do I make myself clear?"

"Yes, Oleg. Completely."

She felt as smashed and crushed as the debris on the floor. She'd been convinced she could get away from the past, and now this. As he looked at her, haggard and distraught, he felt he'd got it right yet again. He'd manipulated the Millers and he'd manipulated Dandy not once but twice. The SVR would have to think more of him now.

"Unlock the door, please," she asked dejectedly. "I can't take any more right now. If there's anything else, tell it to me tomorrow."

He did as she asked, and as soon as he'd waved her goodbye, he put in an encrypted call through to SVR headquarters in Moscow's Yasenevo district.

"Zembarov," came back down the line.

"It worked," Dvorski said, trying not to sound triumphant. "She'll do as we say. She's done a lot of damage to the dacha though. She went through it like a mad bull."

"Get it repaired and send me the bill. I'll sign it personally. I'll speak to Andrey Ivanovich as well. He'll have things to do now you're joining him. And one thing more – Torelli nearly cost you your career, now you must believe she can make it a success. It's up to you. We'll be watching you constantly."

Chapter 5

Storm Clouds Start to Form

Torelli landed in London in November, and a Klemmsley Oil and Gas chauffeur drove her to the furnished cottage in Essex that was hers till she found a home of her own. A Volvo Estate came with the cottage. She wasn't at the top yet, but she was on the way.

Klemmsley's data centre – called Klemmsley Marine – was just twelve miles away down a dead flat country lane. It stood in eleven hundred acres Klemmsley had got cheap in the post-war science boom. Klemmsley had been independent then. Now it was part of CDB Global, a mixed multinational headquartered in London. Global had upgraded the labs, landscaped the grounds, and put a Henry Moore bronze outside the main entrance. On the roof, a red and white Klemmsley banner fluttered proudly whenever the wind sprang up. To the east of the site was the Essex Way – a grass-covered levee with a footpath on top. Beyond the Way were salt marshes and the North Sea, and to the west were fields used mostly for growing wheat. Torelli was soon liking the people she worked with. Like Global, they crossed state boundaries, and a lot of them were young and male. Time was seeping away and, loving soul that she was, she was yearning for someone to be close to. It would've been easy if it hadn't been for Dvorski.

Dvorski arrived in London the day after Torelli and moved into a Russian Embassy flat in Kensington Church Street. It was the one he'd had when he'd come over to see Valkov. It was small and the heating was erratic, but it was secure, and it had all he needed, including a computer, an internet connection and an encryptable phone. The Embassy listed him as a Junior Attaché in the Department of Industry and Trade. It kept quiet about his SVR membership, and Valkov drilled into him that if he played his cards right, the British would leave it at that. They were permanently hard up, surveillance cost money, and they saved where they could.

Dvorski put a month or so into making genuine contacts all around the country, then he asked the Klemmsley board if he could speak to some of its specialists. Gazprom was expanding, he wrote in a letter, and Klemmsley could be in for a deal. He named the people he had in mind, and Torelli came near the bottom of the list as if she was just one more staffer he'd like to have a word with. The board said yes and made it clear to Dvorski's *invités* what they could and couldn't say. When Torelli's turn came, she met him in a security-screened sub-basement room. White-faced, she stuck to banalities, and he didn't tighten the thumbscrews. He didn't have to. Just being shut up with him in an undersized room without windows was enough. She couldn't begin to hide her fear, and when they finished, he raised his hands as if he was coming for her. She shrank back terror-stricken and had to stifle a scream. He laughed in her face and, still grinning, held out his hand to shake hers. But she clasped her hands behind her back and shook her head mutely. That made him laugh again.

When they reached Reception, he asked her to show him round the grounds. It was still only midday, he said, he had three more appointments to keep him on site, and for once the sun was shining. The receptionist was right there, so Torelli said yes. Anything else might have made the receptionist wonder. She got clearance from above, fetched her coat and outdoor shoes, and they set off together.

"The general rule is," he said when they were clear of the building, "you don't contact me, it's up to me or someone else to contact you. If it's me, it'll be just like this time, here and up front, and if you've got something for me, I'll take it from you. The problem is, I can't come as often as I'd like, even if I keep the Gazprom thing running, so I've brought you these."

He took a buff envelope from under his coat and discreetly passed it to her.

"What's this?" she asked, slipping it deftly into her handbag. It was, she thought dismally, just like old times.

"You like arty things, so these are subscription tickets to the Festival Hall, the Barbican and the National Theatre. They're all in London and they're all good for passing things on. The person on your left will always come from us. You will say, 'Could I see your programme, please? I forgot to buy one when I came in' and the other person will say, 'You can have this one if you like. I bought two by mistake.' I've written these words out for you, and both of you must say them exactly. The people we send will know you from photos, but we can't have you recognising our people in advance, so it's the right words or nothing. If ever you absolutely have to contact me, you can leave a coded message addressed to Fox in a dead letter box in Kensington Place. You'll find a one-off code book in with the tickets."

He explained where the letter box was and how to signal she'd used it. Day or night, she had to scratch her forehead with her left thumb in sight of a surveillance camera in nearby Edge Street. It was above some steps. Her biometric data would do the rest and he'd get a red alert. They strolled on some more. As they turned back, he said,

"Bring something useful to every contact or you'll find life turning nasty. But don't remove anything physically. Use a memory stick, your own memory or a camera. Do I make myself clear?"

He did.

Before they went inside, he asked her to list and write out full summaries of the key personnel she worked with. Note form would do to save time. He wanted private as well as professional information, and he'd collect it – sealed – from Reception before he left. She felt deeply ashamed, but she gave it her best shot and duly handed it in.

She had enough status to work her own hours, so it was no big deal when, after a snatched lunch she didn't want, she told

Reception she was going into Chelmsford, Essex's county town, for the rest of the afternoon. She was going round the estate agents. Her colleagues lived mostly in Chelmsford or London, but she was looking for properties near Klemmsley Marine, one for herself and one close by for Irma, because Irma, who couldn't cope with being on her own, wanted to come over and live near her. Irma would have capital for her own place, and part of Torelli's deal with Klemmsley had been an interest-free loan for herself. It was time to call it in. The weeks before Christmas were always a buyer's market.

All the estate agents were in the same part of Chelmsford, but it still took Torelli a while to find what she wanted. Christmas lights were everywhere, carols as well, and the shop windows shone brightly in the early dark. But Torelli became more and more despondent until, in the seventh agent's, she struck lucky. The satellite picture showed a selection of modern bungalows patchworked between aging cottages and farm buildings, just three miles south-west of Klemmsley Marine. They were scattered round a crossroads formed by two narrow lanes as if they'd been spilled from a bag. A bungalow and a not-too-distant cottage were both up for sale there. The estate agent took her through the specs.

"The bungalow's called Oaklands and it's in perfect nick. You could move in tomorrow if you liked."

He glanced about him, but there were no other customers around.

"I shouldn't tell you this," he said, breaching a confidence to bring on a sale, "but it belongs to a local builder. He built it from scratch and now he can't sell it. The cottage is called Dove Cottage. It needs freshening up, but your mother could move in and get it done when it suits her." Torelli waited for the second indiscretion, half-amused and half-ashamed to see someone else betraying secrets. It came dead on cue. "The owner's retired to Spain and she'll be glad of the cash. Her pension's less than she thought it'd be."

He unfolded a large-scale map on his desk and used his biro to point with.

"Oaklands is here," he went on, "this is Dove Cottage, and these broken lines show a footpath going past Oaklands and the cottage. The footpath goes through a smallish wood here, but it's never overgrown, so there's no problem there. It's dark, that's all."

"How do you know it's never overgrown?" she asked.

It was a reasonable question on the face of it, but hatred of her own deceptions was behind it.

"I walked down it during the summer when I took the photos. There wasn't a bramble out of place."

They agreed a viewing time for the upcoming Saturday morning, and as Torelli re-entered the street, she felt she'd got somewhere at last.

Saturday dawned with a hoar frost that was only partly melted as she waited outside Oaklands for the estate agent to arrive. She gave the place the once-over, took to it straight away, and while the agent was locking up, she said she'd rather walk to Dove Cottage than drive there. She wanted to see the footpath and the wood for herself.

The footpath was clear all right, the puddles in it were filmed with ice, and in amongst the trees it was very dark. She'd need a flashlight at night for sure. It was also deathly still, and since the quiet made them stop talking, there were no sounds except their footsteps and the occasional crackle of ice. When they reached Dove Cottage, the agent showed her in. The problems were all cosmetic, the gardens looked the right size for her mother, and there were neighbours on either side – probably with children, if the toys on one side and the swing on the other were any guide. Irma would like that a lot.

"I'm interested in both of them," she said and offered two prices. "If the vendors play ball, I'll firm up. Then we can get things rolling."

Despite Christmas and New Year, the dealing went fast, but the conveyancing was snail's pace, so it was March before she could move in and tell Irma to get her things containerised for air-freighting. During that time, she'd leaked a constant flow of information and Dvorski had called by twice more –

he had his own car now, a dark green Skoda Octavia. But what she couldn't know was, he'd also been to Peterborough. Still calling himself Sanderson, he'd told the Millers he liked the cautious way they were handling their money – they'd got their bank loan, they'd done a deal on new premises, and that was more or less it. He didn't say where his information came from, but it impressed them he had it at all. In fact he'd got it from Valkov. He'd also told them he might not need them for a while, so they could get on with their lives till he said. They wouldn't get a retainer, but they'd see business look up, which was just as good. And if either of them thought of breaking away, they should remember Jethro Torelli and think again.

As the months passed, Dandy Torelli found out more and more about the people at the top of CDB Global. It was public knowledge CDB stood for Cyril David Burney, and it was also public knowledge he was very, very rich. *Forbes* magazine put Global's assets at $420·8 billion and Burney's personal fortune at $53·2 billion. From various bits of gossip she gleaned he was the wrong side of mid-fifty, he had heart trouble, and he'd started making money by selling blemished crockery – 'seconds' – off a stall in Roman Road, East London's famous street market. His wife, Enid, was reckoned to be nine years younger, and she didn't have anything to do with Global. There was one child, Russell, and the consensus was he was in his mid-twenties. As Klemmsley's CEO, he was Torelli's immediate boss. She'd met him at interview, but he'd disappeared to Alaska and Japan before she'd arrived in England.

"So what's he like?" she asked the person who told her most, a software designer by the name of Anders Alstad. They were at a corner table in the canteen taking a morning break. "He's a bit young for a CEO, isn't he?"

She ached for the affable Norwegian, but she despised herself so much, she forced herself not even to hint at it. He finished his coffee and when he answered, he kept his voice down.

"His father wanted a Burney as a figurehead, so as soon as our Russell got his degree, he plopped him in at the top. In fact,

Russell's pretty good, he just lacks experience, but it doesn't matter too much. The rest of the board know who the real boss is, so they cover for him as and when. It's as a person Russell doesn't tick right, and the problem isn't his age, it's his father. CDB is a pig. He picks people's brains, but he doesn't let them have any glory. That includes his son. Russell's on a straight salary with no bonuses, and he has to crawl for everything. So far he's held up, but any real pressure and he'll fall apart. The signs are small, but they're there. Like cracks in the San Andreas Fault."

"Such as?"

"He clings to fixed points. For example – don't laugh! – the BBC late news. If he isn't watching when it comes on, it's like a personal loss for him. He told me so when we were working late once, and we had to stop till he'd seen it. It's completely irrational, but that's the way he is. He drinks too much as well."

Glumly she thought Dvorski should know all that, but she needed to fill it out a bit first, and two days later a phone call gave her the chance. It was a warm Friday evening in May, and she was about to walk over to Irma's, when she found herself talking to, of all people, Russell Burney. He sounded excited.

"I'm ringing from my parents' house in Ascot," he said. "Would you like to come over for Sunday lunch? We want to put something to you."

She pounced on it.

"Their house is called The Crofter's Hut," he went on – she was getting used to houses with names, not numbers. "It's about two and a half hours' drive from your place, three at the outside. Shall we say twelve o'clock?"

That was OK, too. She'd be there.

The weather stayed fine, and as she worked out her route, she wondered what a house called The Crofter's Hut might look like. She tried guessing – it was close to Windsor Castle for a start – but it turned out to be lavish even by Ascot standards. It was a massive gabled mansion and, she learned, it was set in over one hundred acres of parkland, with nine bedrooms, seven bathrooms, a music room, a library and a stable block. At the end of the long road through the estate, the paved approach to the house had a garage complex off to one side, and in front of one of the garages, a venerable-looking chauffeur was washing a white Rolls-Royce Phantom with CDB number plates. She told him her name, said she was expected, and asked where she should park.

"Right here will do, Ma'am. Leave the keys in and I'll put it away for you. My name is Quilter, by the way. Derek Quilter. Mr Cyril likes people to call me Derek."

As she got out, she glanced into the next garage and glimpsed the eye-catching bonnet of a Morgan Plus 8 in British racing green. Time was on her side, so she asked what kind of car it was and whether she could take a closer look. The top was down, and if she'd been anywhere else, she'd have asked whether she could get in.

"I guess you'll be washing this one next," she said.

It looked as if it hadn't been cleaned for some while.

"I'd like to, but it's more than my job's worth. It's Mr Russell's car, and Mr Cyril says if he wants it washed, he's got to do it himself."

"And will he?"

Quilter looked embarrassed.

"I'm afraid I can't say, Ma'am. Now, if you'll excuse me, I must finish Mr Cyril's Rolls."

The front door to the house was opened by a maid in uniform. Behind her stood the butler, also formally dressed. He led the way to the morning room and announced Torelli's arrival to the Burneys, who were sitting inside. When he'd gone, Russell stood up and, not altogether comfortably, did the individual introductions. One other guest was already there. She looked slightly younger than Enid Burney, and Russell introduced her as Miss Shayler, Global's Head of Finance. Both there and in the dining room it was Enid who did most to make Torelli feel at ease. Cyril, whose laboured breathing was relieved by tablets he took with water, talked mostly about himself, while Russell, who was subdued and twitchy, seemed bonded only to his mother. During the meal he was allowed a single glass of wine. When he looked towards the wine waiter for a refill, Enid gave him a kindly smile, placed a hand over his glass before his father could speak, and motioned the waiter back. Thereafter he had water. Shayler said almost nothing, and when she did speak, it was usually to Enid. There seemed to be some kind of friendship there. Torelli had little ear for English accents, but she noticed Cyril and Enid both sounded the same, although the way Enid put her sentences together was smoother, as if, unlike Cyril, she'd polished her English up to blend in better. Later Torelli learned Enid came from the same East End background. Alstad thought she was a gold digger and, Torelli discovered over time, he wasn't the only one.

Over coffee, Torelli drew some silent conclusions. Cyril wouldn't last forever, and repressed and twitchy Russell wasn't being groomed to take over, that was as clear as day. Kewpie doll Enid was out of it too. She still had her looks, but an empty-head like her wouldn't get a look-in. Then there was Shayler. Fern was her first name, she'd gathered that much, but she seemed to be finance and nothing else. She was so turned in on herself, Torelli would have found it easy to forget she was there, even when she was looking straight at her, if she hadn't been so irritated by her. She was sure she was as chaste as a nun, whereas she – Torelli – was burning for a man but was forcing herself to keep him out of her life. So what *would* happen to Global when Cyril went? And how would that affect Dr Amanda Torelli? She could always go to another company, everyone knew how good she was, but that wouldn't get rid of Dvorski, and that was what mattered most. She had no real answers for the moment. Perhaps they'd come when she and the Burneys got down to business. That would be in the conservatory, and when coffee was over, Cyril suggested they go there.

Cyril walked slowly with a stick, and Shayler walked dutifully next to him. Torelli and Russell trundled behind, and Enid, who wasn't invited, said she was going out to one of the outhouses. She had a little place of her own out there, she explained. The Crofter's Hut's corridors were sombre and dull, and that, plus Cyril's invalid pace, made Torelli want to rejoice out loud when they reached the conservatory. It was bright and sunny, and the Edwardian stained glass made the carpet glow with inner fire. Cyril told them all where to sit and asked Russell to operate the blinds. He said the light was hurting his eyes.

In the artificial shade, Russell looked expectantly towards his father, saw him nod curtly, and got things under way.

"Since you joined us last November" he said to Torelli, "you've got to know all our domestic fields except one."

"Cockerel Field. The one off the coast of County Durham."

"That's the one, and since you know that much, let me fill in the rest. It's east-southeast of Blackhall Rocks to be precise, and to date we've been running it as one more methane gas field. But there's a lot of methane hydrate down there as well, so about eighteen months ago we drilled in a place called Dassett Point to see if we could convert some into methane gas and sell it. We sank two trial boreholes, one to drop the pressure through a regulator valve, and one to let out any methane the new pressure generated. But instead of a gentle outflow we got an uprush like I've never seen before. It nearly took out a supply ship, that's how strong it was. So panic, panic, and we only just managed to cap it. We tried two more boreholes into the same pocket, but all we got was two more panics, so that was that. The pressure's been restored, the regulator valve's out, the boreholes are all plugged, and that's how they'll stay till we get us some better technology. That's why I've been in Alaska and Japan, but that's for another day.

"What's for right now is this. Just before you joined us, we detected a giant methane gas bubble poking out from under where the methane hydrate is. That bubble's worth billions, and now Klemmsley has had time to look at you, we want you to help us exploit it. The project's called Harvest Home, it'll be a top promotion for you, and you won't be working on anything else. I mention that now, because on our website it'll say you're Chief Marine Geologist for the whole of Cockerel

Field. Secrecy's everything in our business, but you know that anyway. So, what do you say? You'll get a pay rise to match, if that's any help."

Before she could answer, Cyril put in.

"I'm a dealer, not a scientist, Miss Torelli," he wheezed. "So tell me, what exactly is methane hydrate?"

"It's really just methane gas, Sir – what you'd call natural gas – but it's in a very weird form. If the sea temperature's a squeak above freezing and the pressure's what you get at two thousand feet down, the methane gets trapped in like tiny cages of ice. That's methane hydrate. It's under the Caribbean, the Atlantic, the North Sea, you name it, and there's more gas in it than the whole world can use for hundreds of years. The downside is that it's hard to gather in, as Mr Russell's found out."

"Thank you. Now, my son isn't always truthful when he wants something, so you tell me. Is this new project dangerous, yes or no?"

She knew the answer was yes, methane hydrate was top-risk just from being there. She guessed Russell had kept that back, but his father had found it out and beaten him up with it. She didn't want to get beaten up as well, she had a career to make, so she was about to tell him yes, it was dangerous all right, when some fast thinking involving Dvorski flagged her down. The way Russell had described Harvest Home recalled a study she'd come across when she'd been writing her doctorate. It had analysed an area well north of Cockerel, but the pattern was identical and it told her straight away: Harvest Home wasn't just dangerous, it was deadly. It'd be like an atom bomb exploding once they went full into that gas bubble, the expansion zone would be gigantic, and everyone in it would be wiped out.

That was where Dvorski came in. She'd been hurt beyond endurance resisting the Russians, so why not try being helpful? She'd keep the study to herself, she'd work on Harvest Home till she was sure of all her facts, and then she'd use them to deal for her release. Western Europe under water would be like a gift from the gods to the Russians, and all they'd have to do was let it happen. It'd be mass murder, there was no question of that, and she'd be the crucial factor. But she was so uptight about Dvorski, it bounced right off her.

"There *are* dangers," she said, feeling miserable she could lie so readily, "but because Mr Russell's going for the gas bubble and not the methane hydrate, they're perfectly manageable. Harvest Home sounds safe to me, and it'd be a privilege to do my best for it."

She got a look of relief from Russsell, a grudging "Very well" from his father, and a salary quote from Shayler that made her eyebrows shoot up. All the while after that she kept imagining having sex with Alstad to celebrate. She'd stop holding back, she'd ask him round Monday after work, and they'd start a new life right there. Between fantasies she wondered about Enid. She was made for sex, that was obvious, but she couldn't be getting it from Cyril, not these days anyway. So was she getting it at all? Suddenly, aging, silver-haired Quilter popped into her mind, she could see them doing it in the back of the Phantom, he in his chauffeur's cap. It was all she could do not to giggle. She saw it all again as she drove home after tea, and this time she laughed till the tears ran – then she stopped herself abruptly. Thoroughly frightened, she pulled into the next lay-by, switched the engine off, and gazed sightlessly through the windscreen till she calmed down. She'd signed up to mass murder in The Crofter's Hut and now it was catching up with her. But she couldn't go on being afraid of Dvorski, he'd ruin her whole life if she let him, and reminding herself of that made the pendulum swing back. She blew her nose on a tissue, restarted the engine, and drove off with her teeth clenched and her mind made up. She'd see her plan through because she had to. She was in for the long haul.

Chapter 6

Torelli Says Too Much

The long haul took close on six years and some things went better than others. Torelli mapped Harvest Home in 3D, plus a broad mantle of the surrounding seabed. She also asked for, and got, a dedicated lab built right on Blackhall Rocks. On Teesside would have been better, and there were only a few miles in it, but she felt a brooding affinity with the Rocks' bleak magnesium limestone, so that's where it had to be. The Rocks were a shade further from Dvorski as well, but that didn't make the difference she'd hoped for. She was still completely afraid of him, and wherever she went, her fear went with her.

She had other ups and downs. Russell Burney treated her like royalty, and Alstad moved into Oaklands with her. She got untold happiness from having Alstad with her, but Dvorski's dark shadow and her murderous secret pursued her like Furies, and finally Alstad had had enough of the nightmares, the fault-finding, the rows and the clinging. Statoil bought up his notice and he went back to Norway, relieved to get away from her. It nearly destroyed her. She felt she'd driven him out, and she didn't even think of finding someone else, since she was convinced it would all happen again. Instead she threw herself into her work, commuted relentlessly between Essex and the Rocks, and made sure of time with Irma by drawing up a schedule.

"I'm glad she's around," she told Dvorski one day when he was in Klemmsley Marine, still talking Gazprom up. She was determined to be nice to him till she could make her big move. "If I'm working here, I walk over every weekday evening I'm free, plus every Saturday and Sunday evening. And if I'm in Blackhall, I still get back for Saturday and Sunday evening with her. I guess it sounds schmaltzy, but I need someone to love, and she's the only one I've got right now. Here, I'll show you a picture of her. The hole in the top edge is from a thumb tack. I had it pinned up in my clothes closet on Sakhalin Island. I saw it every day."

She reached into her handbag as she spoke and took a passport-size photo of a smiling, whitish-haired lady out of her wallet. It was a poignant moment. Torelli was so lonely, she desperately wanted to share something personal with someone, even Dvorski, who'd made her mother a widow. She hoped maybe he'd feel remorse, though she knew he wouldn't.

"You can keep it if you want. Please, I've got others," she said wretchedly, and she held it out to him. She was close to tears.

"I appreciate it," he said, slipping it into his diary. "She looks like a lovely lady. But," he moved on, wanting to lift the tension in case she broke down openly, "surely you don't walk to your mother's when the weather's bad. And then there's the dark. Why don't you use your new car?"

She'd bought herself a jet black Jaguar Sovereign. Her hair was greying early and her face was getting worry lines, but she was earning top dollar, and she took a destructive pleasure in spending like a teenager who'd inherited a fortune.

"I walk because I have to. If I'm fighting the weather, I'm not fighting myself. And I like the dark, it wraps me up like a blanket. I've got a flashlight for the worst bits anyway. So all of that's why I don't use my car."

Finally, with one more January come and gone, Russell Burney took the big decision. In an in-house e-mail synchronised with a press release, he announced Harvest Home would pierce the gas bubble on 15th September – a Saturday – and go fully on stream the following Saturday. Gazprom had renewed an interest, he wrote, and after consultation with Mr Cyril Burney, CDB-TV would be broadcasting the event world-wide.

The dates were what she'd been waiting for. Now she had them, she could act. So, at four o'clock in the morning on a bitterly cold Wednesday – it was the 7th February – she dumped a heavily-laden grip into the back of her car, hauled herself behind the wheel, and set off on the two hundred and ninety mile journey to the Rocks. When she got there, she parked in her bay and took a leg-stretcher to where she could look out over the sea. The tide was in, a haze shut the horizon off, and the wintry water gave off the menace she needed. When she went inside, she took her grip with her. She told staff, now Harvest Home's dates were out she wanted to re-run some seabed data. Just to make sure. Then she bought a muffin and some coffee in the canteen and shut herself in her workroom. Nobody gave it a thought. That was how she was.

With the slats of the blinds closed and the neon tubes humming, she powered up her computers and arranged her monitors on her desk so she could flip between them. Then she took a laptop and a clutch of memory sticks from her safe. These she arranged on her desk as well. Finally she pulled an old-fashioned ledger out of her grip and laid it open on a table near her writing hand. She was ready to go.

Using the computers, she worked her way through Harvest Home's core-sample and sonar datasets. Like her 3D mapping, they covered all the Harvest Home site plus a wide part of the surround; they were Klemmsley's, and anyone with the right codes could access them. She'd used a lot more core-samples than someone else might have done, and while most marine geologists put in gaps to save money, her gaps were often in unexpected places. The people she worked with had muttered about it, but she wasn't just in charge, she was a star, so no one had challenged her outright.

Every so often she referred to her private data, using her laptop and changing the memory sticks as she went. Then she checked the results against her ledger.

The ledger was her secret treasure. It had taken her virtually since the Sunday lunch with the Burneys to put it together, and it contained page after page of text, calculations and diagrams, all entered by hand. It had never been near a computer, so no one could hack into it, call it up by accident or reconstruct anything she'd deleted. As far as Klemmsley was concerned, she'd been doing the job she was hired to do. But on the quiet she'd assembled the evidence to show Harvest Home meant death on a catastrophic scale. That evidence was now in the ledger, but every so often she'd kept a page blank except for the heading – 'Summary'. Those pages were what she had to fill in now. Using a fountain pen she'd had since her school days, she wrote everything out in numbered points. And when she'd filled the final blank page, she added in caps, 'IT HAS TO HAPPEN! THE PHYSICS SAYS IT ALL!'

That was it. She closed down Klemmsley Marine's programmes, yawned luxuriantly, and put her ledger back in her grip. The laptop and memory sticks went in as well. She'd lose the hardware for good as soon as she had the chance – there was plenty of deep, silent water in Essex. With her snack litter cleared up, she encoded a note to Fox saying she needed to speak to him urgently, put it in an envelope, and destroyed the codebook in her top-security atomiser. When she opened the blinds, she was glad to see there were still some streaks of daylight about. She couldn't say why, but it gave her a lift.

Feeling suddenly hungry, she stopped off in the canteen for an overdue lunch, made a point of saying she was going home now, and set off not for Essex but for London.

It was well into the evening when she squeezed her car into a school gateway in Kensington Place and walked to a drop box for unwanted spectacles that stood in the entrance to a twenty-four hour convenience store. Select Russian Embassy staff had a key to it, so did the manager, and the system was simple: the spectacles went to Moorfields Eye Hospital and the messages went to the Embassy. She slid the envelope in, heard it hit the wadding inside, and set off for Edge Street, her breath white in the freezing air. The steps she was looking for were well lit, and a surveillance camera was openly attached to the wrought iron bracket arching over them. She gave it a quick look, scratched her forehead with her thumb, and carried on round the block till she was back to her car. It was up to the Russians now.

Midnight had come and gone by the time she reached Oaklands. She was entirely depleted by this time, but she was still fizzing as well, so she heated some milk, put some shortbread on a plate, and did her best to let the day drain away. She wasn't expecting to hear from Dvorski till after she'd had some sleep, but as she was rinsing her cup and plate her land-line phone rang.

"Fox here," she heard. "What's up?"

She guessed he was using a stolen mobile, it wouldn't be the first time. Its next stop would be the Thames. It was all part of the paranoid lives they were leading.

"I need to talk to you," she said. "I'm not in trouble, but it can't wait too long either. When can you come to Klemmsley Marine? Can you make it soon?"

There was a pause at the other end.

"Give me a day or two, I'll see what I can do." Then, "You don't usually want to see me."

"That's true, but try me this time. Will you ring me back?"

"I doubt it. Just don't go shunting off anywhere."

"To hear is to obey. When you come, bring an empty briefcase with you. I've got something bulky for you."

On Friday 9th February she was working in Klemmsley Marine when her desk phone buzzed. It was Russell Burney, he was on site as well. He said Oleg Dvorski had called him on behalf of Gazprom, they wanted some back figures for Cockerel, and Dvorski would be the messenger boy. If he looked in at one thirty, could she talk him through them? He detailed which figures and rang off.

When Reception buzzed to say Dvorski had arrived, she was so tense, she went dizzy as she stood up. With her grip in her hand, she took him down to the sub-basement room they'd got into the habit of using. He'd borrowed an expanding briefcase from Valkov and it went onto an empty chair. The Cockerel print-outs were waiting in a pile, and sitting opposite him across the table, she launched straight into her own thing, while he tilted his chair back and did his best to look bored. He was wearing better than she was. His appointments calendar was bulging, he was looking sleekly pleased with himself, and a female secretary in Economic Development was asking him to her place. The only shadow was the SVR – it still had doubts about him. He knew it from hints from Valkov.

"I've got the deal of a lifetime for you," she said briskly. Her bad temper was absent for once, she was sure she was onto a winner. "The price is high, Oleg – it's my release from you and everything to do with your lousy country – but if you buy, you'll be the Kremlin's favourite son. Are you interested?"

Inwardly he groaned. Not that again.

"Keep going," he said dourly. "I'll tell you when you're through."

"In other words, you're not, so let's see if Harvest Home makes a difference. You think you know as much about it as I do. Do you know when it starts?"

"I read the press release. The lead-in starts September 15th. You go max the following week."

"Correct, but what you don't know is, Harvest Home's a killer. It'll take lives on a scale you'll never see outside of wartime, and I'm not talking guesswork, I'm talking physics. Do you want the details, Mr Know-it-all? It'd strike you dead to say it, but I'll put money on it that you do."

"How can I stop you, Dandy?"

"You can't, so listen instead. Cockerel Field starts on what the Brits call their Continental Shelf. That much even you know. You also know the field runs out beyond the Shelf and where that happens, the seabed drops off like a mountainside. It's a sheer drop and the new seabed's a lot further down than the old one. It isn't sand either, not any more. It's prehistoric sediment and it's packed with methane hydrate."

He yawned and looked at his watch.

"How many more times are you going to tell me all this? Next you'll say, if I go down even deeper, heat from the earth's core stops the methane icing up, and that's how I get the gas bubble you're calling Harvest Home. There's no deal here, Dandy, you're just rattling your cage."

"That's where you're wrong, Russian, because what no one knows except me and now you is this. When we go max on that bubble, we'll disturb the sediment above it, and then do you know what'll happen?"

"Surprise me."

"A great chunk will break off and slide down like an avalanche. And if you've ever seen an avalanche on TV – a really big one, I mean – you'll understand what I'm saying next. That chunk will cause a tsunami so big, it'll deluge vast swathes of England, Holland, Belgium, Northern France and Northern Germany."

"Including where you and your mother live, I suppose."

"Absolutely. We won't be there, I'll see to that, but everyone else will be, and if you think you'll be safe in London, think again. The Thames Barrier will help, it's what it's there for, and my calculations say your precious Embassy will get away with a wet basement. But everything nearer the river will be inundated, and if you're in a tube train, which I very much hope, you'll drown like the rat you are."

Dvorski felt doubts growing. She was too good a scientist to walk away from.

"How long would it take to happen? Have you worked that out as well?"

She looked straight at him.

"Not 'would' but 'will'. Just piercing the bubble won't make much difference. We do that to test we've got our pressures right, and not all the platforms will do it at the same time. But when we go max, it'll be fifteen platforms all going hell for leather, and I tell you straight, Oleg, that chunk will slide down within hours."

"You're sure of that, are you?"

"I've done the maths."

"Will the tsunami take out the rigs?"

"No, the pressure wave will spread east and south. That's why it will do so much damage. Look at a map and see for yourself."

"Experts can be wrong," he said, but he was thoroughly shaken now. "What makes you think you're so different?"

"I've told you, I've done the maths. What's more, it's happened before. Eight thousand years ago a great chunk broke loose off Norway. That caused waves nearly seventy feet high, and they ran all the way to the Atlantic. There was no drilling in those days, I grant you that, but the rest fits like a glove."

"So you say, but the past isn't the future, and County Durham isn't Norway. Even if I believe you, I still have to convince other people. I can't do that with a history lesson, I'd get laughed out of the room."

She took her ledger out, put it midway between them, and took him through some sample pages.

"All my stats are in this ledger and so are my conclusions. Anyone with the right kind of knowledge can check them out. The stats from the Norwegian tsunami are in it as well. You can take it with you when you go. You can also ask your Moscow Einsteins to check the sums for themselves. They'll soon see I'm right. In fact you can have it right now, Russian. Go on, take it. It's yours."

That knocked him completely off guard. In his world no one gave anything away.

"If I take this ledger, you've got nothing to bargain with!" he exclaimed. "Unless you've got a copy stashed away somewhere."

"There's no copy, there's only this ledger, and like I said, you can have it. But don't get me wrong, I've still got plenty to bargain with. I can tell Cyril Burney about the tsunami any time I like, and he'll kill Harvest Home stone dead because he doesn't like it. I can also trash you, Oleg. All I have to do is say I've been spying for you all these years, and you're blown right there. You'll be finished, junked, chewed and spat out – pick your own word, they all mean the same thing."

That scared him outright.

"You wouldn't do that, Dandy. You'd be finished too."

She gave him a look of pure evil.

"You've damaged me so much, I'd let myself be finished ten times over just to pay you back. If I go down, you go down with me, and you'll hear me laughing all the way. On the other hand, if you get me my release, you're the one who'll be laughing. I'll keep Harvest Home on track for you, and when Western Europe goes glug, you'll get a chestful of medals and a Red Square parade."

He took his time before he responded, but she could see she'd won. She slid the ledger towards him.

"Put it in your briefcase," she said. "Put the Gazprom print-outs in with it."

He did as he was told, but then he had to ask her.

"Why do you think the Kremlin will love me so much?"

"Russia is weak but it likes to act strong. It can only do that if the competition's even weaker. And don't think you can double-cross me after you get your Moscow medals. If I get even a hint that's what you're up to, I'll have my Daddy's death re-opened. Remember this, Russian, and remember it well. America looks after its own. It always has done and it always will."

She let him take that on board, then,

"I've told you a lot of things, now you tell me just one, if you can manage that much: What do I do right now?"

"Be patient. We'll check everything, then it's decision time, and I can't say when that will be. I wish I could, but I'm not as free as I was. You won't get your ledger back, that goes without saying."

"I can live without it. It's there to do a job, that's all."

He got to his feet, tapped the table thoughtfully, and gathered in the Gazprom papers.

"You're sure no one else knows what you've told me?" he asked before she could open the door. "Or can ferret it out for themselves?"

"I've told absolutely no one, and no one else has my data. So, no to both. It's between you, me, and whoever you show that ledger to. No one else."

"But why no one else, Dandy? If you don't keep copies and you don't tell anyone either, you're all on your own."

"That's how I have to be for me to take you on. I've burned my bridges, every single one. From now on I've got no choice. I have to get my way."

"Ah, yes, of course. In a better world I'd wish you luck."

She shouldn't have answered like that; it was exactly what Dvorski wanted to hear. Once he got clearance, he'd act on it.

Chapter 7

Dvorski Sees for Himself

As soon as he'd put distance between himself and Klemmsley Marine, Dvorski pulled over to contact Valkov, and at seven o'clock that evening he was in Valkov's corner room, with Valkov pouring the coffee. Dvorski placed the ledger on his desk and took him word for word through what Torelli had told him. Then he spelled out what he wanted to do.

"You want her killed straight away, do you?" Valkov ruminated smoothly. "Tell me again why."

"So she can't have second thoughts about keeping it all to herself. Or let something slip by accident."

"Well, that makes sense. But why have her mother killed as well?"

"To fool the police. If it was just Dandy, I'd be one of the first to get looked at."

"And you want them both shot by the Millers. Well, that makes sense, too. You'll be miles away, and if anything goes wrong, they can carry the can. They can't get through you to us, can they?"

"Not a chance. They think I'm Russian mafia."

Valkov thought for a moment.

"I need to clear this with Moscow," he said. "Fortunately I know who to speak to."

He looked at his watch and tutted.

"It's getting late over there, but I'll try all the same. If you'll just step into the corridor and close the door …"

He took a long time over his call, or so it seemed to Dvorski. Finally he called him back in.

"You're in luck," he said as he filled the cups again. "You've got a provisional OK and fast track treatment as well. This ledger goes to Moscow tomorrow in the diplomatic bag and – let me see, today's Friday – you'll get a yea or a nay through me today week. That means you have this weekend to find out how to get to Dove Cottage without being seen and when Torelli walks home from her mother's. Then you can ready up the Millers. If you get the green light from Moscow, they can shoot the Torellis the night after that."

"I'll need a stolen mobile again. With a voiceprint neutraliser. And the Millers will have to be paid."

"How much?"

He was afraid of pushing Valkov too far, so he pitched his number low.

"£50,000 between them," he answered. "That's more than enough. They're doing well these days, thanks to us."

"You're in charge. You can pick up the money tomorrow. And I'll see about a mobile. Anything else?"

"What they're going to shoot with."

"They can't use our guns – that's far too dangerous. See if they've got any of their own. You said you'd noticed some photos."

"I'll sort something out. If there's a problem I'll let you know."

The next day Dvorski waited till the sky was darkening, then he drove off. He'd used a rambler's map to pinpoint where to head for – he wouldn't leave any electronic fingerprints that way – so all he had to do was point his car in the right direction and take his time. Two and a half hours later, he was pulling off a deserted country lane and halting behind a derelict public house called The Manningtree Ox. The windows were boarded up, the door was padlocked, and the 'For Sale' sign looked as if it'd been there for a very long time. No one would see his car there.

The sky was cloudless, it was still bitterly cold, and all the forecasts said it was going to stay that way. He knew because he'd checked, and he was pleased about it. He needed a big freeze.

He had the best part of a three mile walk in front of him, but the lane was flat, so he could do it fairly fast. There was just enough starlight for him to see where he was putting his feet, but walking in the dark was something he'd have to raise with the Millers – torches weren't an option. The lane twisted and turned, so he saw the headlights of the three cars that approached him before they picked him up, and each time he lay face down in a ditch till they'd gone. When he reached the footpath that led to Dove Cottage – not from Oaklands but from the other side of the wood – he checked how long he'd taken and then started down it. Trees on one side and a high hedge on the other cut out most of the starlight, so it was seriously dark now. There were no sounds at all and the ground was like granite.

The high hedge marked the edge of a field, and just beyond where an even narrower footpath turned off were Dove Cottage and its two neighbouring cottages. The drawn curtains were all lit up from inside, and the front gardens were marked off with picket fences that were so low, there was no point bolting the gates. As he continued along, he saw that the front doors – as the English persist in calling them – were round the side, with paths made of paving slabs between them and the gates. He knew from Dandy that when she went home from Dove Cottage, Irma came out with her and stood at the gate till she entered the wood. When he got to the wood himself, he kept on till he knew how it was in there and, in particular, how dark it was. It was pure black. Because Dandy might just come from the other direction while he was still in there, he got out quickly, and when he reached the even narrower path again, he turned into it. It tracked round the cottages' back gardens, and he saw that they, too, had paving slab paths, low fences and gates with no bolts. There were other cottages about, he could tell by their lights, but they were a safe distance away. It couldn't be better. Becky, who struck him as being faster on her feet than Chris, could take up a position where she'd be hidden by the nearest cottage, but where she'd still be able to see enough of Irma's porch light when it came on. When Irma saw Dandy off, she'd give Becky her chance to cut round to Irma's back garden and get through her front door while it was unlocked and unalarmed. Then, when Irma came in, she could shoot her dead. Chris, meanwhile, could wait in the wood for Dandy, take her out, and move on to collect Becky. Then they could walk back to their car together.

Because Dvorski saw no sign of Dandy, he assumed she was in Dove Cottage, so he positioned himself where he wanted Becky to stand and waited. He froze through rapidly, but he forced himself to stay put. After what seemed an age, Irma's porch light came on, and as soon as he sighted Dandy and her mother, he slipped round to the cottage's back gate. From there he could make them out as they stood by the front gate, and he could hear them talking as well. Then the front gate sounded twice as it was opened and shut, and Irma finally went indoors without using a key, putting the porch light out after her. In his imagination, Dvorski saw her being gunned down in the hallway with almost no noise at all, while Dandy, all unsuspecting and, better yet, with a torch in her hand, was making things easy for Chris. He had no doubts – it couldn't fail.

Chapter 8

Two Murders and an Invitation

The days merged into one after that, and the following Thursday, around mid-morning, Dvorski was in the Embassy typing pool dictating letters when Valkov opened the door and beckoned him outside.

"You've obviously made an impression," he said. "Your OK's come through a day early."

Without being asked, he handed Dvorski a fresh mobile phone.

"You'll need to resurrect the Millers. Why not this afternoon?"

A single call was enough, and at half past three Dvorski set off north. In the Skoda's boot were four hundred used £50 notes, this time in a code-locked security case. He didn't take a gun. Things had moved on.

The Millers had gone up in the world. The garage in Queen of Scots Lane had been sold, and calling themselves Chrisbeckmill Motors, they were now in deluxe premises in Westgate, near the town centre, where they had a Toyota franchise and a lengthening list of fleet contracts. Periodically a courier replaced their mobiles, but that was all. Threatening phone calls and menacing shadows were securely part of the past.

They stayed open till six because they were earning so well, and it was half past the hour when, by pre-arrangement to let the staff get off the premises, Dvorski pulled onto the forecourt and flashed his lights. Becky came out to greet him, told him he hadn't changed a bit, and said Chris wanted him to park round the back – he'd be out of sight there. She'd show him where to go, she said, and got in, filling the front space with perfume. As she did so, she leaned against him just long enough to suggest it wasn't accidental, and glanced his way as well. When they got out, she ushered him in through a back entrance and led him to The Manager's Office (as it said on the door). She'd dyed her hair amber, she was wearing quartz dangle earrings, and her tailored two-piece was intended to show her body lines. Ditto her high heels. She had bangles on both wrists, and her nails were green.

The Manager's Office was large, well-lit and spotless, and Chris, lounging casually behind his polished teak desk, looked like a rich man getting richer by the day. While Becky was making coffee, Dvorski, in his Sanderson accent, asked to see the CCTV.

"It's been shut down since six," Chris said. The old deference was gone. "We hadn't forgotten. Becky did it."

"I'd still like to check."

"Please yourself. It's just along the corridor."

He led the way into a windowless room that housed a bank of screens. They were all blank.

"Start it up," Dvorski said.

As Chris had said, it had been shut down at six. Dvorski ought to have been pleased, but Chris's arrogance made him edgy.

Becky gave them a big smile when they got back. After she'd poured the coffee, Dvorski unlocked his security case and opened it on his lap. The office had one-way glazing, but there was no one about anyway.

"I've got another job for you," he said, "and the deal is the same as before. If you look after us, we'll look after you, but if you make trouble, you'll wish you hadn't. You'll get £50,000 between you, and we'll keep on seeing you right. I've got £20,000 here. The rest is yours when the job's done."

He watched them as he spoke, and there was Chris's arrogance again. £50,000 bounced right off him, and Dvorski saw he'd got it wrong – it was peanuts these days. Becky was different. Just fleetingly, she looked worried, as if something she'd been dreading had turned up at last. Then the smile came back.

"What do you want us to do?" she asked, unconsciously twisting her bangles.

He took them through the murders of Dandy and Irma Torelli, told them they were the daughter and widow of Jethro Torelli since he had no reason not to, and said Saturday night was when it had to be. They looked surprised to hear the Torelli name again, especially after so long, but they didn't ask what it was all about. They knew what the answer would be.

"The younger Torelli looks like this," Dvorski said, showing them a copy of a photo he'd brought with him from Sakhalin Island. "And her mother looks like this."

It was an enlarged version of the photo Dandy had given him. The drawing pin hole was clearly visible. He gave them time to memorise them, then took them back.

"The old lady looks sweet," Becky couldn't help saying. "But I'll still kill her for you," she added quickly.

Was there an overtone in her voice he couldn't quite catch? Dvorski thought there might be, but Chris didn't seem to notice anything, so Dvorski went on with saying his piece.

"Use a dark-coloured car. I don't want it seen while it's parked. There'll be a bit of a moon, but basically you'll be walking in the dark. Get used to the idea. You can't use torches at any time."

"You forget we fish," Chris said. "We've both got night goggles."

Dvorski had never worn night goggles. They hadn't been in his training.

"What about in the wood? It's completely black in there."

"Not a problem. The sea hasn't got streetlamps either."

Dvorski willed himself to be patient.

"Point taken," he nodded. "Now, the ground will be too frozen to take tyre marks or footprints, but you could have a long wait, so you'll need warm clothes and footwear."

"Understood."

"The bodies can stay where they drop, and don't steal anything. Leave everything where it is."

"Understood again."

"You'll need an alibi for the evening."

"We'll be at home watching TV. We'll put the recorder on and catch up later."

"And you have to supply your own guns. Can you do that?"

Without answering, Chris stood up and unlocked a side door. It opened into a much smaller room. He beckoned Dvorski in and Becky followed.

"Top people always have a private office," he said with no trace of irony. "This is mine."

There were a couple of lockers in there, a desk that had seen better days, a computer and, dominating everything else, a massive safe. Chris opened the desk's top drawer, placed his palm over a reader, and tapped in the opening code. As soon as a red light in the safe's top right hand corner was winking, he swung the door open to reveal shelves full of carefully sorted papers and enough cash to make £50,000 seem like pocket money. On the floor of the safe, behind some box files, were two locked strongboxes. He took them out, stood them on the desk, and opened them. One contained two pistols and two silencers, all in bubblewrap. The other one contained ammunition in magazines.

"These are Walther P22s," he said. "Someone bought them in America, and they found their way to us because we were going to do a job which, thanks to you, went ahead without us. Becky can handle one of these as well as I can. As you see, they're nice and small. They've also got a red laser sight, so shooting dead is pre-programmed, a chimpanzee can do it. The barrels are ready-threaded for a silencer. No one will hear you shoot unless they're standing on your foot."

"Has anyone seen you use them? Like at your club?"

"We tried them out on a closed range, and afterwards we picked up the bullets. So no, no one's seen us use them, and they can't be traced back to us, because they're not registered to us. It'll be good to fire them again. Just looking at them makes my fingers itch."

He locked everything away, swung the safe door shut, and worked the palm reader again. The red light went out.

"There's explosive in that door," he added, preening himself. "When the red light goes out, it's primed for if anyone tries to open it up who shouldn't. The explosive's supposed to be a stun grenade, but I've done something about that, so anyone trying his luck has had it. You'll need tweezers to put them together again."

"You know about explosives, do you?"

Out of the corner of his eye, Dvorski saw Becky look fixedly ahead. He was convinced she moved her lips to say, "No."

"I get around. I put the palm reader in as well. My palm print plus the right code de-primes the explosive and unlocks the door. The same goes for Becky's palm, but not for anyone else's. "

"You're sure of all that? I mean, that's pretty high tech."

"I know what I'm doing, I tell you. Even if someone gets past the reader, they won't know the code because that's between me, Becky, and no one else. Two wrong digits and they're dead. I'm like you, Mr Sanderson. I look after myself."

Dvorski had said all he wanted to say about murdering the Torellis, but he needed to take a closer look at how the Millers felt. Control was one thing he couldn't afford to lose. So when they were back in The Manager's Office, he asked if he could have some more coffee before he hit the road. Becky seemed pleased at the idea and so did Chris, which seemed odd after the business with the money. It was as if something had jogged his memory.

"You must be hungry as well," Becky said. "I've got stacks of sandwiches in the freezer upstairs. I'll put some in the microwave, and we can eat them with the coffee."

She came back from their flat with a plateful of slightly warm turkey sandwiches and a basket of fresh fruit. They ate in chrome-and-leather easy chairs round a low marquetry table. It was patterned with a Chinese dragon.

"I like what you've done here," Dvorski said, waving his hand vaguely in the air. "What do you spend your profits on? Anything special?"

"A cottage in Brancaster Staithe for a start," Chris answered, trying now to sound sociable. "Do you know where that is?"

Dvorski shook his head.

"Try the North Norfolk coast near The Wash. Becky's readying it up for the summer."

"It's been let go a bit," she put in, "but we still snapped it up when it came on the market. They're as rare as gold dust these days. I've done the inside, but the garden's still a mess, and so's the outside woodwork. Chris doesn't need me in the garage anymore, so it gives me something to do. We've bought a new fishing boat as well, an Ala 500. She's lovely, isn't she, Chris?"

"Why don't I fetch my laptop, then you can see for yourself?" he said, completely amiable now. It was as if he'd pulled a stocking mask over his true feelings. "We're logging everything as we do it. It'll give us something to look back on."

He didn't ask whether Dvorski wanted to see their pictures, he just disappeared through the door. As soon as Becky thought she was safe, she pushed it to without closing it fully.

"I'm glad he's gone, I was getting worried," she said softly as she moved her chair and put her hand on Dvorski's thigh. "I'll be in Brancaster next Wednesday. You can come over if you like. We'll be all on our own and I can vouch for the beds. I bought them myself."

He'd have said yes anyway, just to find out what was going on, but his friendly secretary in Economic Development was in Ekaterinburg on leave, and Becky's fondling, he had to admit, was having an effect.

"What time will you get there?" he asked.

"It's about two hours from here, give or take the traffic. Say eleven o'clock?"

"I'll be there."

Hastily she took paper and a biro from Chris's note-bloc, wrote out the address, and tucked it into the top pocket of his jacket. Then she moved her chair away and re-opened the door. When Chris came back, she was on her feet tidying up.

"Sorry about the delay," he said. "Things are never where you think they are."

He could hardly say he'd got Dvorski to park round the back because he wanted to fit a tracker to his car. The monitor was in his private workshop, a small closed-off unit in the main workshop with only one key to it – his. He'd been thinking for some time he could get some very large sums out of Sanderson if he could find out more about him. The £50,000 just made him more determined, and he'd keep Becky out of it for once. She got enough for doing nothing as it was.

Chris had no inkling he was being kept out of something himself. He didn't believe Becky could do anything for herself, but she was bored rigid now they were wealthy. She didn't do much more than fiddle with the CCTV, and Dvorski aroused her because he was dangerous. That alone made her want him badly, but she also had a practical reason for getting him all to herself – she wanted his help. Sex first, then the big ask. That, in her world of *Bella*, dyed hair and bangles, was how to get her way.

Dvorski stayed another hour before driving off into the night, still unsure what to make of Chris's change of mood. He'd have to be more careful from now on, even if he didn't know what about.

When he was gone, Chris said,

"I'm going to change the safe's combination. I feel nervous now Sanderson's seen how it works."

"Hang on a minute, I'll write it down. I'll get my little book."

As soon as she was back, he said,

"I'll change all the 3s to 5s, all the Ps to Zs and the two hashes to question marks. That should be enough. I'll do it when I've got a minute."

"Aren't you going to write it down yourself, Chris?"

"No need, I'll remember it, it was my idea in the first place, don't forget. Just stay out of the safe till I say. You've got no business in there anyway; you don't do the paperwork any more."

Saturday evening was cold and clear, and the fragment of moonlight helped a bit, but the Millers still put their night goggles on after they parked behind the Manningtree Ox. They'd come in a black Avensis Chris kept as a garage run-about. No one would check the mileage, he always did it himself, and since they were parking out of sight, he'd left its real plates on. Like Dvorski, he and Becky lay flat when a car came past, but it only happened twice. They had no trouble finding Dove Cottage, and they reckoned Dandy must already be in there.

"You wait here," Chris whispered, keeping to Dvorski's instructions. "I'll go into the wood. How are you feeling?"

He'd noticed she was shaking.

"I'm all right. I'm cold, that's all."

He raised her chin with his gloved hand and kissed her on the nose. His night goggles made everything look green, but he could still see how pale her cheeks were. They should have used blacking, he thought, but it was too late now.

"We can do a lot with £50,000," he came back, wanting to give her a lift. "Fix your mind on that."

She gave him a wan smile, and as he set off, she unsafed her Walther and settled down to letting the time pass. Again like Dvorski, she had a long cold wait before the porch light came on and Dandy and Irma came out. She moved swiftly round to the back of Irma's cottage, and waited till Irma was watching Dandy walk away with her torch on. Then she slipped up the side of the cottage and was about to open the door when she realised – it was something Dvorski had missed – that she'd let a dangerous amount of light out if she did. With her nerves jangling, she yanked her goggles off to see where the shadows were, and just as Irma turned to come back, she slipped behind a yew bush. Irma was happy and sad all in one. It meant a lot seeing Dandy so often, but there was no Jethro to go back indoors to, so there was always pain twice over when Dandy left. Knowing she'd shed a tear or two, Irma put her hand on the door handle, and just as she was stepping in, Becky rushed out at her, bundled her inside, and shut the door, taking care not to slam it.

Swept off balance, Irma thudded onto the floor, and by the time a scream was forming, Becky was standing over her, pointing her Walther at her. Her goggles were in her pocket, and suddenly she and Irma were just two human beings who'd never met before, one of them knowing she was going to murder the other one.

"Don't make a sound," Becky ordered, and Irma stifled her scream at the very last second. Without taking her eyes off her, Becky reached back and switched the porch light off. She didn't want anyone to think anything was wrong.

As Becky stood there, still panting, she realised she should have shot Irma when she'd bundled her inside. Now she'd have to do it in cold blood, and she didn't think she could. Irma had looked sweet in Sanderson's photo, and she looked even sweeter in real life; and heartrendingly vulnerable as well. Maybe Becky should just knock her out, run away, and make up some excuse for Sanderson. He must know things could go wrong; maybe that and some sex in Brancaster would be enough. But the woman on the floor knew what Becky looked like, she was staring at her petrified right now. And there was Chris as well. He'd kill Irma just like that, and Becky knew it. So she had to do it, too.

"Get up," Becky ordered – she had to see Irma moving before she could shoot her – and as the terrified old lady clambered painfully to her feet, Becky tensed up, pulled the trigger, and put a bullet into her chest, hurling her against the wall. The second bullet pierced her stomach, and the third destroyed much of her head. Becky was staring-eyed with horror, but she couldn't stop shooting till the magazine was empty. She'd never seen anyone who'd been shot before, and she couldn't believe the damage she'd done. There were blood and bits of body everywhere, and what had once been Irma was now a slaughtered heap. More than anything, Becky wanted to bring her back to life, and she knew she'd lose it altogether if she stayed there any longer. Her silencer wasn't cool enough to go in her bag, so she tugged her goggles on one-handed, and with her gun still exposed, she hurried outside, forcing herself to shut the door silently.

Dandy, meanwhile, was well into the wood when she thought she half-saw something move further down the footpath. Instinctively she slowed down and shone her torch ahead of her, but it didn't show anything, so she kept on walking, uncertain whether to go faster or slower. But Chris could see her clearly. He locked his red laser sight onto her, waited until she was twenty paces away, and shot her through the heart. When he was certain she wouldn't move, he walked up to her and shone her torch onto her face. It matched the photo he'd seen. He switched the torch off and, just to be sure, shot her through the head from six paces. He'd been told to leave her where she dropped, so he did. As he walked back up the footpath, he wondered how Becky had got on. He soon found out. As soon as he came out of the wood – he was no more than a movement in the dark – she broke into a run towards him. When he saw the state she was in, he took her back into the wood and gave her time to calm down.

"She's dead, that's the main thing," he said after she'd told him what had happened, and he gave her a squeeze and a kiss. "Now, put your gun away and let's go. I reckon the bodies will be found tomorrow morning, and the media will go viral. We've got to be ready for that."

Dandy's body was found at 7.03 am by a vicar taking his dog for a walk by torchlight before a busy day in two rural churches in two different places. Horrified, he called the police on his mobile, who went on to find Irma's body at 8.17. Radio and TV carried the story through the day, and on Monday first thing the print media took over. Chris always had newspapers in his showroom and waiting room. He fetched them himself as usual, agreed with the newsagent it was 'awful' what had happened, and was in The Manager's Office flicking through them when Becky came down, already prinked for the day. When she saw the papers, she gasped out loud.

"If you carry on like that," he said sharply, "we've had it. *We* know they're writing about us, but *they* don't. We spent Saturday night watching TV, and no one can prove we didn't. As long as we stick to that, we're safe, and Sanderson's money's ours."

She fretted helplessly all through the day, finding things to go out for, then walking straight past the shops because she thought her face would give her away. Guilt and remorse didn't come into it, what bothered her was not knowing. Three years before, she'd gone through a red light she hadn't seen early enough, and for days she'd hung around the letter box expecting the summons that never came. This was the same only a whole lot worse. She was still fretting on Tuesday, but she did her best to stifle it because she was desperate to go to Brancaster on Wednesday. Chris noticed she didn't look so edgy, but he didn't think to ask why.

"You've been more your old self today," he said in his male dominant way as they ate their evening meal. The TV news was on. It was Becky who'd said she wanted to see it. "You're still going to Brancaster are you? It'll get all this out of your head."

"That's what I think," she nodded. "I'll leave straight after breakfast and stay the whole day. The next time you come, you won't know the place."

"Well, it won't be tomorrow, we've got two deliveries due. But I'll get there when I can, don't you worry. I want to see what you've been up to."

Dvorski was intent on going to Brancaster as well, but he hesitated whether to tell Valkov or no. If he told him and it went wrong, it would make him look a fool, but if it went right and he told him afterwards, he might get some glory. In the end, he plumped for the second option, and when he signed out a Honda Civic from the Embassy car pool, he logged the loan as 'Private', not 'Official'. Chris checked his tracker through the day, but all he got was the mews Dvorski parked his Skoda in.

When Dvorski arrived in Brancaster, Becky had been there for over an hour and was rubbing the outside paintwork down. She was wearing white overalls over a thick pullover against the cold, and a cherry red scarf covered her hair, which was light brunette with darker streaks.

"Be making some tea," she called down the ladder. "This is the last frame. I'll come in as soon as I finish. We're keeping the heating on at the moment, so you'll be all right."

It didn't take her long.

"I'll paint what I've sanded later and photograph it," she said, feeling the mug nice and hot in her freshly washed hands. "Then Chris won't start getting ideas."

She asked Dvorski to come into her and Chris's bedroom while she undressed for a shower in the ensuite. When she was naked she turned her head sideways on, put one hand up to the back of it, and stretched the other arm out.

"Do you think I'm pretty?" she asked. "I bet you do. You wouldn't be here otherwise."

"I think you're very pretty," he said, only half-lying. "As you say, I wouldn't be here if I didn't."

When she'd showered, they made love on the brand new bed, and afterwards they lay under the covers and talked.

"It's funny," she said, snuggling up to him. "I thought I'd never get over shooting that old lady. I was nearly out of my mind at the time, but not a ripple since. It was the same when old man Torelli went. Have I got a gift? Being able to kill like that, I mean?"

"You must have. Most people couldn't even do it, let alone put it behind them. They'd be nervous wrecks."

She gave a contented sigh and nuzzled his shoulder.

"It makes me nearly as good as Chris, then. He was cool as you like, and he still is. I'm completely over the shooting, but I'm afraid of being caught. I was even afraid before I knew what the job was, it broke out when I knew you were coming. I like you a lot, that's why I asked you here, but there's something else as well."

So she was moving away from Chris and finding she liked it. Valkov had said there was no one else on the horizon, but there was now. He was. What was the something else, he wondered. He soon found out.

"You're Russian, aren't you?" she asked, but it didn't sound entirely like a question. "And your name isn't Sanderson. It's made up."

Had she been spying on him? He went tense and wary.

"What *is* my name then?" he asked, forcing a smile.

"I don't know and it doesn't really matter. But you are Russian, aren't you? I need you to say you are."

"All right, I'm Russian and my name's Oleg, you can have it for free. What's the panic all of a sudden?"

"Like I said, I'm afraid of being caught – terrified, to be honest. The police have only just started, but they'll get to me all right, I'm certain they will, I know what they're like from … from the old days; and I'm a murderer now, even more than in Florida. So I want you to promise me, when they get close, you'll get me out of this country and into Russia. You must be able to do it. You've got money and contacts, I know you have."

He kissed her and cupped his hand over one of her breasts.

"Of course I'll get you out, word of honour. You've earned it and more besides. But what about Chris? Don't you want me to get him out, too?"

She hesitated, then said,

"I'm not sure. Normally I'd say yes straight out, but you've made a difference, and part of me says I don't want you to. You've got to understand, Oleg, this is all new for me. Maybe I'd better say no, then you won't get confused. Now tell me how I can reach you in a hurry."

Dvorski felt uneasy, this was definitely Valkov territory. On the other hand, Valkov did seem to be letting him off the reins a bit. Surprisingly so, in fact, and he didn't know whether he liked it now he thought about it. There'd be no hiding place for him if anything went wrong, and he could hear the wolves howling already.

"I'll give you a number," he said finally.

She got out of bed and fetched her little book from her handbag. He dictated the number and added,

"You'll be told it's unobtainable. Ring off and wait for a call back. It won't be from me, but whoever it is can get me quickly."

That should keep Valkov happy. He'd still be in final control.

They fondled each other and made love a second time, then Becky, anxious again, said she'd better get on with the painting.

"Shall I stay or shall I go?" he asked as they got dressed. "I can get something to eat on the road if I have to."

"You'd better go. I don't want you being noticed, someone might say something to Chris. You've told me what I wanted to know. If you want to come again, get a message to me, and if it's safe, I'll arrange it."

She put her arms round his neck and kissed him.

"You made me happy doing what you did to me. I want you to do it again and again. I want you to say you'll help me again as well. I'll do anything you like for that. Cross my heart I will."

Gently he pushed her away, letting go of her hands last.

"Save yourself the trouble," he laughed. "I'm as nice as they come, really I am. It's in my nature, I'm afraid. There's nothing I can do about it."

II
A Murder in Stages

Chapter 9

A Trip to the Peak District

When Dvorski arrived in the Embassy the next morning, he found a brusque note on his desk from Valkov's secretary: Valkov wanted to see him the moment he came in. Sensing trouble, Dvorski hung his coat up and made his way queasily up to the corner room. There was no coffee for him this time, only Valkov's face like an ice pick. He wasn't invited to sit down either.

"Where were you yesterday?" Valkov asked.

He had the car pool register open in front of him. It showed where Dvorski had borrowed the Honda and called the trip private. The car pool clerk had phoned up as soon as Dvorski had left.

Dvorski's heart sank like lead. He'd lived and breathed getting on the right side of Valkov, and now this. There was only one thing for it. He grovelled abjectly and unpacked everything except the rescue plan and the phone number. Yes, he should definitely have cleared the visit first. And it would never happen again.

"You're a fool, Oleg Aleksandrovich," Valkov came back at him. "Nothing you do is private, absolutely nothing. I could pack you off to Moscow for this. I thought you'd put your free-wheeling ways behind you, but I was totally deceived. Well, it's on your record and it stays there."

He slammed the register shut, but when he spoke again, his tone had lost its harshness. He didn't need a psychogram to run Dvorski. He could do it in his sleep.

"We've been having a little think," he purred, as if Dvorski's beating up had never happened. "There's always the chance Torelli's replacement will eventually turn up the same disaster scenario she did and this time tell Russell Burney; so I'll ask you to listen carefully. You'll deliver the rest of the Millers' money tomorrow. We don't want them wondering where it's got to, it will only put their backs up. You can also wave a new job in front of them – no details, just the general prospect of more money – and we want you to see the Miller woman again in approximately three weeks' time. That will bring us to the middle of March. We're taking a chance not acting straight away, but we think time's on our side, and we want to get things absolutely right."

"Why do you want me to see her again?"

"I've told you once, she's got an anxious streak, but it seems to have slipped your mind. The police are buzzing mightily at the moment, that can't be cheering her up, and her anxiety might dampen her enthusiasm for helping us in future; her husband's enthusiasm as well, come to that. But if you tighten her attachment to you before we use her again, you'll bind her in, and him with her. I should have thought that was plain enough, but I see I was mistaken."

Dvorski saw Valkov was right. Why hadn't he thought of it himself?

"I'm sorry. Sometimes I need help with these things."

"So it seems. Now, book the same Honda out as last time when you go to Brancaster, a different car will only give rise to gossip. And this time say it's official."

Valkov poured himself more coffee, while Dvorski stood and listened as he spoke.

"This is your very last chance, my friend, and I hope you can see why you're getting it. If we replace you with someone the Millers don't know, they might not want to play any more, and if that happens, we won't have time to ease in any substitutes for them. So you still matter."

"Thank you, Andrey. I do keep trying."

"So you must. Now, shortly after your next fling with Mrs Miller, you'll go and see both of them in their garage. By then we'll have a better idea of what we want you to tell them about their new job. That's all I wish to say for the moment. You can go now."

But he couldn't. He had to tell him about the flight to Russia and the phone number first.

"You'll be pleased to know I'm binding Becky in already," he began, as if all he ever did was think like Valkov.

Valkov was all sweetness and light when he heard what he'd promised.

"You did well there," he said affably. "Now do the rest."

The Millers were all sweetness and light as well. They didn't even look like complaining when Dvorski handed the money over, and when he said a new job was in the offing, they jumped at it. Dvorski was surprised the way everything went so smoothly. Becky he could account for, but he still couldn't make Chris out, and he didn't know how much that should bother him. Then he thought he did know. When he said he had to be going Chris, male dominant as always, told Becky to see him out.

'What an arrogant fool you are!' Dvorski thought to himself. 'Letting me alone with your wife like that!'

It allowed them to pick a day for Brancaster, but more than that, it told Dvorski Chris's arrogance wasn't just a tic, it was a blind spot. So Chris needn't bother him at all. With a blind spot like that, Dvorski could run rings round him any time he liked.

North Norfolk was at its best when Dvorski hid his Honda in the cottage's double garage, and it stayed at its best all day. He made love to Becky first – she was all fired up from the moment he tapped on the door – then they did enough in the garden to make it look as if she'd really got stuck in. Finally she took him to see the new fishing boat. The tide was in, so she pulled a buoyancy aid over her violet tinted hair, told Dvorski to put Chris's buoyancy aid on – but he didn't – and, tight-lipped now, rowed him out in the by-boat.

"Can you swim?" she asked peevishly as they crossed the tranquil water.

"Yes I can. I used to win trophies at school."

"So did I. But I still wear one of these things."

She pointed to her buoyancy aid with her chin.

"I wish you'd wear one as well. You make me jumpy sitting there like that. What if you're not there when I need you?"

So that was it. He did as she asked. It cost him nothing.

He had zero interest in fishing, but he could see why the Millers liked their boat. And although a picture book sky, fresh sea air, and the powerfully scented Becky were simply perks in the game he was playing, he didn't see why he shouldn't enjoy them. By the time he left, he felt she was entirely committed to him. And if she believed he was committed to her, so much the better.

Dvorski arranged to return to Chrisbeckmill Motors on Monday, March 19th, a day of high winds and heavy showers. For the new job, he had £60,000 in his security case, with £20,000 to follow, plus expenses – a deliberate improvement on last time. He also had some print-outs and a map. The Millers were all smiles yet again. Briefing them didn't take long, and all Becky had to do afterwards was put the percolator on. She'd made the sandwiches shortly before, so this time they tasted bakery fresh. While they ate, they chatted about the Toyota franchise, the cottage in Brancaster, and sea fishing, then Dvorski moved to the second part of his agenda.

"I had a policeman round last Friday," he said, and they stiffened visibly.

"What, from Essex?" Becky croaked, because her voice wouldn't function properly.

Anxiety was fountaining in her.

"Yes and no. He was from the National Crime Agency. It's still Essex's case, but the Torellis were non-UK, so the NCA's joined in. Do you want to know his name?"

"We'd better have it. The Torellis in Essex connect to Jethro Torelli in Florida. He'll get to us through our witness statements," said Chris.

"My thinking, too. His name was Detective Inspector Farrell. Leo Farrell. I'd never met him before, but his first name was on his ID. We're all people-friendly these days, even the NCA."

"How did the police get to you?" Becky asked, twisting her bangles.

"They'd done their homework, that's all. Dandy Torelli and I went back a long way, and they'd found that out. They hadn't had to search very hard, a lot of it was out in the open, so I had more than enough to tell Mr Farrell. And the more I told him, the further I moved into the clear. As you'd expect, my alibi for the night you killed her was as fireproof as yours. I was in a London club playing canasta with some business friends. A lot of people saw me, and I signed in and out at the desk."

"Where does that leave *us* though?" asked Becky. She was hugely frightened. "Like Chris says, they'll find out we were in Florida if they haven't done that already, and they'll come hunting for us. They'll have to."

"So what? Farrell or someone else will turn up here, and all you have to say is, you came across Miranda Cove in the *Angling Times*, you paid for everything yourselves, and you happened to meet Jethro Torelli there but not his wife and daughter. In fact you've never met either of them, not ever. Stick to that and, like me, you'll be in the clear."

"What about Busch? Someone must have seen him with us when Torelli was there."

"Why shouldn't he be seen with you and Torelli? Busch used the same bar and grill you did, and he and Torelli were buddies. It would be strange if you *weren't* seen together. There is one thing, though – the guns you shot Dandy and Irma with. I take it you've got rid of them. If the police find them here, you've had it."

Chris looked straight at him.

"They're at the bottom of the North Sea," he said, defiant and smug.

Dvorski wasn't convinced. Was this Chris's blind spot again? He wanted to wring the truth out of him, but he daren't take him on, not right now. Valkov had described him as a 'shrewd operator'. It would have to do.

"You'll go into action Easter Monday," Dvorski went on after a pause. "There'll be excursions running by then, and someone will call in about times after you've made your booking. Easter Monday's three weeks from now, and you can expect the police to have been here by then. Been and gone, I should say, you can bet this garage on it." He added that in for Becky. "Chris, that Buy-Of-The-Week stand out front: Keep a Toyota on it unless something goes wrong. If it does, put another make on it, and someone will get in touch."

As soon as Dvorski was gone, Chris rang a hotel in Matlock, the Fleur de Lys, and booked a double room from Good Friday to Easter Monday inclusive. Matlock was on the south-eastern fringe of the Peak District and about a two hour drive from Peterborough. The Millers knew the Fleur de Lys well; they often stayed there when they fancied an inland fishing break. Next, while Becky was studying an Ordnance Survey map, he scratched around for a coach firm that did trips from Matlock to a twelfth century ruin called Saxley Castle. It was about a twenty-five mile run. When he'd found one, he booked two seats online and filed the times of the trip in his memory for collection. Finally he told Becky to bring him one of her handbags, and he made it clear which one. It had a shoulder strap with a metal buckle for adjusting it. The buckle's cross-span was flat and straight. It was also longer than the buckle was wide, and it had plain, squared off ends. It was just what he wanted. He took the bag down to his private workshop and measured the cross-span with a laser scan micrometre.

"You'll take this with you for Easter Monday," he said when he brought the bag back. "If you forget it, I'll make you come back for it."

All he had to do now was shuffle his staff to cover for him. He had software for that. It was done in minutes.

The Millers liked to photograph each other holding up fish they'd caught, so they both owned top quality cameras, and they went into the luggage along with a laser distance measurer. When Easter Monday arrived, they had all three items with them as they drove to the coach park. The Fleur de Lys's receptionist thought they were going fishing again.

"Just the thing for a sunny day," she said as they pre-ordered their evening meal, and they agreed with a friendly smile. They might yet get some fishing in anyway.

They were completely relaxed. As Dvorski had warned them, the police – Detective Inspector Farrell, in fact – had called by to enquire about Florida and the Torellis. They'd stuck to their story, dug their bank statements out to prove where the money had come from and, when they were asked, they talked about the TV they'd been watching on the night of Dandy and Irma's murders. Neither Farrell nor anyone else had come back. They had to be in the clear.

The run to Saxley Castle took an hour and every seat was taken. There were quite a few families and two elderly ladies as well. They all sounded English. There were also some Americans, some Australians and a small group of Japanese. All that was left of the castle was a crumbling rectangular keep and fragments of the once-mighty wall that used to surround it. There was no permanent staff – the site wasn't big enough for that – the car park was more earth than asphalt, and access was free to anyone who simply wanted to wander round. But anyone wanting a closer look and a commentary had to book onto a guided coach trip. Like the Millers.

'Gina Wavell (Miss)' was on their driver/guide's name tag, and Wavell took her job very seriously. She asked them to keep together because there were other trippers about, then, after she'd gone through the history of the place, she took them to the top of the keep to enjoy the famous views. The castle overlooked the Hope Valley, and just two wind-swept and twisty roads led up to it. One was the one everyone used, including Wavell. The other one, behind the castle, looked as if it had been a trail for pack-horses before it had been asphalted. There was no CCTV visible anywhere, and there were no notices about it either. That meant there wasn't any. With one exception, nothing was locked up. Like the keep, the remains of the wall could be reached at any time.

The Millers worked their cameras just like everyone else, and when anyone wanted a photo of themselves, they obliged there, too, if a selfie wasn't enough. The wind was strong, but it added to the fun. All Wavell seemed to do while they were up there was drift out of the way and keep smiling, while at the same time making sure no one who hadn't paid joined her group. When they went down, she shepherded them out of the keep towards one of the remnants of the wall. It was relatively well preserved, and it had twin wooden doors in it. They were black with age and on the small side even for a time when most people were shorter than they are now. They didn't reach to the ground, and they were locked together with three antique padlocks made of bronze, each about six inches by five with a pivot-flap over the keyhole. An aging glazed-and-framed poster next to the doors proclaimed 'THE SAXLEY HOLE OF DEATH!' in shock-horror caps. Discreetly Wavell told the parents what she was about to say could give children bad dreams, and two families separated off. As they went, Becky moved near the doors as if she wanted to see them close up, and Chris took some quick shots that just happened to have her in them. Then she moved away again. Whenever Chris took photos from now on, Becky, wearing her handbag so the shoulder strap showed, was always somehow in them. And his camera's supersmart rangefinder logged her distance from the camera as well as the distance from the camera of what else was being photographed.

"Behind these doors," Wavell told the trippers who remained, "is something truly horrible. I think so anyway. I'll show you what it is, and we'll see if you agree."

She tried to sound awesome as she squinted into the sun. People came on her coach trip to see the Hole of Death, and they had to have their money's worth. It was a point of honour for her.

She made sure no freeloaders had closed in, then she ceremoniously took an antique bronze key out of her rucksack and held it up. It was something under four inches long, and the business end was a thick square tab with a branched pattern cut into it. It fitted all three locks, and when she parted the doors, her trippers saw a modern safety railing and darkness.

"People didn't walk through this doorway," she intoned. "They were forced through it, usually feet first. When you get closer, look down, and you'll see the top of a shaft that falls away at an angle. Anyone jammed into it might cling to the sides for a bit, but even if they managed to get back to the doors, they'd be doomed because they'd be locked in. They'd be in total darkness as well."

She pointed towards one of the doors.

"If you look closely," she said, "you'll see a whole load of scratch marks where my hand is pointing. There are some on the other door, too. That's where people scrabbled at the wood. They were crazy with fear, and you can understand why. I'd be the same."

That was one for the cameras, and Chris's was just one more.

"So what happened next?" someone asked.

"Their strength would give out and down they'd slide. We're talking about limestone here. When it's wet, it's slippery, and it's virtually always wet. Eventually they'd fall into a cave they couldn't see, and quite likely they'd break some bones when they landed. That cave was the end of the line. They'd never get back up because the roof is too high, and there was no other way out. So they'd die down there, and if they were lucky, they'd go mad first. You had to be careful who you fell out with in those days, because it all happened just as I've described it."

"Yuk," someone said, but they all had to take a peek so, with the sun on their backs and the grass warm under their feet, they moved towards the black hole and fired their flashes into it. Wavell drifted out of the way again, and before long the group was sub-dividing. Some stood around gossiping, some wandered off to see other parts of the wall, and in the lull Chris said quietly to Becky,

"I need to get close-ups of the locks and the key before we go. Can you ask to see them or something?"

"I don't like to, Chris. It'd make us noticed."

"I can't help that. Go on, ask the guide. She'll be finishing soon."

But the two elderly ladies got in first. They were, one of them told Wavell, retired history teachers, and her raised-volume way of speaking reminded several listeners-in of sitting in the back row trying to look interested. "I'm Madge," she added helpfully, "and this is Florence, my companion. You may remember our names from your passenger list." Might they have a closer look at the padlocks? And the key, too, they'd not seen one as fine as that for a *very* long time. Their prim and proper accents as well as their permed grey hair and sensible shoes chimed exactly with Wavell's idea of private boarding schools, so she was more than happy to oblige.

"They're genuine sixteenth century," she said as she unhooked the locks. "They were the earliest the trustees could get that would do the job. Anything older would've been balls of rust by now."

Seeing what was happening, Becky moved in as if she was interested too, and Chris, getting ready to shoot, made doubly sure she was in the frame and the rangefinder was doing its job. Madge held the locks up one at a time, Florence photographed them, and Chris did the same from behind her and a bit to one side. The key, which Madge held up by the butt of the shaft, got the same treatment.

"Do you need the key to lock these locks as well?" Madge asked Wavell as Florence carefully went through her shots.

"No. When you push the top bit in, they lock themselves. You can hear them do it."

"We keep a record of things like that," Madge said, handing the key back after a nod from Florence. "When the book we're writing comes out, we'll send you a copy through your employer. Thank you very much for your help."

It was time to go. Wavell got them all in the coach and set off for Matlock. Chris looked at his watch.

"We can still get some fishing in," he said, as Becky pulled some rolls and two cartons of apple juice out of her rucksack. "How about the lake near the Derwent?"

She was for it, and they brought two fat carp back for the kitchen that they should have thrown back – as a gift, no questions asked, and thanks for a lovely stay. When they were in their room, they went through all the measurements Becky had made and then the photos they'd taken. The twin doors, the locks and the key, plus Becky's handbag with its buckle – they were all diamond sharp. They enjoyed their dinner the more for that, and when they left Matlock the next morning, they felt on top of the world.

"Handy those old biddies putting in when they did," Chris said as Becky scanned the stations for some music. "The guide scarcely noticed us."

Becky looked his way, suddenly thoughtful.

"I'll be in their pictures though," she said. "Do you think it matters?"

"You won't be. Their angle was different from mine, and they were taking full-screen close-ups. I saw them when – What's her name? – Florence checked them through."

"What, all of them?"

"She was so slow I saw every single one. You get like that when you're old."

Becky didn't argue, she had insurance. Oleg made her feel better than safe, he made her feel glamorous. Being whisked off to Russia by a mafia man – that was something to dream about. Then something else crossed her mind.

"I wonder how Sanderson knew about that death hole. I'd never heard of it before."

"It was on TV a year or two back. I expect he saw it when I did. Or maybe someone told him about it. Will that do?"

"Why didn't I see it? We always watch the same programmes."

"You were out. Playing bingo, I shouldn't wonder. Or losing some fat in that keep-fit class of yours."

"I wish I'd stayed in now. I'd like to have seen inside it."

"It's like the guide said. Once you're in, you can't get out. And when you die, you can't see yourself do it. That's all."

Chris was a mechanic of the old school. A car's electrics he'd mend any time he had to, but handling metal was his great joy, and it rose another notch if he could grind and shape it as well. He'd done a lot of that back in Queen of Scots Lane. Now Toyota supplied everything ready-made, but he'd built up a sideline in old-timers, and his private workshop still contained everything he needed, including some high-tech machining gear he could never use enough. Once they were back in Peterborough, he waited till his staff had gone home, then he took his camera out, let himself into his private workshop, and transferred his pictures of the padlocks and the key into a high precision programme. Becky's buckle put a known fixed length into every picture and, thanks to the rangefinder, the dimensions of everything else could be calculated from it. He generated the stats of the padlocks' keyholes, including their depth, followed by the stats of each of the pins that slid into the top end of the key so it could rotate properly. He put the key through the same process, taking extra care with the branched cuts in the tab and the hole in the top end of the shaft that received the pin.

With all of that done, he used a hacksaw to cut six thick strips of brass to something beyond the right length, clamped them one at a time inside a cutting box, put his ear protectors on, and let it fashion six padlock keys, with slight variations in five of them just in case. While he was waiting for the box's ventilator to finish, he tilted and moved a corner cupboard to access the floor underneath it. The floorboards in the workshop were all shorter than normal, and three under the cupboard were even shorter because of the wall. Apart from that, they didn't look anything special till he eased them out, and he was able to do that because the nails didn't go through to the joists. They were cut back on the underside and filed flush. All that kept the boards in place was their carpentry, and under them was an underfloor safe. Becky knew the combination as well as Chris, and when he opened it, the Walthers, the silencers, and what was left of the ammunition lay in front of him. He made a bit of space and added in the padlock keys. Then he put everything back where it should be and locked his workshop up. He had no idea who was being lined up for the Saxley Hole of Death, but knowing what it was like down there, he was glad it wasn't him.

Chapter 10

Russell Burney in Trouble

In a lifestyle entirely remote from the Millers', Fern Shayler and Enid Burney were fond of meeting up together when Shayler had the time, and one evening in early May, when they were in Shayler's conservatory leafing idly through some furniture catalogues, Enid said out of nowhere,

"I must tell you something, Fern. In strictest confidence, mind. You'll know Cyril's called a meeting for August 21st, but I'd be surprised if you know what it's about."

"Right and right again. So what do you know that I don't? Mr Burney doesn't tell you anything as a rule."

"I can't go into details, but this once he's had to bring me in. I'm sure you'll be there, I don't see how you can't be, but my Russell is being kept completely out of it. He doesn't even know it's taking place. The thing is, it's being set up for a yes-or-no decision, and if it's yes, Cyril will want Russell kept in the dark till everything's cut and dried."

"Why should he want that?"

"To stop Russell putting his oar in while he's still got the chance because, mark my words, that yes will do my son enormous damage. And that is why I'm asking a big favour of you, Fern. If Cyril gets his yes, please tell Russell everything you learn in that meeting straight away. But don't let anyone know you've done it. No one at all."

Shayler didn't know how to answer. She'd always been loyal to Cyril, but over the years she and Enid, the spinster and the grass widow, had blended their half-lives into something approaching a whole one. In the end, she said,

"It would take a lot to make me go behind Mr Burney's back. I'd have to be damaged myself for that to happen. The best I can say is, I'll see what happens and decide on the day."

It sounded feeble, and she expected Enid to come back at her, but Enid just smiled her meek smile, told her how grateful she was, and went back to the catalogue she had open on her lap. It was as if the topic had never been.

Time drifted for the Millers as well. The police tried and got nowhere again, and Dvorski looked in just once – on the second day after Easter Monday. It was all very relaxed. He handed over the £20,000, Becky saw to the sandwiches, and she and Chris told him about the Saxley Castle visit.

"Can I see the keys, please?" he asked.

It was framed as a request, but it was clearly more than that, so Chris went and fetched them.

Dvorski was pleased with the keys, and he said so. He studied the photos and was pleased with them as well, and Becky had made a computer mock-up from the measuring she'd done which, he said, would definitely help the next stage. He didn't say what it was or when it would be, he simply told them not to go away for longer than a weekend till he gave the all clear.

During the weeks that followed, he spent two days with Becky in Brancaster – 'binding her in', he called it, Valkov-style, though it was really mostly for fun. The second time – it was shortly after the summer solstice – he used his own car. The Honda needed servicing, and Dvorski thought his Skoda would be safe enough this once. Becky wanted to see him even more often, but he told her what she'd once told him – someone might say something to Chris. She could see he was right, but it still made her pouty.

"You're like a drug, Oleg," she said, cosying up to him in bed and rubbing her hair – it was bright copper for the occasion – against his chest. "Each time I get you, I want another fix."

Dvorski kissed her for that. It was like having her on the end of a rope.

Chris went rigid when he saw the Skoda was in Brancaster. If Becky had been in reach, he'd have beaten her up – he'd done it often enough before – but leaving her or turfing her out were a different story. He couldn't live without her and he knew it. Sanderson was another matter. He had to have vengeance.

"This castle job means a lot to him," he reasoned. "I'll do the follow-up as if nothing's happened, then I'll track him down and squeeze him till he bleeds. After that, I'll kill him in my own way. And I'll enjoy doing it."

Some eighty miles to the south, Russell Burney was edging towards panic. It wasn't because he'd lost Torelli. Steve Hallavy, her Second-in-charge when she'd been Number One, had the top job now, and he was having no trouble at all keeping Harvest Home on track. Twenty years older than Torelli, he lacked her imagination; but he was a rock-steady worker and his experience ran deep. He had no idea Harvest Home was dangerous, the data said it was looking good. It would take something special for that to change.

Russell's panic was about money or rather, his lack of it. It was frightening him even more than his drinking, which was veering seriously out of control. Alstad had been right when he'd said Cyril paid him a straight salary, but it was still enough to make him a millionaire. Unfortunately, he liked to spend like a billionaire. He found women difficult, so he lavished hugely expensive gifts on them for the brief while they put up with him; and when they left him, he holed up in his multi-million pound mansion till the next one came along. His mansion was called Five Beeches, and it was situated in Stanmore, Middlesex, near Harrow public school. It had four acres of prime-value land and seven thousand square feet of living space. In the multiple garage were two E-Types, a 1938 Bugatti, an Alvis short chassis tourer and a modern Bentley, as well as the Morgan Plus 8. He bought incessantly, he liked the kick he got from it, and nothing he bought was cheap.

Directly or indirectly, everything led back to his father. Although Russell spent money like water, he was desperate to fight Cyril by making a fortune of his own. For a long while he'd had no idea how to do it, but shortly after the Sunday lunch with Torelli, he unlocked his Five Beeches letter box and found a letter addressed to him personally from a sender he didn't know. It was headed Pilling, Fayerl and Partners, Private and Corporate Broking, and their Throgmorton Street address meant they had the Bank of England as neighbours. So, stocks and shares. Why hadn't he thought of them before? They could make big money for him – millions, in fact. That would show his father, he might even get some respect out of him. The letter was signed Jocelyn Patrice, Head of Private Broking, and a coloured photo showed the pallid face of a bespectacled, balding man in his late fifties. His personal statement said he specialised in developing markets. He'd spun a lot of money out of the BRIC countries – Brazil, Russia, India and China – and his current long shot, thanks to global warming, was Greenland.

Russell checked the firm out and the word was it was solid. He phoned for an appointment, and within a week he was talking to Patrice in his office under the stern gaze of Sir Thomas Gresham, the black-clad Tudor father of exchange dealing in London. His ornately framed portrait hung above Patrice's head.

Patrice began by recommending the usual – a balanced portfolio with safe returns – but Russell wanted jackpot money, so Patrice suggested some, but not too many, private loan certificates. They were traded in Stuttgart, he explained. German small and medium businesses needed constant liquidity, and they were prepared to pay through the nose for it.

"You can get, oh, twenty percent with ease," Patrice said blandly. "But beware. If your borrower defaults, you lose the lot – your loan as well as your interest."

The certificates had done well, so well, in fact, that Russell had moved on to buying great bundles of them with money he didn't have. It was like a one-man Ponzi scheme. Patrice kept warning him things could change, but Russell insisted he knew what he was doing, and Patrice, always taking care to protect his commissions, kept brokering new deals. When the crash came – around the time Dandy and her mother were murdered – it came like a hurricane. Insolvencies cascaded in, and Russell found himself paying old debts by running up new ones that were even bigger. Patrice got him an emergency loan against Five Beeches at a murderous rate of interest. He also got him part of his debt mountain re-scheduled. But Russell knew all he'd gained was time, which was why, on a muggy Tuesday morning towards the end of July, he picked up his mobile and called his mother's number. It was a long shot, but he'd always been close to her, and anyway, he was heading for the buffers.

"Where are you?" he asked. "I'm ringing from home."

"I'm at The Crofter's Hut."

"Is Dad there?"

"No, he's gone to London for the day. Did you want to speak to him?"

"No, it's you I want to see. Can I come over now?"

If it was that important he better had.

"I'll expect you in an hour or so," she said. "I'll be in my rest room."

He did his best to smarten up before he set off, but he still looked dire when the butler announced his arrival. He couldn't keep his hands still, and he'd have been sweating even if the weather hadn't been so close. His mother rang for tea and, in fits and starts, he told her that unless he got some fresh money, he was on schedule for the bailiffs.

"I've been sensing you're in some kind of trouble, Russell. The truth is, I was going to send for you, so I'm glad you've come of your own free will. So tell me, how long's this been going on?"

"I was on the up for ages – you'd have been surprised," he answered. He sounded like a schoolboy talking up failed exams. “But then I took some really bad hits, and it’s been downhill ever since. Sorry.”

“So how much do you need?”

“£14·9 million before one minute past midnight on Monday the 27th of August. In other words, I’ve got till the end of the 26th.”

“Russell, that’s dreadfully close for such a large sum. Have you got any savings?”

He shook his head.

“Not like that. Not remotely. Easy come, easy go, you might say.”

He shrugged his shoulders helplessly.

“And you’re drinking too much as well, aren’t you? Come on, you might as well admit it.”

“It helps me hold my job down. I’m on a big project right now, it’ll bring in billions. I keep hoping Dad might help me out till it comes on stream.”

“He won’t. You know what he’s like, he’ll see you broke first. Then he’ll sack you.”

“What about you then? Can you help me?”

“I wish I could, but I can’t. I don’t have that kind of money, and I’d be wasting my time asking your father for it.”

She gave him her meek smile.

“You know how it is, Russell. I’m a kept woman, as they used to be called. I don’t have my own income, I own no part of CDB Global, and your father’s the sole owner of our homes. I have a spending account which is very generous, but your father goes through it monthly, item by item. If I skim off anything for you, he’ll see it and call it back.”

“I see.” Then, “It’s grotesque the way he treats you. Why do you stick it?”

“Your father and I come from a long way down. That makes a difference. He’s spent a lifetime making money, and now he’s immensely rich. When he began to take off, he needed someone with – I can still hear him say it – a big round bum and juicy tits to be on his arm when his photo was taken. That was me, and the pay-off is what you see now. I live in luxury houses, I wear the best clothes, I even have the use of a CDB Global helicopter. If I want to go anywhere or if I want something fetching, a phone call brings it virtually to my door. If you think that's grotesque, that's your business, I think it's wonderful. I couldn't have got any of it on my own."

He wiped his palms on the knees of his trousers.

"If you really can't help me, I'd better be going. I don't want to waste your time," he couldn't stop himself adding.

"No, wait a minute. Let me think. I may have an idea."

It seemed a long while before she spoke again.

"Your best plan is to ask your Mr Patrice to try to sell your debts. Your father owns one of the biggest companies in the world, and he's right up there on the *Forbes* list. On the other hand, he's not so young and his health is poor. I don't know who or what's in his will, but even if you're out of it altogether, the law says you'll still have a claim on his fortune when he goes, and it will be much, much more than the amount you owe. What you have to do, therefore, is get someone to pay you £14·9 million plus Mr Patrice's commission before your debts become due, and when you inherit your father's money, you will repay that sum. Plus a very large surcharge, of course."

"Why the surcharge?"

"Because your buyer, quite rightly, will expect to make a profit. And he – or she – may have to wait some time for his money as well. All that has to be paid for."

"You'll have a claim, too, a big one," he came back. "It's certain what you say, is it?" he added.

He was seeing Enid with new eyes.

"Absolutely. I've been finding things out, you see, and I've asked about you specifically. I've had to. Your claim on the estate will affect mine."

"And you think there are people who'd take a chance on my debts?"

"The surcharge would be high, but yes, there certainly are such people. Have a word with Mr Patrice and see what he thinks."

He didn't know what to say, so he took his mother's head in his hands and kissed her on the forehead.

"I never knew you were a witch," he laughed loudly as his nerves slackened. "I'll bet Dad doesn't know either."

"It's not for me to upset him; I owe him too much, so it's the sort of thing I keep from him. Now, before you go, there's something I want you to do for me."

"How can I say no? You've made my day."

"You might regret saying that, but anyway. If you keep pouring alcohol into yourself, you won't hold your job down, you won't see your project through, and you're quite likely to kill someone with one of your cars. So you'll phone a clinic I know of and start drying out from the first day they'll take you. After that, you'll stay dry. If you don't do as I say, you can forget about selling your debts. I'll tell your father, and he'll block any deal Mr Patrice can come up with faster than you can draw breath."

For a long moment Russell was silent, then,

"I'll give it a try, just to please you. What's this place's name and number? And how do you know about it anyway?"

"It's called the De Macey Clinic and it's in Oxfordshire, not far from Chipping Norton. I've never been near it, but a lot of my friends are like me – they've got money and nothing much to do, so some of them wind up in clinics like this one. The success rate isn't perfect, but it's better than average, I understand. You have to be determined, that's the main thing."

Russell was feeling a whole lot more cheerful when he set off for Stanmore. As a bonus, the air had cleared and the sun was shining brightly, so he put the Morgan's top down. When he left The Crofter's Hut's grounds, he normally blasted straight into the road – that was how much the place got on his nerves. This time he waited amiably for a gap in the traffic to make his right turn. Not even the prospect of spending time in a clinic – doing time, as he called it – could depress him. Dearest Enid had got it right again.

To the left of the T-junction where Russell turned right was a hill. It stopped him seeing Mike, who was parked in a lay-by on the far side, just below the crest. He didn't know Mike, but Mike knew him and his car. Mike saw him as well, because he'd got out of his Renault and walked till he could see down the hill without being seen himself. Once he was sure Russell wasn't coming back, he started the Renault and cruised down the hill. As he approached the T-junction, he signalled, slowed down and, as if he had every right to be there, turned off into The Crofter's Hut's grounds.

Chapter 11

In the De Macey Clinic

Burney made two phone calls when he got home. The first one was to Patrice, who said he'd be available at five o'clock sharp. The second one was to the De Macey Clinic. They said they could take him for a four day block from Thursday morning. Apparently they'd had a late cancellation, and better yet, they were running a promotion, so he'd get 50% off his bill. He could download everything he needed to know, and could he check in Wednesday evening, please? He said he could.

He called a taxi for the fifteen miles from Stanmore to Throgmorton Street. It saved him hunting for somewhere to park, but he was still nervy as he sank into the all too familiar chair in Patrice's office. After he'd explained what he'd come for, Patrice took off his gold-rimmed bi-focals and rubbed his eyes. It had been a busy day, and his sight wasn't what it had been.

"I'm sorry it's come to this," he said, meaning he was well aware who was in trouble and who wasn't. "I warned you repeatedly things could change, but you wouldn't listen."

Sir Thomas Gresham stared down accusingly.

"That's true," Burney replied, "but you always had another deal on offer. Looking back, I wish you'd just stopped me in my tracks."

"You'd only have gone elsewhere. We brokers are servants, not masters, Mr Burney. We give advice, but it's our clients who decide. And now you want me to clear the slate by selling your debts. Is your father likely to die very soon?"

Burney wanted dearly to say yes, and it wasn't just the money. Thanks to his father, he carried an unbearable pile of resentment around with him.

"All the signs are there," he said finally, "and they're worse every time I see him."

"It's a pity you can't be more precise. As my Continental friends say, if you write someone off, they live forever."

"So it's no deal, is that what you're telling me? Selling my debts, I mean."

"Not at all, but an uncertain time scale and an inheritance that can only be guessed at do create problems. I'll see what I can do though. Let me have a look."

He brought up Burney's debt schedule on his computer.

"Hmm, August 27th is the killer, and it's closing in fast. I'll be honest with you, it could be touch and go; but if you really want me to, I'll do my best. I'll be discreet, but you must let me mention the Burney name. It could make all the difference."

"So be it. When will I know?"

"Well, there'll be appointments and travelling to cope with, and they all take time. But I'll be as quick as I can."

"And your fee?"

"Seven percent. That's – let me see – £1·043 million. That's very reasonable in the circumstances. Most brokers would charge more."

Burney looked embarrassed.

"I don't think I can manage that much. In advance, I mean."

"Not to worry, not to worry. We'll add it to the sale price of your debts."

"And your time now?"

"The usual rate. I tell you what, I'll dictate an agreement before I go home, and you'll get it by courier tomorrow morning. Can you tell me where you'll be?"

"At home. Make sure the courier comes early."

"You won't be kept waiting. Now, is there anything else I can help you with while you're here?"

Burney bit the bullet.

"Not as such, but I'm booked into a clinic from tomorrow evening to all day Sunday. You may need to know that. It's called the De Macey Clinic. It helps people who drink more than they should."

"Will it do the trick, do you think?"

"I don't know; it's my mother's idea. I'd never heard of it till she mentioned it. I can't say I want to go there, but she thinks I should and, well, I owe it to her."

He felt acutely ashamed as he wrote down the details. Then they shook hands, Patrice rang for his secretary, and Burney was ushered out. As soon as the office door closed, Patrice switched off the mini-camera and microphone in the frame of the Gresham portrait and opened a connecting door Burney had never really looked at. Dvorski was sitting behind it with headphones on and a monitor in front of him. Patrice's profits in Russia had come at a price.

"Did you get everything?" Patrice asked as Dvorski slipped the headphones off.

"Loud and clear. You'll get further instructions this evening. Make sure you're available."

Dvorski stood up and stretched while Patrice went back to his desk, entered the times of Burney's stay on his computer, and ordered 'Erase'.

"Always delighted to help," Patrice said. "I owe Mr Zembarov a lot. Mr Valkov too. Such gentlemen, I've always found."

"As have we all," Dvorski replied neutrally. Then, "You can let me out now."

Patrice took him down a set of back stairs and unlocked a side door for him. It was the way he'd come in. Reception hadn't seen him or logged him. He was gone within seconds.

Outside, the air was hot after the air-conditioning in Patrice's office and Burney, wondering how he wanted to spend his time, had dawdled down to London Bridge. But the throng of people, many of them holiday-makers, made him feel lonely and out of place. He could always go back to Stanmore, but he didn't want to go back to an empty house, so he stood with his back to the upstream cityscape and worked his way through the restaurants an app was putting his way. Eventually he found one in Old Broad Street that had a table free. He took his time while he was there, and knowing he'd go home by taxi, he had two bottles of wine with his meal and whisky with his coffee. When he got back to Five Beeches, he watched the ten o'clock news with a bottle of vodka and fell asleep in his clothes. He knew what he was doing, but he didn't care. He'd make a fresh start Thursday. It would come round soon enough.

The next morning he felt like death, but he forced himself to get going. Patrice's courier delivered the agreement early, and after he'd read and signed it, he drove gingerly over to Klemmsley Marine to organise his four and a half days off. It didn't take him long. Alstad had said the rest of the board was always ready to cover for him, and that's how it was. He was still feeling bilious at lunchtime, but he managed some canteen shepherd's pie to keep in with his staff, politely declined the prunes and custard to follow, and then he was off to pack.

He had an idea what the De Macey Clinic looked like from the download, but he was still surprised how well it blended into the Cotswold Hills when, with some daylight still remaining, he rounded a bend and saw it nestling in a fold in the landscape. It consisted of two storeys of pale Oxfordshire stonework with flat, dark-hued tiles and billiard-table lawns framing the drive.

"A lot of money's behind this place," he thought casually as he lost speed for the gatehouse and waited for the wrought iron gates to swing open. He'd switched to his Bentley and was glad he had. The Morgan would have sent the wrong signals.

Checking in was painless, and since his appetite was creeping back, he asked for a table in the restaurant. He'd be down in half an hour. As he turned to reach for his suitcase he realised someone had come up behind him. Instinctively he looked to see who it was, and the impact was profound. She was the type of woman who'd obsessed him when he'd first entered puberty – he'd collected magazine photos of them and hidden them in a drawer in his room. Her brown hair was waved, her cheek bones were high and delicate, her skin was pale, and her poise was textbook perfect – an English rose. He guessed she was about thirty, but he didn't have to guess about her clothes. They were expensive and they looked it, as did her shoes and her suitcase which, however, she was pulling herself. If she was a drinker, it didn't show, so perhaps there was something else wrong with her, the clinic treated a range of complaints. As he followed the bellhop to the lift, he heard her speak, but it was the way she spoke, not what she said, that caught his ear. He'd never heard English spoken live like that, not even by royalty. It was like hearing a voice from a 1940s film – clear, precise and glinting like a diamond. He was in such turmoil, he had to find out who she was. The only question was how.

He got his answer in the restaurant. He was sitting at a table laid for one when she came in, just as he was looking up for the waiter. He caught her eye instead, and before he could think, he was inviting her to share his table with him. While a second place was being laid, he felt himself going red.

"My name's Russell Burney and you're making me blush," he said, smiling wryly.

It broke the ice.

"Mine's Toni, Toni Aubrey," she replied. "If I blushed easily, you'd be doing the same to me."

They talked non-stop through the meal, and since everyone who checked in had to sign up to the stimulants ban, they were still talking when the decaff rounded it off. It was as if she was passing into him. He'd noticed early on she wasn't wearing any rings. That helped as well.

"Let's go next door," he suggested when they'd finished their coffee. The way she said yes told him he'd said the right thing.

'Next door' was a room for quiet socialising. There were knee-high tables with easy chairs round them, voices were subdued, and a gently lit bar vended De Macey soft drinks. They made themselves comfortable in a bay window, made fun of the jargonised bar list, and settled for more decaff. Before long, they were into Guess-who-I-am. Burney was lost outside of CVs, so he adapted what his mother had said.

"You're single," he began, "and you've got lots of money. I think you're an heiress, you live in the country, and you don't know how to fill your time up. Am I right?"

She laughed, but not aggressively.

"Not even a little. My divorce has just come through, I used to live in Manchester, and my ex, who makes things out of plastic like downpipes and dustbins, has sole custody of our twins till the court thinks again. He's the sweetest of men, he took endless trouble over me, but the children had to come first. I was always drunk, you see. I couldn't take them to school, I couldn't fetch them back, I couldn't shop without falling over, and if I took my car, I would hit other people's. That's why I'm here. I'm starting afresh with no ring on my finger and the name I was born into."

"Do you still live in Manchester?"

"No, I'm with my sister in Pinner at the moment."

"Pinner? That's near where I live. I live in Stanmore."

"I thought you did. I had to make a detour through Stanmore, and then I was behind this Bentley all the way here. It turned out to be yours. Didn't you see a gunmetal Range Rover in the traffic behind you?"

"Sorry, no, I can't say I did." He wondered how he'd missed it. It made him feel inadequate. "What's it like at your sister's?" he scampered on quickly.

"Not very nice. The house is small, I've never got on with her, and her husband detests me. When I left to come here, she said quite openly she was glad I was off their hands for a bit. I have to go back to them though. I've got nowhere else, and I'm not as rich as I was. Now, what about you?"

He was afraid he'd lose her if he told her about his father and his debts, but he went ahead anyway. He talked about Klemmsley Oil and Gas, but he kept Harvest Home to himself. It wasn't a secret any more, but he had a superstitious fear it'd go wrong if he talked about it more than he had to. Nothing he said seemed to put her off, and that made him even crazier about her. As the evening drew to a close, he asked her if they could spend more time together.

"I'd like that a lot," she said. "What have you got tomorrow?"

"A medical, some psychology rubbish, an interview with Dr De Macey, and therapy. It'll take most of the day."

"I've got the same in a different order. That leaves the evening though. We could have dinner together again."

"We'll have earned it, that's for sure. The download alone frightened the wits out of me. I nearly cried off right there."

She touched the back of his hand with her fingernails.

"Alcohol destroys the body as well as the mind," she said, suddenly ominous, "so do exactly as they say. I don't want to die before I have to. Neither should you."

The download's motto was, 'First we take you apart, then we put you together again'. De Macey kept coming back to it in the interview, and by late Sunday afternoon, when Burney checked out and paid his cut-price bill, he felt taken apart with a vengeance. But he also felt very happy. He was deeply in love with Aubrey, and she was going to move in with him just as soon as she could detach herself from her sister. When he got home, he rang his mother to tell her about Patrice and also about Aubrey. But he asked whether his father was listening in first.

"He's in London again," she said, so he went right ahead.

"I'm glad on both counts, of course," she replied. "Does this Toni of yours know you're running out of money?"

"I've told her everything, and she still wants me. I've never really been wanted before, except by you. I'm enjoying it."

"It's all up to Mr Patrice then, is it? Well, I'll keep my fingers crossed. For both of you, I mean. And I'll tell your father about Toni when I speak to him next."

"Thanks, I was hoping you'd say that. What's he doing anyway?"

It was an awkward question, since in a general way she knew; but she couldn't tell anyone.

"It's business," she replied evasively. "Now you know as much as I do."

"I wish you were as happy as I am. I know how you see things, but even so ..."

"Never mind that now. Just hang onto this Toni of yours, and stay dry as well. She's quite right; no one wants to die before they have to. Bear that in mind, Russell. You may come back to it one day."

Chapter 12

"He's Had My Life… Now I Want His."

CDB Tower stood in London's Canary Wharf, and it took the VIP lift exactly thirty-eight seconds to get from the top to the ground floor. The August 21st meeting had come to an end, and when the team of four men and three women spilled out into the lobby, they took care not to say anything that might even hint at what they'd been discussing. But they all had that smug look that said they were onto a winner. It was afternoon already, they'd been there since six that morning, and as they split up to go back to their offices, none of them expected to get home till well after midnight. A run of secret meetings had led up to this one, and now it had all come good.

Up on the fifty-second floor, only Cyril Burney was left at the conference table. If he was exhausted, he was also grimly satisfied. Breathing noisily, he raked his papers together, while Shayler, self-effacing as always, brought him some iced water for his medication, killed the computers, and cleared the table. She'd lock his papers and her own away when he said she could go. She expected it to be straight away, but instead he told her to go back to her place, he wanted to talk to her. Obediently she went to the far end of the table and Burney, looking at her between two rows of empty chairs, let her stay there. The silence in the room was absolute. The air conditioning was soundless, and although whole segments of London were visible through the windows, nothing could be heard through the armoured glass.

"So now it's definite," he said, drying his mouth with a monogrammed pocket handkerchief. "CDB Global will be broken up, the sale of its parts gets launched next spring, and I'll retire a very rich man. I'm sorry you've been kept in the dark till now, but you're not the only one. The tiniest leak, and this meeting couldn't have happened."

Her unmade-up face was expressionless.

"I'm sure you're right, Mr Burney. I'm only sorry you're not well enough to carry on."

"So am I, but at least I'll go out with a bang. It'll be the sale of the century. There'll be consequences for you, of course, and you won't like them. The pension and lump sum you've been counting on were based on a lifetime's service. That won't happen now, so they'll be cut pro rata. If I can, I'll find you a present from somewhere. Nothing grand, but you've done a good job over the years. Don't let me forget."

"That's kind of you, I've never done less than my best. What about Mr Russell?" she probed without appearing to. "He's salaried like me, but he carries the Burney name."

"I've no idea, whoever buys Klemmsley decides that. Quite likely he'll be out on his ear. It'll do him good; he's had it far too easy till now."

"Does he know what's going on yet?"

"No, and I don't want him to. The only people who know are me, now you, and the bean counters who swanned out just now. Oh, and Enid. I didn't want her seeing something was up and prattling the way she does, so I told her what was in the wind. She's never been bright, but she can keep a secret if she's handled right. You're gagged as well, of course. Not a word to anyone."

"You know me better than that, Mr Burney. Do you know where you'll retire to yet?"

"I do, but no one else does, and you can be sure the taxman won't get me. I started with nothing, but I'm not going to finish with nothing. And when I finally clap out, my money goes into a foundation I'm starting with my name on it. Enid will get a bit, I've provided for that, but Russell will get nothing. I'm not having my hard-earned money lining his pockets."

He paused for breath and drank some more water.

"Enid thinks I'm staying in Britain. That suits me, it'll make life easier for both of us till she finds out she's wrong, and by then it'll be too late. She also thinks I'll still want her to live with me, and that's something she *is* right about. I don't want some paid stranger doing for me what she can do for nothing if she's hanging around with time on her hands. The fact is, I'll need someone I don't have to watch all the time. She's good enough for that."

He drank his glass out.

"You can finish clearing away now. You won't be doing it for much longer. It'll be a big change after all these years, but you'll get used to it. When you've locked everything away, you can go. I'll be off myself shortly."

It was close on six when Shayler pulled onto her drive and garaged her Lexus with barely contained ferocity. Her late Tudor house in Sunningdale – The Wool-Staple – was just a seven-minute drive from The Crofter's Hut and an hour or so from Five Beeches. That meant her home was as much part of CDB Global as her place of work was. Or had been till now. She was livid about her cut-down lump sum and pension, but what hurt her even more was the feeling she was being junked as a person. Well, she could do something about that, something deadly. She'd been damaged all right, damaged a lot. Now it was her turn.

She wasn't hungry, she was too angry for that, but she felt she ought to eat something, so she made some porridge in the microwave, and while it was cooling, she put a call through to Russell Burney in Stanmore.

"Can you come over?" she asked. "It can't wait. And don't let anyone know you're coming. If you have to say anything to anyone, make it something that can't be checked."

He said he'd try for eight, though it might be later. What he didn't say was that he was helping Aubrey into bed. He'd got home from Klemmsley Marine at the time he said he would, and he'd found her retching into their ensuite lavatory. An empty gin bottle lay on the bedroom carpet, a tumbler stood on her bedside table next to some mix that was hardly touched, and the whole room stank of vomit. He was shattered. He'd stayed dry so far, more for her sake than anything else, and she had as well. And now this. Once she'd finished throwing up, he ran some warm water into the wash basin, cradled her in one arm and tenderly freshened her face with his free hand. She was rag-doll floppy and she dribbled instead of speaking, but she clung to him as if she wanted to show she loved him, and that moved him so much, he felt his eyes prickle. Holding her carefully, he'd just got her onto the bed when Shayler's call came on the extension. After he'd rung off, he put a clean nightdress on her and took good care she was lying safely before he carefully closed the door. Seeing Aubrey like that made him feel his whole world was giving way, so from downstairs he called Patrice on his mobile. He didn't know his home number.

"Have you got anywhere yet?" he pleaded desperately.

"I'm doing my best, Mr Burney," the unruffled voice came back. "And we've got a few days left."

It wasn't enough. Russell had to do something just to relieve the pressure.

"Can I come and see you anyway? To talk things over, I mean."

There was a short but definite pause. Then,

"I'm busy all day tomorrow. How about Thursday at ten thirty?"

Russell said he'd be there and thanked him warmly. It was only a straw, but he clutched at it like a drowning man. He was half-sobbing as he set off for Sunningdale in the Bentley.

"Please don't leave me behind, Toni," he whimpered. "I'll get you well again, I promise. I just want to see you smile and hear you say you love me. Truly, that's all I ask."

As soon as Patrice had finished talking to Russell, he put an encoded call through to Valkov, and Valkov, following a brief call to Zembarov, summoned Dvorski from his flat.

"Patrice has had the sense to keep tomorrow free," he said, with his usual mixture of languidness and force. "You'll use the time to see Florence and Madge in person, then you'll go to the Millers. I want everything set up before Thursday. If you care to sit down, I'll tell you what to say. My secretary is getting some background papers ready, make sure you bring them back with you. It's a shame we have to sacrifice Patrice, but if you and he do your jobs properly, we'll have Russell Burney exactly where we want him – like a butterfly pinned to a board. That will be in your interest too, of course."

It didn't take long for Shayler to tell Russell what his mother had said about the meeting as they'd sat in Shayler's conservatory, nor yet how she'd responded at the time. Then, vibrating with a fresh upsurge of rage, she told him about the upcoming sale, her hands constantly moving and her cheeks inflamed. But at a deeper level she was weaving a killer web, and she knew exactly how to draw Russell into it.

"I can't see whoever buys Klemmsley keeping you on," she said when she'd got her breath back. "They'll bring their own people in, it's what they always do. And if your father holes up outside English law, as I'm sure he will, you can hire all the lawyers you like, you won't get a penny piece compensation. So that leaves his estate, and you'll lose there as well. Your mother will get the pittance he's promised, his foundation will get the rest, and a legal challenge from you will get you nothing – I repeat, nothing – except a very large bill. Think about it, Russell. Think about it hard."

He tried, but it wasn't easy. What his mother had said about selling his debts still seemed well-meant, but what she couldn't have known was that when Cyril died, his fortune – made even bigger by the sale of CDB Global – would be beyond the reach of English law. But if he – Russell – failed to inherit, he wouldn't be able to redeem the sale of his debts, he'd be bankrupted instead, and that would mean no money for Toni either. So what could he do? His only option was to place himself in Shayler's hands, which was what she'd set out to achieve. It meant spelling out his money problems, which filled him with embarrassment. But, like his father, he'd always trusted her, so he went ahead.

"You can bust the sale any time you like by leaking it before next spring," she said when he'd finished, "That'll keep your father in this country, but it won't do you any good."

"Why not?"

"Because CDB Global will carry on as before, but your father will stop you carrying on with it. Then he'll start another sale, and you won't hear even a whisper about it. He'll make absolutely sure of that."

"So what can I do instead?"

He was caught in her web.

"First, don't leak the sale whatever you do, you'll be worse off than you are now if you do. Second, you've got to get past August 27th. When are you seeing this Patrice again?"

"The day after tomorrow, at half past ten. It's all arranged."

"Don't let him drag his heels, get those debts sold straight away. It can't be that difficult to find a buyer."

"I'll put pressure on him, I give you my word. Now, since you're working in numbered points, what's the third one?"

She paused before she answered. When she did, the room seemed to ice up, and for a fraction of a second he thought the lights turned a sort of blue colour.

"The third one is this," she said evenly. "Don't just hope for your father to die. Make sure he does before Global goes up for sale and he moves out of English law."

The shock was total. He understood the words, but try as he might, he simply couldn't absorb them.

"You mean kill him?" he stammered. "Kill my own father? What's up with you, Fern? It's wrong and it's crazy. Even if I did it, I'd never get away with it. What do I know about murder?"

But Shayler's calculation was, if she let him struggle enough, he wouldn't find it crazy. He might not even find it wrong.

"Either you destroy him or he destroys you," she came back. Her hands were motionless and her face wasn't inflamed any more. "If you destroy him before he can make a move, Enid will get her share of the estate, you can't avoid that, but you'll get Global and the rest of the money. You'll be an extremely wealthy man, Russell, wealthy enough to be in *Forbes* like your father. And you'll be powerful like him, too"

"What about you, Fern? Where do you come in?"

"I want you to keep me on when you take Global over."

"What for? You can't need money."

She waved her hand round to take in the room they were sitting in. It was chock-a-block with expensive furniture, there were oil paintings on the walls, and the carpeting would have graced Buckingham Palace.

"Global's been my life, and my house is what I've got out of it. It's luxurious because it has to be, it's in one of the best parts of England, and I want to kiss the walls every time I think about it. Every room is furnished as richly as this one, the gardens are faultless, and I've got a Bentley on order that will put yours to shame. But in cash terms I'm almost spent out. My remaining years with Global, my pension and my lump sum were going to put that right between them, but if your father has his way, that won't happen. So I want you at the top instead, and me there with you. Then it will."

"It's not just money though, is it?"

She'd been so wound up, it couldn't be. She wondered whether she should tell him, then she did. She hoped it would strengthen the bond between them.

"I want revenge, Russell. I want it so badly it's burning like a fire inside me. I was straight out of school when I started working for your father, and now I'm gone fifty. He's had virtually my every waking moment in between, and now he wants to throw me out like a cat that's died. He's had my life and he's done well out of it. Now I want his."

She stopped there, clasped her hands round her knees, and waited. What she'd said about destroying or being destroyed had gone in – Russell was thinking in her terms now. All he had to do was say the fatal words. Just getting rid of his father would be bliss, and he'd inherit Global as well. It *had* to be better than waiting for Cyril to die naturally.

But could he kill him without being caught? His mind stayed blank at first, but then he thought he could. Methane hydrate was the answer, he just had to work it right, and he was sure he could. Killing his father didn't seem crazy or wrong any longer, it seemed rational and just. But instead of saying yes, he said,

"I can't do it, Fern. I'm afraid."

"Don't worry, I'll be brave for both of us."

"Second hand courage is useless. I'd still be afraid."

"Fear and courage go hand in hand, and I'll repeat what I said just now: either you destroy your father or he destroys you. And you've got a dependant these days, I hear. Are you going to let her down?"

That was the question he couldn't bat away. In his mind's eye he could see Aubrey sleeping peacefully. But she'd need him totally when she woke up.

He crossed the line.

"You win," he said. "It'll happen when Harvest Home is due to go max. My father won't be on the rig, he'll be dead. Don't ask me how, what you don't know, you can't pass on. Have you said anything to Enid, by the way?"

"No, you're the first person I've spoken to since the meeting. What shall I tell her when I get back to her?"

His answer came quickly, more quickly than he'd expected. Could he think like a killer already?

"Say you've told me what she wanted you to, and I'm so upset, I have to have time to think about it. She'll believe that and, yes, tell her I don't want to talk about it. That will stop her getting at me. Don't say anything about killing my father, that's strictly between ourselves. And now there's something I must come back to before I go."

Her face hardened. Was he leaving himself a way out?

"Tell me what it is," she said carefully. "If I can help, I will."

"If I can't sell my debts, August 27th will see the end of me. Hanging on till Harvest Home won't be an option."

So that was all.

"Listen, Russell. Instruct Patrice to take whatever terms he can get. It doesn't matter what the surcharge is, just get yourself solvent now. You'll have so much money, you won't know what to do with it once your father's gone. I don't see what the problem is. You're worrying over nothing."

When he got back to Stanmore, Aubrey was out to the world. He kissed her lovingly and whispered he'd got things all worked out. He'd missed the ten o'clock news, which made him feel crumbly, but he'd done his deal with Shayler, and that sort of made up for it. He kissed Aubrey a second time and disappeared into a spare bedroom, hoping to fall asleep straight away. He had a lot to do in the morning.

But sleep wouldn't come – he'd learned too much about his mother, Shayler and himself for that. He didn't get overwrought like Shayler, but they both thought in straight lines, so they had that much in common at least. It was his mother who was different, and she disturbed him profoundly. Looking back, it dawned on him she'd only ever showed him those parts of her personality she'd wanted him to see, but he realised now, there was much more to her than that. As he dozed off he saw her half-walking, half-floating down an ill-lit corridor towards him. She was a strange white colour, she carried a bunch of lilies in her hand, and her face was completely immobile. He was only a small boy, he held out his hands to greet her, and he called out, "Mummy!" But she simply stared at him and, as she got nearer, she terrified him so much, he awoke abruptly and started up in bed. The same dream came back to him twice more. Then it left him in peace, and he less slept than passed right out.

Chapter 13

Hallavy Gets a Phone Call

Wednesday came and Russell Burney was up with the sun. He was grievously overstrained, but he was keen to look at his 'murder weapon' – he woke up calling it that with fascinated guilt – and that gave him the momentum he needed. Before he drove off, he looked in to see how Aubrey was. She was more awake than asleep, and what really pleased him, she seemed in far better shape than he'd feared. He wanted to say something about the previous evening, only he didn't know what. In the end, in her crystalline way, she filled the blank in for him. She was sorry, she explained, but it was always the same. Once she opened a bottle, she had to empty it. If he hadn't come home when he did, she'd have opened another one and drunk it out, too. Being sick didn't matter. Once she started, she had to keep drinking till she fell into a coma.

Burney was distraught. It was as if behind her wish to get better, there was a stronger wish to get worse.

"Where did the gin come from?" he asked, trying not to sound as if he was blaming her. "Did you go out and buy it?"

"No, I got it from your drinks cupboard. You forgot to take your indoor keys with you yesterday morning. I found them, and then I could only think of one thing. I hung on and hung on, but it was hopeless. You know the rest."

So it was his fault after all. And she'd done her best to hold out, of course she had. He'd have succumbed straight away if it'd been him. He kissed her on the cheek and told her he loved her more than ever, now he knew how she'd struggled.

"It's me who should apologise," he said, checking his pockets. "If you get into any kind of bind again, phone me, and I'll get home as soon as I can."

He couldn't stop himself, he had to kiss her again.

"I have to go now, but I won't be away for long."

"Where are you going?"

"Klemmsley Marine. I want to go over something with one of my staff. Something I think will help us."

He kissed her a third time, she gave him her English rose smile, and then he was out of the house with Hallavy on his mind. He felt nothing but love for Aubrey as he accelerated away in the Morgan, but he also chiselled it in stone that if he caught her drinking again, he'd take her money away. Love sometimes had to be tough. He'd have done it this time, if it hadn't seemed like punishing her.

He reached Klemmsley Marine by mid-morning, but when he swung into the senior management car park, a graveyard chill made him shudder. His father's Rolls-Royce was standing in one of the bays.

"Have you come to haunt me before you're dead?" he whispered, and parked as far from it as he could.

As he got out, Quilter caught his eye, so he gave him a wave and a smile he didn't feel. But he didn't go over to speak to him.

"Mr Hallavy's in Visual Data," Reception told him brightly. "He logged in there – let me see – exactly fourteen minutes and six seconds ago. Mr Cyril's with him. Mr Hallavy pre-arranged it. They've got the place to themselves."

He went straight up to the first floor, and he was very angry. His father owned Klemmsley, so he could do as he pleased, but, even so, he felt humiliated. Cyril had obviously got someone to contact Hallavy, or maybe he'd done it himself, but Russell Burney, the CEO, hadn't even had the courtesy of a text message. And unlike his father and Hallavy, who'd been switched through by Reception out of deference to the owner, he had to go through palm recognition, iris recognition and face biometrics in three separate gateways before he could tap his personal code into the door lock. That did nothing to improve his temper. Nor did the fact that Visual Data was his personal pride and joy. One of the first things he'd done when he'd been made CEO was have Cockerel Field cabled up so every key site could have its hardware close by, permanently plugged in, and ready to go. And it could all be controlled from the room he was about to enter. Security meant it was windowless, and the ceiling lights were dimmed down to brighten the oversize HD screens taking up most of the wall space. Each HD had a cluster of mini-screens showing what was available for seeing on one of the big ones.

"Hallavy said you might look in," Cyril half-coughed, taking a deliberately long look at his watch. "You can stay if you like. He was just going to show me Dassett Point. I'm making sample inspections of some of my holdings. I want to see how my money's being spent."

"What lies you tell," Russell thought venomously. "It's the sale you're fretting about."

But he didn't let it show. From now on he was going to keep out of trouble with his father. He couldn't afford to look as if he had it in for him.

"How are you feeling?" Russell asked, but he got no answer, and Hallavy cringed. Russell sat down next to him on the side away from Cyril.

"Get on with it, man," Cyril ordered Hallavy, and glad to be given something to do, Hallavy brought up a 2D graphic of Dassett Point on one of the UHDs. It showed where the four boreholes were that Russell had told Torelli about, plus their underwater hardware cage. The boreholes formed more or less a square, and a point of light was pulsating across it, apparently in the same plane.

"That point of light, it's on the surface really," Hallavy explained. "We've got inverse sonars on the seabed and a support ship's moving over them." He switched into 3D mode. "That's better," he said. "This simulation shows what you'd see if you could look up from the seabed, and this one" – he switched again – "shows what you'd see if you could look down from the support ship. Clever, eh? It was Mr Russell's idea."

Cyril sat stony-faced, his breathing laboured but steady. Russell noticed him put a finger to his collar. Then, ignoring Hallavy, he leaned forward and turned towards his son.

"Get me some water, will you? I need to take one of my tablets."

'I wonder what you'd do,' Russell thought as he walked over to the dispenser, 'if you knew you were looking at where I'm going to kill you. There's all the water you'll ever need right there.'

While they were waiting, Cyril asked Hallavy to show him a plugged borehole for real.

"What are these plugs like anyway? I can't say I've ever seen one."

"They're like a piece of metal piping. They're about two feet long, they're narrower than the borehole you want to plug, and they've got gas-tight seals set up inside them. Once you've lowered a plug to where you want it, you use a tool called a retrieval tool to give it a twist, and the seals expand outwards through the sides. That's all there is to it. When you want to take it out, you twist it the other way, the seals go back in, and if the plug is deep down the borehole, you pull it out on a line. Ours are made to sit in the top. They're easier to get at there."

Russell handed Cyril his water and sat down.

"It'd help if you could speed things up," Cyril said to Hallavy as he put his tablets away. "I've got a meeting in London later today, and I don't intend to miss it."

'I bet you don't,' Russell thought, again taking care not to let anything show.

For a moment it looked as if Hallavy had pressed a wrong key. The 3D images had gone and the only thing on the screen now was 'Dassett Point' top left. Then a metal framework about the size of a three-storey house lit up. It was brighter at the bottom than at the top, and what looked vaguely like a portcullis wound up to provide a way in.

"There's a plug in here, Mr Burney," Hallavy explained. "I've fetched a Remotely Operated Vehicle out of its hardware cage to clean it up for us. It's carrying a de-silter to do that." He paused, but there was no response. "The pics you're seeing now come from the ROV's front cameras, and I've got its lights going as well." He switched some more images through. "These pics are from the side cameras. See how dark it is where the lights don't reach." He switched again. "And this is looking behind."

"What's that trailing out of the back?"

"That's the power line, what we call the tether. It carries the telemetrics as well. Humans need lights, but ROVs use sensors and scanners. That's a lot more efficient. Would you like to see some pictures of one?"

"If you must."

Hallavy split the screen, fed in some file pics, and talked his way through them. Because he wanted Russell to look good, he added, "NASA holds the patents on the traction and suspension. Thanks to Mr Russell we can use them under licence. That's why our ROVs look like Mars rovers."

It didn't work.

"How many of these things do you keep down there?" was all that came back.

"In the cage this one comes from? Four usually. One for each borehole. Silting up's a permanent problem."

"That's three too many in my book. Now let's see one of these plugs."

Wishing fervently he was in any other part of the building, Hallavy was reaching his hand out to move the ROV in when Cyril pressed on his forearm and stopped him.

"Let me clear something up before you start fiddling around," he wheezed. "If you lower the pressure through a regulator valve and unplug even one of the other boreholes, you've got instant panic on your hands. Is that right?"

"One hundred percent. It's what the plugs are there to stop."

"And you've got not one but four plugged boreholes down there, all close together, with no regulator valve to slow things down. You've taken it out, I know you have, my son told me once."

He had an aging man's obsessive memory.

"That's true, but they're all safe. They've been there for years and nothing's even looked like happening."

"That's not what I'm asking. What I want to know is, why the panic?"

"It's a vicious circle, Mr Burney. The gas pouring out makes the pressure drop, and that frees up even more gas to come gushing out."

"I can work that out for myself, but so what? Why doesn't it just evaporate?"

"It might catch fire," Russell intervened quickly. He didn't want Hallavy saying what else it could do. "And four boreholes at once would make one almighty blaze. I shouldn't want to get caught in it."

Cyril let go of Hallavy's forearm, leaned across him, and poked Russell in the side with his stick.

"So this stuff is a lot more dangerous than Torelli let on," he said. "Or you, for that matter. I've caught you out at last, Russell, and you didn't see it coming. Which reminds me. Have the police been to see you lately?"

"Not lately, no."

"They called on me last night. I expect you were enjoying yourself somewhere, you and that drunk you've picked up with. They wanted to know why Torelli applied to us, if Exxon loved her so much. If I were you, I'd re-read her papers before you go home. You don't want the law to catch you out now you've been caught out once already."

He tapped Hallavy's hand and Hallavy, back in unsplit format, steered the ROV inside the framework, set the de-silter to work and, in the eerie undersea light, cleared a massive steel roundel set into the seabed. To stop the spoil clouding the water, a reinforced flexi-pipe whisked it away.

"Can I open the lid?" Hallavy asked Russell.

Russell nodded, and Hallavy made the roundel fold itself back through one hundred and eighty degrees. That laid bare the borehole's concrete collar, and wedged firmly inside it was an Archer plug customised for Klemmsley Oil and Gas. Above the plug and with plenty of room to spare was a splay-footed metal bridge, and mounted into its cross piece was a vertical rod. Its carefully notched end pointed directly towards a socket in the plug.

"That rod's the retrieval tool," Hallavy said, sending some extra lighting in its direction. "The notched end can find its own way into the socket as soon as it gets the order. Then twist, retract, and out comes the plug."

"But you can't give the order because you'd get a blow-out if you did."

"That's right, Mr Burney."

"So you're stuck with a clutch of very expensive non-earners down there. It's obvious, those holes should never have been bored."

He looked across to Russell with contempt.

"Is there anything else I should see?"

"Go automatic," Russell said to Hallavy, "and – let me see – park the ROV in the dark."

He needed to get his father right away from methane hydrate.

They stared silently at the pictureless HD till 'Task ended' came up, then the hardware cage lit up from the inside. The ROV was back in, complete with de-silter, the tether was spooled to stop it fouling, and the cage had closed itself.

"That was just to show you, Dad. The fact is, ROVs can do just about anything, with or without anyone watching."

If Cyril was impressed he didn't show it.

"How many command centres have you got?" he asked instead.

"Just this one. It's enough for where we're at right now."

A look at Harvest Home came next, and then Cyril had to be off. No, he wouldn't be staying for lunch; Shayler would have something ready on his desk for him. He didn't say what his meeting was about, and Russell, who thought he knew, didn't expect him to. As they were making their way at Cyril's slow pace towards the main door, Hallavy's mobile pinged, and he stayed back to take the call. Quilter was already waiting – Cyril had paged him once they were through the security gates – and the Rolls was parked right outside.

"I'll tell you again," Cyril wheezed at Russell, as Quilter moved in close in case Cyril needed help. "Get Torelli's papers read. You won't want to look as foolish as you really are."

The police again. While Russell was waiting for Hallavy, he wondered what it was like to know the police were hunting you down. It'd be more than his nerves could take. Whoever had killed the Torellis had used guns, and that was a big mistake. They might as well have left their names on bits of paper. He, Russell Burney, would use science and stay in the clear. But he couldn't keep his confidence up for long, and by the time Hallavy was standing next to him, it was dipping again. And what if Patrice couldn't sell his debts in time? That didn't bear thinking about.

"I've been talking to the Rocks," Hallavy said, mightily relieved Cyril had gone. He was totally amiable by nature – it went with his tweed jackets and personally hand-knitted cardigans – but he'd been tried to the limit in Visual Data. "They're bothered about Dandy's core-samples. She used masses of them, and now there's a space problem. What do you think?"

Russell nearly lost it without knowing why.

"I was sure the police had sealed them off," he managed to say. "Weren't they bringing in some scientists to have a look at them? You remember, when they put the Rocks' computers off limits along with ours."

"I thought you knew, the scientists have been and gone. They copied everything and released the core-samples back to us. We can do what we like with them. I was there when they said so."

So probably the Rocks were just fussing. But Russell had to be certain.

"Do me a favour, Steve," he said. "Drive up and get this one sorted. And make it soon. We don't want any foul-ups at this stage."

"I'll go later today, if you like. You can always give me a call if you need me back here."

He left to clear his desktop and Russell was thinking about lunch when the phone on the Reception console buzzed and the receptionist waved him over. It was Essex Police. Would he mind if they came and saw him?

"Of course not," he replied down the line. "I was just going to lunch. Can we name a time after that?"

He had to read Torelli's papers first.

"Let's say two fifteen, Sir. I don't think it'll take too long."

"It's about Miss Torelli, is it? And her poor mother, I suppose."

"Not directly, Sir. It's Mr Dvorski we want to ask about. Mr Oleg Dvorski from the Embassy of the Russian Federation."

He nearly lost it again, but this time he knew why. It was guilt. He hadn't done anything yet, but all it took was seeing his father's car or being wrongfooted in some way. Roll on tomorrow then. The police would be gone, Steve would start sorting the Rocks out, and Patrice would see him right about his debts. That left taking care of Toni. On impulse he stepped outside and called her on his mobile. She seemed bright enough when she answered.

"Get a couple of tickets for a West End show," he said. "Yes, for this evening. Call me back when you've got them, and I'll meet you there. We'll have supper afterwards, and make love when we get home. How does that sound?"

He heard kissing noises, panting noises, and Mmmmm noises.

"That's how it sounds from me," she giggled. "Now let me hear how it sounds from you."

He did the same and they both laughed. But his mood was dipping again as he went inside. Things had to go well with Patrice, if not he'd lose everything. And time was nearly up.

Chapter 14

Left to Die in the Dark

They saw *High Society* in the West End and thought it was 'divine'. It was Aubrey's word, and she used it again after the supper and the love-making. It struck Burney as dated, but it went with her accent, and she used it so naturally, he was happy to go along with it. But he hardly slept that night, and when Thursday's dawn put an end to his fitful dozing, all he could focus on was things going wrong. It worried him Patrice hadn't fitted him in the day before, and he invented one malignant reason after another why Patrice should want the extra day. The police worried him as well. They thought he knew Dvorski better than he did, or so it seemed to him, and when he'd told them he was hoping for a deal with Gazprom, they'd asked to see the paperwork as if he'd been lying. They'd even taken copies. He knew he was frightening himself, but knowing it didn't stop him doing it, and the big trouble with Patrice was, he might let him down for real. Aubrey was sleeping soundly next to him. He squeezed her shoulder gently – out of love, out of protectiveness, but also to feel he wasn't alone. Then he stole out of bed and, moving slowly to use up time, he got ready for Throgmorton Street.

Patrice got in first. He was polite, but determined to dominate.

"My sincerest regrets, but you caught me on the hop Tuesday," he began, without any opening pleasantries.

Burney was perched on the edge of his chair. The Gresham portrait might as well not have been there, likewise the connecting door.

"If you'd called a bit earlier, yesterday might just have been possible. But at that hour …"

Patrice spread his hands, smiled benignly, and let his voice trail away. Then, changing tack, he asked whether Burney would like some tea. Burney shook his head.

"Not now," he said distantly. "Maybe later."

He wanted massively to tell Patrice he was lying, that he'd deliberately been playing for time, but he didn't dare risk it. Instead he blurted out,

"How have you got on? Selling my debts, I mean."

Patrice took his bi-focals off, wiped them on a cleaning cloth, and put them back on again. If he could see without them, it was plainly only just. He sucked his teeth.

"Bad news, I'm afraid," he said. "I've made enquiries – discreetly, as I promised – and the word is, your debts are unsaleable. The unknowns are simply too great."

Burney thought he'd stop breathing.

"That can't be true," he forced out. "What about my name? Did you use that? You said it would make the difference."

"'Could' is what I said, not 'would'. I'm sure of it."

"But if you can't sell my debts, I'll be ruined. Don't forget," he went on, hoping against hope, "we've got till the beginning of Monday. If you'll keep trying, I'll wait till then. Can I ask you to do that? I've, er, talked things over with a close friend, and she says you mustn't cap the surcharge. Whatever's on offer is good enough."

"Never say die, eh? Well, I must admit I *have* been strict about the surcharge. I can't have you taken advantage of, we've got on so well together. I tell you what. I'll go back to a certain person whose offer I've declined and ask him to reconsider. After what you've just said, I'm sure that's what he'll do. With a fair wind we could turn this round as soon as tomorrow."

"I truly hope so. It would be wonderful if we could."

"Don't talk of hope, my dear Sir, talk of expectation. Land is almost in sight, believe me."

Burney's mind flashed across to his father's murder. He couldn't tell Patrice about it, but in his desperation, he felt if he hinted at the outcome, it would help things along.

"That certain person may not have to wait very long – to get his money back, I mean," he said nervously. "I'll be very rich before the end of the year. You can pass that on to sweeten the pot."

"I shall, I shall! May I ask where the money's coming from?"

"I've got a big project on. I'm, er, going to ask for a rise."

Patrice clapped his hands with satisfaction.

"Better and better!" he exclaimed. "I'll do exactly as you say. Now, about that cup of tea. I could certainly use one myself now things are settled to your liking."

Tea was the last thing Burney wanted, but he was so relieved, he gave in and spent an awkward fifteen minutes trying not to say more than he should.

"I don't like to admit this," he nevertheless came out with at one point, "but I'm entirely dependent on you. And if you don't succeed, it won't be just me who's finished."

"But I shall succeed, Mr Burney, there is no reason why I shouldn't. I can feel it in my bones."

As Patrice's secretary led Burney down to the exit, he couldn't help himself, he felt more optimistic with each succeeding stair. It was Patrice's manner that did it. He made it seem the debts were sold already.

It was raining when Burney stepped into Throgmorton Street, so he was glad to see a taxi cruising past. He could guess his father's visit to Klemmsley Marine had set tongues wagging, and then Hallavy had shot up north at short notice, so he'd go home, see if Toni was all right, and if she was, he'd make a point of working in Klemmsley Marine till late to show he had everything under control. As his taxi toiled through

London, he kept wondering how Hallavy would make out. If anything wasn't right, Hallavy would flush it out. He might lack imagination, but point him in the right direction, and he'd get there in the end.

Even before Burney had left Pilling, Fayerl and Partners, Patrice was in the adjoining room, beaming with pride at his performance. He was about to ask how Dvorski liked it, when he spun round and shot back into his office, leaving the connecting door open. He'd forgotten to switch off the Gresham camera and microphone.

"It's all right," he called through as he put the times in and ordered 'Erase'. "It's all wiped off now. My fault entirely. It won't happen again."

"I'm sure it won't," Dvorski called back amiably. "That was quite a show, Jocelyn. I'd rate it Golden Globe at least."

Patrice had in fact been *too* good, since although he didn't know it, all that remained for him now was to be murdered in a deliberate and well-organised way, then his part in a plan he knew nothing about would be over. The turning point had been when Burney had admitted he was entirely dependent on Patrice. From that moment on, Patrice was dead.

They gave Burney time to get clear, then Patrice took Dvorski down the back stairs and let him out through the side door. Unlike Burney, Dvorski had checked the weather.

"A nuisance this rain," he said as he opened his umbrella. "I'm glad I've got this with me. What time are you going home?"

"Two o'clock on the dot. Joel's due back from Abu Dhabi. I'm cooking something special to celebrate."

Joel Purdy was Patrice's partner, and their love for each other was total. He'd started out as a trauma surgeon, then he'd seen there was more money in running hospitals than working in them, so he'd bought into a private string and finished up the owner. Abu Dhabi was his first Middle East venture. There were others in the pipeline.

"You might make it in the dry then, it's not supposed to rain much longer. And have fun this evening. You can tell me the decent bits over lunch next week."

Dvorski walked briskly towards Bank underground station, but before he got there, he stepped into a doorway and made two calls on yet another stolen mobile. He'd read in *Time Out* 190,000 mobiles got left in London's taxis every year, but he was still surprised Valkov was dishing them out so readily. Someone in the Kremlin must have got at him. It was just like the old days, when Yeltsin was calling the shots.

His first call was to Chris Miller. It was a pre-arranged enquiry about a faulty Toyota Yaris. Mixed in were the words 'two o'clock'. The second call was to Madge. This time it was about a history lecture starting at two.

Punctually to the minute, Patrice went out through the main entrance and headed for Bank station. The pavement was still wet, but the rain had stopped, leaving a covering of low grey cloud. Madge was just one more pedestrian as she walked down Throgmorton Street, and Florence was the same as she window-gazed near Bank station. They both recognised Patrice from Dvorski's briefing papers. They checked the time and faded away to report back to Dvorski. For them it was task ended.

Patrice had a house in Essex not far from the end of the Central Line. In the mornings he'd park in Epping and take the underground to Bank, and in the evenings he'd do the same thing in reverse. The last part of his journey home took him through a web of country lanes till he was almost in the village of Abbess Roding. His house, which he co-owned with Purdy, was five-bedroomed Georgian on a three-acre site. Its main attraction, more important even than its style, was the privacy it provided.

He drove a white Porsche Cayenne – it was a birthday present from Purdy, he kept a head-on photo of it on his office desk – but he never parked it on the station car park. Like a lot of wealthy people, he saved pennies when he could so, as he liked to boast to Dvorski, he left it for free in Marlborough Close, a tree-lined side street where there were no yellow lines.

It was quiet there, the homeowners all had driveways to park on, and he'd been doing it with different cars for years. When he approached his car this time, things seemed the same as always. Automatically he unlocked it as he got near, but his mind was on the meal he'd be cooking for Purdy. He scarcely saw Chris Miller open the passenger door of a Toyota Prius hybrid that was parked six cars further along and start walking towards him with his hands in the pockets of his raincoat. Looking both ways, Patrice stepped into the road, got in, put his briefcase on the back seat and closed the door. As he clicked his seat belt on, Chris opened the passenger door, slid onto the seat, and keeping his thinly gloved hand low, pointed the silencer of a SigSauer P239 at him. The Walther was Chris's favourite gun, but he could see, if he shot Patrice with it, the police would link the corpse to the Torelli murders and that wouldn't be clever. So he'd smuggled two SigSauers and their gear out of his shooting club – one for himself and one for Becky. If they didn't use them, they'd be smuggled back in. If they did, they'd disappear.

"Don't move and don't call out," he told Patrice quietly. "Rest your hands on the steering wheel and keep them there."

Patrice was almost paralysed with fear. He did exactly as he was told.

"In a moment I'll count to three," Chris went on. "On three you'll get out with your briefcase, go round the front of your car to the pavement, lock up as soon as I've got out, and walk to the smoky grey Prius that's six cars up from here. You'll do it all at normal speed. If you try any heroics, I'll kill you. Do you understand what I'm saying, especially the last bit?"

Patrice nodded. Speech was beyond him.

"When you get to the Prius, open the passenger door, put your coat and jacket on the back seat with your briefcase and sit next to the driver. I'll be directly behind you, and the Prius's driver is armed like me. Behave yourself and you'll be all right. Get ready now."

He waited till a small boy had scampered past on his scooter, then he made his count, and when Patrice got out, he did likewise. His gun was in his pocket again – the lining was holed to take the silencer – but if Patrice had jumped back in, he was poised to jump back in with him and start again.

The Prius was a trade-in, it was fully tanked, and this time the number plates were fakes. When Patrice was belted in, Chris got into the back, and while Becky held her SigSauer ready, he opened the briefcase and looked for a smartphone or mobile. There was neither the one nor the other in there, but he found a mobile in the inside jacket pocket. He switched it off, asked Patrice for his electro-key, and walked back to put it in the Porsche's glove box. They had a four-hour drive in front of them. Becky would keep the wheel and Chris would stay in the back with his SigSauer at the ready.

It wasn't completely night when they reached Saxley Castle, but threatening cloud and the sun low down made it almost that. Patrice had started to talk as the miles had passed. He was chatty by nature and he thought, quite wrongly, that if he was nice to these people, they might yet be nice to him. Chris was used to talking to strangers, it went with his trade, so it cost him nothing to chip in the other fifty percent. But he didn't say where they were going and he didn't say why they were going there.

The keep and the fragments of wall were looming silhouettes as they got out and eased their cramped limbs. The Millers knew where everything was, the photos and the computer mock-up they'd made from Becky's measurements were fresh in their minds. There was a lull in the wind, but the air was chilly after the warmth of the car, and Chris and then Becky slipped their coats and gloves on. But they kept Patrice standing in his shirt.

"Give me your glasses," Chris said, holding out his free hand, while Becky pulled Patrice's belongings out of the car.

"Please, no. I'm as blind as a bat without them."

"So I've been told," Chris said, keeping his hand where it was, and Becky pressed her gun into Patrice's back. He knew what it was without asking, and submitted straight away. His glasses came off, and Chris slipped them into his trousers pocket. It didn't matter if they got damaged now.

"This way," he ordered Patrice. "Don't take all night."

He seized his wrist, pulled him towards the twin doors and soon, with the wind picking up again, they were standing in front of them. Patrice wanted to run away when his wrist was let go, but it was too dark and anyway, he couldn't see anything in focus. Becky pressed her gun into his back again.

"What are you going to do to me?" he gasped, but no one answered.

"Keys," Chris said, and Becky, dropping Patrice's belongings, put the brass copies into his hand. Working more by touch than by sight, Chris felt each padlock through his gloves, slid the flaps to one side, and found a key that fitted all three. Using a centre punch from his coat pocket, he marked it with three vertical scratches. Then he slid the padlocks out, laid them on the grass in order, and opened both doors. Finally he brought the side of his fist down hard on Patrice's head. As it jerked forward, he did it again, leaving Patrice too dazed to resist as he yanked him to the ground face down.

"Take his feet, Becky," he rapped, and he took his shoulders.

Patrice's feet went over the railing first, then the rest of him. As he felt himself slide, he grabbed hold of the railing, but Becky brought her gun handle down on his fingers. That made him let go, and he slipped away, his fingers too damaged to grasp at the edge of the hole. He was screaming at the top of his voice by this time, so Becky stuffed his things into the shaft after him, then Chris lobbed his glasses in and shut the doors. Patrice must have stopped sliding somehow, possibly a piece of rock had caught him, because he could still be heard screaming when Chris was putting the padlocks back on. But the doors were a good fit, and once they were locked together, the noise more or less disappeared. Before they left, Chris tried the other keys, and found two more that fitted all three locks. He marked these as well. The rest he'd destroy in Peterborough.

He took his time driving back, it seemed the sensible thing to do, and he felt relaxed anyway. He didn't want anyone to notice the Prius arriving at the garage so, with about a hundred yards to go, he told Becky to shut down the burglar alarm. That was routine. Then he switched to battery and cruised silently onto the workshop car park with just his daytime lights on. Once they were parked, Becky went ahead to erase the CCTV and ready up something to eat while Chris, making the most of the scatter light from round about, changed the number plates. He'd destroy the fakes in the morning along with the redundant keys. He'd take care of the tyres as well; they must have left quite a few tread marks behind. He wondered vaguely how long Patrice would take to die. Two days, three, maybe four even. Or straight away, if he hit the floor of the cave hard. He didn't know and he cared less, Patrice was part of the past. All that mattered now was the pay-off. Then it was Sanderson's turn for some dedicated attention.

Chapter 15

The Trap Is Set...

When Purdy arrived home he expected to be greeted with love and the odours and sounds of cooking, but instead the milk was in the cooler on the step, the house looked as if it had been empty all day, and there was no trace of either his partner or a meal of any kind. Anxiously he tried to reach him on his mobile, but he couldn't get past 'Currently unavailable', so he put a call through to Pilling, Fayerl and Partners.

"Mr Patrice left at exactly two o'clock," Reception told him. "I've got the log in front of me."

His third call was to Jenny's, the convenience store on Epping underground station. Every time Patrice came home, he stopped off for some chocolates or sweets to see him through the evening. It was a cast iron ritual. Jenny's trade card was pinned to the kitchen notice board.

"He looked in and bought some Black Magic," Jenny told him. "No, he was laughing and joking. He said he'd keep the chocolates in his little store, he had something special lined up for tonight. That was why he was early."

That did it. Purdy rang the police, described the Porsche, and told them where Patrice usually parked it. Sixteen minutes later they rang back to say two officers were on their way to see him and more would be coming later. They'd found the Porsche in Marlborough Close, unlocked and, suspiciously, with the electro-key in it, but there was no sign of Mr Patrice. A full search was under way.

Some fifty-five miles north-east of Epping, Russell Burney was in his office with enough paperwork to keep him busy, and keep him seen to be busy, till as late as he cared to stay. He was checking some bills of lading when a thought struck him: he hadn't fixed a time when Harvest Home would go max. He should have done, but he hadn't. With his confidence slipping again, he pressed 'Encode' on his phone and tapped in the Site Controller's number. There was the usual lag till the encoding kicked in, then,

"Tilman here."

"Alice, it's Russell Burney. I'm calling from Klemmsley Marine. Can anyone hear if we talk?"

"No, I'm in my car on Teesside. What's up?"

He said he wanted to mark September 22nd with a big festive event, like with dignitaries, politicos, that sort of thing. If she could come up with a starting time, he could take care of the rest. Could she do that?

"It's more up to you than to me. How about 11 am? That will give people time to get here."

"Alice, please, it's got to be after dark. I want fire ships with searchlights and great curtains of water, the drilling deck bathed in multi-coloured lights, and everything so bright, you can see it from outer space. Mr Cyril's getting CDB-TV in, and CDB-Media is marketing the images. Everyone will see us."

"Make it 11 pm then. Technically it makes no difference."

"11 pm it is. Thanks for that. It's official as of now. I'll put it on the website and do a full press release. We can't get too much publicity now."

"Will you be coming yourself?"

"Try and stop me. And since we're talking September 22nd, I'll say this. You don't go max till I give you the go-ahead face to face. Not on the phone, not via a messenger, but face to face. Is that clear?"

"As crystal. Face to face it is."

"I've got a plan for Mr Cyril as well, if he'll agree to it. He'll be on a supply ship at Dassett Point. It'll have all its lights off except its navs. As eleven o'clock approaches, he'll come out of the darkness and be transferred onto the rig in a blaze of glory. How does that sound?"

"Couldn't be better. I hope he thinks the same."

'Someone wants to keep in with his old man,' she thought. 'I don't blame him with a father like that.'

He stayed talking to show he really was the CEO, then he put in a call to Hallavy, who didn't sound too happy.

"The Rocks people were right to phone," he said. "Dandy's core-samples are seriously in the way. The cold store's clogged up with them."

"So what? Can't you just thin them out?"

"It's not as easy as that. Some of them must be redundant, I don't see how they can't be. But off hand I can't say which ones, and I don't want to junk the ones we need to keep."

"You were her Second-in-charge. Didn't you see this happening?"

"Not a chance. She was totally secretive about her samples. 'I get the mud, you get the data' was what she used to say, and she was Number One, so that's how it was. Even now I don't normally come up here. I do everything from Essex."

"Someone should have told me, I'd have soon knocked her off her perch. Can you sort things out?"

"I can try, but it'll take me a day or two. There's a lot of working out to do."

"It'll have to be. If anyone gets in your way, let me know, they won't do it twice. By the way, I've been talking to Alice Tilman and we've agreed to go max at 11 pm on the 22nd. I'm organising a knees-up, and I want you in with the VIPs. You've earned that. I'll introduce you all round and say what a good job you've done filling in for Dandy. Seamless takeover and all that."

He could sense Hallavy blushing into the phone. Amazing the loyalty a pat on the head could generate.

At half past seven he'd had enough. He still had plenty of paper in front of him, but he wanted to get back to Aubrey. Just the thought of her made him feel good, and as he left, he asked Reception to phone ahead for him to say he was on his way. He was still feeling good when he got home. His front lawn – moist from the rain earlier in the day – glistened a welcoming emerald green as he swung the Morgan off the road, and there were enough lights on in the house to confirm his belief that some things at least were going right. The silver Volkswagen Polo that had been hanging back behind him was past the end of his drive before he reached his garage, and it kept on into the night. As he killed his engine, he automatically glanced at his watch. It showed the same time as Florence's dashboard clock.

As soon as he got indoors, he called Aubrey's name, but she didn't call back and she didn't come running. He called again and there was still no response, but so what, she might be in the bath or something. He put his briefcase on the umbrella stand, slipped his coat off, and made for the stairs. He'd soon find her and they'd make love there and then. He'd been up for it since he left Essex.

When he opened their bedroom door, the stink of vomit hit him first. As before, it was coming from the ensuite. When he looked in, there was some in the sink, some more in and around the lavatory, and Aubrey was lying face down on the bath mat. At first he thought she was dead, but then she shuddered, and he could see she was just about breathing. When he turned her over, the front of her dress was wet and smelled of urine. He did his best for her. He sponged her clean, laid her face down on the bed, and spread a light duvet over her. She didn't help him, she was completely inert, and she didn't seem even dimly aware he was there. It intensified the fear that constantly haunted him – that one day she'd leave him completely behind. On the bedside table were two gin bottles, one empty and one halfway there. Once again, the mix was hardly touched. Just to be sure, he patted his pockets, but he knew his drinks cupboard was locked and he'd taken his indoor keys with him. She must have gone out and bought the stuff. That made it his fault again. He should have taken her money away while he had the chance. He sat down on the bed and held his head in despair. The high hopes he'd come home with had crashed to the ground.

Finally, he kissed her lovingly, dragged himself down to the living room, and put the TV on. There was still a while to go before the ten o'clock news, so he went to the phone to check Reception had done as he'd asked. The call had come in all right, but no one had answered, so Reception had left a message. She must have been drunk already. Well, he just had to keep fighting for her, and from there he drifted onto how he was going to kill his father. One of the things he'd learned about methane hydrate blow-outs was that ships sank like a stone in the water they bubbled up through. He'd nearly lost one himself at Dassett Point, and this time he'd make sure one did go down there. The blow-out would be all four boreholes at once, and his father would drown in the dark. Better yet, he'd drown believing his son was about to make it big, and that would torment him even more than the sea water he'd be breathing in. Afterwards, there'd be legalities to get through, but his mother was right – he'd inherit a fortune. And Fern was right as well. If his father died on September 22nd, there'd be no sale, his estate would stay within reach of English law, and he – Russell Burney – would have Global all to himself.

But he had to get to September 22nd first, and that made Patrice key. He was glad he'd seen him that morning, the turn-around looked guaranteed, and remembering that kept him on the up. So when he zapped the news on, the headline story struck him like a bullet. Jocelyn Patrice had disappeared, his car had been found in a side street in Epping - empty and with the key in the glove box - and the police were appealing for witnesses, though none had come forward as yet. Patrice's partner was at home helping the police. There'd be a statement in the morning at the police press conference.

The key in the glove box sluiced two chilling thoughts into Burney's head – something dire had happened to Patrice and without Patrice, he was finished. Transfixed, he watched the story right through and stared sightlessly at the screen through the next item – the *Leonid Golovin*, a Slava-class Russian battle cruiser, was making a goodwill visit along the Channel in September on its way from the North Atlantic to the Baltic. Then, automaton-like, he turned the set off – he didn't want to see anything else. But he couldn't stay still, so he went back upstairs to see how Aubrey was. She looked to be out for the night. He kissed her on the cheek and was clumping aimlessly down the stairs when the living room phone rang. He ran to answer it before it woke Aubrey, and he recognised the voice straight away. It was Dvorski. What on earth did he want? It was well past ten o'clock.

"I'm sorry to eat into your evening like this," said Dvorski, who knew exactly what time it was, "but I've spent the last hour talking to Gazprom. They've made a proposal, and they want a response within twenty-four hours. If you come to the Russian Embassy at nine thirty tomorrow morning, I'll be there, and I'll go through it with you. If it goes ahead, I can promise you a nice fat commission for your trouble. So, will you be there, or shall I say no deal?"

Burney didn't have to think.

"I'll be there," he said. "And thanks."

The commission alone could run to millions, and there'd be other palm-greasers as well, there always were. And a response within twenty-four hours? That had to mean big bucks were just around the corner. Maybe he wouldn't have to sell his debts; maybe he'd get enough from Gazprom to pay them off. He spent the night in a spare bedroom again, and every time he woke up, he checked his watch and wished it was already morning. He couldn't believe his luck. Suddenly everything would be fine, and Toni would get all the care she needed.

Back in Essex, Purdy had forced himself to watch the same TV news as Burney and then, devastated with grief, he'd gone to bed and wept deep into the night. The police had been gentle, but they'd also been thorough. When they left, they took the Porsche's duplicate electro-key and a toothbrush and hairbrush belonging to Patrice. They were for Trace Analysis. They also emptied his workroom into a stack of cardboard boxes and took them, devoid of life and context, to join the boxes from his office in London. They'd all be combed through item by item.

Chapter 16

…and Sprung

While Russel Burney was greeting the new day with a morning shower in Stanmore, Chris Miller was pulling on his overalls in Peterborough to clear some jobs before anyone else showed up. It was something he often did; he liked to look better than the people who worked for him. He collected the fake number plates from his safe, destroyed them with a welding torch, and ground up the unmarked keys in his cutting box. Then he brought the Prius into the main workshop and put the odometer back to what the trade-in documents said. The tyres came next. He changed them all and rolled the old ones out to the heap at the end of his lot. He'd picked the right day – they'd all be gone by the end of it. Finally he drove through the wash tunnel and sprayed off every last speck of dirt from the bodywork. That included the wheel arches and the underside. The petrol didn't matter – no one expected much in a second-hand car. While he was bringing up a shine, the two part-timers who valeted the used cars arrived.

"Clean the inside and put it on the Buy-Of-The-Week stand," he said without stopping. "I'll put a good price on it. If it's still for sale tomorrow, I'll ask why."

That left the SigSauers and their gear. Well, lunchtime would do for them. He'd book half an hour on the pistol range and take them in with him. It was a question of nerve, that was all.

Burney, too, was keeping his nerve. Aubrey seemed unharmed again, and before he could say anything, she gave him a big lift by ordering him to lock her money and cards away. She could still buy on account, she admitted that, but she thought she could rein herself in if she tried. And she'd feel like a child if he took every decision for her. He told her where he was going, he was too excited not to, and anyway, he'd booked a taxi. When it arrived, he gave her the sort of kiss that says it all, ran his fingers through her hair, and then he was gone. He had no clear idea what she did when he wasn't there, but she had her own computer and she seemed to read a lot, so she must be keeping busy in her way. All he ever read was what he had to, but as soon as she'd moved in, she'd asked him to register with the Middlesex Mobile Library Service. She couldn't do it herself, she'd explained, she hadn't been in Middlesex long enough, so she ordered in his name, and a van delivered the books. He'd offered to get her an e-book reader, but she'd said no thank you, she preferred a real book, one she could feel in her hands. Burney was happy with all of that, but he figured, if he could get her out more, maybe she'd forget the gin entirely. He'd see what he could do once he'd relieved Gazprom of some of its surplus millions.

The Russian Embassy was its usual inscrutable self as he paid his taxi off and waited patiently for clearance. He'd been inside several times before – Industry and Trade was never slow with vodka evenings when it came to oil and gas. Dvorski was all smiles as he shook Burney's hand and led him down to what looked like a briefing room. It was in the basement, away from the street. It was oppressively still, and an unsettling hint of dust hung in the air. A table in the middle had a PowerPoint projector on it, and at the far end, a screen had been pulled down from the ceiling. The flaked tubular chairs that went with the table were stacked on either side of the screen, leaving four worn easy chairs set out in a semi-circle. They'd be comfortable to see the screen from and they could easily form a ring. The windows had thick curtains drawn over them, so all the light came from some yellowing standard lamps that were controlled from a dimmer by the door. Two large flasks of coffee, some thick plain cups, a jug of cream, and a bowl of brown sugar stood on a tray on the table. Dvorski invited him to sit down but he – Dvorski – soon seemed to run out of small talk, and as the silences grew longer, his smiles became more mask-like. Burney had had no idea what to expect, but he hadn't expected this. Maybe things would pick up when the rest arrived. He wondered how long they'd take and, for that matter, who they'd be.

There turned out to be three of them, and it was Valkov, who Burney knew, who led the other two in. Valkov was all smiles, just as Dvorski had been, and he too shook Burney's hand as if he was glad to see him. Behind Valkov was a petite, smartly dressed woman in her early sixties. She was carrying a leather hold-all, and Valkov introduced her as Professor Bondareva from the St Petersburg Institute of Oceanography.

"But," he added unctuously, "you can call her Galina. I'd like us all to be on first name terms this morning."

The third person wasn't introduced. Sombrely suited and closely cropped, he locked the door and seated himself in front of it on a tubular chair he'd fetched for himself. He didn't say anything and he didn't need to. He clearly wasn't there to talk oil and gas. So who was, then? Just Bondareva, Dvorski and Valkov? That didn't seem right. Perhaps more would turn up as the morning wore on.

Valkov served the coffee – "from my private stock," he simpered in his great man way – and Bondareva got the PowerPoint going. When she joined the rest, Valkov was ready to start. His smile evaporated, his face set hard, and he moved his chair to close the circle before he sat down. When he spoke, it was straight at Burney from close range.

"You've been deceived," he said glacially, not bothering with his name. "There's no one from Gazprom here, they were warned months ago never to come near you. And there's no Gazprom deal either, it's been a trick all along."

"No Gazprom deal?" Burney managed to echo, and the follow-up came fast.

"Oleg promised you lots of money last night. I know because I told him to. I also know why you need it. You're facing bankruptcy."

Burney felt as if he'd stepped into the street having forgotten to put his clothes on. All his privacy had been stripped away. But he could see denial wouldn't work.

"How do you know?" he came out with instead.

"Let's say someone's been touting your debts about, complete with the Burney name. And let's say that someone's called Jocelyn Patrice. Strange he's gone missing, just when you need him most, you'd think it was deliberate. But with no Gazprom, no Patrice and, I tell you straight, no sale of your debts, you're a ruined man, aren't you? Come on, you might as well admit it. Say it out loud."

Burney believed him, but he refused to speak. It was the only defence he could think of.

"I said, Russell, you're a ruined man. Now come on, say it out loud."

He felt trapped by the ring of chairs, by the guard on the door, by the Embassy and, most of all, by his now unpayable debts. Then there were Valkov's actual words. He'd heard some of them before somewhere, he couldn't remember where, but they made him feel as if he'd never grown up properly. But he still wouldn't say anything. Instead he pressed his palms against his knees, hunched his shoulders, and screwed up his eyes. No one spoke, and when he opened his eyes again, everyone was staring at him. He ran up the white flag.

"All right," he mumbled. "Have it your way. I'm a ruined man."

"Thank you. Now tell us why you're a ruined man."

"Do I have to?"

"It could be in your interest."

He took a deep breath.

"Very well. I've made some bad investments, and I need £14·9 million by Monday first thing, otherwise I lose my house, my cars and my job. There, will that do?"

"Your pride's in this as well, isn't it? Your father's a success, but you're a total failure. You want to compete, but you haven't got it in you. Am I right?"

"You are. I wish you weren't, but you are."

"And not too long ago," Valkov ploughed on relentlessly, "you made an acquisition. If I don't know her name, you'll forgive me, I'm sure, but she's a pretty little thing, I'm told; an English rose, some might say. We've been watching you closely, you see. Tell us, where did you meet her?"

This had to be the final humiliation. They know I can't protect her, and now I've got to tell them she's a drunk like me. It was too much.

"I want to leave," he said tersely. "I want to leave right now. Unlock the door, please."

Valkov looked across to the guard, who unlocked the door and stood out of the way.

"You're free to go," Valkov said, "as you have been since you came in. But before you leave, tell me, why do you think we've taken so much trouble over you? And why has Galina set the PowerPoint up?"

He wanted to say it was up to them what they did, but Valkov's questions made him feel, if he walked out now, he'd be leaving with nothing but a heap of unsolved problems. On the other hand, if he played along, there might yet be something for him in all this.

"Very well, I'll stay," he said. "I'm in your hands."

"It's your choice entirely. Say that, please."

"It's my choice entirely, it's my choice entirely, it's my choice entirely!" he almost shouted. "There, will that do?"

Valkov looked at the guard again. He relocked the door and resumed his position in front of it.

"So tell us," Valkov persisted, intending to take Burney completely apart. "Where did you meet this young lady?"

"In a clinic. She's a drunk and so am I. That's why we were there."

"Yet you love her all the same."

Burney flushed angrily.

"You take that back," he snapped. "You speak of her with respect or not at all."

It was the response Valkov wanted – it was unguarded, and it betrayed how intensely Burney felt about Aubrey. Valkov had made quite a haul so far, but from his point of view, the best was yet to come. He moved his chair to one side, refilled the coffee cups, and asked Bondareva if she was ready to go.

"*Da*," she said curtly.

She went to the PowerPoint, Dvorski dulled the lights, and she zoomed in on an Industry and Trade archive picture of Torelli waving from a support ship in the Sea of Okhotsk.

"I don't have to say who that is," she began, just as Valkov had told her to. "She was feeding us information all the time she was with ExxonMobil, and she kept it coming when she transferred to you. She told us one thing especially, and we think you still don't know about it. We'll see if we were right."

Torelli a traitor? It was another shock opening, and again the follow-up was instant. Using the data Torelli had given to Dvorski and speaking fluent American-accented English – Bondareva had used the Yeltsin years she now spat on to land a Princeton research fellowship – she explained to Burney why Harvest Home would cause a tsunami when it went max. Then she detailed the devastation it would cause, first in terms of national economies, then in terms of human life. Burney was horrified. He could cope with killing his father – to his mind it was a way of righting personal wrongs. But he couldn't answer for this.

"It can't happen," he countered, as pale as death. "The seabed's knee-deep in sensors, and we can always put in more. If they show anything, we stop drilling. It's as simple as that."

"You won't have time. What we're talking about is a sudden catastrophic subsidence. One minute everything's fine, and the next it's all happened."

He still didn't want to believe it.

"Show me the fault lines again," he said.

She did.

"Now the pressure lines."

Likewise.

"Now superimpose the two."

Likewise again.

"Now Dandy's figures. The results ones."

She screened them, too, and he had to accept what he saw – Dandy had got it right. For form's sake, Bondareva added in the prehistoric tsunami, but it didn't matter now. Dejectedly he turned towards Valkov, who met his gaze in the odd mix of light from the standard lamps and the PowerPoint.

"So we were right to think nobody had told you this before," he murmured smoothly. "Neither Dandy nor anybody else. Say that we were, please."

Burney nodded. His face was sweaty.

"You were right. I had no idea till now."

He dabbed his forehead with a handkerchief.

"I suppose you want me to abandon my project, that's what you're driving at, isn't it? Another Western flop you can crow over."

"Not so fast, not so fast, Russell. All you've heard is between ourselves, and that's where we want it to stay, because I'm going to add to your surprises. We don't want you to abandon your project at all, we want you to keep it going, since we want that tsunami to happen. To help you agree, I'll tell you how we see things, then you can tell me whether you'll play ball or no. Are you ready?"

Burney knew he should have walked out right there, but he didn't. The old problems hadn't gone away, and a big new one had joined them. So he said he was ready, and Valkov set to work. Dvorski watched him in admiration. It was a masterclass.

"To begin with, there's no risk to you, Russell, none at all. When the great flood takes place, you'll be able to say you took every precaution. You even put Dandy Torelli in charge to make sure everything was perfect. Second, we'll get all your debts paid – not just your Monday ones, but your long-term ones as well, which we also know about. There are plenty of Russian billionaires in London, and I might even have talked to one already. If you give Oleg an itemised list of your debts, he'll make sure enough is banked to cover them."

"You can stop right there, Andrey. My bank would have to report a sum like that. I'd never hear the end of it, let alone get my hands on it."

"Who mentioned your bank? It's Sberbank we're talking about. All you'll have to do is sign the papers, and they'll do the rest. You can do it tomorrow if you like. As for your project, it's always been doomed, it's just that you know it now. So, get shot of your debts, let Harvest Home run its course, and start living again. Come, Russell, what do you say? Do we have a deal?"

"Start living on what?" he asked morosely. "Klemmsley will get hit all ways. In the courts, I mean. So will CDB Global, it's the parent company. And I'll get the sack."

"What nonsense you talk! If Torelli couldn't get it right, no one could. That covers Global, Klemmsley and your job as CEO. You'll be all right, Russell. No one will be able to touch you, not even your father. He'll have no cause to."

Burney warmed to all that, it fitted his needs exactly. But there was one question he had to ask.

"What if I say no?"

If Valkov had been using a bear trap, everyone would've heard it shut.

"Oh dear, Russell," he said. "You should have left while you had the chance, because it isn't that you've learned a lot this morning, it's that you've learned too much. If you say no, or if you say yes but go back on your word, we'll not only hunt you down and kill you, we'll hunt down and kill your sweetie-pie as well. We're good at that sort of thing. Don't ask us for demonstrations."

He was sure Valkov meant it. That sent him back to the positives in the deal. And, seeing no way out, he said it was on.

Valkov, all smiles again, found more coffee for him in the bottom of one of the flasks. While Dvorski put the room lights up, Bondareva repacked her hold-all, and the guard unlocked the door.

"I'll leave you with Oleg," Valkov said. "Round figures will do on your list, these oligarchs don't think in less than millions. Oh, and one last thing. If you ever get asked why a Russian billionaire and Sberbank bailed you out, say you confided in Oleg and he did the rest."

"Why should he do that?"

"Because it makes sense, that's why. He keeps you solvent and you put business his way. Just make sure you stick to it, because it's what Oleg will say if he has to."

Then he was gone, taking Bondareva and the guard with him. Dvorski, who just happened to have pen and paper to hand, kept Burney for as long as it took him to spell out his debts, then he saw him into the street and went up to Valkov's office. The guard and Bondareva had gone to the staff canteen, and Valkov was perusing the menu for senior officials. He was also wondering just how tightly he'd really stitched Burney up. The trouble was, Burney's passion for Aubrey could go either way. It could make him co-operate or it could make him rebel, there was simply no way of knowing. On balance, Valkov decided, it would make him co-operate, but he couldn't rule a backlash out entirely. It was something he'd have to be careful about.

He took Dvorski's list from him, but he didn't ask him to sit down.

"That went very well," he said smoothly, hiding his doubts about Burney's passion for Aubrey. "From now on, if anyone tells Burney Harvest Home is lethal, it won't matter because he already knows. And he'll make sure the tsunami happens, unless we tell him otherwise. It's been a good morning's work."

"I'm glad you're pleased, Andrey Ivanovich," Dvorski replied.

He'd been hoping for a word of praise.

"Yes, I *am* pleased. It's cost us Patrice, but it's been worth it."

He returned to his menu, then looked up.

"You can go now. I expect you're wanting your lunch like the rest of us. I shouldn't want to keep you waiting."

Burney didn't phone for a taxi when he left the Embassy, he wanted to spend time out in the open first. As he soaked up the August sunshine, the questions floated up. Had Patrice tried to sell his debts to Valkov? It didn't seem likely, but if he hadn't, how did Valkov know about them and that they hadn't been sold. From Dvorski perhaps? But how would *he* know? Patrice had said he'd be discreet, but half London seemed to be in on his shame. Then there was Toni. Did Valkov really not know where he met her? Or what her name was? Valkov, he decided, knew a lot more than he let on, and behind the mask he was deadly. Like a stage magician in a horror movie. Did he know who killed Dandy and her mother? Why not? Or who'd got at Patrice just when he needed him most? Why not again? Burney was in Kensington Gardens by this time, and they were so green and peaceful, the new Russell Burney he was discovering himself to be made him feel like an alien species. He was frightened, he admitted that, and, try as he might, he couldn't quieten his conscience. On the other hand, a man as powerful as Valkov could protect him as well as harm him, and the lift that thought gave him let him take some basic decisions. He wouldn't tell the Russians about his intention to kill his father; that would stay between him and Shayler. He wouldn't tell Shayler about the tsunami – she lacked Valkov's cool, detached insight, so she might have one of her flare-ups. And if Hallavy found out about it, he'd stifle him with flattery.

There was no turning back, he was convinced of that. Between them, Shayler and Valkov had made him a different person. Now he had to live out the consequences, one of which was, straight away, to lie to Shayler. She'd know from the news Patrice had disappeared, but she wouldn't know whether he'd sold Burney's debts or no. She might try to do something about that and somehow give their secret away. So he waved down a taxi in the Bayswater Road, and when he got home, he wrote by hand on his personal stationery, 'Rest assured, the sale we discussed has been put through successfully. All outstanding payments will be made on time – Russell.' Then he dated it, put in the time, and added, 'Destroy this when you've read it' before he sealed it in an envelope. Aubrey was in the room she'd made her own – it looked out onto the back garden and had a permanently tranquil air about it. He gave her a loving kiss, told her his meeting had been a total success, and put on a big smile to match, confident she wouldn't see past it. His words triggered a big smile in return. It had to be because she was pleased with what she'd heard, but fleetingly he felt he was being humoured or even ridiculed. But she couldn't possibly know more than he'd told her, he must be feeling an after-shock from the mauling he'd had from Valkov. Sensing his uncertainty, she switched to mock-solemn and held up a book on Patagonia he hadn't seen before.

"The Mobile Library has only just gone," she pronounced, sounding like a headmistress in Speech Day mode, "and here is your prize for a good morning's work."

He took the book with a bow, and they both burst out laughing. Then, smothering his disquiet, he kissed her again and set off to put his note personally through Shayler's letterbox.

III
End of a Key Witness

Chapter 17

A Problem with a Hard Drive

When New York architect Avery Scrite wanted to expand into London, he toughed out the endless security checks and leased part of a Crown property near Chelsea's Royal Hospital. The weathered namestone said 'Ashell House', and Scrite got a kick every time he read 'Scrite and Associates' on the steel plate next to the glass swing doors. It was fame by association. Chelsea was ever London's big name borough.

The rest of the building housed the UK's Serious Risks Office. As a Crown institution, it was above the law. In practice it answered to the Prime Minister and Parliament. Access was through a roll-up door round the back that looked like the door to the garbage bay. When it went up, an armoured portcullis went up with it, but the barriers inside stayed down till final clearance came through. No one got in who wasn't meant to.

One of those who *was* meant to was Willem van Piet. His office was on the third floor down from the top. The top floor housed Signals, plus bed-sits for emergencies, and the floor underneath it was where Luke Benjamin, the new Director General, had his room, as his office was traditionally called. His predecessor, Alex Trilling, had been unmasked as a years-long traitor, and Benjamin, a no-nonsense ex-field man, had been promoted to make a fresh start.

Van Piet was British by birth. His mother, Daphne, a senior lecturer in the London School of Economics, was British as well, but his father, Joost, was Dutch. Joost owned

Van Piet Banking, a private bank headquartered in Amsterdam, and Willem was being trained to take it over when the SRO asked him to join its ranks. Joost respected his son's new career, but he also put him on his advisory council. He said he'd done it to keep his pay up. But he also reckoned a Crown agent who had one foot in international banking was better placed than one who didn't.

While Valkov was taking Burney apart in Kensington, van Piet was in Chelsea re-adapting to office life. He'd been mostly in Jordan since January, and he still looked reddish as, through the slats of a venetian blind, he peered idly over the Ranelagh Gardens towards the Thames. At least he didn't have to write a report. He'd agreed a text with King Abdullah before he'd left Amman, and a copy had preceded him to London via the Jordanian secret service. His mind was drifting back to the Sandhurst-trained monarch and the dangers his kingdom faced when his desk phone buzzed. It was Tom Garry, his secretary.

"Mr Benjamin wants you in his room, Sir. He'd like me to be there, too."

"I'm on my way. Any idea what it's about?"

"Well, Mr Snape from Essex Police and Detective Inspector Farrell from the NCA are with him. My guess is it's the Torelli murders, the Patrice disappearance, or both."

Van Piet was aware of the Torelli murders. He lived on the Blackwater Estuary, less than forty miles from where they'd happened, and Célestine, his wife, had phoned him in Jordan when the news broke. Patrice he knew about from the media.

"You could be right, Tom. Let's find out."

Benjamin seated them all round a conference table, the blinds were already down, and as soon as the tea came in, he locked the corridor door from his desk, sketched in enough to get things started and asked Snape to take over. Eddie Snape was easy to misread. He didn't have a degree, he wrote in block capitals, and his spelling would have made even Shakespeare blink. But he'd made it to Chief Constable, and every stat said his force was either top or near it. He also liked to take cases on personally. He said he was too much of a policeman to push a pen all day. Van Piet had a lot of time for him.

"There's no mystery why we've come here," Snape began, addressing van Piet directly. "We've been putting in the hours, but we still don't know who shot the Torellis or what's happened to Patrice. There's an international angle as well. The Americans are getting restless about the Torellis, and a Russian with diplomatic status is also mixed in somehow. His name's Oleg Dvorski, he's with their Embassy's Department of Industry and Trade, and Russell Burney's told us they've been discussing a deal with Gazprom."

"Is it documented?"

"Just about. We've taken copies, but there doesn't seem to be much. They're in this file if you want to see them."

He reached over a box file marked 'Burney, R./Gazprom'. There was plenty of room inside it when van Piet opened it up.

"There's nothing from Gazprom itself," he said after a look-through. "It's all Russell Burney and Dvorski. I don't see a deal, either. Routine enquiries, statements of intent, yes, but that's about it. And this is Dvorski, is it?"

He took a newspaper cutting from Snape showing Dvorski at an Anglo-Russian trade fair in Coventry. He was right on the edge at the back, with a glass of champagne in his hand. Snape pointed out his misshapen ear.

"My deputy's doing my job so I can move things on," he went on, taking the box file and the cutting back, "but the truth is, I'm getting nowhere, and time's running out for Patrice. We think you can help us. You're better with the spooky side than we are, and your command lines are shorter. Mr Benjamin says, if you want to, you can come to us on secondment. So, do you want to?"

"Talk me through it and I'll tell you."

It was a typical van Piet answer. In his heart he was a home-lover, and that was all he wanted to be. But he also had a Calvinist sense of duty. If he took something on, it wasn't because he wanted to – it was because he felt he had to. It could make him hard to work with, but once he started a job, he saw it through.

The talking through, which was constantly interrupted by calls from police HQ in Chelmsford, lasted till late afternoon, then Snape and Farrell took questions. There was a set of photos of Dandy Torelli amongst the back-up they'd brought. Van Piet picked out two, moved a used paper plate, and placed them side by side. One was a print Jethro Torelli had made from the Sakhalin Island photo. On the back he'd written 'Great shot! Just what I wanted. – Love, Daddy' followed by 'Sakhalin Island/Nikon D100' and the date the photo was taken. The other one had 'Univ. Glasgow' stamped on the back. It was a 30,000 times magnification of part of Dandy's left eye as shown on Torelli's print. The image was blurred, but there was no mistaking who'd been working the Nikon. It was the Russian in the press cutting – the one with the damaged right ear. Torelli's eyeball had acted as a mirror, and Glasgow had done the rest. Van Piet looked across to Snape.

"You said this print comes from Dandy Torelli's place. She's kept it for a long while then."

"She and her father were close. There's no surprise there."

"I don't suppose the Nikon's turned up."

Snape shook his head.

"Her father took it apart and now it's gone."

"How do you know?"

"We've had access to his research log. It says, 'Parts analysed and photographed. Originals not retained.'"

"That's too bad. But this" – he indicated Torelli's print – "might yet tell us some more."

He went back to a file marked 'Cyril Burney/Enid Burney/Russell Burney' that he'd glanced through earlier.

"Three well-known names with faces to match," he observed. "But I wonder how many people know the family's only one generation out of Poland. Eddie?"

"Leo can talk you through that," Snape answered. "He put the file together."

Farrell didn't need the file. He'd been on top of his data all meeting.

"Cyril Burney's father was a Warsaw plumber and his name was Marek Bulinski. Bulinski knew Hitler had his eye on Poland, so the day he finished his apprenticeship, he fled to London with Johanna, his wife, and started plumbing near what's now Roman Road. He was twenty-one, she was nineteen, and they'd only just got married. When war broke out, he said he was younger than he was and trained as an RAF pilot. Later he transferred to a Polish fighter squadron, and he finished the war with a row of medals. Then he went back to plumbing in East London."

"So he was a war hero as well as a plumber," van Piet put in. "That could take some living up to."

"Correct, and some people say that's why Cyril's so driven. They also say it's why he kicks his son around. Apparently he doesn't even pay him bonuses, just a salary – like doling out pocket money. Anyway, Cyril stayed well clear of Marek's plumbing. He helped the street market traders instead, and as soon as he could, he got his own stall, changed his name to Burney, and the rest is public domain."

"What about Enid Burney?"

"Her parents came from Lodz. Her father was an unskilled labourer named Pawel Sakowski and her mother was Zuzanna Yanta before she got married. They tied the knot straight after the war, but they didn't like what the Russians were doing to Poland, so they also took off for London. They settled near the Bulinskis, and the two couples got to know each other. The Sakowskis took their time to produce Enid, but one way or another, when Cyril wanted some totty about the place, Pawel's daughter was right there."

"Did any of these people go back to Poland?"

"Cyril spent a week in Warsaw with an uncle and aunt when he was twenty, and when she was eighteen, Enid spent ten days with an unmarried sort-of-aunt in Lodz."

"Sort-of-aunt?"

"She was Zuzanna's foster sister and everyone called her Aunt Yanta. Anyway, Cyril's done a lot of business in Poland since the Soviet Union folded, but Enid's never gone with him, or so Fern Shayler, his Head of Finance, told me. Apparently Enid couldn't stand Aunt Yanta, so she said she'd never go to Poland again, and she's stuck to it ever since. Shayler's sure there's more to it than that, something the family keeps under wraps, but she's never found out what it is."

"Thanks for that, Leo. I take it it's all in the file."

"It is. There's all the pictures you'll need as well."

Van Piet was about to move on when Benjamin's secretary tapped on her door as she opened it.

"Excuse me, Sir, but there's another call for Mr Snape from Chelmsford."

Snape went out into the office. He wasn't gone long, and when he came back, he looked flattened.

"You'll remember Patrice had this spy room next to his office," he said. "We've been trying to recover the erased bits from his hard drive, but I've just heard we can't, and I have to say that's bad news. Patrice and Russell Burney met yesterday morning, it's in the log. If we knew what they said, we might get a lead on where Patrice is now."

"Russell Burney's drowning in debt," van Piet put in. "Patrice's stats show that. Was this meeting scheduled?"

"No. Burney rang Patrice on his mobile Tuesday evening – we've got the metadata – and Patrice booked him in for yesterday morning."

"Why not Wednesday?"

"We don't know. Patrice's diary was always pretty full. That could be your answer."

Van Piet turned to Benjamin.

"That hard drive. Can I ask Millie Bayliss?"

Benjamin nodded the go-ahead, and while van Piet tapped a direct number into his mobile, Benjamin spoke to Snape and Farrell.

"Millie Bayliss heads the Department of National Security Support at Cambridge. If there's anything to find on your hard drive, she'll find it."

A woman's voice came out of the mobile. Van Piet turned the volume up.

"It's Willem van Piet, Millie. Can you be in your department an hour and a half from now? It's urgent."

"Can do. What's it about?"

"The missing stockbroker, Jocelyn Patrice. Be ready to take a hard drive from Essex Police. I want all the erasures restored fast. Don't wait for me, start as soon as you get it. And can you call Pamela Wole in? Tell her it involves her project."

"If I can reach her I can. Anything else?"

"Yes. I want to bring Essex's Chief Constable with me. Is that on?"

"Sorry, no clearance, no entry. The best I can offer is a viewing room."

Snape whispered it was fine.

"That's good enough. Tom Garry's coming as well. Give us time to arrive, we're coming from Ashell House. I'll tell you more from the road."

He terminated the call.

"I've made my mind up," he said to Benjamin as he put his mobile away. "I'll take this assignment, I don't see how I can't. Eddie," he went on without a pause, "have that hard drive and the rest put into a marked car and say it's for Professor Bayliss personally. Mr Benjamin, can you get Eddie her lab address, please? Leo, call the Met and get a marked car and driver for me, destination Cambridge. Lean on them hard to make it quick, then go back to Chelmsford and make sure every lead, however slight, gets followed up. Tom, my apologies to your wife, but you could be out all night. Eddie, that goes for you, too."

He gathered up the photos of Dandy Torelli and handed them to Garry.

"Bring these, Tom. They're for Pamela."

Not long after, Benjamin's secretary came back in. A car from the Met was pulling up outside the roll-up door, she said. Van Piet took the passenger seat and told the driver to make for Cambridge West.

"I asked for a marked car," he added, "because you have to drive fast. A man's life is at stake."

"I understand, Sir."

He put his blue lights and siren on, accelerated through the first hints of rain and, with ice-cold precision, drove risk-free as fast as the roads and the traffic allowed. He had sixty-three miles to go, including London. He took just over an hour. While they were still in London, van Piet waited till Garry and Snape had called home, then he put in a call to Célestine. He told her he'd taken on a new assignment and he'd be out most of the night. As always, he didn't tell her what it was and, also as always, she didn't try to find out. Then he asked,

"Is Jackie about? With her smartphone?"

Jackie was the van Piets' adopted daughter. A smartphone was much better than a mobile for her. She was profoundly deaf, and there was a lot more to life than texting.

"She's mucking out. Her smartphone's not far away, I saw her take it with her."

The van Piets' home was a manor house called Gorris Hall. Célestine, a former international showjumper, had opened a riding school in the grounds, and Jackie knew, if she wanted to join in the riding, she had to join in the rest. Van Piet switched to his smartphone and put the camera on so Jackie could read his lips. She could say anything she liked back, he just liked to have her talking to him. He told her he'd taken a new job on, so he wouldn't be home till late. It hurt them both, she liked her Daddy about the place, but it was what she'd grown up with, so she didn't complain. Not out loud anyway. Finally he shaped his lips into some goodbye kisses, terminated, and turned round to speak first to Garry, then to Snape.

"I'll be in Chelmsford a lot from now on," he said. "I want you and Mr Snape to set up a secure link between Mr Snape's office and Ashell House. Not Chelmsford's Ops Room – we have to control who hears things. Eddie, Leo needs to understand I'm not police. I don't trust him because I don't know him, and I don't pass on information unless I see fit. You know that, but he doesn't. I'll ask you to tell him."

"He won't like it. He's a hard worker, you've seen that for yourself. And he's got a lot of pride."

"Then he'll have to lump it. Pride's nothing, Eddie. It's duty that counts."

Snape didn't have to say he agreed, they knew each other too well.

The evening sky promised more rain as the driver sped through Cambridge and halted outside the Department of Materials Sciences, where the NSS had a suite of its own in a sealed-off annexe. This was the new Cambridge – purpose-built, cutting edge and internationally staffed. The world-famous Cavendish, which it replaced, was now a museum.

"Shall I wait, Sir?" the driver asked van Piet.

"Thanks. Pull up on the forecourt. Someone will let you know."

He led Garry and Snape towards the main entrance and gave their names to the receptionist, who typed them into a computer. He was a rotund, affable-looking man in his fifties. Not too long ago he would have been called a porter.

"Professor Bayliss will come and collect you," he said, reading the answer.

As he finished speaking, Bayliss came through a door in the back of the lobby. She looked young to be a professor. Her CV said she should have been one sooner.

"Two pieces of good news," she said briskly. "First, the hard drive's not damaged, and we think we can get what you want. Second" – and she gave her attention fully to Snape – "I'm sure Willem's explained, we're security services only. But the colleague Willem asked about – Pamela Wole – she's preparing a project for the police, so when she gets here, you'll be able to see how it works. That could be any time now. She's been lecturing in Nottingham, but she said she'd get here as fast as she could. I must get back and I'll take Willem and Tom with me. You can either wait here or go through to the coffee shop. When Dr Wole arrives, we'll see how things stand."

He said he'd wait in the lobby.

"I'll send the Met car away," he told van Piet as they split up. "We can get one from Essex when we finish."

Snape was trying not to look glum, but Patrice was weighing him down. He was glad he'd involved van Piet, he was making things happen already. But the odds on finding Patrice alive were lengthening fast.

Chapter 18

Analysis of a Face

"We'll go into my office," Bayliss said as she shepherded van Piet and Garry through the security gates. "We can get an update from there, and you won't have to change into lab gear."

Bayliss's world of secrets was like a science fiction nightmare. There were no windows, the impact-absorbent floors deadened every sound, and the doors, which had code boxes instead of handles, only had numbers on them. Cameras and sensors monitored everything, the air was piped, and regardless of day or night, the lighting was the same.

"Here we are," Bayliss said as she opened her own numbered door. "Willem, make some coffee while I find out what's doing."

She slipped on a headset, put her questions, and memorised the answers. It didn't take long.

"First," she said, stirring her coffee, "the hard drive and the software are Russian, and the software's been rejigged for an English user."

"Do you know how old they are?" asked van Piet.

"The hard drive matches a model the Russians produced mid-July. It's restricted-use, I should add. We think the software was produced at the same time, and dates in the files support that. It's also restricted-use. Anyone not an apparatchik would have to be special to have this stuff."

"What about the files that were erased?"

"We're getting them. We're going as fast as we can."

A lull set in, then a message from Reception flashed on a monitor: Dr Wole was in the lobby. Bayliss typed in, 'Thanks. We'll come through' and stood up.

"We'll go to Pamela now. As soon as she's finished, you'll come back to us."

Wole, who was a good ten years older than Bayliss, gathered up Snape and whisked them all through the coffee shop – she hadn't eaten either – then she hurried them into her part of the building. Garry laid out the Torelli photos on her desk, leaving a gap between the Sakhalin Island one and the rest.

"This is the big one, is it?" she asked, and Garry nodded.

While she was getting organised, she explained how things were to Snape.

"Face muscles are the only muscles that connect bone to skin," she began. She couldn't help it, she always sounded as if she was giving a lecture. "When they contract, your expression changes. When they relax, it changes again. It's like dominoes falling. You get emotions in your brain, your brain tells your face muscles to contract or relax, and the expressions they produce tell everyone what those emotions are."

She took a bite from a sandwich and powered up a flatbed scanner.

"I'll model this lady's skull to start with."

She scanned the photos one by one, the software drew its conclusions, and Torelli's skull emerged life-size and in 3D on a monitor.

"Next I'll see how her muscles were. These photos you've brought cover a range of expressions, so it shouldn't be too hard."

Working steadily, she covered Torelli's skull with virtual muscle groups to represent the ones she must have really had.

"It's inference software," she said to Snape. "And come the spring, every police force will be able to get help from my lab. That's why I'm not in with Millie. You're allowed in this far, but go any further, and the SAS storms the place."

While she spoke, she overlaid the muscle groups with Torelli's various expressions, and each time she made Torelli's skin, eyes, lips and teeth all see-through. It was uncanny. With each overlay, the muscle groups contracted or relaxed as if they'd really constructed those expressions. She reached for another sandwich.

"So far, so simple. Now let's go for broke."

She reset all the muscle groups to relaxed and overlaid them with the Sakhalin Island photo, again using see-through. Spontaneously they moved to how they would have been for real when Torelli prepared her face for the Nikon. Wole split the screen and brought up the strain measurements. A lot of them were flashing scarlet.

"I thought so!" she exclaimed when she'd finished. "This face is completely inconsistent. Everything about the eyes says triumph, but everything about the mouth says fear. You can forget about the fixed big smile. That was strictly for the camera."

She picked up her desk phone and told Bayliss she was rounding off.

"You want them in Viewing Room Four, do you?" she repeated. "I'll bring them along."

"Ring for two cars, Eddie," van Piet put in. "They can be getting here while we're watching. Make them marked again. And use Pamela's desk phone – three sevens, then your number. Mobiles are a hanging offence in here."

Viewing Room Four was up a floor, and Wole disappeared as soon as Bayliss unlocked the door. Wole was after promotion before she ran out of years. That meant finishing the textbook she was writing soonest.

"We've made the whole drive playable again," Bayliss said, "and everything you sent us is ready to go back to Chelmsford. Because you're in a hurry, I'll play you a copy of just the erased bits. We've enhanced the clarity, by the way, especially at the end. You'll see why when we get there."

The pictures were black-and-white and the sound was echo-y, but there was no problem tracking Burney's last two encounters with Patrice. And then came Patrice's slip. He opened the door of the spy room and left it open with the camera switched on. From the computer-enhanced glimpses, Snape made out someone who had to be Dvorski.

"Can we see that last bit in stop-frames, please?" he asked.

It was Dvorski all right. His ear gave him away.

Then it was over. Van Piet was tired, Snape was exhausted, and while they'd learned a lot, Patrice could still be anywhere. Bayliss saw them to the lobby, where they sat waiting for the cars from Essex to arrive. Patrice's equipment, neatly boxed, stood on a table in front of them. There was a technical note inside.

"What now, Eddie?" van Piet asked.

Disappointment was etched into Snape's face, but he wasn't giving up before he had to.

"We go where the evidence leads," he said.

"What Dvorski? Right now?"

"Certainly. We can see why Burney and Patrice go together, but what Dvorski's doing there is anyone's guess. We've got to talk to him."

"How are you going to get to him? He's a protected species, don't forget. He's probably sound asleep as well."

"We'll take him by surprise. We'll drive to his flat, phone him from outside his door, and ask if we can come in. Then it's up to him. I can't let a face-to-face with him go, not now. He could be the lead we're after."

When the Essex cars arrived, van Piet and Snape got into one and set off for Kensington, while Garry was driven home to Barnet via Chelmsford. Patrice's equipment was in the boot, and it had priority. Van Piet and Snape hadn't gone far when van Piet took a leather wallet out of his inside pocket and went through the IDs inside it.

"I don't want Dvorski to know who I am or who I work for," he said, "so for now I'm Detective Inspector Eric Blaker, and I'm with the NCA like Leo. He knows Leo. That should get me in."

Kensington Church Street was eerie when they got there. Nocturnal stillness draped it like a shroud, and daylight seemed banished forever. The Essex car pulled up on the kerb, the driver turned the engine off, and Snape took out his mobile. Dvorski answered almost at once. It was as if, even in his sleep, he was on full alert. Snape told him who he was and said he'd got an urgent lead on Patrice. Could he come in and bring a colleague with him?

"Of course, Mr Snape. When you hear the door buzz, push it open. I'll be getting dressed."

And switching on the sound recorder.

The front door gave into a hallway and Dvorski – unshaven, bleary-eyed, but smiling determinedly – was standing at the bottom of the stairs as Snape and van Piet came in, their IDs in their hands. The carpet had seen better days, the floor creaked, and in the low wattage light, the floral wallpaper looked faded and grimy. Once the civilities were out of the way, Dvorski led them upstairs to his office, a small paper-stuffed back room with the curtains drawn.

"Tea or coffee?" he asked, and when they said tea, he used a tea set on a filing cabinet to make it. The milk came from a mini-fridge, and since there were only two easy chairs, he moved his computer monitor out of the way, got hold of an upright chair on the far side of his desk and hoisted it over.

"Now, gentlemen," he said as he sat down on it. "What can I do for you?"

"We've been examining the CCTV in Mr Jocelyn Patrice's office," Snape began, "and you're on the hard drive in a spy room next door. The day and time make you one of the last people to see Mr Patrice before he disappeared. We'd like you to tell us what you were doing there."

Dvorski stopped blowing on his tea. He'd had his answers ready, lies and all, since he'd left Patrice's office.

"My pleasure, Mr Snape. When Russia opened its economy up, it needed to broker its shares in the West. We got to know Mr Patrice, and he's helped us ever since. We like to stay informed, so we set up the spy room you mentioned. I expect you've noticed the hard drive and the software came from us. We keep them up to date and tailored to Mr Patrice's needs."

"As you say, we'd noticed."

"Mr Russell Burney of Klemmsley Oil and Gas has been seeing Mr Patrice about a downturn in his investments. Mr Burney and I have a developing business relationship, so Mr Patrice has alerted me to Mr Burney's appointments. He doesn't bring me through Reception in case Mr Burney learns I'm on the premises. That's one of our little ways, and Mr Patrice is always discreet."

"How did Mr Burney come to know Mr Patrice?" asked van Piet.

"Not long after I'd been transferred to London, I had dinner with Mr Patrice in Knightsbridge. We were talking contacts, and he asked me whether I'd met anyone who might welcome his services. Mr Burney came to mind, Mr Patrice wrote to him, and Mr Burney followed it up."

"And the De Macey Clinic. You must have caught the name. What can you tell us about it?"

"Not a lot. I hadn't heard of it before, but I earn my money from trade, so I looked it up. It belongs to a former compatriot of mine, a Mr Anatoly Dobrynin. He made his billions when Mr Yeltsin was our president, and now he lives in your lovely country. There's no secret about the clinic. It's all in Companies House."

"Mr Burney asked to see Mr Patrice Tuesday evening, but he didn't get to see him till Thursday. Do you know why Wednesday wasn't on?"

"Mr Patrice said Mr Burney had called him too late. I can't add to that, I'm afraid."

Snape felt they were getting nowhere, but he tried one last question anyway.

"Have you any idea where Mr Patrice is now? Even a guess might help."

"None at all, I wish I did. I like Mr Patrice and, to be honest, I also like his contacts, so I want you to find him as much as anyone. Tell me, if I hear anything, how can I reach you?"

Snape gave him his Chelmsford number and was about to round things off when van Piet said,

"You arrived in this country the day after Dandy Torelli. Was that coincidence?"

Dvorski gave him the smile people use when they've done something tricksy they're proud of.

"Of course not. Dandy and I got on well on Sakhalin Island, so the thinking was, if I come to London at the same time, I'll have instant access to some very valuable contacts. And it's worked. I'm in and out of Klemmsley Marine like an old friend. As you British say, it's not what you know, it's who you know. And I knew Dandy Torelli."

That was it. Snape thanked Dvorski for getting up for them, and Dvorski showed them to the door.

When they were back in the car, van Piet said he'd like to talk things through instead of driving home in his own car, so Snape said he'd drop him off on his way back to Chelmsford. Before they'd put Hyde Park behind them, Dvorski was contacting Valkov.

"That was beautiful," Valkov enthused after he'd listened to Dvorski's recording, and Dvorski swelled with satisfaction. "Not a word out of place. You realise, of course, the Millers have to be thought about now; they could be reaching their sell-by date."

"Can't we just annihilate them? It's not up to me, of course, but such things have been known."

"Indeed they have, but the trouble is, if anything happens to them, there's no one between you and four murders plus a kidnapping. And if you get dragged in, so do we. It's a delicate situation, Oleg Aleksandrovich. We think about it constantly."

The Millers were on van Piet's mind as well as they motored through London.

"You won't break Dvorski down, Eddie," he said. "He's too well prepared. De Macey's didn't faze him, and if I hadn't seen that photo of Dandy Torelli, I might have believed what he said about following her over. What about that pair from Peterborough, the garage owner and his wife? How hard have you looked at them?"

"Chris and Becky Miller? Not hard enough, but not for want of trying. We've questioned them twice and got nowhere. I've asked for permission to make a search, but I haven't got the evidence to get a warrant. I've had the FDLE report gone through, and the advice is, while they *could* have been up to something, I'd have to force the facts to say they were. Tallahassee says the same. I know because I've asked."

He brooded for a while.

"First the father, then the wife and daughter. There ought to be a connection, but I'm blowed if I can see it."

Exasperated, he called Farrell in Chelmsford. Nothing new had come in.

"You can go off duty now," he told him gloomily, "but don't go home. Get some sleep in the station."

"Do you think we'll find Patrice alive?" he asked van Piet, who was following his own thoughts.

"I've no idea, and neither have you. The fact is, we're one card short of a flush. Until we get that card, we're stuck, and it may take too long to get it. You've got to accept that, Eddie."

The sky was beginning to pale when van Piet unzapped the locks on Gorris Hall's great outer gate and put the lights on that were on either side of the drive. There was a dawn freshness to the damp air, and the familiar crunch of gravel made him feel he was where he belonged at last. There was a light in the downstairs living room, and with a weary smile, he guessed why. Softly he let himself in. The living room door was open, and Célestine was asleep in one of the armchairs. She was fully dressed, an empty coffee cup stood on a side table, and the book she'd been reading was lying where it had fallen. He kissed her on the forehead and she stirred. When she woke up, her face gleamed with love.

"I feel happy now you're back," she said, yawning and stretching. "I kept awake as long as I could. I've laid out something in the kitchen if you're hungry."

"Thanks. By the time I get to it, it'll be breakfast time. When's your first riding class?"

"Eight o'clock for me, eight thirty for Jackie, and nine o'clock for the riders."

"We're all in it together then. I've got an early start, too."

He gave her another kiss, and this time he made it last.

"I'm glad you waited up, though I shouldn't be," he went on. "I left my car in London, so I need to book a taxi, then I'll take a shower and pretend I've had some sleep. It's been a long day, Cissie, and there'll be plenty more like it. It's all starting up again."

Chapter 19

A Fall in the Dark

Chris Miller lost as much sleep Friday night as Snape and van Piet did, and Becky was the trouble. Since he'd tracked Dvorski to Brancaster, having her in bed with him had been agony– he wanted her and he didn't want her, both at the same time. And it so happened, she'd dyed her hair black, which made her look sexier than she'd looked for ages. So, seething with frustration, he lay awake in the dark and focused all his rage on so-called Sanderson. He didn't want to wait till he'd been paid off for Patrice, he wanted to start on him right now, and gradually he worked out how to do it. If Patrice was so important to Sanderson, maybe Patrice could say who Sanderson really was, and there was a chance Patrice might still be alive enough to do it. Even if he wasn't, there was always his briefcase. He probably had an address book, and Sanderson could well be in it. It was worth a chance – he'd go to Saxley Castle that evening, and tell Becky he was going somewhere else to do a deal in case she sneaked a look at his odometer. That would keep her right out of it.

Satisfied he'd got it right, he paused his own breathing and listened to Becky's. She didn't always sleep well, but it sounded deep and steady right now. The bedside clock said three twenty-two. Slowly he eased himself out of bed, felt his way into his dressing gown and slippers, and headed for his private workshop. If Becky woke up before he got back, he'd say he'd been for a pee. The bedroom door closed and Becky, who'd been awake for some time and was just fading away nicely, came to again and, suddenly suspicious, forced herself to count to ten before she made a move. Then she got into her own dressing gown and slippers, and crept down to the CCTV room.

A lot of the vehicles Chris sold in Queen of Scots Lane were so far gone, he kept a permanent supply of towropes for when the call-outs came. He also had a cycle lamp he could fit round his forehead so he could rope up in the dark. When he moved into Westgate, he brought his rescue gear with him. He still had it.

First he took the ropes out of their storage bin. He wasn't sure how deep the Hole of Death was, but he reckoned, if he tied all his ropes together, it should be enough. Maybe Patrice had got stuck before he reached the bottom, or his briefcase was caught somewhere along the way. Quickly he tied handknots in the ropes, then he tied them together. That made them heavy, but he could half-drag them, so it wasn't a problem. The lamp came next. He put new batteries in and it lit up like day. Finally he went to the corner cupboard, uncovered the safe, and fetched out one of the padlock keys. He wondered about taking a Walther, but thought better of it. He didn't expect to need one, and if the police stopped him for anything, he wouldn't have a gun to explain away.

Becky knew where he was. The cameras were showing Chris's workshop, and light was leaking past the blinds. Then the lights came on in the main workshop, and she saw him load the ropes into the boot of his Avensis. It had been serviced the day before and was standing ready to go. It was fully tanked up, too – she knew that because that was how Chris was. He kept her vehicle, a RAV4, tanked up as well. After the ropes came gloves, a slate-grey pair of overalls, and – she saw it clearly – the cycle lamp on a headband. It reminded her of potholers she'd seen on TV and that made her guess instantly where he was going. Just the thought set alarm bells ringing, especially as he was keeping her out of it. Was he going to shop her? Was he going to save Patrice and try for some deal with the police? She couldn't wait for any of that, she had to get in first. By the time Chris had put all the lights out, she was clear what she had to do. And when he slipped back into bed she was, to all appearances, as sound asleep as ever.

Chris got up at daybreak as usual. When his mechanics arrived – he made them work Saturday mornings – the Avensis was in its usual spot outside, and he was behind his desk talking to customers on the phone. When Becky got up, she cancelled a sun-bed appointment – she told Chris she'd heard bad things about the rays on the radio – and settled down to keeping an eye on him. She guessed he'd set off after the sales staff had gone home, since they were there for the whole day; but she wasn't sure till, over lunch, he said he was going to Sheffield as soon as everyone had finished to discuss some used vans. She'd better not wait up for him, he'd be late getting back. That confirmed it. Sheffield was as far as Saxley Castle, roughly reckoned, and he could always say there'd been no deal. During the afternoon, she worked out an alternative route to the castle from their angling maps. She also found the navy blue tracksuit she'd worn to her keep-fit class plus some gloves, dark trainers, an angling knife and an overnight suitcase. She left her hair as it was. She must have had second sight when she'd gone for black, she told herself; she'd read about second sight waiting for a body wax, so she knew all about it. At six o'clock Chrisbeckmill sales staff were on their way home, at six fifteen Chris drove off into the evening light, and at six twenty-five Becky locked up and did the same. She'd see to the CCTV when she got back and, like Chris, she wasn't taking a Walther.

Chris had a clear run and reached the castle at nine. It was dark and star-lit by now, distant villages in the valley were glowing like fire-flies and, as he'd hoped, the car park was deserted – no lovers, no nothing. The wind had dropped, and although the weather had dried out, the ground was still soft. He pulled his overalls on, adjusted the cycle lamp round his forehead and, wearing his gloves, hauled the rope out. Then, after locking the car, he made his way to the twin doors, where he undid the padlocks, opened the doors wide and pocketed the key. With no wind there was no chance of their blowing back – not that it mattered if they did – and the silence let him listen for any sounds coming out of the shaft. There weren't any, not even when he nerved himself to shout Patrice's name into it. He knotted the end of his improvised climbing rope firmly round the railing, and he shook the rest down the shaft. Despite himself, he was feeling afraid now, so he cut his plan back. He wouldn't go right to the bottom any more, even if he could reach it, he'd settle for finding Patrice if he was near the top. If he wasn't, he'd try for his briefcase. He tugged the rope a couple of times and it held, so with his lamp switched on, he lowered himself into the shaft. It was claustrophobically tight - it was like squeezing into a chimney - but there was just room to slide on the wet limestone and brake with his feet when he had to. He was soon breathing hard, but he kept pausing his breathing in order to listen. Still not a sound. When he got moving again, he'd look up and use his lamp to gauge how far he'd come. Going down was hard enough. Coming back up would be harder.

Becky reached the castle at five minutes past nine. Her route had brought her to the back road, and she'd parked in the last passing bay before the top. There was moist dirt about, and she tried not to tread in any as she got out. With her black hair and navy tracksuit, she was virtually invisible as she moved off on foot. The Avensis confirmed Chris was there, and with the coldness she'd come to associate with killing, she hid behind a separate piece of the wall and waited. She'd nearly got caught when Chris had switched his lamp on. She'd moved out a bit to get a better view, and the beam had flitted across her. But Chris had been glancing down, so he'd missed her.

Thereafter the lamp was her beacon. Every time Chris raised his gaze, light showed more and more faintly in the recess at the top of the shaft. Then it wasn't reaching that far any more. Sure she was safe, Becky tip-toed across the grass to the doors and, by the light of a pocket torch, gathered up the padlocks and slid them silently into place. Then she tackled the rope. The angling knife made short work of it, and suddenly it slipped away, yanked down by Chris's weight. He thought his knot had unravelled, it couldn't be anything else, but before he could react, he was sliding down painfully, and the rope had collapsed in his face. He stopped when one of his feet jammed against some rock that poked out, but by that time Becky was removing the tied end of the rope – she'd discard it on the way back - and relocking the doors. Her dashboard clock showed a quarter to ten when, after a tension break, she finally switched the RAV4's engine on, so she reckoned to be home by half past midnight. As she drove, she tried to imagine what it was like to be locked into the Hole of Death. "It must be horrible," she said out loud, but that was as far as she got. She had a lot of things to think about and Chris wasn't one of them. No point thinking about the dead.

Chris had scraped himself badly, and he was terrified he might fall further. But at another level he was thinking that if he could work his way up the shaft, he'd at least get out alive – he had some light, his trainers gave him traction even on the wet limestone, and Patrice and his secrets didn't matter anymore. But first he had to attend to the rope. He had its dead weight in his face, he couldn't properly see through it, and the more he tried to move it out of the way, the more it kept falling over his nose and mouth, making him feel as if he was drowning. His lamp was also askew, so the beam was shining too much to one side. The only solution was to feed the rope past his body and let it continue down the shaft, but he scarcely had room to crook his arms, and the knots kept getting in the way. He had to use his teeth as much as his hands, and by the time he'd finished, he'd just about had it. But he hadn't slipped any further, and once he'd laboriously straightened his lamp with his upper arm, he could see plenty of finger- and toeholds in its beam. They'd get him out. All he had to do was stay cool.

He worked his gloves off to get a better grip, but the shaft was too narrow for him to reach them down to a pocket, so he let them fall onto himself and then keep falling. They'd probably be found along with the rope when Patrice was eventually found – he'd *have* to be dead by then – but the gloves wouldn't tell any tales any more than the rope would, and anyway, he wasn't going down after them. As he struggled upwards, the sweat coursed into his eyes, and every time he slipped, he thought he was going to die. But somehow he managed to catch himself and begin again. The fact that the shaft wasn't vertical all the way up helped him, and after what seemed like a lifetime, his bleeding fingertips felt the top. But he could also see the doors were shut. A breeze must have done it, he told himself, but when he pulled himself up enough to give them a push, they didn't open, and when he tried again, it was the same thing. He panicked. He found enough strength to make his legs push him up further, then he beat and scratched at those places – he could see them clearly in the lamplight – where others had beaten and scratched before him. The doors were locked, he had a key in his pocket, but he couldn't use it. There wasn't enough room for him to get out of the shaft and sit till someone came, whenever that might be, so the best he could do was half raise himself out and stay there by clinging to one of the safety rail supports. But he couldn't do that for long. Gradually his grip slackened, and he slid back into the shaft. At first he was able to stop his fall and struggle upwards again, but it was a losing battle, and before long he was on the rocky outcrop that had helped him before. He didn't recognise it, he was too far gone for that, but he dimly sensed it would give him some rest. At first it did, but when he tried to go upwards again, he couldn't sustain his own weight any more, and he went into a non-stop slide. The shaft went straight down now, and it was only a matter of time before he spilled into the cave. He landed clumsily, breaking his lamp and fracturing his skull, his left wrist and his collar bone. He passed out on impact. Next to him was the body of Jocelyn Patrice. He'd landed even more badly and broken his neck. Not far from Patrice was his briefcase. It had lodged in the shaft, and Chris had helped it down without realising it.

Chapter 20

A Fatal Mistake

It was thirty-eight minutes past midnight when Becky got back to the garage. She went to the CCTV room first, meaning to scrub the entire hard drive – that way there'd be nothing at all to help the Old Bill. Or would there? They could work miracles, it was in the papers all the while, so she took the drive right out. That would stop them; they wouldn't get past that in a hurry.

She intended to call Dvorski and tell him Chris had tried to get into the Saxley Hole of Death. He might have been trying to rescue Patrice, so she'd cut the rope he was using and made him fall down the shaft. He had to be dead, no one could survive a fall like that, but they'd have to hide till they could get out of the country, because Chris's car was still on the car park. Someone was bound to see it, and she'd be first in line for questioning when Chris was found. And Patrice, he'd be found as well now. She was convinced Dvorski would do what she wanted, he'd given her his word, but they'd probably need money, and she couldn't ask him for everything.

So, still carrying the hard drive, she fetched the overnight case from its hiding place and let herself into Chris's private office. She didn't like it in there. She believed firmly in ghosts, a friend of hers had actually seen one, and she felt Chris's could glide right through the nearly shut door while she was in there. But she was also sky high from starring in her own real-life drama, and that made her reckon, if she was quick, she'd be all right. She slipped the hard drive into the case, got her little book and her mobile out and, holding her breath, put in the call. It was like James Bond and *Bonnie and Clyde* rolled into one. Sure enough, she was told the number was unobtainable, so she terminated, all fired up for the call back and keeping a wary eye on the door.

It seemed forever since Chris had said he was going to change the safe's combination, and since then she'd done as he'd told her and stayed away. But she knew he kept big money in there, and she wanted to take as much as she could pack in her case. Chris had never told her he'd made the change, but she was sure he had, because he always did what he said he'd do. She didn't know he'd decided, in his male dominant way, not to bother and not to tell her either. As he saw it, there was no real chance of Sanderson getting to the safe, and Becky would never step out of line, so there was simply no point. To save precious seconds, Becky placed her hand on the palm reader and was about to tap in the combination she'd written down when the call back came through. She thought using Dvorski's first name would give her status so, speaking extra clearly and emphasising 'Oleg', she said,

"I'm Becky and I'm in Chrisbeckmill Motors. Tell Oleg Chris has gone to Saxley Castle and I've killed him in the Hole of Death because – "

While she was speaking, she started tapping in, and her second mistake coincided with 'because'. The explosion was instant – it blew her apart and incinerated her remains, leaving only dispersed bits of bone. It also destroyed her mobile before it could transmit more than the first nanoseconds of the bang. The walls, the floor and the ceiling were blasted out, and in no time at all, Chrisbeckmill Motors was an inferno. The size of the blaze, its location, and the possibility of fatalities made the national news pick up the story early and cover it at shriek level.

At the time Becky was blown apart in Peterborough, Dvorski was in the Russian Embassy attending a reception for a trade delegation from Moscow. He'd been there all evening, the vodka had flowed like the Moskva, and it was well past one in the morning before, seriously the worse for wear, he toiled back to Kensington Church Street. Out of habit, he went into the internet to catch up on the news, and the fire was the top story. Struggling to think straight, he put a coded alert through to Valkov and asked: had Becky Miller tried to use the number he'd given her? Valkov saw at once why he'd asked, and within minutes a terrified Interceptions clerk was playing the tape of what Becky had said before the cut-off. He'd had to put reporting the call on hold, the clerk stammered, because a stream of other traffic had come in right then and he was the only one on duty. He didn't say a lot of the vodka had been finding its way upstairs and the call had been drowned in the process.

So Becky Miller was dead. She had to be.

The Interceptions clerk was in deep trouble, that was as certain as snow in Siberia, but Valkov's overriding concern was an old one revisited – there was, quite possibly, no one now between Dvorski and his murders. It was something Valkov couldn't handle, he'd have to call Zembarov. Then there was Miller's car, it must still be on the castle car park. He knew from Dvorski Miller drove a black Avensis, and it would have to be moved fast. He got back to Dvorski, told him what he'd heard on the tape, and said he was to carry on as normal – no cancellations, no postponements, no changes of venue – till they both knew more. Then he woke Florence and Madge. They lived in Wolvercote, a village near Oxford on the Cheltenham side. He gave them their instructions and set them three hours maximum to get to Saxley Castle. Being late wasn't an option.

Mike was next. He was sound asleep in Witton, a Birmingham suburb where he lived on his own. He was given two hours to get to the castle. He took seven minutes less, and his dipped headlights picked out the Avensis straight away. It was the only car there. Using a scanner, he disabled the alarm, unlocked the doors and got the engine started. Then he set off for Birmingham, leaving his Renault locked and the keys by the inner side of the rear wheel on the driver's side. Florence and Madge arrived at five to five in their Volkswagen, grateful for the absence of traffic. Madge found Mike's keys and set off in the Renault for Witton. She got to Mike's house at seven twenty-two and silently rolled up one of his double-garage doors with his in-car remote control. Hoping the neighbours hadn't been looking through the window, she parked next to his trade van, let herself into his house through a connecting door and settled down to wait for him.

Mike didn't take the Avensis to Witton. A winding route through Birmingham brought him to an independent garage on the west side called Cars For The World. As soon as he got there, the workshop doors opened and he drove straight in. He was expected. The Avensis would get a make-over, its identifiers would be altered or replaced and, with forged documents and a respray, it would be in Bulgaria within a week, where a happy buyer was waiting. Cars For The World gave Mike a lift to Witton, dropping him a few streets away from his house. As soon as he reached it, he ran Madge over to Wolvercote, where Florence had arrived in the Volkswagen at three minutes past eight.

While the Avensis was being disposed of, Valkov was on the Embassy's secure link to Zembarov. Being woken up didn't stop the old man thinking rapidly.

"To me it's the best possible news," he said. "Now Dvorski's lost the Millers, we can use the situation he's brought about to get rid of him altogether. At long last, I might add. It will be risky, but the gain for the Motherland will be immense. The last thing it wants is free thinkers like Dvorski."

The old hardliner was lusting for it. He'd given Dvorski a lot of rope since Sakhalin Island, always hoping he'd hang himself with it. Now that time had come. The tsunami had been a nice idea, but it was nothing compared to destroying the man who stood for everything he loathed.

"What about the tsunami?" Valkov asked. "Will it still go ahead?"

"No, of course not. We could too easily get blamed for it, even if there wasn't any proof. But Dvorski mustn't know we've changed our minds. On the contrary, I want you to commit him to the tsunami by every means you can. If you do that, I can set him on a collision course that will smash him."

"What about Russell Burney? Shall I whisper to him the tsunami's off?"

"I forbid it. Harvest Home gives us a unique chance to crush Dvorski with maximum benefit to the state, so they've both got to believe everything's going to plan. But since you mention Burney, do you see any problems with him? You must say so if you do. We need to get this right."

Valkov remembered how Burney had flared up over Aubrey, and his suppressed uncertainty came back. But he hadn't survived for as long as he had without knowing how to guard his back, so he said,

"He's taken a beating, but he's got reserves of willpower left.. I'd say he could cross you when you least expect it, and do the one thing you don't want him to do."

"Then we'll have to break this willpower of his. It should be easy enough."

There was a silence from Zembarov, then,

"As I see it, I need to have this collision with Dvorski securely set up, and I also need someone to break Burney's willpower. One person will do for both, and I have that person in mind. I'll get back to you when I've thought things through. I'll want you to pass on instructions."

"Before you hang up, Grigory Viktorovich, what if Miller's alive after all? We've only got his wife's word he's dead."

"The police have got to find him first, and thanks to your good work, they won't know where to start. Nevertheless, I shall allow myself a day or two to see how things turn out. We Russians are chess players, not dice throwers. We think ahead, and we play to win."

It took much of the night to put out the Westgate blaze, and investigators were moving in while damping down was still going on. They rapidly sifted out bone fragments – they looked like a woman's, including what was clearly part of a jawbone.

A co-ordinated wake-up of Peterborough's dentists soon found Becky's, and his records confirmed the part of the jawbone was hers. That satisfied the police she was dead, and the news was made public in a bulletin. It wasn't yet known, it went on, whether her husband had been on the premises at the time. A gas explosion hadn't been ruled out, and the police had contacted Chrisbeckmill staff overnight. Some of them were being brought in to help on site.

Anxious not to be beaten by television, the print media were chancing photos of Becky on the front page before the police announcement, and some carried Chris's as well. They came mostly from the *Peterborough Telegraph's* archive and they weren't always best quality, but one of them was good enough for six year old Edgar Straw to say out loud, "I know her, I've seen her before" when he picked a *Sunday Mirror* up from the doormat to take to his father.

Edgar's parents were separated. His father, a tiler, lived in Debden on the Central Line, and his mother lived two stations further out in Marlborough Close, Epping. His parents got on well, and because they lived close to each other and to Edgar's school, Edgar shuttled contentedly between them. He'd been hurrying on his scooter when Chris had let him pass because his mother was waiting to take him to his father at Epping underground station. When the police had rung her doorbell she'd said no, she hadn't seen anything suspicious and no, there was no one else in the house. She had a son, but he was in Debden with his father. They were separated, you see.

Becky's photo earned Edgar £5.00 from his father for his money box.

"When did you see her?" the nice policewoman asked him in his father's living room, and he told her.

"How did you know the lady in the photo was the lady you saw in the car?"

"She had big earrings and sort of rings round her wrists. Her hair was coloured as well."

"Was anyone with her in her car?"

"No. She was on her own. She was in the driver's seat."

"Was the engine switched on?"

"I don't know. My mummy was waiting for me. I had to catch the tube."

The policewoman asked him to look at her laptop as she ran through different makes and colours of cars from a national database. He picked out the white Porsche straight away. It was like the one parked near his mother's house. He thought there was a man in it near the path, but he hadn't really noticed him. When they got to Toyotas, he picked out a grey Prius. The lady had been in one like that. His best friend's father had one like it as well, he confided. He'd been for rides in it.

The policewoman radioed her report in as soon as she got in her car. It was typed up as she spoke, and a print-out went straight to Snape in his office. He was talking to Garry, who was in Ashell House. A TV with the sound off was covering the Peterborough story.

"Hold on, Tom," Snape said, breaking off to read it. When he'd finished, he asked, "Is Mr van Piet there?"

"He's with Mr Benjamin. Is it urgent?"

"Yes it is."

Snape held the print-out up to the camera.

"Copy this in shorthand and get it to him now. He needs to know it straight away."

He was white with anger when he reached Farrell's office along the corridor. The door was open and Farrell was on the phone to Cambridgeshire's Chief Constable.

"I'm getting an update on Peterborough," he said, cupping his hand over the mouthpiece.

Snape took no notice, and as soon as Farrell put the phone down, he started. There was menace in his voice.

"Have you heard of Edgar Straw?" he asked

Farrell looked surprised.

"No, I can't say I have. Who is he?"

"He's a little boy whose mother lives in Marlborough Close, Epping. He was with Mrs Straw the afternoon Patrice's

Porsche was found there empty. That boy saw Becky Miller – your very own Becky Miller of Florida and Chrisbeckmill Motors – in a Toyota Prius a few cars up from the Porsche around the time we're interested in. He quite likely saw Chris Miller in the Porsche as well."

He put the print-out on Farrell's desk.

"It's all in there," he said. "You can read it for yourself, but not yet. You were in charge of the house-to-house, Leo. You took it on because, you said, Patrice's disappearance might just have something to do with the Torelli murders and I couldn't say it didn't. But when you, personally, spoke to Mrs Straw to show my country bumpkins how to conduct a police enquiry, you entirely missed the only eye-witness we've got. If you'd asked the simplest questions, we could have got after the Millers right then. Now it looks as if at least one of them is dead, and we still don't have a lead on Patrice. You can read the print-out now. Your name's not in it, but it should be."

Snape had said Farrell had his pride and it was true. It made him not just a hard worker but a compulsive one. He'd been passed over for promotion twice, and he was obsessed with proving it was the others who'd got it wrong. As soon as he read the print-out, he could see he'd bungled badly. It devastated him.

"I have to hold my hand up," he said. "I'm sorry."

It was a diplomatic reply. Inside he was doing his best to resist what he knew, but he wasn't going to show it. Snape knew what was going on, he could see the man's fault line as if it was marked with red ink. But he also knew the NCA. They wouldn't let one of their own be junked without a fight. Nevertheless, Snape wanted him out there and then.

"I'm going to speak to your boss," he said, taking the print-out back. "I'll see what he says."

From his office he asked to speak to John Lorrie, Director General of Britain's equivalent to the FBI. When he got him, he explained what had happened and asked for Farrell to be withdrawn.

"That's not going to happen, Eddie," Lorrie replied. "He's made a mistake, I grant you that, but it's not enough for me to pull him out. He's a bear for work, that's why we sent him to you. It's your job to make the best of him."

"I can't watch him all the while. I'm too busy."

"That's your problem, not mine, and I'll spell things out since I know what you're like. The NCA is a national agency, Essex Police is a county force, and I have the authority to direct as I see fit. My direction is that Farrell stays. I've said yes to van Piet's involvement, but that's where I stop."

It wasn't Snape's way to go behind people's backs, so he went straight back to Farrell.

"I wanted you pulled, Leo, but Director General Lorrie won't do it. So nothing's changed, except we both know it has. We'll just have to make sure nothing else goes wrong."

"I'll work on it, Eddie. Just tell me what to do and I'll do it."

Edgar Straw wasn't the only one to recognise Becky Miller. It was Gina Wavell's day off, and in her detached house in Matlock Bath she was idling through her breakfast somewhat later than the Straws when Becky's picture came on screen, together with the news she was dead. Wavell knew who it was straight away. She picked her smartphone up and phoned Matlock police.

"Stay where you are, a car's on its way," she heard, and she was only just changed out of her dressing gown when it pulled up outside her gate. While it was taking her to police HQ, the link between Snape's office and Ashell House was temporarily extended to Matlock, Snape called Farrell in, and van Piet hurried down to his office. In her best professional manner, Wavell went through the excursion in sequence, including the locks and the key bit, then she pulled her smartphone out of her handbag.

"I took some pictures while I was up there. I always do that, I've got an archive I put them in, and I don't let people see I'm doing it. I know it sounds sneaky, but they look more natural that way. Would you like to see them? I use templates in my archive, but they're the same pictures."

She talked her way through them. 'The two teachers', as she called them, were in a lot of them, and so were the Millers. There were always people between the two pairs, though sometimes not too many. Snape and van Piet recognised the Millers from file photos. A glance from Snape stopped Farrell saying anything in front of Wavell.

"Those two teachers, can you remember their names?" van Piet asked without identifying himself.

Wavell was impressed by that. It meant he was Secret Service.

"I can do better than that. I always photograph the passenger list as well. It makes my archive more historical."

She held up her smartphone again. In her neat, careful handwriting they read 'Miss Madge Bunting' and 'Miss Florence Penderton', together with their address in Wolvercote. Snape and Garry jotted down the details. The Millers' names and the Fleur de Lys Hotel, Matlock, were on the list as well. It was signed 'Gina Wavell (Miss)' and dated in full.

"And they only asked about the locks and so forth towards the end of the visit, did they?" van Piet went on.

"That's right. I was just about ready to go."

"Had anyone else asked about them?"

"No, no one."

Van Piet thanked her, and the moment he finished, Snape asked Matlock to wait, blanked the link out so Wavell wouldn't hear, and called Cambridgeshire Police's Incident Centre in Westgate. No, there was no sign of a second body. Not yet, anyway.

"Expect a visitor," Snape said. "I'm coming up shortly. Give me two hours or so. I need to know everything you turn up."

He terminated and turned to Farrell.

"Leo, everything says the Millers, Patrice and Saxley Castle add up to a lead, so that's where you're going. I'll arrange it with Matlock right now. I want them to clear the site, cordon off the area, check the tyre prints, and get Gina Wavell there pronto with her key. Derbyshire's used to cave rescues, they'll know exactly how to get down this Hole of Death to take a look, but if they do decide to go down, they'll need the word from you, because we'll be putting rescuing ahead of clue-gathering. I also want a search of the whole terrain, car park included, so make sure the manpower's there. If there's no car there for Miller, we need to ask why. If there is, Forensics gets it first. And have a warning put out: Miller may be armed."

He brought Matlock back in, confirmed Wavell had been moved out of earshot, and squared things for Farrell. As soon as Farrell had said his piece, with Snape listening to every word, he was on his way to the car pool.

That left van Piet.

"What do you make of it, Eddie?" he asked.

"The locks and the key matter. Either those teachers were there to take pictures of them, or they were there to make sure the Millers could. I get the impression the teachers were keeping an eye on the Millers, but the Millers weren't aware of them, so I go for the second option."

"I'll buy that. Anything else?"

"The Millers are working for someone. They turn up in Florida, and Jethro Torelli gets killed. They turn up at Saxley, and those teachers see them right. They turn up in Epping, and Patrice disappears. If Patrice is found in this Hole of Death, I'd say they reconnoitred the place last Easter, made a key to fit the locks, and abducted Patrice last Thursday. I'm sure Dvorski's mixed up in this somehow, and I'm also sure the Torelli shootings tie in. But if you ask me why any of this is happening, you're asking the wrong person."

"Leave the last bit with me. Dvorski said more than he meant to when we got him out of bed, and Patrice's hard drive had some useful things on it as well. But right now, what do you want me to do?"

"Go to Wolvercote, those teachers are in this up to their necks. Same as with Dvorski, don't phone first, just turn up. And use the Blaker ID again. If they're in with Dvorski, they might compare notes."

He paused for a moment and cleared his throat.

"Do you want to say anything about Edgar Straw before you go?"

Time was pressing, but Snape had to ask. He felt badly about a police blunder, even if it wasn't his. He'd give him the full story about Farrell when they had more time.

"Try this, Eddie. Miss Wavell saw the start of an operation, Edgar Straw saw the end of it or close on, and what strikes me is the dates. Miss Wavell took her photos on April 9th and Patrice disappeared August 23rd. That's a long time, and the question is why that should be." He stopped to think things through. "My advice is, keep Russell Burney well out of sight, Dvorski as well. And two more things. Get onto Leo and say Derbyshire Police must keep Miss Wavell and her pictures away from the media. Also, she needs close personal protection. She may have seen or photographed something she shouldn't have. That could cost her her life."

Snape stopped in the Ops Room to radio Farrell, then he was off. Van Piet turned to Garry, who'd been taking notes.

"These teachers I'm calling on, Tom. I need a driver in uniform and a marked car, they'll help me look the part. While I'm gone, ask around whether they're on anyone's files. Top secret and no third parties to know you're asking. And while you're at it, see if you can find out who Dvorski answers to. When we know that, we'll know a lot more. I'll call you when I've finished in Wolvercote. Stay here till then."

Chapter 21

Two Retired Teachers

Van Piet arrived in Wolvercote at two forty-eight. On the car's back seat was the late edition of a morning newspaper he'd bought on the way. His driver, Police Sergeant Sadie Severn, soon found the bijou thatched cottage they were looking for. The five-barred gate stood open as if they were expected. The hedges on either side were immaculate.

"Go right up to the door," said van Piet. "I want whoever opens it to see the car straight out."

Severn eased the car onto the gravel drive. Beyond the cottage was a detached garage. Its door was raised, and the Volkswagen was standing half out. It looked as if it had recently been cleaned, but so did a lot of other cars they'd passed.

Madge Bunting opened the pseudo-weathered oak door as soon as the bell rang, and van Piet had his ID and his lines ready. Her smiled response was instant, and she clucked him in as if he'd come about jam making. He took the newspaper with him, keeping it folded.

"Do call your driver in," Bunting went on. "She can sit in the kitchen."

The floor of the kitchen, like the floor of the hallway, was made of well-worn mock-rustic boards, and the driver was shown to a wooden table and benches, while van Piet stayed by the door. The sink taps were brass, a keg of cider stood on a stand, and the ceiling was heavily beamed. Penderton came in through a side door, saying she'd heard a car draw up and wondered who it was. She was wearing gardening clothes, and she had some herbs in a basket on her arm. After she'd made the tea and found some seedcake in the larder, Bunting took over again. She led van Piet into the sitting-cum-dining room, and Penderton followed with the serving trolley. The sitting room was also heavily beamed, the open fire place was brick, and the floorboards had knot-patterned scatter rugs on them. Bunting was about to sit down when she said,

"It seems rude to leave your driver on her own. Why don't I go and fetch her? I don't suppose we'll say anything she mustn't hear."

She installed Severn in a far corner and made herself comfortable in an easy chair.

"I don't think we've had a visit from the police before," she went on. "Not an official one anyway."

"We had that policeman from Crime Prevention, Madge," Penderton put in. "Such a very nice man, we thought."

"You're quite right, Florence. My memory's not what it was, Inspector, I'm growing old, I'm afraid. Yes, it's thanks to him we had our shatterproof windows installed. No burglar will get in through them, I'm more than relieved to say. But to business. Tell us, Inspector, to what do we owe the honour this Sunday afternoon?"

Van Piet unfolded the newspaper and showed them Becky's photo, together with the report of her death. Near it was a smaller one of Chris. Van Piet had no intention of mentioning Wavell.

"This lady, Mrs Becky Miller, died in a fire in Peterborough during the night," he said. "I can't comment on her husband's situation since it's still being investigated, but last Easter Monday they both went on a coach trip to Saxley Castle in Derbyshire, and records show you went on that trip as well. We'd like to know more about Mr and Mrs Miller, and it's possible you can help us."

"We'll do everything we can," said Bunting. "We're well aware of what we owe to society."

"Thank you, I wish more people were. I'll ask you about yourselves first, if I may. That will give me a context. Then I'll ask you about the Millers."

The atmosphere seemed totally relaxed. The only interruptions came from the tea things clinking and an Edwardian mantel clock chiming the quarters.

"You were heard to say you're retired history teachers," he said to get things started.

"Whoever it was heard correctly," Penderton replied proudly. "Miss Bunting and I taught history all our working lives and always in the same school."

"Which one was that?"

"Cheltenham Ladies' College, one of the finest in the country. Miss Bunting was Head of History at a very young age and I was her Second-in-charge. Madge," she went on, "show our visitor some of our photographs."

Bunting left the room briefly and came back with a box file marked 'Miscellaneous'. Inside were single-person, whole-form and whole-school photos, some black-and-white and some coloured. One showed Bunting as Captain of a Staff Hockey XI, another showed Penderton holding a croquet mallet. The College formed the background to most of them.

"That's a fine collection," van Piet said. He had no doubt they were genuine. "I expect you miss the place now."

"We attend reunions, and many of our Old Girls stay in touch," Penderton replied as Bunting reboxed the photos. "But we keep very busy as well. We've begun a book on castles and their prisons, and it so happens that Saxley Castle was our very first field trip. It was an ideal place to start."

"Why was that?"

"Because of its oubliette. That's a technical term, it means a prison you're thrown into and forgotten about. You can see the photos we took if you care to enter our study. We mustn't forget your driver of course. Everyone likes castles."

They went back into the hall and from there into their study, which was between the kitchen and the back of the cottage. There was the mock-rustic floor boarding again, the walls carried portraits of distinguished historians, and rows of file cards covered the desk. The computer must have been in sleep mode, since a touch of a key from Penderton brought the control panel up. Instinctively van Piet expected a chime or a dong, and when there wasn't one, he glanced at the free-standing speakers. Their pilot lights were off. Bunting saw him do it.

"We don't have the speakers on unless we need them for a purpose," she said primly. "The world is noisy enough as it is."

Penderton found her file and turned the monitor so they could all see the screen. A draft title page came up, then a florid Introduction, a list of sites with Saxley Castle at the top and, finally, the photos. They included the keep, views over the Hope Valley, bits of the wall, and the Hole of Death with its locks and key in close-up. The Millers weren't in any of them.

"You haven't got any with Mr and Mrs Miller in them?"

"I'm afraid not. Their pictures in our newspaper rang a distant bell, but that was as far as it went. You must understand, Inspector, we lead very sheltered lives."

"Can you recall anything about them now?"

"Mrs Miller's hair. We didn't approve at all. And her earrings were unspeakable. But her husband seemed quite interested in what he was looking at. He certainly took a lot of photographs. Not that we were watching them, you understand, but one does perceive these things. What about you, Madge?"

"I agree with Miss Penderton, Inspector. There were a lot of people on the trip, and the Millers were just two more. We talked to other people of course, one should always be civil, but we were there for our research, and that's what we concentrated on."

"Have you been to any other castles since?"

"We have indeed." It was Penderton again. "We've been to Berkeley Castle, where Edward II was murdered, and the Tower of London. You can see the photos we took there too, if you like."

He looked at them for form's sake and thanked them for letting him see them.

Eventually they all went back to the sitting room, where van Piet took them through every angle he could think of, and then he was ready to go. On the way back, he sat in the rear of the car, closed the partition and talked to Snape. Then he called Garry. Had he found out anything about the Wolvercote pair?

"Not a thing, Sir. None of our services knows anything about them."

"It doesn't surprise me. I suspect they've got used to being careful."

"I asked about Dvorski while I was at it. Apparently he's having trouble with his own side. With Mr Yeltsin gone, his face doesn't fit any more."

"So he's doing his best to make it fit, is he? Well, it's a thought. What about his minder? Do you know who it is?"

"It's the Principal Attaché in his Department, a man called Andrey Ivanovich Valkov. He's into his sixties now. Almost all of his career's been in London."

"Is that so? Anything else?"

"He was KGB when he came here. He's SVR now, but we haven't followed it up too closely. Scant resources and all that. Dvorski is SVR as well."

Van Piet terminated and opened the partition.

"Stop as soon as you can, Sadie. I'm coming into the front."

Severn pulled into a lay-by, and as the M40 left the A40 behind, van Piet asked her what she'd made of the afternoon. She allowed herself something between a laugh and a snort. She didn't have to say it: she'd seen it all before.

"They were waiting for us, complete with open gate. Their car was poking out for us to see, squeaky clean and, I expect you noticed, with brand new tyres. You can bet they wanted you to ask about it, so they could get their story in. They must have been close to tears when you didn't."

"It wasn't worth it. I could guess what they'd say. Anything else?"

"They kidnapped me when we arrived and kept me where they wanted me. Their box of photos was pre-selected, and just fancy their research starting with Saxley Castle! Then there were their photos, which just happened to be Miller-free. They'll have reported back by now, of course."

"Who to?"

"Whoever wrote the script for this farce. You gave them an easier ride than I'd have done."

"I wanted to let them talk. I hoped they might say more than they should."

"And did they?"

"I think so. We'll have to see."

Bunting and Penderton weren't the only ones affected by the Peterborough blaze. Dvorski couldn't sleep after he'd alerted Valkov, and as he stared into the darkness, the same clutch of anxieties kept pushing past the vodka fumes. Someone in Brancaster would see Becky's picture and remember noticing him when her husband wasn't around. If they tipped off Norfolk Police, which they were sure to do, it would bridge the gap between him and the Millers. Badly rattled, he finally crawled out of bed and opened up the internet to see what was doing. Becky's picture was on the first site he visited. She was at some kind of party. Her dress was cut too low and she was wearing earrings like bunches of grapes. Chris was next to her in a suit and tie. They both looked drunk. He riffed through some more sites and she was on all of them, sometimes with Chris and sometimes without.

He put his computer back on sleep and sat in his pyjamas gazing at the blank screen. As long as no one could connect him to the Millers he was OK, and he'd been very careful in Peterborough. But now they probably could, since he couldn't so easily get out of knowing Becky in Brancaster. And that, he suddenly saw, meant he could *safely* bridge the gap between himself and the Millers. It was light at the end of the tunnel, but then it flickered. Had Chris found out he'd been seeing

Becky in Brancaster? He was crazy about her, Valkov had told him that. Was that the reason he'd gone back to Saxley Castle? To use Patrice against him somehow? But how had he found out about him and Becky? Some nosey neighbour in Brancaster must have rung him up to tell him. Or – wait a minute – he'd gone there once in his Skoda. Had Chris put a tracker on it? He was a mechanic, so he could have done. There'd been that strange change of mood that time when he'd had to park behind the garage and Chris couldn't find his laptop. Or said he couldn't. He should have seen something was up, but he hadn't. Not then and not later, when he was crowing over Chris's blind spot. Now he could well be paying the price.

Close to panic, he scrabbled his clothes on and hurried through the night to the mews he parked in. He was well up on trackers, they went with his SVR training, and he wished he'd thought of them before. His Skoda looked innocent enough when he rolled up the door, but as soon as he closed it, he was on his knees in the yellowy overhead light, feeling under the sills. It didn't take long. He fetched the heaviest screwdriver he had, prised the tracker off, and locked it in a cupboard where it could signal harmlessly till the battery ran out. Valkov would have to know, of course, there was no way round it, and his big, big fear came back – he'd lose Valkov's support and be kicked out of the SVR. He didn't bother to undress when he got back, he knew he wouldn't sleep. He made himself some coffee and sat surfing the internet for the rest of the night. He saw the blazing garage with turntable ladders silhouetted against the flames, a never-ending stream of people being interviewed, and again and again pictures of Becky and Chris. It was self-torture, but he couldn't switch off. Finally, at about the time Edgar Straw was gathering up the *Sunday Mirror* in Debden, he stood up stiffly, made some more coffee, and started to get cleaned up. He had a fully worked out plan. He was ready well before he usually set off for his Sunday stint in the Embassy, but he was frightened of arriving early, since Valkov would see it as free-wheeling. So he switched on breakfast TV and stolidly watched the investigators in their overalls, more interviews, and yet more pictures of the Millers, till it was safe to go. It was during this time he learned part of Becky's jawbone had been discovered.

Valkov seemed more subdued than angry as he listened to Dvorski in his corner room. He wanted to take Dvorski apart, but he had to be careful not to get on the wrong side of Zembarov.

"It was a bad mistake letting yourself be tracked like that," he reflected, pouring coffee for both of them against his will. He had an unnerving fantasy Zembarov was watching him through the window gauzes.

"What will happen to me?" Dvorski asked apprehensively.

His voice was trembly. He'd heard the whisper the Interceptions clerk was already at Heathrow, waiting to be flown back to Moscow. He didn't want the same thing happening to him.

"You say you can finesse your way out of this," Valkov replied evasively. "Tell me how. It'll influence what I decide."

It didn't take Dvorski long. When he'd finished, Valkov let him stew for a bit, then,

"So you're going to speak to Snape, are you?" he mused. "When are you going to do that? He won't have much time at the moment."

"I'll ask if I can see him this evening. Things might have settled down by then."

"Well, do your best. If your plan works, we may still be able to use you. I hope so, for your sake. It would be a shame to lose you now."

Chapter 22

Only One Survivor

Derbyshire Police followed Farrell's instructions to the letter. Visitors on site had their tyres photographed, and after the site was cleared, all the tyre marks were photographed, and the entire package was streamed to Chelmsford to be analysed, sorted and relayed to Peterborough. Tyre marks and half a footprint were found in the back road's last passing bay before the top of the hill. They were photographed as well. No car for Miller was found.

Wavell arrived in a police car while a team of cave rescuers was unloading its Land Rovers, and two hearses from Matlock glided in shortly afterwards. Wavell had collected her key on the way. After she'd been fingerprinted, she unlocked the Hole of Death, and Forensics made its first sweep of the entrance while the cave rescuers were being briefed. As soon as they were ready, the Team Leader switched his helmet light on, dropped his rope into the shaft, and worked his way down as fast as the cramped space allowed. The air in the cave was cool and clammy, and it smelled of something he didn't want to be there – human putrefaction.

"Doc One, Doc Two, stand by to descend," he radioed up after he'd taken a first look at Miller and Patrice. "I've got two adult males. One's alive but unconscious with an impacted left-side temple. The other one may have been dead for some time, my call is a broken neck. There's no danger from firearms. Tell the police these could be their missing persons. They both match the photos we've seen. I also see a pair of gloves, a heap of knotted rope, a pair of glasses, a jacket and a briefcase. I'm leaving them where they are."

The Site Officer, Chief Superintendent May Docherty, radioed the finds through to Farrell and got permission to bring up the casualties before Forensics claimed the site.

The two doctors descended, their Medipaks came next, then a pair of drag stretchers with harnesses, and finally a police photographer. Working by helmet lamp, the doctors quickly confirmed Patrice couldn't be revived. Moving to Miller, they readied him up to be lifted out. When his stretcher got near the top, the shaft was too narrow for it unless it was folded, so one of the hauling crew was lowered head first to meet it. Hardly able to move and leaking sweat into her overalls, she clipped ropes onto Miller's harness and freed him from the stretcher. She was pulled out first, then she helped pull Miller out. One of the paramedics checking him over felt something spikey in his overalls pocket. He called to a CID man who was about to go down, and together they took out Miller's key to the Hole of Death locks. It went to Docherty's caravan for safekeeping. By the time Farrell arrived, Miller had been airlifted to the Special Care Hospital in Buxton. He'd been unconscious the whole while, and Buxton said he'd be kept that way for two to three days because fluid was squashing his brain. One of the hearses started back to Matlock as the air ambulance took off. The other one stayed for Patrice.

Docherty was working out of an Emergency Incident caravan. She was doing her best, but media pressure was getting to her, so while Farrell was walking the site, she snatched a minute to call her Chief in Matlock.

"I'll bring some more people out," she heard. "What's Gina Wavell doing?"

"Drinking tea in the Back-up Tent. Don't worry, someone's keeping an eye on her."

"She's a head-ache we don't need, May. Don't let her go till I get there. I want to speak to her personally."

Snape's drive was less than half as far as Farrell's, and when he got to Peterborough, he could see for himself,

Chrisbeckmill Motors was a write-off. Burned out car shells stood around forlornly, and everywhere there was the smell of wet rubble and smoke gone cold. Demolition crews had had to bring down near-by brickwork before it collapsed on its own, and steel beams shored up much of what remained. The site was marked with different coloured flags, and the last of the fire engines was getting ready to go, its crew drained by the heat, the tension, and the non-stop graft.

Cambridgeshire Police had an Emergency Incident caravan similar to Derbyshire's. It was in amongst a cluster of caravans towed in for communications, fire and rescue, and police back-up respectively, and they all had their own generators. The media mobbed Snape's car as it slowed for the cordon, then it was through. The Site Officer, Chief Superintendent Trevor Hawley, apologised for the scrum.

"We're not giving them much at the moment," he said. "We wanted you here first."

"Have you found any more?"

Snape had been talking to him from his car, and he knew from Saxley, Miller and Patrice had been found.

"Come inside and I'll tell you. They're using distance microphones, so we're running the generators hard."

As Snape was closing the door, his mobile buzzed. The number showed Chelmsford Ops Room.

"A request from Mr Oleg Dvorski of the Russian Embassy in London," he heard. "He'd like to speak to you urgently, but he wouldn't say why. I told him you were in Peterborough, and he offered to drive over. I said I'd call him back."

Snape hesitated. Van Piet wanted Dvorski kept away from the media, but that wouldn't happen if he came to Peterborough. They were there in numbers.

"Tell him I'll be in Chelmsford at nine thirty tonight. Get a plain-clothes car to fetch him from London, and when he gets near us, put a cover over him on the back seat. Say it's an order from me. If it's that urgent, he'll put up with it."

He terminated and gave his attention to Hawley.

"There's a lot to get through," Hawley said. "It's helped that the back of the garage was hit a bit less than the front."

"Talk me through it. Have you got any pictures?"

"On my smartphone for now."

He made some space, poured tea from a flask into two paper cups, and got under way.

"Chrisbeckmill staff have inventoried the vehicles out the back. They include Becky Miller's RAV4. It's badly damaged, but there was enough of her tyres left to match to fresh prints in a passing bay on a back road leading to Saxley Castle." He was moving the pictures along as he spoke. "Part of a footprint, also fresh, was found near them. We've matched it to fragments of footwear from the Millers' flat, and we think it's Becky Miller's."

"What about Chris Miller? Saxley hasn't found a car for him."

"He's a car missing here as well. He normally drives an Avensis. It was here all day yesterday, but it isn't here today."

"So it must have been moved during the night. Do we have a time fix?"

"Not exactly, but there are tyre marks on Saxley Castle car park it could have made, and Saxley is just over a hundred miles from here. Say two and three quarter hours, roughly reckoned."

"I wonder where it is now. What else have you got?"

"Miller had his own workshop and its floorboards got burned out. Underneath them was a safe which we've been able to open. It contained two Walther P22s and two silencers that would fit them. The ammunition with them exploded from the heat, but everything's gone for testing because—"

"—the Torellis were shot with silenced P22s. Trevor, this is major!"

"Calm down, Eddie, there's more to come yet. These little numbers were in the safe, too, which is just as well, because they're made of brass."

He showed what looked like two old-fashioned padlock keys. They were distorted, but three deliberate scratch marks could still be seen.

"May Docherty says they match Gina Wavell's key. They also match a brass key found in the pocket of Miller's overalls. We think the keys were made in this metal cutter – it was in Miller's workshop – and we think the scratch marks could have been made with this centre punch, which was also in his workshop. All that's being tested. You'll know for sure as soon as I do."

Snape leafed through his notebook. Saxley Castle, the keys, the Millers in Marlborough Close, and Patrice going putrid in the cave. And now the Walthers as well. But why had Chris Miller gone back? And why had he gone down the Hole of Death on a home-made climbing rope? If Farrell had been on the ball, a lot of this could have been avoided. But Miller was still alive. Suddenly, he was the key witness.

"Do you know what Chris Miller kept in the safe that blew up?"

"Money. Lots of it, his staff's told us. Trade documents as well. It had a palm reader and a combination lock to open it, and Miller and his wife were the only ones with access. There should have been a stun grenade in the door in case the wrong people had a go, but it seems Miller put in plastic explosive instead. The signs are it's Semtex."

"Where did he get that from?"

"He was on the wrong side of the law in his early days. He probably asked his connections for it. He probably also thought he knew more than he did. Hence the big bang."

"So Becky Miller wanted to get what? – Money? Papers? – out of the safe after she'd been to Saxley. Can we add to that?"

"Could be. Try this."

Hawley moved his picture gallery along some more. First came some fragments of an overnight suitcase plus its ripped off handle, then the mangled casing of the CCTV's hard drive.

"Becky Miller had this suitcase with her and the hard drive was inside it. Chrisbeckmill staff have told us she looked after the CCTV, and that was about all she did do. Quite likely she removed the hard drive herself and slipped it into her suitcase. Was she taking it to someone or did she intend to destroy it? Either way, it looks as if she was covering her own tracks and possibly someone else's."

"Is there anything left of the hard drive itself?"

"Not an atom. Too close to the blast, I'm afraid."

Snape decided to stay on as long as he could. Farrell, who was being careful to stay in touch, called him when Patrice's briefcase was opened. He kept his voice neutral, and Snape compelled himself to do the same.

"It contained a flask that once had coffee in it, a *Times* dated August 23rd – that's the day he disappeared – a packet of tissues, and an unopened box of Black Magic with a 'Jenny's of Epping' price sticker on it."

"No documents, diaries or letters? An address book, maybe?"

"None of those. He wasn't intending to work that evening."

"True. What about Gina Wavell?"

"She's got a will of her own and she's showing it. She doesn't want anyone in her house with her, and she doesn't want to move into anywhere else, thank you very much. She also doesn't want a police car on her doorstep in case the neighbours see it, and she'll talk to the media if she feels like it."

"So what's going to happen?"

"She's asked to be taken home. She's been told she's at risk, but she's enjoyed being important, and she wants to stay that way. Derbyshire Police will do what it can, but frankly it's not a lot. She hasn't even got a boyfriend to move in with her."

Snape sighed. Maybe she'd see things differently in the morning.

"I've got a relief team for you, Leo, they're on the way now," he said. "They'll be there in about two hours' time. I've got one for myself as well," he thought he'd better add. "I want you in the Ops Room by seven thirty tomorrow morning. There's a lot to get through already, and there'll be a lot more by tomorrow."

"Will Willem be there?" Farrell asked, doing his best to sound like a team man. "We can't overlook Wolvercote."

"I'll be talking to him before the day's out," Snape replied, ignoring the wheedling. "I'll find out then."

He didn't tell him about Dvorski. There seemed no point right then.

Chapter 23

An Account is Settled

The afternoon was on the wane as van Piet was dropped off in a side street near Ashell House. He gave his wristwatch to Garry to transcribe the recording he'd made on it and caught up with the latest information from Saxley and Peterborough. Then he said he had some phoning to do, so Garry disappeared into the back room he called his office.

Joost van Piet came first. Since it was Sunday, van Piet rang his home number in Amsterdam. To his surprise, his mother answered – he didn't know she was over there. His father was at the bank, she said. No, he won't mind you calling him there, he's shuffling paper for tomorrow, that's all. They gossiped a bit, then van Piet said,

"You study rich Russians, it's part of your job. Have you come across an oligarch called Anatoly Dobrynin? You'll keep this to yourself, by the way. No one must know I've asked."

"Anatoly Dobrynin? Willem, I've done better than come across him, I know him personally! And his charming wife! He's funded a whole Graduate School of Governance for us, so he's always in and out, and their at-homes and garden parties, well, people fight for invitations. They've got this delightful house in Hampstead, and when London gets too hard to bear, they've got a stately pile near Chequers. They travel on Cypriot passports, but if you ask me, they're more English than I am. What else can I tell you?"

"What he's worth and where it comes from."

"That depends on how you do your sums. He's usually listed as £9·8 billion, but that strikes me as low-ish. It comes from aluminium, oil and gas, telecommunications, and property. He's also a director of Sberbank."

"He owns a clinic in the Cotswolds, I understand."

"The De Macey Clinic. Yes, it's doing so well, he's thinking of opening a chain. If he goes public, buy in. I shall."

"What about staff? Are they Cypriot as well?"

"Not the last time I checked. Not a single one."

"So no pro-Cypriot policy, you'd say."

"Definitely not. He takes whoever's good enough."

He brought the call to a close, then tried for his father. There was no mistaking Joost's slightly ironic voice, and Willem instinctively switched to Dutch. It made the bond tighter.

"I want permission to ask Kasper Filipek to help me with a non-bank assignment," he said, and explained what it was.

Filipek was the bank's agent in Warsaw and an old friend of Willem. He happened to be attending a conference in London. If they hadn't both been so busy, they'd have arranged to meet up.

"I don't see why not," Joost replied. "Anything else on your shopping list? There usually is."

"Anke Sweelinck. I'd like her to do some foraging for me."

Sweelinck was the bank's Head of Intelligence. She was one of nature's night owls, so it was par for the course when Joost said,

"She'll be here before I go home. Tell me what you want and I'll ask her."

Van Piet told him about Patrice's involvement in Russell Burney's finances. He wanted to know why they went sour when they did. He had a list from Patrice's safe. He'd ask Tom Garry to fax it over.

Joost wryly observed it'd been hard to avoid Patrice's name in the last little while. The Dutch media had carried the story when he disappeared, and Dutch television had been taking feeds from Saxley Castle through the day. But, Joost added, he knew the name anyway.

"Patrice fell in with the Russians when Boris Yeltsin was in charge. Someone in government wanted to show Russia was safe for foreign investment, so certain companies were fattened up with subsidies, and Patrice got to sell shares in them. They were like loss leaders in a supermarket, and Patrice couldn't go wrong. He got a commission for every share he sold, and as a bonus he was allowed to buy some for himself. And sell them on, of course, once their value was pumped up. He must have made a fortune."

"Did you ever hear he was trying to sell Russell Burney's debts for him?"

"No I didn't. I can't say I was bound to, but somehow I think I would have."

"One more thing, Dad. You said 'someone in government' just now. Can you say who it was?"

"No, it's confidential. But this person had an old-style Stalinist fixer called Grigory Viktorovich Zembarov. I don't think Zembarov liked the Yeltsin years, but he was a patriot, so he got on with it. He's a colonel in the SVR now. You could do worse than follow that up."

Van Piet always enjoyed talking to his father, but there was still Filipek to contact. He struck lucky. Filipek's conference was over and he was getting ready for the farewell dinner. He'd be flying back to Warsaw in the morning.

"I want you to do some non-bank digging for me," van Piet said. "It's about Cyril Burney and his wife, Enid. Yes, *the* Cyril Burney. Mr Joost says it's all right."

He took him through the Burneys' backgrounds then,

"When he was twenty, Cyril Burney spent a week in Warsaw with one of his mother's brothers and his wife. Their names were Fryderyk and Monika Labuda. I want you to find out everything you can about them. When she was eighteen, Enid spent ten days in Lodz with her mother's unmarried foster sister. Her name was Isabela Yanta. Again, I need all the information you can get. Speedy, speedy, please, and keep it totally secret."

"I'll see what I can do, Willem. How do I get back to you?"

"The usual. Encoded message to Gorris and destroy all notes. Thanks in advance, Kasper. Enjoy your dinner."

Snape called almost immediately afterwards.

"I've had a call from Dvorski asking to see me. I told him nine thirty tonight in Chelmsford, and I want you there as well. Come as D.I. Blaker. It'll make life easier."

"I'll be there. What's on his mind?"

"No idea, that's why I said yes. While I've got you, I'm calling a meeting for seven thirty tomorrow morning. Can you be there, or do we link you in?"

"I'll be there as well."

"Good. Leo will be back from Derbyshire, and speaking of Leo, there's something you need to know now I've got a minute."

He detailed the Marlborough Close fiasco and his run-in with Lorrie.

"How's he feeling, do you reckon?"

"What, Leo? Full of good intentions is what he wants me to think, but as sore as an open blister is more likely. That may have consequences, and I'll add this while I'm at it. He's just come through a very nasty divorce. His wife left him for one of his juniors, then she took him to the cleaners in court. You can guess how it was – everyone was laughing at him and he knew it. His self-respect must have hit zero, and if it's much different now, I'd be surprised."

When they terminated, van Piet went through to Garry to get the Patrice list sent off. To his surprise, Garry had stopped transcribing and was checking through the FDLE report on Jethro Torelli's death, including the witness statements. An A4 block, a pencil and a calculator were on his desk where he could reach them. A nautical map of Miranda Cove was on his computer screen. It had a grid superimposed on it.

"You're free to go when you've sent this list off and put the transcribing to bed," van Piet said. "Use my JvP code and there's no reply to wait for. I'm off to Chelmsford before I go home, Mr Snape's meeting Dvorski there at nine thirty tonight. Looking to tomorrow, I'd like you here by seven thirty. There's a meeting in Chelmsford and I'll be sitting in on it. Now it's your turn. Why the FDLE report?"

"Since the Millers and the Torelli shootings seem connected, I faxed a copy to the Crown Actuary and asked her what she thought about Jethro Torelli's death. She did her own maths and said she'd never insure the Millers against a conviction because it was almost certainly murder. I've been checking her sums while you're still here."

"And?"

"I agree. Few things in life are certain, but this is as good as."

"Mr Snape needs to know that. E-mail him the details before you do the other things. I'll make sure he knows about them."

He put his hand on the door handle, then took it off again since Garry hadn't finished.

"Go ahead, Tom."

"I'm wondering how the Millers knew how to organise a shark attack. It must require specialised knowledge. I fancy someone's been instructing them – someone who knows Miranda Cove as well as sharks."

"I think you're right. We'll call this person Suspect X. With luck we'll get a name now we know we've got a gap to fill. Is there anything else?"

"Would you know the name Grigory Viktorovich Zembarov?"

"I've just heard it from my father. Apparently Zembarov knew Patrice back in the Yeltsin days."

"Yes, he did. MI5 tells me the Russians routinely sounded out stockbrokers as useful strategic targets; Patrice saw the glint of gold, and then came the handcuffs, which he was happy enough to wear. MI5 also tells me Zembarov knew, and still knows, Valkov and Dvorski. Valkov's a sort of protégé, they see eye to eye, and they keep in close touch."

"But Dvorski's face doesn't fit, that's what you told me, and my father said Zembarov was an old-style Stalinist patriot. If he still is, and we have to assume that, where does it leave Dvorski, the Yeltsin-man?"

Rain set in and then came on hard as van Piet motored to Chelmsford. He showed his Blaker ID to the media when he got there and told them he'd come for an update. He wasn't high-profile like Snape, so he got away with it. The heavy rain helped. No one wanted to stand in it longer than they had to.

Snape was waiting for him in the lobby.

"We'll go straight to my office," he said. "Dvorski's being smuggled in. He should be here any time now. I suppose we ought to ask for some tea for him."

Dvorski looked sheepish and confident at the same time when he arrived, and the same mix of opposites was in his voice when he spoke. He settled into an easy chair, drank his tea, and sounding like an actor who's fresh from learning his part, he said,

"I've been watching the news for much of the day. I was appalled when I learned Mr Patrice was dead. And in such circumstances, too. However, it's Mrs Miller I'm here to talk about. I've got no choice now she and her husband are being investigated. Was she really blown up opening their safe? That's what the media are saying."

"That's what it looks like. Now, what would you like to tell us?"

Dvorski studied the floor slightly longer than necessary, then,

"Well, the truth is, I've been seeing Mrs Miller more than I should have. I first met both of them not long after I was posted here. I went to a meeting of the Peterborough Chamber of Commerce, the Millers were there as well and, as you English say, we struck a chord. I called into their garage once or twice after that, there were always deals to discuss, or so I pretended, but the truth is, Mrs Miller and I began a relationship."

"How long did it last?"

"Not long. I was in a foreign country and she was bored, so it started well enough, but the strain of getting to hotels without her husband knowing took its toll. In the end, we called it quits while we were winning and let it gently fade away. More recently, however, I met Mr Miller at a Toyota promotion. He'd got his grand new garage by then, and he naturally wanted to show it to me. He'd also got a holiday home in a seaside town called Brancaster, and to cut a long story short, Mrs Miller and I started to meet there. I'd call in at the garage the way I used to, and we'd fix a day on the quiet."

"Were you seen in Brancaster, do you think?" van Piet asked. "By local people, I mean."

"I must have been. It's only a small place and Mrs Miller's appearance was striking, to say the least. I also think Mr Miller found out. I say that because instead of using an Embassy car, I drove there in my own on one occasion, and I fancy it had a tracker on it, because I was asked to park near Mr Miller's workshop when I called round once, and not too long ago I actually found a tracker on the underside of my car. Has a tracking monitor been found in Peterborough, by the way?"

"No, but we're not finished there yet," Snape answered. "What did you do with this tracker?"

"It's still in my garage, signalling away I shouldn't wonder. You can have it if you want it."

"Thanks. Your driver can collect it when he takes you back. Tell him to bring it here so we can have a look at it."

"What would you and Mrs Miller have done if Mr Miller had caught you?" van Piet put in.

"We talked about it, of course. Mrs Miller wanted me to whisk her off to Russia, but that was clearly not on. I said I would, but the truth is, I'd have simply got out of the way and left her to it. It sounds bad, I know, but I'm not here to talk myself up."

"Mrs Miller seems to have removed the CCTV's hard drive before she was killed," Snape said, "so let me put this to you. She was covering her tracks prior to going away with you, as she imagined, and she blew herself up getting the money to make it work"

"She hadn't contacted me, but it's perfectly possible. Her grasp of reality left a lot to be desired."

"Do you know whether she'd been out of Peterborough before she got blown up?"

"No I don't. And I don't know why her husband went to Saxley Castle either. Did he know Mr Patrice?"

"We're looking into that."

"There was a link between yourself, Mr Patrice and Mr Russell Burney," van Piet took over. "Mr Patrice was going to help Mr Burney sell his debts, and you were listening in. Did Mr Patrice do anything about those debts between when you last saw him and later that afternoon?"

"I've no idea, but I doubt it, he had other things on his mind. However, I mentioned Mr Burney in the Embassy when Mr Patrice disappeared, and you'll be pleased to know, Sberbank is going to keep him solvent till his big project comes on stream. It's a very good investment for us. I also see it now as a memorial to Mr Patrice."

"That's a kind thought. Will Sberbank be putting its own money up?"

"I ought not to answer that, but I expect you'll find out. No, one of our oligarchs is putting the money up, and Sberbank is acting as middleman. You'll know the name. It's Mr Dobrynin, the De Macey Clinic owner. He's made a lot of money in gas. He knows exactly what he's doing."

"So Mr Burney's project looks good, does it?"

"Immense is a better word, Inspector. The gas he's going for is worth billions."

"Will it make him rich? He told Mr Patrice he was going to ask for a rise."

Dvorski wondered why he'd been asked that, but there was only one answer, so he gave it.

"He deserves one, I'm sure of that, but between ourselves, I can't see it getting past his father. As you know, no doubt, they don't get on very well. A young man's wishful thinking, I fear."

Things wound down after that, and before long Snape was calling Dvorski's driver to take him back. As soon as they were gone, Snape switched the taping mike off and brought the flat of his hand down hard on his desk.

"What a liar!" he exclaimed. "He had his answers on tap. All he wanted was the questions."

"Just like Bunting and Penderton this afternoon. Tom was transcribing what they said when I left, and that reminds me. He went through that FDLE report using different maths. He says it's just about certain the Millers enticed the sharks in, and so does the Crown Actuary. It should all be waiting for you to download."

"I'm grateful for all this," Snape said, as his printer did the necessary, "but it won't be enough to get Dvorski with. He's been giving the orders, I'm sure of it now, but proving it's like nailing jelly to a wall. I can't wait to talk to Miller. If he's found out Dvorski's been seeing his wife, he might have a tale to tell."

He stood up, put Garry's report into his briefcase, and held the door open for van Piet. Van Piet had a half hour's drive to get home, Snape had less, and he was glad of it. He was knackered. Wearily he switched his light off, code-locked his office door, and they set off down the corridor.

Dvorski wasn't the only one who'd been watching the news. In the Georgian house Purdy and Patrice had made their home, Purdy switched on at breakfast time and kept watching through the day. When there was no news on TV, he pressed the mute button and went into the internet on his smartphone. He had a round of toast for breakfast and another one for lunch. He didn't want any more. Occasionally he'd make some coffee, then let it go cold in his cup.

He was bitterly angry. No one was saying outright Miller had killed Patrice, but Purdy was certain he had, and that certainty ate into him as one hour followed the next. Finally he knew what to do. He powered his computer up, went into the website of the Special Care Hospital and studied the way the wards were laid out. From there he went to the Trauma Department page and clicked on 'Staff'. The Head of Department was a Mr Clive Manessa, his photo-portrait showed him in sky blue operating clothes, and his career was spelled out under his cheery middle-aged face. 'Publications' came at the end, and when Purdy clicked it open, it listed what he expected – articles co-authored with specialists in other hospitals. British hospitals were Purdy's recruiting pond, so he knew who was where. That included a consultant who'd published with Manessa – Aidan Brightside of the Royal Liverpool Hospital – and Purdy looked like Brightside. Purdy also knew Brightside was out of the country – he was on a guest-lecturing tour in Switzerland. He printed the article and went down into the basement, where he kept a store of medical odds and ends. One of them was an ID card maker. He photographed himself, typed in 'Aidan Brightside, Consultant Traumatologist, Royal Liverpool Hospital', edged the card in dark blue – the Royal's house colour – and plasticised it. He found a neckband in the same colour and that was that. Upstairs, he changed into the kind of lightweight clothing doctors wear in warm wards, pulled on an overcoat, and headed for his Aston Martin. Before he left, he made sure everything was washed up. He also straightened the curtains and left a note in the milk cooler cancelling the milk. The right sum of money went in with it.

The drive to Buxton took him a good four hours. It rained ceaselessly and the night was pitch black, but he was so concentrated, he hardly noticed till he got out at the other end. The main entrance was blockaded by the media, so he walked to Accident and Emergency via a dimly-lit covered way. It could have been midday instead of late at night in the waiting room. The lights were bright, most of the chairs were taken, and the moving about was constant. He joined the queue for registration, then left it to go into the gents'. He stayed in there long enough to be forgotten, and when he came out, he didn't rejoin the queue, he sat down next to an elderly man who was on his own. He was in a wheelchair with one of his legs raised.

"I'm Dr Brightside," he said, taking the ID card out of his jacket pocket. "What's up with you?"

"I've turned my ankle, the triage nurse thinks I've cracked something. I went to cross the road and it gave way under me."

"That's dreadful. Look, I've got a minute before I'm officially on duty. When you get called, I'll wheel you in. A place like this isn't nice if you're on your own."

Once he was into the treatment rooms area, he passed the wheelchair man on and found another gents'. His coat went into a waste bin and his ID card went round his neck. In the busy corridors he looked like one more professional going from A to B. The dark blue edging didn't matter. On the night shift there were people from everywhere.

He needed to go up four floors, then down a long corridor with single-patient wards on either side. Garth Ward - the media hadn't so much as tried to conceal the name - was right at the far end in a kind of cul-de-sac. He'd have to be careful up there. There wouldn't be many people around, just night staff working their routines. He'd be very visible.

He crossed and re-crossed the vestibule where the lifts were until he saw a nurse in a plum coloured uniform get into one of them. The colour said she was agency, and she might just be new to the place. She was.

"Going up to the trauma wards?" he asked as he followed her in.

"I think so," she laughed, leafing through a file while she spoke. "It's my first night in this hospital. Everywhere looks like everywhere else."

"I'll tag along. I'm from the Royal Liverpool. I'm seeing what makes Mr Manessa so good. Courtesy of Mr Manessa, of course."

She laughed again but didn't say anything. Consultants were like gods. They could talk to nurses, but it was best not to say much back.

When the lift door opened, he saw an armed policeman standing against the opposite wall, so he made sure he was talking traumas to the nurse as they got out. Like the nurse, he held out his ID, and because the policeman had seen her before, he let them both go through.

The long corridor was next.

"I got this thing right this time," she said as she tapped in a code and the entrance doors swung open. Whispering now they were inside, she added, "It was so embarrassing, I had to get someone to help me last time. They must have thought I can't even open a door."

He took the corridor in at a glance. The lighting was night-time dim, and looking into the wards through their windows, he saw patients lying at angles, their limbs raised, sometimes their heads bandaged, and enveloped with wires and tubes. Purdy knew there was one nurse to three patients, he'd got it off the website, and he could see the nurses' station down the corridor. Beyond it was Garth Ward, but guarding the approach to it were two police officers. Like the one outside the lifts, they were armed.

"I don't suppose Garth Ward is one of yours," Purdy said to the nurse. "I'd like to see how the Saxley Castle chap's being treated."

"Sorry, mine are all this end. You'll have to speak to Mr Betts, he's looking after Mr Miller. I'll ask at the desk for you, then I'll have to go."

This was crunch time. Frank Betts was a Senior Specialist Nurse, and if he knew Brightside personally, Purdy had had it. Manessa had worked with Brightside, so Betts could have as well. As Betts approached him, Purdy made sure his ID was visible and held out his hand.

"Aidan Brightside," he said with a confident smile. "Consultant Traumatologist. Pleased to meet you."

Betts shook his hand.

"I know you from your website," Betts said. "I'm sorry we haven't met before. I've been wanting to come over to see how you do things, but something's always got in the way."

It was a struggle for Purdy to keep the smile on his face. It had been that close.

"And now you want to see how we're treating Mr Miller," Betts went on. "I think you'll be impressed. I'll get his notes for you, then you can have a look at him."

They made themselves comfortable in a storeroom, and Purdy struck lucky again. Betts had been around a long time, he knew as much as a lot of doctors, and when Purdy took out the article the real Brightside had co-authored, Betts ran his finger down the list of contributors' names. At the end of Manessa's helpers was his own. By the time he closed Miller's notes and suggested going into Garth Ward, he and Purdy were colleagues enough for him to get Purdy seamlessly past the police.

Miller's eyes were closed and his breathing under his mask was peaceful, as Purdy noted with fury. He ran his eyes over the monitors. There was none he didn't know. He could work them all.

"The big trouble's the skull injury," Betts said. "We've cleared the blood clot, but fluid keeps gathering faster than Mr Manessa likes. He'll decide what to do when he comes in, if you can stay that long."

As Betts spoke, his radiophone buzzed.

"I'll come along now," he said and terminated.

He returned his attention to Purdy.

"You'll have to excuse me, one of the nurses needs help," he said. "I'll be ten minutes at most. You can stay here if you like. If his brain pressure changes, let the nurses' station know. They'll send for me."

He went out, shutting the door behind him.

Five minutes was enough. First Purdy switched all the acoustic alarms off. Then he turned Miller's breathing-assist off, removed his mask, and slid one of the pillows out from under his head. It disturbed the tubing fixed under the flap in his skull, but that didn't matter now. As he was bringing the pillow down over Miller's face, Miller's eyes flickered open, and they seemed to look pleadingly into Purdy's. For Purdy it was a moment of unexpected joy. He pressed the pillow down and watched the monitors. One by one they started flashing, but there was no sound to raise the alarm. Miller's heart worked harder and harder, trying to compensate for the lack of oxygen, then it surrendered, and the line went flat. His brain signals were the last to go. When they did, he was dead. Deeply satisfied, Purdy laid the pillow neatly across Miller's chest, sat down on one of the bedside chairs, and relaxed. He was serene. When Betts came back, he said calmly,

"I've just killed your patient, Frank, and you won't be able to revive him. It had to be, he brought it on himself. You can ask the police in, I won't make a fuss. My conscience is clear."

IV
Closing the Ring

Chapter 24

Shayler's Secret

Snape was dragged out of a deep sleep with the news his key witness had been murdered, and his frustration level went through the roof. He tried to get back to sleep, but it was hopeless, so he got cleaned up and, profoundly angry, he drove in to police HQ through the last of the rain. A pile of flimsies from the Ops Room was waiting on his desk. Still bleary-eyed, he skimmed through the top one. It confirmed the Walther P22s from the Peterborough blaze were the ones that had killed the Torellis. Well, good news at last, he yawned. It'd get the Americans off his back for a start. The remains of a tracking monitor had also been found, but it was too damaged to do anything useful with. Some gas bottles had been near it, and they'd exploded from the heat.

"That's more like it," he muttered bleakly as he thumbed through the rest. "It wouldn't do for too much to go right."

By seven thirty van Piet and Farrell had joined him. They both knew what Purdy had done, it had been on the early news, and when Snape coupled it with the Marlborough Close bungle, the atmosphere went Arctic. Tight-lipped, he passed the tea round and waited with studied patience while Farrell speed-read what Dvorski had said the night before, then what Bunting and Penderton had come out with in Wolvercote. Van Piet added a few carefully chosen words of his own, and Snape summarised the flimsies. There were hot bacon sandwiches on a serving-plate, but no one wanted them, so Snape let them go cold.

"So, gentlemen," he said when they were ready. "Chris Miller's dead as well. Any suggestions where we go from here? Leo?"

Farrell dropped his gaze to the table they were sitting round.

"We could pull in Bunting and Penderton," he said, half-looking up. "Willem's just said their Volkswagen had been very carefully cleaned. It had new tyres on it as well. Maybe they helped to shift Miller's car."

"I'm against that," van Piet said sharply. "If we show our hand too soon, we've had it."

It wasn't meant personally, but Farrell took it that way.

"I hear what you say, Willem," he heard himself answer. "Who comes next then?"

"Russell Burney, I'm sure of it. Leo, I want you to go back to Miss Shayler. Get her to prattle about Burney, we need to know everything about him that we can. Ask her about his father and mother, his drinking, his love life, his spending habits, that sort of thing. Nothing's too trivial now."

"It'll have to be after hours and at her house, she won't want to talk to me at work. I'll set it up now if you like. I'll speak to her personally."

Anything to get out of Snape's office. Snape gave him the nod and, seething inwardly, he went off to make his call.

"You'd better bring Sal Gulliver up to speed," van Piet said to Snape as the door closed. "We'll likely need her before long."

Sal Gulliver was Head of Essex Police's Armed Support Unit. Van Piet had worked with her when she was in Kent Police. They'd hunted down Alex Trilling, the SRO traitor, together.

"One more thing," van Piet went on. "I'll be at GCHQ for most of today, following up a lead from Wolvercote. I'll ask you not to contact me unless you have to." He turned to the Ashell House camera. "Tom, you're coming as well. I'll pick you up on my way."

In Sunningdale, Shayler was up well before seven thirty and getting another Monday under way. She usually drove to Sunningdale station to commute into London, but this time, just as she was nearing the car park, a slight figure in a raincoat stepped off the kerb and waved her down. It was Hallavy. She put her flashers on and halted just long enough for him to jump in.

"Don't go into the car park," he said as he buckled up one-handed. His other hand clutched a well-worn Gladstone bag. "I've got to talk to you, but I don't want the CCTV to pick me up."

She wound her way through to Sunninghill. From there she could loop back to Sunningdale station in her own time.

"I've been to Blackhall Rocks," he said. He had anxiety written all over him. "Did you know I'd been there?"

"I'd heard but that's all. What else do you want to tell me?"

"Nobody knows I'm here. I said I was going home when I finished there yesterday, but I came this way instead and spent the night in Windsor. I figured I'd catch you if I waited where I did. Fern, can you get home early this afternoon? Without anyone noticing, I mean. I know something terrible. You're the only person I can trust with it."

"I can be home by five twenty unless someone has a bright idea. Park round the back out of sight of the road. I'll do my best."

She dropped him off near where he'd street-parked and motored on to the station. The platform was full when she got there – her train had been delayed – so she didn't have to cover for why she was late for work. The morning and her diary stayed more or less in sync, and towards mid-afternoon she made sure she had some head-achey papers on her desk.

"I'm going to take these home and work on them in peace," she told her secretary as she gathered them up. "I'll not be in for anyone, regardless."

"What if Mr Farrell calls again?"

He'd phoned in as he'd said he would. Shayler was there the second time he'd tried, and they'd agreed on eight thirty.

"Either he comes as arranged or he rings in again tomorrow. I'm only seeing him because he's police."

Hallavy was already there when she got back. He must have been sitting with his window down, because he was round from the back of the house before she'd closed the garage door. He'd left his coat in his car. His Gladstone bag should have blended in with his baggy tweed jacket and his hand-knitted cardigan, but the way he gripped it made it seem as if he'd brought the crown jewels with him.

Hallavy and Shayler were old friends. Aging and single, they felt comfortable with each other. Without thinking, Shayler showed him into the same room she'd persuaded Russell Burney to murder his father in. While she was in the kitchen slitting rolls open, he let his eyes drift over the furniture and the paintings. Normally they would make him feel at home and easy. Not this time.

"You're the last person I want to see the back of," Shayler said as she wheeled a trolley in over the deep-pile carpet, "but I've got the police coming round at eight thirty. You may want to be gone by then. We'll eat first, then you can tell me what's bothering you. That way I'll know you've had something."

They ate in silence. When they'd finished, Shayler pushed the trolley to one side and let him sort himself out. He didn't take long, and the maps and graphs he pulled out of his bag were all in the right order. He'd put a lot of thought into what he wanted to say.

"I've been checking Dandy's core-samples for Harvest Home," he began. "The Rocks wanted to thin them out, so Russell sent me up to have a look. I didn't think there'd be a problem when I started out. The police boffins had been happy with them, so why shouldn't I be?"

"But there was a problem."

"Dandy was top of the range, so when she did things differently, no one argued with her. She tested way beyond Harvest Home, she prioritised core-sampling over sonar, and some of the gaps she left weren't where I for one would have left them. But she produced the goods, so we all went along with it. Normally we keep all our core-samples, but when I checked the depository log, I found she'd written 'Irrelevant' against some of them and had had them destroyed. She could do that because she was in charge, but she'd taken so many samples, she'd still kept enough to cause problems further down the line. The obvious thing was for me to junk some more. I just had to work out which ones."

He leaned towards Shayler and lowered his voice.

"She'd been clever, Fern. Some of the ones she got rid of were irrelevant by any standards, but others were only irrelevant if Harvest Home was safe. But it wasn't safe and it isn't. She used these other samples to prove how dangerous it is, and then hid the danger by writing them off. Or sometimes she put in gaps if she knew what the samples there would show, and that had the same effect. To cut a long story short, she worked out, when Harvest Home goes max, it will trigger a tsunami so big it will swamp everything round the North Sea basin, eastern England included. There'll be no escape. It'll be millions drowned and billions of pounds' worth of damage."

"And billions of pounds' worth of lawsuits," Shayler put in. "It'll destroy us completely." She didn't have Valkov's need to hide the truth. "But what I don't understand," she added, "is why your police boffins didn't pick this up."

"They saw what Dandy wanted them to see: a well-researched field with an emphasis on sampling. I'd have been the same. It was only because I had to take her on, so to speak, that I saw what she'd really done."

"Have you told anyone else?"

"Not a soul. I'm not a hero, Fern, I'm a jobbing scientist plodding towards retirement. This is too big for me, and then there's the fact that Dandy was murdered. I think she was murdered because she knew what I know now and told somebody. I'm not going to make that mistake. I've told you because I trust you and I had to tell someone, but that's where it stops. I'll be honest with you, Fern. I'm frightened."

"So you haven't told the police."

"No. If they start asking questions, everyone will know I started them off." He paused. "Do you think I should?"

She didn't have to think.

"Better not, it might not be necessary. I'll keep an eye on things for you. What about Russell? Have you told him?"

"No."

"Do you think he knows?"

"No. He wouldn't go ahead if he did, and going ahead is what he's doing. I'd be the first to know if he was pulling out."

Shayler still wanted Cyril Burney murdered, nothing had changed there, but she didn't want CDB Global destroyed, she'd lose everything if it was. Somehow she had to have the murder but not the tsunami, and that meant two things: keeping Hallavy's mouth shut and staying informed what the police were up to. Farrell might yet come in handy.

"You've done well, Steve," she said, putting warmth and affection into her voice, "and we'll keep this between ourselves. We don't want you with a bullet through you." She looked at her watch and tutted. "You'd better be going soon, the police might get here early. What will you do now?"

"I'll go home. I've already sorted out which core-samples to junk, so when I get up tomorrow, I'll go straight to Klemmsley Marine, tell Russell the space problem's solved, and ask him to authorise the clear-out. I'll leave everything else to you. I couldn't have managed if I hadn't told you, but I feel I can now. Thanks, Fern, you're a friend."

He gathered his documents up carefully – "These go in my safe at home and they stay there," he said – and she saw him out of the grounds. Back in the room he'd just left, she sat and thought it all through. Getting Farrell to help her, that was the hard bit, and she couldn't see how she could do it. For a while she sat motionless, then a strange idea came to her. She loathed Farrell profoundly. It wasn't his questions, he had to ask those, it was a basic sexual pull he had, quite possibly without knowing it. He wasn't a charmer – he had a reddish face, two chins and a beer belly. But to Shayler he was bullish – her word – a modern-day Minotaur with a mighty pizzle and big hanging testicles. And that was why she loathed him. His bullishness stirred up fears and desires she didn't want anyone to know about. Until now. Calculating by nature and with the prize of a lifetime to play for, she'd use them to get control of him.

After she'd removed every trace of Hallavy from the room, she went upstairs to her bedroom and tugged an aging acid-wash denim suit out of her wall-length wardrobe. She used to wear it when she was just out of her teens, and she still put it on when she wanted to be her most secret and private self. A button-front shirt came out next, followed by maroon and white banded socks and open-toed sandals. The shirt and suit went on over filmy black underwear, then she combed and brushed her fading hair till she had an old-style big hair look. When the doorbell rang, she was ready. She stood her collar up, left the flap of her jacket pocket casually undone, and let Farrell in. He was nearly half an hour ahead of time. She thought he was hoping to catch her out, but all he wanted was to finish early. He was sure he'd been sent on a nothing job. Well, he'd get it over with and disappear.

He noticed what she was wearing, but he thought she was freaky anyway. She was so locked into herself, a paper clip had more going for it. Pretending to like her Lapsang Souchong tea and eating chocolate truffles from a porcelain plate, he laboured dutifully through the Russell Burney agenda. Toni Aubrey caught his attention.

"She's a reclaimed drunk, you say."

"Not me, his mother. Apparently he's crazy about her."

"Did anyone know her before he took up with her?"

"No. We don't think Russell knew her either till she stepped out of her space ship. That was last July."

"And where was it?"

"In a clinic his mother knew about, the De Macey Clinic. It's near Chipping Norton."

He put it all into his notebook. Years of giving evidence made him write things down virtually word for word.

"I suppose we ought to do something about her," he said wearily. "Thanks for that."

He was clearly heading for the exit. Shayler was panic-stricken at what she was about to do, but it was now or not at all.

"Please don't go," she said, and held out her hand as if to stop him. "You've finished your questions so … so now we can relax and talk a bit. I'd like that. I get lonely here sometimes."

He cringed inwardly.

"What do you want me to say?"

"What you like, really. Tell me about yourself. Start with what sort of house you live in."

She didn't know it, but the chip on his shoulder had just got a whole lot bigger.

"I don't live in a house. I used to have one in Lewisham, but my ex-wife's got it now, along with most of my money. So I live in a one-bedroom flat in Croydon when I'm not in a police bed-sit in Chelmsford."

"I'm sorry. Would you like to see round my house or would it be too painful?"

It was the surprise factor that made him say yes. Suddenly he was curious. Cautious, too, but mostly curious.

They started on the ground floor, and each room told him the same thing: she was loaded. The staircase was grand, and his entire flat would have fitted into each of the bedrooms, or so it seemed to him. In her own bedroom she opened one of the leaded windows and lit up the grounds near the house with a zapper kept on a chest of drawers. The lawns sprang into life, and a fountain in an ornamental pond played over lighting that made the water look like glass.

"I've got two and a half acres," she said. "They're fully landscaped, and the gardeners keep their things in what used to be a coach house. Do you like what you see?"

He said he did, but 'like' wasn't the word. He was overwhelmed. She turned the outside lights off and shut the window.

"I ride to hounds," she said as she showed him onto the landing. "I also shoot and scuba-dive. And I play golf, of course, I'm on the Sunningdale committee. I'm single, you see, so I do what singles do. It's compensation really, but I enjoy it, and since it tires me out, it makes me forget what I'm missing."

"So what are you missing?" he asked.

They were outside a room they hadn't been in and the door was shut. He thought she'd say 'sex' or 'a man', and he'd be able to tell her no. He didn't realise the clichés didn't apply.

"If you come in here, I'll show you," she said. "It's my special room."

She opened the door, brought the concealed lighting up, and the curtains closed automatically. To one side was a neatly made single bed, and near it was a recliner armchair that was facing a large HD screen. There were what looked like pictures round the walls, but they were covered with mini-curtains. There were cupboards as well, and each one had its own lock. The rest of the furniture consisted mainly of two matching armchairs that didn't recline. She invited him to sit down in one of them.

"What would you like to drink?" she asked, waving her hand towards a well-stocked bar. "I usually drink cherry brandy or Tia Maria when I'm in here, but you can have whisky, brandy, vodka – anything you like except beer, because I don't like it."

"I'm driving," he said, still cautious. "A tomato juice will do."

She poured herself some cherry brandy and a tomato juice for him.

"If you change your mind," she said, "I can put you up for the night. I've got a razor and a new toothbrush you can use. I might even find some pyjamas if I look hard enough. They'd be my deceased father's in case you're wondering. He was big like you."

"Thanks, but I'll have to be going soon. I've got a long day tomorrow."

But he didn't sound in a hurry now, and she felt less on edge as she caught the change of tone.

"I want you to know some things about me that nobody else knows," she said. "All I ask is that you don't say anything till I've finished, otherwise I'll lose my nerve. Let me start with some pictures. I don't like them, but I force myself to look at them before I look at anything else. They're my inner me."

She brought up some photos of herself on the HD screen when she was five, nine, fourteen and seventeen. The clothes and the hairstyles changed, but one thing didn't: the big blotches over her face, arms and legs. On the colour photos they were red.

"I hated myself when I was growing up, and you can see why. I was teased mercilessly at school, and when my friends started going out with boys, I knew none of the boys would want me, so I shut myself up. I often wanted to kill myself, only I was afraid I'd fail and be laughed at.

"The blotches went when I was twenty, and I bought these clothes to be the new me, but by then the damage was done. I craved sex immensely, but I was terrified of everything to do with it, except for one thing. I can't say the word out loud, it makes me embarrassed even now when I say it to myself, but if I say I touched myself and got pleasure from it, you'll know what I mean. I've led a double life, you see. I've buried myself in my work and become very rich. And I attend to my sexual needs up here. Let me show you some more."

She stood up and uncovered the pictures on the walls. There were six of them, they were art-quality black-and-white photographs, and they formed a matt-finish sequence entitled *Better and Better*. They showed a naked woman. Her face was blurred, but the rest of her body was sharp. Three showed her sitting with her legs apart, three showed her lying on her back, and in all of them she was fondling herself with completely natural pleasure.

"I like these a lot," she said. "She looks so happy. Her face is blurred to make you see her whole body is happy. I don't know who she is, and it doesn't matter. I like what she tells me."

She took some keys off a shelf and unlocked one of the cupboards.

"I've got books in here," she went on. "They're all about having sex, and most of them have pictures in them. When it's just words, I try to imagine what they're doing so I can enjoy it, too. When it's pictures, I like to see penetration so I can feel it as well. Orgasmic faces don't interest me. They always look faked."

She opened a second cupboard.

"I've got DVDs in this one. I buy them from a shop near Foyles, it's safer than buying online. I like to watch people having sex, it makes me feel I'm having it, too. Two women having sex is boring. It has to be a man and a woman. Men's—" She broke off, afraid of the word, and she lost the struggle. "Men's you know what, I've never seen one for real, and if I did, I'd back away. But in DVDs they attract me in the same way dangerous animals attract me in a zoo. Like lions. I have to go and look at them, but I'm always afraid one will leap over the moat and claw me to death."

Just briefly, a years-long desperation showed in her eyes. Farrell kept perfectly still. He was afraid he was being filmed.

She opened a third cupboard. It was full of sex magazines, some in 3D. The fourth was crammed with erotic novels, and the last one contained four vibrators and a range of accessories.

"You're probably wondering what I do when I'm watching my DVDs or reading my magazines," she persisted. "I drink a lot, it gets me in the mood. And I usually wear this denim suit. It takes me back to when I still hoped for a sex life, even though I knew no one would ever come near me. If I want an orgasm, I slide my trousers down, there's no one here to stop me. I can come quickly if I want to, two or three times in a row, but usually I like to come slowly, either in my recliner or on the bed. If I've had a frustrating day, I like to come fast, otherwise I take my time. Sometimes I drift without coming at all, and that's nice, too."

She refilled her glass, he covered his with his hand. He couldn't help himself, he wanted her, but he was nervous about the price tag. She read his face carefully. She was almost there.

"I'm going to make you an offer shortly, and part of it is me," she said. "So I want to know what you think of me. I'm older than you are, you see, I'm over fifty and it shows. My hair is going grey, my throat is stringy, and my thighs are mottled and lumpy. See for yourself. If you find me repulsive, you must say so."

She slipped her suit and shirt off, leaving only her black underwear and, deliberately, her unsexy banded socks. The way she'd described herself was true but, as she'd reckoned, it didn't make any difference. He was fully sexed up and finding it unbearable.

"You're not repulsive at all," he managed to say. Then, "I want you badly."

"In that case I'll stop," she said and began to get dressed again. "We'll go downstairs and we'll talk. Then we'll see."

"Was I being filmed in there?" he asked as she opened the door for him.

"No, I hadn't even thought of it. Desire is stronger than fear. I want your desire."

She took him back into the room he'd asked his questions in. Over coffee she said,

"You've seen how wealthy I am, and with your help I'll go on being wealthy. My aim is to give you so much money, you can leave your little flat and live in the style you want to. You can move in here and live in luxury with me, or you can buy a place of your own and I'll pay the mortgage. You've also seen how my personal life is. I want you to give me what I've been missing for a lifetime. That means you can have as much sex with me as you like and whenever you like. You said yourself you wanted me badly, and I take you at your word. But you must say you'll help me first."

Farrell's certainties were shifting. He'd not had sex for a long while, and now he could have it on demand. He'd soon get her past her hang-ups, she'd be going like a rattlesnake in no time. Then there was her money and, best of all, he wouldn't be kicked around by the likes of Snape and van Piet. Not anymore.

"What sort of help do you want?"

"I want to know everything there is to know about the investigations you're working on. I'm not going to tell you why, but unless you agree, I won't do any of the things I've promised. I've got some cryptophones in my safe, as Global's Finance Director I lend them out from time to time, and I'll let you have one before you go. The deal is, you phone me with everything you learn, and I'll make you rich and happy."

"I'd lose my career if I got found out."

"There's no reason why you should get found out. And anyway, I can always get you a top job with Global. You wouldn't have to bow and scrape to anyone then."

He'd taken such a drubbing lately, he said yes and meant it. They tried some sex, it didn't work, but it didn't matter, they could always try again. With a cryptophone in his pocket, he drove off into the night. To cover his tracks, he pulled into a service centre on the M25 and radioed in his report. It consisted almost entirely of Aubrey and the De Macey Clinic. The further he got from Sunningdale, the weirder Shayler struck him, but so what? Her money wasn't weird, that was the main thing. And sex on demand, that wasn't weird either.

Punctually at six the next morning – it was Tuesday, 28th August – two white vans marked British Telecom drew up opposite Russell Burney's house and set about getting their workplace organised. The footpath was closed, cones were put round, and an all-weather tent protected the lines where a metal cover had been removed. A junction box a little further along was opened up as well. The engineers moved about as the work jogged along, but the peephole in the tent was constantly manned; and when a woman with wavy brown hair and high delicate cheekbones kissed Burney goodbye, the superfast camera did its work. It had to be Aubrey, it couldn't be anyone else, and the images were in Ashell House and then on to Chelmsford before Burney's Morgan had cleared the drive. After that, the door stayed closed till eleven thirty-three, when a van from Middlesex Mobile Library pulled in and the same English rose opened up to exchange some books. She wasn't seen again. At five o'clock the site was cleared, and the phone tap installed in the junction box was left to its silent ways.

Chapter 25

Wavell Has a Visitor

Fern Shayler and Gina Wavell – they were like chalk and cheese. Where Shayler was repressed, Wavell was upfront, and where Shayler was calculating, Wavell was instinctive. In summer, Wavell chauffeured tourists around, regardless of what they were like, and in winter, she worked for a football club in Crowd Control. No one was too large or too drunk for her to manage. If they tried it on, she sent them packing with a flea in their ear.

Her father had a lot of money to his name. It came from speculation building, and when she came of age, he bought her a rambling mid-Victorian house outside Matlock in Matlock Bath. He told her it was the last big thing he'd buy her, and she liked that, it showed respect. She put a lot of free time into making it the best-looking house in the road. The large back garden – a wilderness when she moved in – ran up a steep hillside into dense conifer woodland. She put a limestone wall round it with broken glass in the top, cleared the bushes and brambles out, and terraced the gradient to make it 'as good as the ones next door'. In the front garden, which was flatter, she relaid the lawn, put a rockery in, and trimmed the high hedges that marked the property lines. When she needed help, she hired it, but it wasn't often. She could work machinery, she didn't mind taking her time, and she valued her independence, as the police found out when they tried to look after her. She told them flatly they weren't to come onto her land, and when she saw one of their cars parked outside her gate, she rapped sharply on its side window and told them to go away. If there was one thing that made her livid, it was being defied.

The media couldn't get enough of Patrice, the Millers and now Purdy. They'd soon found out about Wavell, her address and phone number were in the directory, and her attitude was, whoever talked to her nicest could have her story. It turned out to be Channel 4 News, which wanted an in-depth interview for its seven o'clock evening round-up. So, less than twenty-four hours after Shayler recruited Farrell, a reporter and film crew from London spent over an hour recording an interview in Wavell's living room. Yes, she said, oozing earnestness, she'd definitely noticed something strange about the Millers, it was the way they kept watching each other. She'd picked it up as soon as they got on the coach. She also explained how her photos had made the breakthrough and then, out of nowhere, came the rage.

"The police have been bossing me about ever since," she said, her eyebrows pulled high and her face taut with resentment. "They don't want me to let the media see my photos, but if they don't stay off my property, I'll do precisely that. I've still got them. The police can see them whenever they like, but they're not having them, not now."

The interview's producer liked that, it was so natural it was gold dust, and they'd definitely use it in the broadcast. Could they blend in some shots of her home, please, and say it was near Matlock? No place more natural than Matlock, Gina. Wavell was overjoyed.

"Say straight out it's in Matlock Bath," she said. "Matlock Bath's got more class."

Channel 4 trailed the interview towards the end of the afternoon, and Derbyshire Police contacted Snape in his office to tell him it was coming. No, they didn't know what she'd say, Channel 4 was keeping that to itself. Sensing trouble, Snape called Farrell in from his office and alerted van Piet, who took the call in his car.

"Call Derbyshire Police," van Piet came back while Farrell listened in, "and get her address from them. Tell them to surround Wavell's house if they haven't done it already, and send Sal Gulliver up to help. Give her a good driver, and make sure they've both got everything they need for night work. If they suspect any danger to Wavell, they can enter her house and grounds. I'll get a Crown Warrant issued as soon as I finish this call, it'll cover all of this case till it's over. Spell out to Derbyshire Sal's Crown warranted, and get it through their heads Wavell's safety is on the line. I'm tied up right now. I'll come in when I'm free."

Gulliver and her driver, Gubby Corbett, had 171 miles to cover to get to Matlock Bath. While Corbett was watching the road, Snape was briefing Gulliver with what he'd found out. It'd be pitch dark round where the house was, he warned. The street lamps didn't run that far, and there was woodland at the back. He explained about the warrant as well.

Valkov heard about the interview from the Embassy's Mediawatch unit, one floor down from his office. Also sensing trouble, he contacted Mike, and while the interview was running, he had Wavell's house located and maps of the area digitised. The minute it was over, he despatched Mike to Matlock Bath with orders to get sight of Wavell's photos. Mike had been at Saxley Castle when Bunting and Penderton had been there, and if Wavell had caught him on any of her photos and she let the media use them, someone might recognise him and say so to the police. If he had to, he could kill her. He had just fifty-three miles to drive and the weather was perfect. It was dry and completely still.

When Snape took a break, Farrell asked him what a Crown Warrant was. He wanted to get it right when he phoned Shayler. Snape put his cup down.

"It means, if we have to, we can invoke defence of the realm as our legal protection."

"I didn't know we were defending the realm."

"Willem thinks we are. He wouldn't ask for the warrant if he didn't."

Farrell looked at him sharply.

"This warrant changes things, doesn't it?"

"In what way?"

"Well, it's a Crown Warrant and Willem's a Crown officer. So he must be in charge from now on."

"We'll still do the policing, he's no good at that, but you're right – he's in charge from now on. It's been on the cards since we brought him in."

Farrell's expression changed again.

"Doesn't it bother you to lose first shout?" he asked.

He couldn't believe anyone would step down just like that. Snape couldn't see what the fuss was about.

"Not if I get the last one," he replied. To him it was obvious. "It's results that count."

Farrell felt total contempt for him. He'd always hated playing second fiddle, and soon, he thought with joy, he wouldn't have to ever again. Not with Shayler footing the bill.

Mike was dressed for the dark, and in a rucksack on his passenger seat he had night goggles, his scanner, a wallet with lockpicks in it, and a Colt Rail pistol modified to take a silencer. After three miles he reached Sutton Coldfield – it was just outside Birmingham – and made for a bottling plant car park he knew. When he wasn't serving Russia he was a self-employed electrician. It was good cover, and he could take time off as and when. About eight months earlier, one of his customers had been complaining that the bottling plant's car park should be in *The Guinness Book of Records*, the number of break-ins there'd been there. It wasn't fenced off, there were no security guards, there was no floodlighting, and no CCTV. The owner of the plant should be made to park there himself, then he'd know. Two nights later, Mike checked the car park out and filed it in his memory as 'Useful'.

The cars he was looking at now were the night shift's, and they wouldn't be needed till six the next morning. He parked his Renault in the middle, picked out a dark blue Mitsubishi, and opened it up with his scanner. The tank was three quarters full, it was plenty enough to get to Matlock Bath and back. When whoever it belonged to got in, they'd think someone had been joyriding, if they noticed at all.

Gulliver and Corbett made good time till they got to Northampton, where a crashed petrol tanker was causing a major tailback. Corbett swung onto the hard shoulder, but he had to drop his speed, and when they reached the crash site, he had to come to a standstill. The carriageway had been foamed, but the still air was dense with petrol vapour. A spark would set the lot off, so they had to wait till it thinned out. Gulliver radioed Snape they'd be late. Snape clenched his fist in frustration and said he'd pass the message on. It was all he could do.

When Mike got to Matlock Bath, he hid the Mitsubishi in an ungated field about a mile from the woodland, pulled his goggles and some gloves on, and set off into the dark. None of his maps had shown any footpaths through the trees, but one for 'Visitors to Derbyshire' had shown a picnic bay and car park in a clearing on the edge. It looked the sort of place the police might find a use for, so before he got there, he pulled a balaclava on and entered the woodland, treading carefully. The ground was soft from years of falling needles, but there were twigs and branches as well that could easily crack if he put a foot wrong. He'd been right about the police. In the greenish light of his goggles he saw a marked car drawn up in front of a picnic table. Standing next to it was a policeman holding a carbine across his chest. He was talking to the driver, who was still in the car, and a torch lay on the car roof. Mike needed to get round behind them and go on down the hillside. He ghosted stealthily from tree to tree, pausing behind each one. At one point the car was only six feet from him, and he froze totally when the driver got out to stamp his feet and stretch. As he moved on, the clearing was suddenly bathed in light – another car and crew were taking over. A minute or two earlier, and it would have had him in its headlights.

The slope gave him a general sense of direction, but he didn't want to risk arc-ing beyond Wavell's house, so every so often he lit up his wrist compass and stuck to what it told him. Eventually he came to a brook he was expecting, then the trees really thickened – he was almost to Wavell's garden wall. He slowed right down, afraid more police were scattered amongst the trees, and when he peered round the trunk of one of them, he saw, about eight paces away, an officer leaning back and staring into the darkness. She too had a torch as well as a carbine – which meant they didn't have night goggles. Moving as slowly as he could, he edged away till he could touch the wall's corner. He couldn't see anyone when he took a peek round, so he made the turn. Still no one. The wall was a good deal higher than he was tall, but he didn't mind that. He knew how to get over it.

Carefully he examined the limestone it was made of. The blocks were different sizes, and a lot of them were just slabs. They had their rustic charm, which was why Wavell had bought them, but to Mike they were handholds and footholds. He stepped back, took a good look at the broken glass, and picked his route. Then he took off the thick tunic he was wearing, put his rucksack back on, flipped his tunic over it with the sleeves tied loosely round his neck, and started to climb. When he was near the top, he used his feet and his left hand to steady himself while he undid the sleeves. Then he dragged his tunic onto the top of the wall and folded it to cover the glass. Holding his breath, he listened intently. No scuffling from a dog, no footfall. She really did keep the police out.

Protected from the glass, he cleared the top and lowered himself down the other side, where he put his tunic on again. The gradient was mostly grassed, and the ends of the terraces were firmed up with more limestone. Beyond them was a patio, the curtains were open, and through the glass door he could see Wavell. She was reading a paperback in an armchair; she must be in her living room. He wanted to corner her in her bedroom, so he lay down by the side of a shed and took in more of the house, especially the upstairs, while he waited.

From where he lay, the house was an oblong sideways on. The left-hand outside wall was straight from front to back, but at some point in the past the middle part of the right-hand wall had been built out to make an extension with what looked like a bedroom in the upper storey. A matching pair of upstairs windows in the main part of the oblong suggested another bedroom, then came windows with frosted glass in them.

They'd be a toilet and bathroom. So, he concluded, there must be a landing running from the bedroom door of the extension to the left-hand outside wall. The stairs would probably join it about half way along, and there'd be a front bedroom on either side of the staircase. He'd know for sure once he got inside.

Before long, Wavell left for another room, and when she put the light on, he could see it was the kitchen. She put a slice of fruit cake on a plate, boiled some milk to make cocoa – he could see the tin clearly – and took them back to her armchair on a tray. But instead of sitting down, she left the room again, and when she came back, she was carrying a saucer and wearing a quilted outdoor jacket. The saucer went over the cocoa to keep it hot, and she vanished yet again. She had to be going outside. Swiftly he moved towards the house, and he was standing in the darkness by the side of the extension when he heard not the front door, as he'd expected, but the kitchen door open. Creeping back, he watched the white beam of a high-powered torch scrutinise every part of the garden, including where he'd been lying. When she switched the torch off to go inside, the darkness was like a blanket descending. She could have been making a security check, but given what she'd said on TV, she could also have been looking for police. In that case, she'd come out of the front door as well.

Moving towards the house's front corner, he almost trod on a hinged cover made of worn wooden planks. It was let into the ground in the angle between the front wall of the extension and the right-hand outside wall. As he reached the house's front corner, the porch light came on and Wavell came out with her torch switched on. She played it over the rockery, then along the front hedge right into the corner, and when she was satisfied there was no one there, she strode down the drive to the road. While she undid the gate, Mike slipped round the back and tried the kitchen door. It had an old-fashioned lock and she hadn't turned the key. He went through the kitchen, took a quick look round the ground floor, then crept swiftly upstairs. The lay-out was as he'd worked it out, and it took him no time at all to locate her bedroom. It overlooked the road between the staircase and the extension. Moving on to the extension's door, he opened it and went in. It was a bedroom all right, and he could smell fresh paint in it. He found what he was looking for without any trouble and returned to the corridor. To his left, a door that was not quite shut gave into the rear bedroom, the one with the matching windows. It was still work in progress in there. The mattress on the bed was bare, there was an empty bookcase, the fireplace had yet to lose its Victorian grate and boxes were piled randomly on the floorboards. He pushed the door back to how he'd found it, sat down on a lumpy ottoman, and screwed the silencer onto his Colt. Suddenly he heard Wavell's voice, it was coming faintly from the road side of the house. Stealthily he opened the door right up and heard her more loudly. Then a car drove off. It must have been police. He didn't think they'd go very far, but she'd still be totally isolated. When she came in, he heard her lock the front door, then go through and lock the kitchen door. She thought she was safe.

She took her time over her cake and cocoa, and when at last she drew the curtains and came upstairs, she brought the book she'd been reading with her. Mike took his goggles off as the staircase light came on and sat stock still while she crossed his line of sight getting ready for bed. She didn't bother to shut her door, and as she pulled the covers back, he prepared to make his move. He didn't want her to put her light out and then on again in case the police were watching the curtains. But instead of reaching for the light switch once she got into bed, she bunched up the pillows and picked up her book again. He watched her get absorbed, and then he was ready. A floorboard creaked as he got to his feet. Startled, she looked up, and to her horror she saw a black-clad, masked figure emerging from across the landing, pointing a gun at her and holding an index finger to his lips. Before she could do anything, he said,

"If you scream, you're dead. This gun is silenced, no one will know it's happened. Now, put your book down slowly and rest both hands on the covers."

When she'd done that, he went on in the same even voice,

"I saw you on TV. You've got pictures of the Saxley Castle trip the Millers were on. Where are they?"

She wanted to resist, but she was afraid to. Fear was a new feeling for her. She didn't even dare ask who he was.

"They're in my smartphone and my laptop. I'm archiving in my laptop till I can buy a new printer."

"Why not in your computer?"

"I haven't got one. The laptop's enough."

"Where do you keep it? And your smartphone?"

"My laptop's next door in my study. My smartphone's downstairs. It's in the living room."

"We'll fetch them together and bring them back here. You're not to put any lights on or off. I'll be right behind you with this gun pointing at you. Put your dressing gown on. We'll start with the laptop."

There was enough indirect light from her bedroom dimly to light up her study. It was the other front bedroom, she'd converted it herself, and the curtains were drawn. Near her printer, which was unplugged and clearly defunct, was a framed photo of her father handing over the keys to the house. And in the middle of her desk was her laptop. They took it back to her bedroom.

"Show me the pictures," he said.

She'd set them in illuminated manuscript templates with captions in Old English lettering, and she'd made the passenger list look as if an eighteenth century clerk had drawn it up. He was partly pleased with what he saw. He was in two photos, but not near enough to Bunting and Penderton or to the Millers for the police to prove anything. But there were still the media to block off, so after Wavell had shut down her laptop, he put it in his rucksack. Erasing wasn't enough. He'd take the whole thing with him.

"We'll fetch the smartphone now," he said, emphasising his words with the Colt. "Don't try any tricks. You sent the police away, not me."

He took a pencil torch out of an inside pocket and followed her down to the ground floor. The front door was solid wood. It had no panes of glass for any light to show through.

As Wavell and Crane reached the bottom stair, Gulliver and Corbett drew up in front of a police cordon hidden from the house by a bend. May Docherty was in charge again – she had a good record in Derbyshire for being a safe pair of hands. Police cars were parked on both sides of the road, and an ambulance was occupying its own coned-off space. People living nearby had been ordered, mostly by phone, to stay indoors and keep away from the windows. They'd kept their lights out as instructed, but they'd moved chairs upstairs, and the couple living opposite Wavell were sitting in the conservatory on the side of the house.

"I've got four armed officers on this side of where she lives," Docherty said in a voice scarcely above a whisper as she and Gulliver walked by the light of Docherty's pointed-down torch towards Wavell's house. "I've got four more on the far side and six in the woodland at the back."

Gulliver was clipping on the radio Docherty had lent her.

"Wavell's still being awkward, is she?" she asked, also keeping her voice right down.

"We've just found it out yet again. That's why we're keeping our distance. At the moment we think she's reading in bed. Her light's been on for some time, and we're sure no one's in there with her."

Gulliver wasn't convinced; it all looked as leaky as a sieve. Derbyshire was one of the most peaceful counties in England and, she figured, Docherty was out of her depth but didn't know it. The torch alone was a bad sign, and the police weren't deployed right.

"These other houses, they've still got people in them," Gulliver whispered as Docherty switched her torch off. They'd almost reached Wavell's drive. "Why aren't they evacuated?"

"I had to make a judgement. We've got Wavell's house under guard. In my view that's enough."

"That we'll find out."

Using her goggles, Gulliver took the best look she could all round then, with her free hand cupped over her own radio, she contacted Corbett, who had stayed in the car.

"Quickly, Gubby. Bring the bag and do the front door. I'll go in first. You take the left side, I'll take the right, and give me cover on the stairs. There's a light on up there, it's the only one."

As Corbett padded silently down the road, she unholstered her Glock semi-automatic and loaded it.

"If we think there's imminent danger to life," she whispered to Docherty as Corbett hustled past, "we go in fast and create surprise. Otherwise we take our time."

"And you think there's imminent danger to life, do you?"

"I can't rule it out. Gubby's sticking explosives to the front door right now. When I give the word, he'll detonate them, and they'll blow the door in. As soon as that happens, I go in followed by Gubby. I want you to cover the exits. Send two of your people round the back, and bring two up the drive as soon as we make our move. Put the rest on alert. And tell everyone to restrain but not to shoot."

"Why not? They're well trained."

"I can't risk it. It's so dark here, they'd be shooting each other. Have any of them got night goggles?"

"No, but they've all got torches."

Gulliver groaned inwardly.

"I guess they'll have to do then. We go now."

She waited for Docherty to talk to her people and move clear. Then,

"Ready, Gubby?"

He nodded. He'd come down the drive to her and was loading his pistol.

"Take the door out."

Inside the house, Wavell's smartphone was lying on her living room sideboard and, with Mike right behind her, they took it upstairs. She found the Saxley Castle photos and took him through them. It didn't take her long, they were exactly the same as the ones in her archive. She wondered what would happen now there was nothing left to do. Mike was looking at her strangely, and it terrified her. If she'd known how close the police were, she'd have risked running downstairs and screaming. But she thought they'd be keeping their distance after what she'd said. And she couldn't just run outside, she'd locked the front door.

Mike had decided to kill her some time ago – she had his voice in her ears and she'd seen the way he moved. He also might have said something that would give him away. So as he tucked Wavell's smartphone into his rucksack, he secretly stiffened his hand, brought it out without warning, and crashed it edge-on into her windpipe. As she staggered back, he rammed her head against the wall, intending to crush her throat by stamping on it when she fell to the floor. At that moment, by the front gate, Corbett pressed the red button on a matchbox-sized detonator. A fractional delay let him and Gulliver get their fingers into their ears, then with an enormous bang, the door leaped off its hinges and slammed into the hallway.

Whipping their goggles on, they were through the smoke and into the house straight away. They cleared the downstairs rooms super-fast with all the lights kept off. They didn't want to be silhouetted in a doorway. Upstairs, Mike scrambled his own goggles on, swung his rucksack onto his back, and jabbed the light out. Then he grasped Wavell's shoulders and yanked her out of the room onto the landing, where whoever came up the stairs would have to see her, if they could see anything at all. She'd just missed being stamped on, but her throat was swelling at a rate of knots and very soon she'd suffocate. Cautiously Gulliver crept up the stairs, her pistol ready to fire. Corbett was half hidden at the bottom, his pistol also unsafed. When Gulliver got to the top, she looked left first. She saw Wavell on the landing looking as damaged as she was, and the door to the extension bedroom shutting. Rapidly she turned her gaze to her right. She couldn't see anyone, but there were three doors, and someone could be behind any of them.

"Gubby! Up here!" she called.

He crowded in behind her.

"Cover me while I clear the rooms to the right. Keep an eye on the other way as well. Someone went through the door at the end of the landing."

It didn't take her long – the three rooms were empty. She rejoined Corbett on the top stairs.

"Wavell looks grim, but it could be an ambush."

She felt guilty about not going to her, but getting trapped wasn't an option.

"Keep your pistol pointing towards that end door while I clear the room she's come from and the one opposite. Watch out for a sudden charge and mind me if you have to shoot. When I've done, move up to me, and we'll see who's in the end room. Then we'll call May and get Wavell seen to. Let's go."

When Mike went into the extension he headed straight for a second door in the left-hand corner of the far end wall. It was what he'd expected to find when he'd gone in there the first time, the hinged wooden cover outside had virtually shouted it out. He'd done the electrics in several houses like Wavell's. Their Victorian owners built them out as they moved up the social scale, and when that happened the maid had to lug the coal up a back staircase in the extension from the cellar rather than up the main staircase. The coal chute from outside into the cellar nearly always had a wooden cover, and while Wavell had modernised the bedroom in the extension, the rear bedroom with the matching windows still had its nineteenth century grate. To Mike it was all familiar territory.

The staircase behind the second door was narrow, dusty and dark. There were a couple of roundel windows in the outside wall, but there was no light outside for them to let in. The trapdoor at the bottom was unlocked, and when Mike heaved it open, switching his pencil torch on to help him see, he had steps into the cellar in front of him. There was no chute and no coal in there now, just red brick where the damp had got into the plaster, plus a snow shovel, a bag of sand, a pair of aluminium steps and a broom that had seen better days. The wooden cover was padlocked but, standing on the pair of steps with his torch in his mouth, he had it unlocked in seconds with his picks. Then he listened hard. No one was following him down the staircase, he'd have heard them on the bare wood. Very gently, he pushed upwards against the cover and felt it give. He had no idea whether anyone was up there or whether, despite the gobbets of grease on the hinges, it would squeak. All he knew was that the hinges were in front of him so he'd be able to lay it flat to get out. He pushed it completely open, and still nothing happened, so he risked a glance round. An armed man in body armour was standing with his back to him by the front corner of the house. He had to be police. To his right, however, there was only the extension wall jutting out. That meant he could get out without being seen unless the person by the corner turned round or someone approached from the back. All he had to do was do it and get clear when he could.

When Gulliver and Corbett burst into the extension, they threw the bed over and ripped the wardrobe open, but only when they tried the second door did they figure out how Mike had vanished. If Wavell hadn't been hurt, they'd have followed him down the stairs, but she'd looked nearly gone when they'd forced themselves to step over her, so they hurried back to her.

"Lights on!" Gulliver ordered, frustrated, and while Corbett worked the switches at speed, she radioed for the ambulance and told Docherty how Wavell's assailant – "We think there's one only, gender uncertain" – had likely got out of the house. Corbett escorted the ambulance crew over the wrecked front door and, standing ready to shoot, he and Gulliver covered them while they kept Wavell alive by feeding a tube down her throat. Outside, Docherty ordered the policeman on the corner of the house to watch the ambulance closely. Whoever had been after Wavell might have one last go while she was being stretchered out. Mike saw his attention shift, and it was all he needed. Softly he worked his way along the base of the side hedge. The light from the extension scarcely touched him, and the ambulance's lights made the darkness darker still. He passed the policeman within seven feet of him, the other officer on the drive being also focused on the ambulance; and when it pulled away with a warning blast on its siren, Crane was on his way towards the corner where the side and the front hedge met. When Wavell had shone her torch there, he'd seen a low gap – it looked like a fox run – between her front garden and her neighbours'. It would do.

As soon as they could, Gulliver and Corbett hurried down into the cellar and climbed out as Mike had done, hoping to get a hint which way he'd gone. But it was futile – just guesswork in the dark – so, shedding optimism fast, Gulliver got back to Docherty.

"Has anyone seen anything, May?"

"Not yet, and I'm getting a build-up of ghouls round the cordons. Word's getting round and the media are here as well. I've talked to Matlock, but at the moment we're under pressure."

"May, there's a potential murderer on the loose. Whatever happens, that person is your absolute priority. You can use your torches if it helps."

Gulliver knew by now it was hopeless. As the torches came on, they showed Mike better where the police were, but not much else. Entirely unnoticed he slithered through the fox run just as Docherty was tightening the ring round the house. Thanks to his goggles, he got back to the Mitsubishi without any hold-ups, and when he reached Witton, he reported he'd brought all Wavell's pictures with him on her hardware. So far as he knew, no one had seen him or his car, and he'd been masked all the time he'd been with Wavell. The only thing was, she'd heard him speak and seen him move. He'd get rid of the laptop and smartphone as soon as he could do it safely. He'd hide them in his house till then.

Gulliver, too, reported in, and Snape took the message. Farrell was still with him, and by this time so was van Piet.

"Whoever it was, we've lost them," Gulliver said neutrally. "Wavell's in Buxton Special Care. The word is she'll live, but she won't be talking for a while. We'll hope she doesn't go the same way Miller did."

"Mr Farrell will take care of that," Snape said. "I'll ask him to have NCA people put in."

"What do we do now?"

Before Snape could answer, van Piet signalled he wanted to take over.

"Can you get back straight away, Sal?" he asked.

"If we share the driving we can."

"Do it then. Armed Support's on standby as of now, and that includes you and Gubby. Before you leave, search the house for Miss Wavell's laptop and smartphone. If they're there, bring them back with you. If they're not, we need to know."

He terminated and stood up.

"Sorry to push in, Eddie," he said, "but it was a priority call. Get the word to Armed Support fast. I still don't know everything, but I know enough. From now on we take the fight to the enemy."

The air in Snape's office was stale, so Snape opened a window while they put things straight. Farrell went as soon as he could. He hadn't had a chance to phone Shayler, but he'd put that right before she left for work. Snape and van Piet went out to the car park together, their coats done up against the early morning chill. They walked slowly and van Piet did most of the talking. He'd had a busy night.

"So you found time to talk to Burney's Site Controller, did you?" Snape said, stifling a yawn. "What name did you give yourself?"

"I didn't, I asked MI5 to broker the call. They checked her out and they think we can trust her. She confirmed the celebrating will be on the main rig only, starting at eleven o'clock at night, and Russell Burney's parking his father in the dark so he can make a spectacular entrance. But we have to know a lot more than that now, so I want Sal and Gubby on Teesside as soon as we know who else is going to be there. Mrs Tilman's on standby for the contact. Their cover will be Health and Safety."

He glanced round instinctively, but there wasn't a soul about.

"I got some big information from GCHQ, too. Russian state television finalised image rights from CDB-Media on Monday just gone, and the grand event will be shown all over the Motherland in real time or recorded, depending on the time zones. It's the breakthrough we needed, Eddie. Whatever we do from now on, that info will be key."

He talked a while longer, and as Snape unlocked his car, he felt for the first time since he'd taken this case there could just be light beyond the next hill. Van Piet walked on towards his own car, and his feelings were more mixed. He had no illusions about the people he was up against, they couldn't be stopped soon enough. But he knew it wouldn't be easy.

Chapter 26

A Letter to the Police

Mike was back in Witton, Wavell was in Special Care, and, later the same morning, at nine forty-two, Reception at Klemmsley Marine called up to Russell Burney to say Mr Hallavy hadn't logged in. He wasn't answering his landline or his mobile. Should they send someone round?

"I'll go myself," Burney said quickly. "He might be ill or something. I'll go right now."

He was frightened straight away. Did Hallavy know more than he'd let on? And had someone found that out?

Hallavy lived in a 1920s half-timbered house near Essex Cricket Ground. The Members' Stand was his home from home, and out of season he played host to past and present heroes till late into the night. But there was no sign of cheer when Burney parted the ivy and rang his doorbell. The house sounded empty, and when no one answered after the second try, he walked all round, peering through the windows and the French doors: Nothing. Either Hallavy wasn't there, or something was very wrong. Burney walked across to the garage. It was locked but it had a dusty side window and, standing on a rubbish bin, he could peer through it. Hallavy's car was gone.

Burney's first thought was to call the police, but he had such a terror of them, he called Shayler instead. She was in CDB Tower sourly compiling data for the sell-off. She kept telling herself it wasn't going to happen, it was what she had to believe, but suddenly Russell Burney was on the phone saying Hallavy had disappeared. That had to be bad news. Or did it? Hallavy had his tsunami papers in his safe, that's where he'd said he'd put them, and if the police got their hands on them, they might find out about the tsunami she absolutely didn't want to happen. Killing Cyril Burney was what mattered, Russell didn't need a tsunami for that. But what if the police found Hallavy, and he said he'd been to see her about the tsunami? Well, let him, she'd deny it to his face. It would be easy enough. He'd put a lot of effort into keeping his visit secret.

"You've got no choice, you have to call the police," she said briskly, her hopes rising. "If you just drive off, everyone will ask why. Call them right now, and don't say you spoke to me first."

He put a call through on Snape's direct number.

"Stay where you are," Snape replied. "I'm on my way. I'll get an ambulance there as well."

He didn't take long. Wan and tired from an early start, he drew up with a CID sergeant from the Ops Room, and she had the front lock picked before the ambulance arrived. Then came a Forensics van and a minibus full of police who'd been hastily dragged off other duties. Hallavy's burglar alarm came on when the sergeant opened the door, so someone must have set it who knew the code, but she soon had it silent again. Across the road, faces were appearing at windows, and by the time the drive was sealed off, several passers-by had stopped to watch. Some were taking photos on their mobiles, others were phoning local radio, the *Essex Chronicle* or the *Chelmsford Weekly News*. Snape asked Burney to wait in his car. He'd send for him as soon as he had something to tell him.

He went through the whole house with the sergeant, and there was clearly no one there. The garage, the shed, the greenhouse and the summer house all got the same treatment. The sergeant opened the safe, but all it contained was a small sum of money, the deeds to the house and some personal documents. On the dining room table was an envelope addressed by hand to 'Essex Police'. Forensics had better have first look, Snape said, and had it rushed back to police HQ along with some samples of Hallavy's handwriting – he kept longhand diaries of every match and signed them off on the last day of play. Klemmsley Marine's Reception told Snape Hallavy had left towards the end of the afternoon the previous day. It was his usual time. Snape radioed for Burney, and standing in the hall under a portrait of W.G. Grace, he told him Hallavy was gone, so was his car, and there was no sign of foul play. They'd found a letter addressed to the police, and it was up to the scientists what happened next. Burney could go back to work, but he'd probably be wanted for questioning later.

"The media will be after you, so keep your mobile switched off," Snape added. "And tell your Reception to intercept all calls. One will be from me about the letter, so don't cut yourself off completely."

The police got Burney through the ruck that had gathered outside, and before he was back in Klemmsley Marine, the media were whooping up another disappearance, this time of the chief scientist of oil and gas magnate Russell Burney. And Russell Burney, they fell over themselves to add, was the son of billionaire entrepreneur Cyril Burney. Dvorski caught it on his car radio while he was driving to a trade meeting in Brighton. He pulled over to contact Valkov.

"What do you think, Andrey Ivanovich?" he asked timorously. Harvest Home mustn't be scrapped, his whole future depended on it.

The Hallavy business had caught Valkov by surprise, but he still knew what his answer should be. He'd rehearsed it with Zembarov minutes before.

"Hallavy can't be irreplaceable, not at this late stage," he replied airily. "So my judgement is, as long as the media don't find out Patrice was Burney's broker, we go ahead as planned. And make sure you get an invitation for September 22nd. We definitely want you there."

"Shall I stay away from Burney till then?" Dvorski asked with a mixture of joy and relief.

"That would be a very bad idea, we don't want him getting a sense of freedom. It's quite possible he'll call you first, in fact, to find out where we stand. If he doesn't, call him yourself and keep him in line."

"You can trust me on that – and thanks for backing me up."

Snape left Hallavy's house as soon as he could and headed for police HQ. Van Piet and Farrell were in Farrell's office talking to Gulliver who, also looking drained, had just reported in. Snape got some tea from the Ops Room and joined them.

"Hallavy's gone all right," he said, before anyone could ask, "and so's his car. He must have gone sometime after he left work yesterday afternoon, and it looks as if he gave it some thought."

He told them about the letter and asked Farrell to ring Forensics to see how far they'd got.

"They've opened it," Farrell said, putting the phone down, "and they've e-mailed you a copy. No one is saying it isn't what it looks like, and the graphologist is happy, too."

Snape asked van Piet to shut the door.

"Let's see what he wants us to know then."

He opened up the in-house e-mail system on Farrell's computer, put his own code in, and there it was in an attachment, all neatly hand-written:

'Dear Essex Police – I was never cut out for the Number One job, and I can't carry on any longer, it's all too much for me. I'm going where no one can find me till I can see my way forward. Please show this letter to Mr Russell Burney with my apologies. I have gone of my own free will.'

It was signed 'S. N. Hallavy' and dated Tuesday, August 28th.

"You were right about when he went," Farrell said ingratiatingly to Snape. "What do we do now?"

"I don't see what we can do unless Forensics has a rethink. There's nothing to stop an adult male downing tools if his job's too much for him. It wouldn't be the first time."

"But someone might have forced him to write that letter. They wouldn't have had to be in the house to do it."

Snape took out his mobile and called Klemmsley Marine. When he had Burney, he said,

"We've opened the letter we found. Can you come over to police HQ straight away? Ask for Mr Farrell's office."

Burney was wound up tight – his father had been on the phone to him and it hadn't been pleasant. He'd been watching the news, and he'd insisted on being told what was going on. When Burney said he didn't know, his father laid into him.

"You don't know what your own staff are up to? You're not fit to make the tea, let alone run a major concern. And what about the Burney name? You're making it a laughing stock. Your mother's upset, too. She keeps making excuses for you, as if that helped. Get this one sorted out fast or you're finished in oil and gas. No one deals with clowns, Russell. All they get is laughed at."

Burney desperately wanted him to stop, but he wouldn't. He went on and on relentlessly, and then he terminated the call before Burney could get a word in back. That left him white hot with resentment but also angry with himself for feeling that way. On top of that, he was worried how Dvorski and Valkov were reacting. They might pull the plug on him now he was bad news. He was on the point of trying for Dvorski on his business number when Snape's call came through, and he gave it priority. He gabbled where he was going as he hustled past Reception, and he would have sprinted to his car, except he didn't want anyone to think he'd lost control.

Snape had printed the attachment off for him to see. He took the date in first.

"He was on site all day yesterday, I've checked the log. I spoke to him myself first thing."

"So we come back to after he left work," Snape said. "Can you confirm this is his handwriting?"

"No question. I'd know it anywhere."

"Now, Mr Hallavy's an important figure in the oil and gas industry, Mr Burney, and I know as well as you do, people like that are expected to put little tricks into their handwriting or use certain phrases if they're writing under duress. Is there anything like that in this letter?"

Burney read it again.

"No, nothing at all. It's all as it should be."

"So he's run away, just as he says. You realise I can't take action against that."

Burney nodded, he didn't know how else to react. But his father was a different matter. After the onslaught he'd had from him, he knew exactly what to do. Snape looked round the room, his eyebrows raised. No one was inclined to argue, so he put the print-out to one side, thanked Burney for his help, and had him shown out. Then it was back to business. Gulliver left to write her report, and van Piet tagged along, saying he wanted to talk one or two things over with her. Snape asked Farrell to ring Buxton Special Care about Wavell.

"Find out how soon she can answer questions," he said, getting up. "I'll be in my office. Let me know how it goes."

He was feeling it was about lunchtime, so he phoned down for some rolls and a pot of tea for when the trolley came round. No hurry, he said, he had some paperwork to be getting on with. He was making good progress when a call came in from Radio Essex about Hallavy.

"No, we're not treating it as suspicious," he said. "Mr Hallavy seems to have had a breakdown, that's all. Unfortunate, but there we are."

As he put the phone down, there was a knock at the door. It was van Piet.

"Something for you to know," he said as he came in. "Tom left Brize Norton first thing this morning for RAF Akrotiri in Cyprus. He should be in Nicosia by now, going through Russian property investments. I've asked the British High Commissioner to lend a hand."

"What's Tom doing that for?"

Van Piet counted the points off.

"One, there are a lot of Russians in Cyprus and they're mostly very rich. Two, 1·5 million euros invested in property buys you Cypriot citizenship, likewise if you found a firm. Three, you can travel anywhere in the EU on a Cypriot passport, including to this country. Four, Toni Aubrey turned up in a clinic owned by a former Russian, now a Cypriot, at the same time as Russell Burney. Five, Tom's taken Aubrey's photo with him. If there's a connection in all this, he'll find it."

He paused while Catering wheeled in its trolley. It reminded him he was hungry - he'd also started early - so he helped himself to a baguette and some spare tea things. As the trolley was being pushed out, Farrell appeared in the doorway.

"Good news, Eddie. Wavell can be interviewed as soon as tomorrow if we do the talking and she just nods or shakes her head. She may be able to write a bit as well."

"Can you take this on, Leo?" van Piet asked him. "It would help a lot."

"I don't see why not. I'll go up tomorrow and be back by the day after."

"Couldn't be better. Two more things. Sal says Miss Wavell's laptop and smartphone weren't anywhere in the house. Ask her if she uses tracker apps. And make sure you get her e-mail address."

Her attacker was plainly clever, but there was a chance he'd been too clever.

"You can take a car from the pool," Snape added.

"Thanks but no, Eddie. I'll use my own for once."

It was a lovingly pampered Morris Minor 1000. His father had left it to him. Now it was a trophy from his divorce.

"I've just had it re-tuned. I want to see how it runs."

It was true. He also didn't want anyone tracking his route.

"I'll get off home early if that's all right," he went on. "I'll need to think through what to say, if I'm doing all the talking."

As soon as he'd gone, van Piet asked Snape for Farrell's Chelmsford address and the Morris's details. Snape knew the address without looking it up, and the Morris's details were in Farrell's personnel file. Van Piet used his mobile to call the

SRO's heliport on London's Isle of Dogs, across the Thames from Greenwich.

"He's using his own car," he phoned through. "It's an almond-green Morris Minor 1000 and he parks it outside his flat. I want it tracked from now till he gets back to Chelmsford, it should be the day after tomorrow sometime. Yes, I know it's a long assignment. I'll get some cars to help out if I can. Someone will be in touch."

"What'll you do if Farrell really does do something wrong, now we've given him the chance to?" Snape asked him when he terminated.

"That depends on what it is. The leak GCHQ caught this morning was the first one it's picked up, so we're still feeling our way. To be honest, I'm as much interested in Shayler as in Farrell. She's been out of sight till now. That's not on any more."

Snape drained the teapot, and they cleared their litter away.

"Speaking of GCHQ," van Piet went on, "we're getting input on another front as well. The people we're up against have to communicate, and I'd been wondering how they do it. Bunting and Penderton gave me a helping hand, and I followed it up Monday with Tom. These dear ladies keep their computer on sleep, but with the speakers on unless there's a reason for turning them off, like having Inspector Blaker about the place. When instructions come through, they get a message in their in-box with a picture attached that they might get anyway – like a castle, or something to do with their school – and the speakers sound a special alert. The message is a decoy, it's the picture that matters, because the instructions are encoded and dispersed amongst the pixels. All it takes is the right software, which they've got, and they can read them off. They can send messages back as well."

"And GCHQ is tracing the network."

"It's trying to. It'll take time, and these people must have other ways of communicating. But we could still get some interesting finds."

As soon as Farrell got home, he put his questions together – it was the sort of thing he was good at – and packed a suitcase. By the time he'd finished, he reckoned Shayler would be heading back to The Wool-Staple, so he got into his car and headed for Sunningdale. She didn't know he was coming, but if she had someone with her, he'd say he was on police business. What he wanted, however, was to be in her house soaking up the luxury. It had been nagging him since he got up. They could try for some sex as well, she might find it easier this time. And he had a whole lot to tell her whenever she wanted to listen.

Zembarov had guessed right about Hallavy's being replaceable. As soon as Russell Burney got back to Klemmsley Marine, he asked Hallavy's Second-in-charge, Marianne Halter, to take over and see Harvest Home through to the big day. She'd worked closely with Hallavy, the project seemed to be running on tramlines, and the money on offer had a charm of its own, so saying yes didn't strain her, and action-man Burney e-mailed the board to tell them what he'd done. Then he called his father, and that wasn't so easy. Doing his best to sound relaxed, he said everything was under control, Hallavy was just a blip, and could he talk to him and Enid about September 22nd, please? It had to be soon, time was slipping away, and he wanted to tell Cyril about the starring role he was arranging for him. Cyril was in a good mood for him – he'd just had some upbeat news about the sale – so he said he and Enid would be in London for the next few days. If Russell cared to call by, his mother would be glad to see him.

Burney's final call was to Aubrey. His battery was getting low, so he used the landline. She answered straight away, and to his relief she sounded sober. He said he'd be home a lot later than planned, and to help her he gave her an approximate time. It'd been that kind of day, he explained, and he still had an errand to run. She'd better eat without him, he'd do something for himself when he got back. He kept his goodbyes proper in case Reception was listening in and terminated. Ashell House *was* listening in, and a tail in a lay-by near Klemmsley Marine got a heads-up. It should have been a three car operation but, as Valkov had said to Dvorski years ago, the British were chronically strapped for funds, so one car had to do.

Rigid with determination, Burney drove to Theydon Bois underground station, between Epping and Debden on the Central Line. He was going to take the tube to Tottenham Court Road. Theydon Bois wasn't a station he knew well – he just remembered the parking was good – and his mind was fixed on what he'd do when he got into London, so he went to the wrong platform. It wasn't till he was standing in the train that he realised what he'd done, and just as the doors were closing, he squeezed out, leaving his tail, who was further down the carriage, trapped and helpless.

From Tottenham Court Road he walked to Wardour Street, and he kept going till he came to a peeling black-painted door with no names on it. It was between a casting agency and a sheet music wholesaler. The door buzzed when he pressed in his personal code, he pushed it open, and stepped into a dimly lit passage smelling of damp. A door to his right needed another code, and then he was going up a flight of stairs to the first floor. People must have lived there once, it still had that look about it, but the rooms were offices now, and one of them had 'Henry Seeler' pinned to the door on a piece of card. Burney knocked and went in. His father had asked for trouble. Now he'd get it.

Seeler was a commercial hacker. He was in his late twenties, and whoever paid him had his loyalty till the pay-off arrived on the Caribbean island of Nevis. Burney had used him before to test his data systems, and he wanted to use him now. He helped himself to some notepaper and drew a sketch of Dassett Point.

"It's another routine check, Henry," he said, trying to look unconcerned. "At ten twenty-five precisely on the night of September 22nd I want you to try to unplug these four boreholes all at the same time. The timing's part of the test. You've got to get it right."

He hesitated, then recalled Seeler had no sense of right and wrong, only of good hacks and bad ones.

"If you get through," he went on, looking distinctly shifty now despite himself, "you may cause a ship to sink. Don't re-plug the boreholes till it's on the bottom. There'll be a great hoo-hah of course, and the police will get involved, but they mustn't get back to me on any account. Or to you, come to that."

Seeler didn't blink.

"Not a problem, Russell. I'll globalise."

"Thanks, Henry, that's perfect. Make it look like a random hack, and too bad about the ship, it just happened to be there. Do you want any of the codes?"

"I can't think why. If it's got to look like a hack, a hack it has to be."

Burney was still full of anger as he walked back to Tottenham Court Road, but it was stabilised now he'd done something and, catching him unawares, his guilt feelings welled up past it – guilt about his father and also guilt about the tsunami. That made him want to go to Shayler's to talk things over, but he still believed she didn't know about the tsunami, and he wasn't going to alter that, so he switched his attention to his mother. She was loving to a fault, and she'd been more helpful than he'd expected about his debts, but he could scarcely talk to her about murdering his father, let alone millions of strangers. That left Aubrey, and he realised she'd been top of his list all the while and anyway, he'd given her a time he'd be home by. He couldn't talk murder with her any more than he could with his mother, but in his beaten up state, just to be with her would be enough. More than anything else – it was clear to him now – he simply wanted to go home.

Thinking about Aubrey made him smile with love, and the warmth she caused in him was still with him when he finally garaged his Morgan and went to unlock his front door. He was hungry as well. He'd put together something quick to eat, they'd sit at the table together, and she could tell him about her day. An envelope under a stone on the outside mat caught his eye. It had his name on it, so he opened it where he stood. It was from the owner of Stanmore's off-licence and general store. Burney hadn't bought any alcohol since he'd been to De Macey, but he still bought plenty of other things there.

'Dear Mr Burney,' he read. 'Miss Aubrey came in just before we closed. She wanted to buy some gin on your account. I let her have three bottles, but I don't think I should have now, because you've never said she could use it. If I've made a mistake, please let me know, and there'll be no charge. Yours truly, Cosmo Healey.'

Three bottles. He guessed what he'd find when he got inside, and he was right. She was flat out on the living room carpet, there was vomit in the hearth, and an empty bottle – but no glass or mix – lay next to her. Her dress was sodden with gin as well as urine. She must have drunk the bottle straight out. Another empty bottle stood on the coffee table, but he couldn't see the third one. He'd have to find it.

Dismayed beyond endurance, he got her upstairs, cleaned her up, and put her to bed. It looked from her vomit as if she'd had something to eat, so maybe she'd held back from drinking as long as she could again. He had to blame himself. If he'd been home on time, he could have stopped her, and they'd have had a happy evening together. Wearily he cleaned the hearth and e-mailed Healey to say he'd pay for the gin, but he didn't want Miss Aubrey to use his account again. He'd thank him personally for his note when he was next in the shop. He was shutting his computer down when his mobile chimed. It was Dvorski saying he wanted to know how the Hallavy business was going. Burney had trouble hearing him, his battery had just about had it, so he kept his answers brief, but yes, Hallavy seemed to have had a breakdown and the police were leaving it there. How did Dvorski see September 22nd?

"It can go ahead without Hallavy, can it?"

"Of course. I've replaced him already."

"Then we don't see any problem. Do I get an invitation?"

"I'll see to it personally. Regard it as on its way."

After Dvorski terminated, Burney plugged in his mobile, heated up a pizza, and sat down to wait for the ten o'clock news. He had to finalise things with Tilman soonest, that couldn't be allowed to drag on any longer, and then there was that third bottle of gin. He daren't leave the house till he'd found it. He had a bit of time, so he put his pizza down and started searching. It didn't take him long. It was in a press on Aubrey's side of the bed under some of the lightweight woollens she looked so lovely in. In case he missed her the next day, he put a note together for her and placed it on the breakfast table.

'Darling,' he wrote, 'I should have come home earlier, I can see that now. Cosmo Healey has told me you took three bottles with you. I've found the third one and emptied it out. Don't be angry, but I've told Cosmo not to let you use my account again. I'm still fighting for both of us, you especially. I won't give up, because I know we'll win. My love forever, Russell. XXXXXXX.'

Hallavy had slipped to third spot on the ten o'clock news. Snape, explaining how stress can get to people, was at his seen-it-all best, and a market analyst said Harvest Home was still on course for a multi-billion pound pay-out. End of report. Burney's pizza was cold, but he finished it anyway, and when the news ended, he found a bar of chocolate and ate it as well. He felt less tense now the Hallavy story was fading. He was certain his father had watched the news. He'd listen to the market analyst, even if he wouldn't listen to his own son.

Over in Sunningdale, Shayler had put some of her clothes back on to watch the same news broadcast, and she wasn't nearly so relieved. Farrell hadn't said anything about tsunami documents to her, so she had to assume the police hadn't found any, and she'd be nervous till she knew where they were. And where Hallavy was as well. But she'd still go ahead as planned, she was as vengeful as ever, and she was desperate to secure her future. Farrell was lounging next to her, his trousers undone and drinking Glenlivet. He noticed she was tense. He thought it was because they were going to try some more foreplay before they went to bed. He wouldn't be upset if she gave it a miss, it was like stroking bricks getting life out of her. He didn't know that, when she took her clothes off, all the self-hatred of her red-blotch years spontaneously flooded back.

And if, despite that, she were to tell him she was unbelievably happy because she had a boyfriend at last, he'd laugh out loud.

Chapter 27

Aubrey Breaks Cover

The next morning Farrell was up and finding where everything was before Shayler so much as stirred. His head felt thick and his eyes were gummy, but he was still too much of a policeman to hang about when he had a job to do. Everything he touched – the soap, the taps, the towels, the fittings – felt pricey. Just handling them told him he'd seen himself right. When Shayler got up, she had a big smile on her face, and instead of slotting into work mode, she fussed round Farrell till he was ready to go. It made her late, but early appointments weren't her style, so when she got in, she said she'd been clearing her e-mails, and it was good enough.

Farrell was put through three identity checks before he was allowed to see Wavell, and two armed NCA officers stayed in the closed ward all the while he was there. A pile of pillows propped her up, and a nurse who had had the Official Secrets Act spelled out to her sat by her bedside while Farrell put his questions. They were mostly yes or no, so all she had to do was nod or shake her head. He found out her attacker was male, about five foot ten tall, fit looking when he walked, and he had a Birmingham accent. When they got to her smartphone, she confirmed the pictures on it and on her laptop were the same, and that her attacker had taken her hardware with him. No, she didn't use tracker apps and, dragging her hand as if it didn't belong to her, she scrawled out her e-mail address. She was fading fast by now, and the nurse was signalling it was time for Farrell to go. Desperately Wavell moved her hand in the air

– she wanted to write something else. Farrell gave her a fresh page in his notebook and lent her his biro again.

"Don't leave on own," she wrote, fighting for every letter. "He'll kill next time."

"You won't be on your own till he's caught," Farrell replied with the grandeur that went with feeling life was good. "And that will be soon, I promise."

He phoned what he'd learned back to Chelmsford and said he'd call on May Docherty before he left Derbyshire to make sure she didn't foul anything else up. That and a well-deserved lunch, he calculated, would soak up most of the rest of the day. He also said he'd overnight on the road. That meant back at Shayler's. He'd hinted as much to her before he left, and she hadn't said no.

Van Piet started the day by waving his family goodbye. Célestine had time off from her classes, so she was taking Jackie to Madame Tussaud's. They also had some shopping planned. It was August 30th already, the new school term was heaving into view, and Jackie was growing fast. Growing up as well. They left van Piet with a chores list, and the cleaners were coming in for the morning, but he was hoping to take some calls as well. No one complained when he kept disappearing upstairs, but it wasn't the best thing for family life.

He began by re-reading the report Anke Sweelinck had sent him. Patrice had manipulated Burney all right, but what intrigued van Piet was when the crash had started. Then he tackled the chores list till Snape called him with Farrell's news about Wavell. The Shayler stop-over he knew about, it was what he'd half-expected and it didn't interest him much, but Wavell's handle on her attacker did, and so did her e-mail address. So, with his study door locked, even though the cleaners were nowhere near, he put a coded call through to a windowless second floor office in GCHQ. It was where he and Garry had been Monday, sorting out how Bunting and Penderton communicated. There was the usual pause and then he was through.

"Kossler."

"Ian, it's Willem."

He told him about Wavell's laptop and smartphone. No tracker apps, he said, but he had her e-mail address.

"The laptop and smartphone will almost certainly be switched off," he went on, "but I still want you to find out where they are. When you've done that, go into them and search all the pictures. You're looking for a set from Saxley Castle in Derbyshire, and they're dated April 9th. Send them and anything else that looks relevant to my computer at Gorris and call me on my mobile when you're done."

"Will do. Switched off's a relative concept, Willem. It should go fairly fast."

By this time van Piet was wondering about something to eat, but his computer was signalling traffic, so he powered it up and opened an e-mail from Filipek. It had come in while he was talking to Kossler.

'All hail the paranoid Polish communists!' he read. 'Nothing escaped their eagle eye! I've pulled some strings, and this is what I've come up with.

'Three cheers for the Labudas! They were good honest Catholics and beamed sunshine everywhere. Boos and jeers for Aunt Yanta! She was a hard-line pro-Moscow journalist, and her favourite male was the local Soviet enforcer, a man named Konstantinov. They produced a son they called Patryk – born out of wedlock, as you Brits coyly say. Patryk was Polish, but he lived with his father and was given his father's surname, so the odds are he spoke Russian as well. He was as sharp as a razor so his school reports say, and somehow he got to know Enid. But then things get murky. There's talk of a hushed-up rape, and Patryk was last seen being bundled off – at dawn, would you believe?! – in a UAZ-469. (That was the Soviets' favourite jeep. Yanta and Konstantinov must have had connections!) After that, Patryk disappeared, I can't find him anyway. Happy days in the People's Republic! Enid must have loathed us by the time she went home.

'I dug up a photo of Patryk from about that time – it's in the attachment. You'd think he'd be in the army, he was the right age, but as I said, Yanta and Konstantinov must have had connections, so our razor sharp young man was doing propaganda work when he vanished. It was – what's the phrase I learned in my English boarding school? – a cushy number!

'Hope this will do, you owe me a dinner for it. Kasper.'

Van Piet re-read the e-mail and opened the attachment. The black-and-white photo came from a Party magazine. Patryk's hair was thick and long, the beard – his first? – needed trimming, and the shirt collar was undone. It was youthful freedom, communist-style. It had been a group picture. Filipek had enlarged the bit showing Patryk.

'You're on,' van Piet e-mailed back. 'Give me a call the next time you're over. We'll bring you back to the Hall.'

He had to wait till Kossler got back to him before he could do much else, so he warmed up a steak and kidney pie he found in the fridge and took it onto the terrace. He could see the rings of Célestine's riding school from there, and although they were empty, they still made him feel good. He was clearing away when his mobile buzzed. It was Kossler. The cleaners had gone and no one else was around, but in his ingrained way, he had to lock himself in his study again.

"OK, Ian. Go ahead."

"Mission accomplished," he heard back. "You can view the pics when you like. The laptop and smartphone are in Witton."

So, taking the hardware *had* been too clever. It'd been like leaving a trail of fresh blood.

"Where's Witton?" van Piet asked.

"It's a Birmingham suburb. It's near Sutton Coldfield."

"Can you say where in Witton?"

"Try 48 Cannington Road. An electrician by the name of Mike Crane lives there. Self-employed by the look of it, man and a van, that kind of thing."

"Where did you get all that from?"

"As I sort of said, smartphones and laptops are never fully switched off, and the e-mail I sent to Wavell's address bypassed the in-boxes and ordered a reply to an address I sent with it. I captured the reply, located where it came from – to within three inches, I might add – and left Wavell's hardware as if it hadn't been touched. The electoral roll for Witton came next, and Mike Crane was the only one listed as living there. After that I googled in 'Mike Crane, Birmingham, UK' to see what came up. It got me his website, complete with his web address, so I went into his other files while I was at it. He's been receiving instructions from a Russian Embassy computer, which may or may not surprise you. The sender's codename is Conger and his is Sentinel. Conger's also been sending stuff to Bunting and Penderton. Their codename is Icicle."

"Does Crane have a pic on his website?"

"He does and it's on your computer right now, along with what he says about himself. But listen to this first. Crane and the Wolvercote pair were given detailed instructions to go to Saxley Castle on April 9th. Early on August 26th they were up there again removing Chris Miller's car from the car park to a code-named destination, unfortunately, and on August 28th Crane was sent to Wavell's house to get sight of the pics she'd been talking about on TV. When Crane got back, he reported to Conger how it went. The encoding's complex, but I've cracked it now. You'll find his report in clear amongst the other stuff."

"Does anyone else send these people instructions, do you know?"

"I've identified a sender called Alder. When I know more I'll get back to you. Bear with me, Willem. These codes aren't easy, and I don't want to leave any traces."

They terminated and van Piet went carefully through Crane's website, taking his time over Crane's cheery, clean-shaven face and thinning grey hair. Then he went through the pics from Wavell's hardware. He knew better what to look for now. First he studied the groups, then each face separately, and yes, one face was definitely Crane's. He enlarged it to see it better, then he switched to the attachment on Filipek's e-mail.

Was that him as well??? Age and the hair made a difference, the beard was in the way, and it was sharp colour versus blurry black-and-white, but it could be. He put a call through to Pamela Wole, keeping his fingers crossed. It was the Long Vacation and she might be anywhere, but when she answered, she said she was at home working on her textbook. He explained what he wanted – the beard removed, the hair trimmed and the two faces compared.

"All pics to my computer," he said mechanically. He felt like a speaking clock. "Call me on my mobile when you're done. You're not to keep anything, and only Millie to know."

Before he went downstairs, he checked Wavell's passenger list, and there was no Crane on it. That figured; he was probably there to keep an eye on things. That meant arriving separately and staying in the background if he could.

Van Piet's afternoon chore was to muck out the horses, and at about the time he was pulling on his boots, Russell Burney was phoning his father in London. Could he come round that evening to discuss September 22nd? He was hoping Cyril would see him early; he didn't want to leave Aubrey alone two evenings in a row.

"Where are you now?" Cyril asked once Russell had got past the butler.

"At work. In my office."

"And that's where you'll stay, Russell. I don't pay you to knock off whenever you feel like it. Be here at seven, that's soon enough for me."

There was nothing he could do. It was as if his father knew he didn't want to be late back.

"You won't be on your own," Cyril finished off. "Oscar Handley will be here."

Handley had been with Cyril for years, he was his personal helicopter pilot. He was close to retirement now, softly spoken and good at his job. If Enid was around, Cyril liked to tell people he'd got his job because she fancied him. Russell sometimes wondered if there was any truth in it. It would be just like his father to employ someone he could use against his family.

When Russell told Aubrey he'd be late again, she sounded well, and she promised to stay that way. She also thanked him for his note. She said it had made her cry, and she sounded as if she'd cry again as she said it.

"What time will you be seeing your father?" she asked. "If I can't be with you, I want to think about you."

He told her. He'd never dared try to bring Aubrey and his father together.

"Will it take long?" she asked. She sounded fearful. "What time do you think you'll be home?"

"Knowing my father, not before eleven. It could be later than that. He'll keep me as long as he can."

Before he left work he changed into a fresh set of clothes– he'd brought them with him especially – and he took a taxi, not the tube, from Theydon Bois to London's Berkeley Square in order to stay spotless. He had a modest dinner in a four star off the Square, and then he walked through to Upper Brook Street and his parents' Mayfair home. It was four storeys high counting the built-out loft, and Russell had to admit it was beautiful every time he went in. The butler opened the door to the reception room for him, where his parents were drinking coffee. Handley had already arrived, he was sitting stiffly on a high-backed chair. He'd brought some of his scrap books with him. Neatly collated, they showed Cyril being greeted by politicians and business grandees on a variety of British and European helipads. Cyril was leafing through them and reminiscing loudly with Handley, while Enid sat smiling politely. She invited Russell to sit down on one of the soft chairs and asked the maid, who was standing near the door, to pour him some coffee. Then she could go.

Cyril was in no hurry to talk about September 22nd. Instead, in his pernickety way, he picked over Hallavy's disappearance, then the murders of the Torellis and Patrice. It was a tactic, Russell knew it, but he kept his patience and strung along with it. When Cyril finally flagged, Enid put in,

"Your father has had his portrait painted. It's hanging in the dining room. Can I show it to him, Cyril?"

Cyril nodded curtly.

"Five minutes and no more," he grunted, dragging his breath in. "We don't want him here all night."

She took Russell into the dining room. The head-and-shoulders portrait was large, and a plaque on the ornate frame said 'Cyril David Burney. Founder of CDB Global.' The sitter stared straight at whoever looked at the painting, the colours were vivid, and the mood was domineering. It intimidated Russell as he stood there. And it made him even more determined to strike back.

"It's good, isn't it?" Enid remarked in her placid way, but before he could answer, she lowered her voice and went on,

"I'm glad I've got you to myself. I have to ask you how you're making out with your debts. I've been desperately worried about you ever since Mr Patrice disappeared."

Dearest Enid. He put his arm round her shoulders, squeezed her lovingly, and thought fast.

"Don't worry, it's all taken care of. He put the sale through just in time. On good terms, too."

"I'm so relieved." She brightened her tone. "We'd better go back to your father now. Our five minutes are almost up."

"Will he keep me here much longer, do you think? I really want to be getting back."

"I doubt it; he's got to go out later tonight. He had an important phone call not long before you arrived."

"Do you know what about?"

"Ministry business, he said. Apparently the government needs his help yet again, and you can imagine how he made it sound. I shouldn't tell you this, but he's booked a taxi for half past ten."

She gave him a quick kiss and a conspiratorial smile.

"So you're in luck," she added quickly, and she hurried him out of the room.

As they sat down, Russell said he was impressed by the portrait.

"It's exactly like you," he said, doing his best to be agreeable. "It must be worth a lot of money."

"It is. I'll have to think hard who I leave it to."

A silence opened up, and Cyril yawned exaggeratedly.

"I've almost forgotten what you've come for, Russell," he said, stretching as well. "Would you like to get on with it before we all fall asleep?"

Doing his best to look eager to please, Russell set out his stall.

"Where will I be when the drills start to turn?" Cyril asked.

"You'll be opposite the most important one. I've instructed Alice Tilman not to do anything till I tell her face to face, so nothing will begin before you get there, and when it does, you'll be centre stage."

"And I'll be waiting in the dark," he said, sounding as if he liked the idea. "What do you say to that, Oscar?"

"Your personal helicopter will be on the supply ship, Sir. I don't see any problems."

"Neither do I. I could wish I got good advice more often, Russell."

Enid sensed his mood was lifting.

"How dramatic to sail to the rig in the dark!" she exclaimed. "I'd like to do that, too. May I, Cyril? I'm sure Russell can manage it."

Russell's blood froze. Handley, the co-pilot and the supply ship's crew – he didn't care tuppence about them. But he loved Enid more than anyone except Aubrey, she'd given him the warmth he'd never had from his father. But if she was on the supply ship, she'd be drowned as well, and he didn't know how to put her off without putting off Cyril. Cyril, in fact, didn't want Enid on board in case she stole some of his glory. But he could see Russell didn't want her there either, so he said,

"I don't see why not. Make it happen, Russell, it's what your mother wants. We'll have radio silence as well, it'll make the effect better. I'll tell the captain. He'll listen to me."

The evening limped on, and Russell hoped he might get his mother on her own for just long enough to say she had to be on the rig, not the supply ship. But when Cyril, with a frowning look at his watch, rang for the maid and the butler, Enid gave him a kiss and left the room before he got his chance. The butler phoned for taxis from the hall, and Russell said he'd wait outside for his. He was frothing with anxiety. He'd felt his old guilt pressing upwards all evening, even though, on a higher level, he absolutely wanted his father dead. But he didn't want his mother dead; she had to live for a thousand years. Somehow he'd have to contact her and, without saying why, get her to think again. If she refused, he'd have to choose between her and Toni. He knew he'd choose Toni, despite the anguish he'd go through, but just thinking about it made him feel sick.

The squad trailing Russell had been beefed up since the Theydon Bois fiasco, and it was an SRO agent who drove him home in the taxi. But Ashell House was still overstretched, so no one had been near Five Beeches at shortly after five that evening to see Aubrey accelerate out in her Range Rover and start on the thirty-six miles to Sunningdale. She knew from Russell where Shayler lived, and she also knew Shayler tended to get home around six. What she couldn't know when she drew up in front of The Wool-Staple was that Shayler had been home since five twenty, getting ready for Farrell just in case he got back early. It was a fantasy and Shayler knew it, but when the doorbell rang she still ran to open it, only to see someone who looked as though she'd stepped straight out of *Cosmopolitan*. And Aubrey, who'd been expecting a dowdy frump in tweeds, found herself talking to someone in a denim suit and open-toed sandals that were decades too young for her. There was the full hair, too. But Aubrey didn't miss a beat.

"Miss Shayler?" she enquired in her cut glass way. "I'm Toni Aubrey, Russell Burney's wife-to-be. I believe you've heard of me. May I come in? I have to talk to you urgently. It's about Russell."

Shayler was alarmed. Had Russell been opening his mouth? Abandoning her fantasies and the hopes that went with them, she reckoned it would be mid-evening before Farrell got back. So she smiled her professional smile and said yes, of course.

"Thank you so much. I see you have a multiple garage. I wonder if I might park in there first. I don't want to sound like a B-picture, but I'd rather no one knew I was here. You know how gossip travels."

Shayler operated the third door with her smartphone and watched the Range Rover back in.

She wanted to keep Aubrey at a distance, so she took her through to a small sitting room at the back of the house where she talked to people who came on business. It was cosy, but it was formal as well, and the glazing made it sound-proof. Shayler felt it gave her all-round protection.

"I might as well draw the curtains while I'm on my feet," she said. "The days are shrinking fast, I'm afraid."

She covered the French doors and the windows, and when Aubrey said thank you, coffee would be splendid, she went to the sideboard and made a cup for herself as well. As they faced each other, Shayler grew more and more agitated. Did Aubrey know Russell was planning to murder his father? Or that Harvest Home would cause a major disaster?

Aubrey, for her part, was nervous as well. She had no reason to think Shayler knew anything about anything, and that was why she'd come to her. Her task was to set up someone entirely above suspicion to collide with Dvorski. And as far as she was concerned, no one was more above suspicion than Finance Director Shayler.

It was time to start lying to her.

"My husband-to-be confides in me frequently," she began, fluent and poised as always. "He holds you in very high regard, and that's why I feel I can trust you. You see, he also tells me about one of his business connections, a man called Oleg Dvorski. Do you know him?"

"I've heard the name, he's from the Russian Embassy. Why do you ask?"

"He terrifies me, Miss Shayler. I know nothing about drilling for gas, but I do know it can go very wrong, and this Dvorski has taken my Russell over. Dvorski's a salesman, that's all, but every time Russell mentions a doubt about Harvest Home, he forces him on as if there were nothing at all to worry about."

Shayler froze. Did Dvorski know about the tsunami? Was that why he was pressuring Russell? Strange Russell hadn't said anything. She had to know.

"Do you know why Dvorski forces him on?" she asked, trying to sound detached.

Aubrey rounded her lying off.

"It's all very sordid. The Russians want Harvest Home to go ahead because they want to buy into it. So whenever Russell has a doubt, their Mr Dvorski bullies him to keep it going." She leaned forward, ringing her hands, and Shayler noticed how skilfully she was made up. "It's dreadful, Miss Shayler, he's destroying Russell, I see it happening daily. That's why I've come to you this evening. I'm desperate to save Russell, but I can't do it without your help."

So that was all there was to it. Dvorski didn't know about the tsunami, and Aubrey was fretting about the man in her life. She could understand that. She'd fret as much about Leo.

"I'll gladly help if I can," she said, feeling herself relax, "but you'll have to tell me how."

"On September 22nd Russell wants his father to be on the main rig for Harvest Home, and when everything is ready, Russell will order the Site Controller to start drilling. Russell has to do this personally, otherwise the Site Controller won't go ahead. Just before he does it, I want you to intervene. You will say you've heard the drilling is too dangerous to go ahead. You won't have to be specific, the word 'dangerous' will be enough, because it's common knowledge Russell's father hates Harvest Home. He thinks Russell and the late Miss Torelli fooled him into letting it go ahead, so if you, the highly respected Miss Shayler, say it's dangerous, he will stop it in its tracks, and this awful Russian will lose his hold over Russell."

"But what if Russell says I'm wrong? I know absolutely nothing about these things."

"His father won't listen to him, he'll think he's trying to fool him again. Believe me, Miss Shayler, his father has built up a fearful head of steam on this."

But Shayler still wasn't satisfied.

"Has Russell told you anything in particular can go wrong?" she probed.

"No, he just knows *something* could. He says all new projects come with risks attached, and he can't always know what they'll be. It's as simple as that."

"It would be an immense risk for me. It could cost me everything."

"Who would you rather have grateful to you, Russell or his father?"

Shayler allowed herself time to think. Aubrey's scenario had a major flaw in it – Cyril Burney would never reach the rig alive. But Russell might insist on going ahead even though his father was missing, saying Klemmsley must come first or something pseudo-heroic like that. So she – Shayler – might still be expected to stop Harvest Home, and Aubrey had told her how to do it. Without Cyril there, she couldn't be sure she'd succeed, but she'd do her very best; and she'd have an ally in the woman sitting opposite. She was Russell's wife-to-be after all. She had to be able to influence him.

"I'll do as you wish, Miss Aubrey – Toni, if I may, and please call me Fern. I can see it will help you and Russell. And Mr Cyril will think well of me, so I shall gain, too."

"Oh, Fern, I thank you from the bottom of my heart! Now, please don't tell Russell or anyone else that I've discussed this with you. If he finds out, he could become difficult."

"Of course not, it's not in my interest to. There, if a finance director says something's not in her interest, it's as good as a written contract."

Aubrey had to go, she couldn't be sure Russell wouldn't get home before he said, and Shayler, who was yearning painfully for Farrell, made no attempt to stop her.

"Your house is quite beautiful," Aubrey said as they stood up. "You must be very attached to it."

She wanted Shayler to feel she'd made a friend.

"I am. It's cost a lot of money, but I don't begrudge a penny. I'm happy here."

Farrell was closer than Shayler knew. Once he'd left Matlock, he'd put his foot down, and while Shayler and Aubrey were draining their coffee cups, he cruised up the drive and round to the back of the house. The drawn curtains meant he wasn't seen, and the glazing kept the sound out. By the time he clunked the driver's door shut, Shayler and Aubrey were moving through the house, and because Aubrey took time to change back into her outdoor footwear, the front door didn't start to open till Farrell was approaching it. Afraid of being seen, he darted behind a box tree by the edge of the drive, but not before he'd recognised Aubrey from the photos that had reached Chelmsford Tuesday. As Aubrey drove towards the gateway she paused, leaned out of her side window, and waved to Shayler with make-believe affection. It was one manipulator waving to another, each one believing the other was as pure as the driven snow. Well above The Wool-Staple, the SRO helicopter that had been tracking Farrell was handing on to its relief. But its high-sensitivity camera just managed to catch Aubrey leaning out, and Ashell House had the image before it swung away.

Farrell gave Aubrey plenty of time to drive off before he came out of hiding and rang the doorbell as if he'd just arrived. Shayler was certain it was him this time and – she couldn't help herself – she put her arms round his neck and kissed him as soon as the door was shut.

"I'm so glad you're back," she said as she snuggled up to him. "I've missed you a lot. I didn't think I would, but I have."

After a leisurely meal and three bottles of wine between them, they sat on 'their' settee behind The Wool-Staple's expensive curtains, and Farrell told her how he'd got on in Buxton and Matlock. He didn't say he'd seen Aubrey driving off. He wouldn't tell Chelmsford either, he couldn't without revealing he was hanging round Shayler. Withholding information didn't come easily, but he'd do it. It was like closing a door on his past.

They moved on to quietly sharing a dwindling bottle of brandy, and Shayler couldn't stop kissing him. Finally she slipped her denims off and unbuttoned her shirt.

"I've been waiting all day for this, Leo," she said, loosening his tie with fingers that weren't quite steady. "I'm sure we can do it tonight. I've gone back to one of my books. It says I just have to breathe right, and then I won't tighten up."

Farrell finished his drink, poured himself another one, and they went up to her bedroom. It was a price he had to pay. She breathed as the book said, or imagined she did, she didn't tighten up, and as she lay in the dark next to a raggedly snoring Farrell, she felt bliss. Gratefully she kissed the nape of his neck, wiped the sweat off her lips and, holding him tightly, slid into a sleep as deep as his with her body pressed against his back.

High over Sunningdale, the relief helicopter was coming to the end of its stint. It peeled away towards London, and a spruce Subaru parked where it could see Shayler's drive. The previous night it had been an Alfa.

At about the time Aubrey was setting out for Shayler's, van Piet was chopping vegetables ahead of his family's return when his mobile buzzed. It was Wole. Yet again he toiled up to his study and settled down to listen. As she spoke, he downloaded the visuals she'd done for him.

"At first sight," she said in her invincible lecture-hall way, "they look like two different people, even with the beard removed and the younger man's hair thinned out. That's normal. But the biometrics I've added in for you make it certain: they're both Mike Crane."

"You're sure they're not twins or something?"

"Good try, but if you look at my enlargements, you'll see the same horizontal scar under the left eye of both of them. I should think your Mr Crane was in a fight when he was young. That scar's typical of a blow to the cheekbone. It scarcely shows on the older man, but it's there all right."

So Mike Crane, the masked man who'd nearly killed Wavell, was Patryk Konstantinov, the Polish love child with the Russian father. But how had he got from Lodz to Birmingham? And why the name change? He thanked Wole for her good work, wished her luck with her textbook, and let his mind run on. Crane must have been around for some while to get a Birmingham accent. He looked oldish on his website as well. Bunting and Penderton, they were oldies too. And so was Valkov. But Dvorski was new – he'd only been around for six years or so. Did that signify, and if so, what?

He went back to Wole's pics, especially the one of Konstantinov minus his beard and some of his hair. He studied it hard.

"Wavell knows how he moves and sounds," he mused. "If whoever's running Crane finds that out, how will they react?"

Wavell was safe, he was sure of that, but what about Crane? Would they kill him? He couldn't answer that, but he could see some heavy surveillance was called for. He had to speak to Snape.

He also had to speak to Cyril Burney. Urgently.

He called Snape first, then, suppressing guilt feelings for not moving dinner on, he called the Permanent Secretary at the Department for Business, Innovation and Skills on his personal number. Could the Secretary get Cyril Burney into the Department as soon as possible? Yes, top secret. Face to face only.

"Say it's about a big transnational trade, he's used to that, and it'll flatter his vanity. Stress no one else must come with him. As soon as you get a day and a time, let me know on my mobile."

The Secretary, who would have felt remiss had he not had Cyril's mobile number to hand, made his call straight away. It was the call Enid had told Russell about when they were standing in front of Cyril's portrait – the one that would get Russell out of his parents' house by ten thirty.

When the Secretary got back to van Piet, he took him by surprise. Van Piet had thought he would take longer.

"Burney's flattered all right," the Secretary allowed himself to remark. "He likes it when governments crawl to his door. He also said he had his son to put up with, so he'd be happy to come over at eleven. By 'happy' I think he meant 'relieved'. "

"What, eleven o'clock this evening?"

Van Piet dearly wanted to ask for another time.

"That's what he said. He'd tell Mrs Burney the Department needed his help yet again. And he'd come on his own in a taxi."

The Secretary terminated the call just as Célestine and Jackie came bustling through the door. Dinner wasn't ready, he confessed, and he had no choice, he had to go out at nine. Célestine found some baking potatoes, they put together some fillings, and while they were eating, he listened totally engrossed to what they'd seen and done. When he left, he said he wouldn't be back till well after midnight, so they'd better have their kisses now. Then he was gone.

Cyril was punctual to the minute. He spent just over an hour with van Piet in a top security room, and when they finished, he was so shaken, the duty doctor kept him for a further thirty minutes before he called a private ambulance to take him back to Mayfair. Van Piet, meanwhile, got to his car as quickly as he could and set off for Essex. Unexpectedly, he was in a good mood. The outturn was better than he'd hoped.

Chapter 28

Treachery

Van Piet awoke later the same day expecting a call from Garry and, sure enough, his mobile buzzed just as his porridge was starting to bubble. He moved the saucepan to a heatproof mat and trod his familiar path upstairs. Everything in the Hall was still. He was the first one up.

"All right, Tom. What have you learned?"

"I'll start with Anatoly Dobrynin, Sir. He's got five companies here and twenty-one million euros invested. That's how he and Mrs Dobrynin became Cypriots. It seems he also bankrolls other Russians who want to get into Europe, and the suspicion is, it's not always his money."

"Whose is it then?"

"The betting is, it's Moscow's. When they want someone in, he pays up front, and Moscow sees him right on the quiet. That could be how Toni Aubrey got in. She arrived from Russia in March under the name of Katya Morozova, and she stayed in one of Dobrynin's hotels while she officially changed her name to Toni Aubrey. Then someone – almost certainly Dobrynin or one of his agents – passed off a two million euro investment programme as the newly minted Miss Aubrey's, and she applied for Cypriot citizenship on the strength of it. Successfully, of course, and her new name is on her new passport. Some people think it all happened rather fast, but it happened. She stayed in Nicosia till the third week in July, when she left for London on a one-way air ticket. I get most of this from our High Commissioner. He recognised Aubrey from the photo I brought."

"Does he know anything about this Katya Morozova? What's her full name, by the way?"

"Katya Danilovna Morozova, and the short answer is, she's a killer. She's a graduate of the Military Institute of Foreign Languages in Moscow, and she learned a lot of her English from British films, so she's got an accent you can't miss. The word is: She's totally loyal to Moscow and ruthless towards everyone else."

"Well, it's good to be warned. She paid a visit to Shayler yesterday, and she was driving herself in a Range Rover. We'll track her as much as we can, but the way things are, it will have to be hit and miss."

"Perhaps Dobrynin helped her with the Range Rover."

"My thinking, too." (As her insurance cover later revealed, she'd leased it from Nicosia as Toni Aubrey and was driving it on a brand new Cypriot licence.) "We've also got a problem with Mr Farrell. He's leaking police information to Shayler. Things are piling up, Tom. When are you flying back?"

"This evening. I'll be in Ashell House tomorrow morning."

"I'll talk to you then. I'm off to Chelmsford shortly. I'll tell Mr Snape what you've said before I go."

Snape was already in his office when van Piet called him, and while he was updating Snape, Russell Burney was phoning Tilman from Stanmore. At the end of his list he added Mrs Burney would be on the supply ship with his father. It was as much as he could do to get the words out without tripping over his tongue.

"Anyone else?" Tilman asked.

"The chauffeur, Derek Quilter. My father never goes far without him. And my father's helicopter crew. That's it, so far as I know. Is there a problem?"

"Not at all, I just like to know what I'm up against. That goes for your party, too. I'll ask you to keep me posted."

"Will do. You can count on me, Miss Aubrey and Miss Shayler, plus Mr Oleg Dvorski from the Russian Embassy. I'll ask my secretary to stay in touch."

As soon as Burney terminated, Tilman contacted Snape on a secure mobile Ashell House had couriered to her and told him what he'd said.

"Your Sal Gulliver and the other one, Gubby Corbett – when are they coming up?"

"Given what you've told me, how about today?"

"I'll send a helicopter. They can look round in daylight and again after dark. Rigs look different under lights. Either something's bright or it's in deep shadow. There's no in-between."

"Point taken. I'll get some Health and Safety coats from Chelmsford Council. Hard hats, too. We can supply our own clipboards, I'm sorry to say. We've got more than enough of those."

He rubbed his eyes wearily. It was time to go back into the Ops Room. After van Piet's call the previous evening, he'd sent a red-line request to the Home Office for information about Mike Crane, formerly Patryk Konstantinov. He still hadn't had a reply, and it was making him tetchy. As he was shutting his door, Farrell came down the corridor. He wasn't late, but he wanted to be seen. It had taken Shayler's alarm to wake him, and all the way to Chelmsford he'd been afraid he might be breathalysed. He hadn't noticed the Subaru when he left The Wool-Staple, and a helicopter had finished the job. Snape signalled to him to stop. He'd agreed with van Piet what to say.

"Hang on, Leo. I've got a job for you. It needs seniority and it can't wait."

He disappeared into his office and came out with three faxes in his hand.

"The deaths of Patrice and the Millers are going to inquest. I want you to collect all the information you can for our legals to package up. Any problems, let me know."

When he went into the Ops Room he caught the smell of fresh toast. He hadn't had any breakfast, he'd been in too much of a hurry, so he helped himself to a couple of rounds and sat down by the secure link to the Home Office. A constable fresh from college was minding it for him.

"They've signalled seven minutes, Sir."

"Can I get you something while we're waiting?"

"Just some tea, please. I've eaten already."

Snape got two teas and, with a professional lifetime between them, they sat chatting easily till the reply came through. He took the print-out back to his office to read it again. Van Piet was waiting for him.

"I've found out more about Patryk Konstantinov," Snape said as they went in. He felt pleased with what he'd got.

"Tell me more."

"After he left Lodz he was taken to Moscow. They made him a Russian citizen there and gave him a PR job in the Ministry for Economic Development. The job meant travel in the West, which we can see now was why he got it, and in short order he washed up in Paris. A young man's dream come true, you might think, but on the last day of his mission he walked into the British Embassy and asked for asylum. There was the usual huffing and puffing, but we took him in, of course. The Cold War was on, and a Ministry man was just too tempting. He re-named himself Mike Crane and became an electrician in Birmingham."

"Whose allegiance to Moscow has never faded. Well done, Eddie. We're near the complete picture now."

Forty miles away, Russell Burney was spending the morning with Marianne Halter. He wanted to run through the big day with her. He managed to look cheerful, but inside he was a bag of nerves, and a lot of it was down to his mother. Ever since she'd asked to be on the supply ship, he hadn't known which way to turn. And then there were the millions he'd murder when Harvest Home went max. It was too many for him to imagine, but he kept hearing children screaming and he thought he'd go mad. As the morning wore on, he found it harder and harder to keep up appearances. Then, out of the blue, a call came from Reception. Miss Aubrey would like to speak to him. He said he'd call her back in twenty minutes.

He beat his deadline by fifty percent. Standing next to the Henry Moore bronze, he put the call in, dreading to know what she wanted. But it wasn't a cry for help, it was sunshine and laughter. Could he come home straight away, she wanted to know. The day was so lovely, it was a pity to waste it indoors. Why didn't they go out in one of his cars? He couldn't believe it, it was like the first flowers in spring.

"Give me three hours, maybe less," he said. "I'll be as quick as I can."

She'd done her utmost to look her best in a crisply ironed blouse and skirt, and she kissed him lovingly when he came through the door.

"We'll take one of the E-Types!" he called out as he ran upstairs to get shot of his suit and tie. "Which one do you fancy?"

"The bright red one. It's a happy colour, and I'm happy, too."

He'd never seen her this cheery before. He had to make it last.

The E-Type's top went down, and once they were clear of Greater London they powered towards the South Downs, laughing and shouting as the 4·2 litre engine surged through the revs. They had a cream tea at Black Down Hill and, holding hands, they sat on the café terrace to enjoy the last of the August sun. Finally it was back to Stanmore. They'd been trailed all afternoon, partly by helicopter and partly by a team of fast cars. But once they were back in the Greater London grind, a single Smart was more than enough to stay with them.

'Break his willpower. Make him so he won't even think of acting on his own' – those had been Aubrey's instructions, and her thinking was, if she could break his willpower in one place, she could break it all along the line, like a single crack making a whole dam give way. So, the blast in the E-Type came first. Second was a surprise gourmet meal, delivered to the door after they got back. Third, well, that would take a bit of skill. When the dishwasher was loaded and they were on one of the settees, she snuggled up to him and said,

"We've not had a better time than this, Russell, and you've been working so hard lately, I think you need a reward. I know you've got some champagne in your drinks cupboard, I've seen it in there. I think we should treat ourselves to two small glasses. It won't do any harm if we stick to two. Please say yes, just for me."

His shirt was open. She moved her fingers across his skin the way he liked it, and it worked – he could feel his hormones running. But he was also thoroughly scared.

"I don't think we should," he stammered. "You know how it is. Once we start drinking, we can't stop."

But he wanted a drink very much now. The idea was in his head, and his whole body was craving for one. He didn't just want to taste it. He wanted to swallow it all in one go and then keep swallowing more.

"We *can* stop, Russell. All we have to do is watch each other. Give me your key. I'll pour just enough, then I'll put the bottle back. Trust me."

He was foundering fast. He couldn't say "No", it was beyond him, so he grabbed at an excuse.

"It'll be warm, Toni. It won't taste right."

She'd expected him to say that. He'd once told her, if there was one thing he couldn't stand, it was warm champagne. And she'd filed it away.

"Then we'll drink something else," she came back. "I know you like vodka and you know I like gin. We'll allow ourselves a teeny little bit – just enough to end the day on a high – and then we'll put it away. It's like sex, isn't it? Once you think about it, you have to have it. That's how I'm feeling about a drink right now, and I know you are, too. Give me your key, Russell. You know how much you'll enjoy it."

He was beaten. He knew there was vodka in there, and there was some gin in there as well – he'd forgotten to get rid of it after he'd found her in the ensuite the first time. He separated the key from his key ring and watched greedily as she walked to the drinks cupboard. It lit up when she opened it, and the back was mirrored to make the bottles seem twice as many. Inside was a narrow counter and she stood two glasses on it. They were larger than he'd expected, they were virtually full-size tumblers, but he didn't want a small glass now, and he was glad there wasn't much mix in them when she brought them over.

The first taste was enough. It was like fire, and all his restraint evaporated. He drank mouthfuls more, and the happy-happy zing he'd nearly forgotten swept right through him. He began to laugh and Aubrey, who'd almost drained her glass, was laughing as well. She was close in to him, and all he could see was her laughing face and her bright, glistening eyes.

"Let's have one more glass and then we finish," he said, and this time he was the one who fetched the drinks. The glasses were brimful when he came back, and they drank into them so quickly, they were half empty before he sat down. His ears were ringing, and she seemed oddly remote as he struggled to steady his gaze, so he draped his arm round her and pulled her clumsily towards him.

"Careful, you'll spill my drink!" she laughed and drained her glass as she half-resisted. "There, it was either that or tipping it over you. Now I'll have to get some more."

She took his emptied glass as well and, swaying as she walked, she filled them both again, adding just enough mix to make it taste. He took his from her with both hands, she put her arm through his, and they gulped down their drinks together. They were giggling as well as laughing, and his default expression was a vacant grin.

"I love you, Toni!" he slurred. "You're more than life to me! Let me kiss your beautiful, beautiful lips."

She pressed her lips against his, and as he squeezed her against himself, his glass fell onto the carpet. Slowly he turned his head and stared at it.

"Stupid glass," he managed to say. "Who needs a stupid glass? We'll open two more bottles, then we'll – Ha! Ha! Ha! – lock the cupboard up like we said. No, I'll get them. A gentleman always gets the drinks."

"You're drunk, Russell! You're drunk!" she screeched, as he tried to stand up with a litre of vodka inside him. But he reeled sideways instead and collapsed onto the floor. He didn't even try to get up.

"Now it's your turn!" he laughed back noisily. "You're drunk as well!"

She teetered unsteadily and subsided next to him, her skirt riding up her thighs. He pawed feebly at her legs, half singing and half dribbling, "I must, I must; I must" as she tried to pull it down. But she was giggling frantically and her hands seemed weak, so she rolled away and began crawling towards the drinks cupboard. Burney followed her, also on all fours, till he lost control completely and flopped onto his face. She heaved herself up and, leaning hard against the cupboard, let her hands circle till they closed on two fresh bottles. Burney was still on his face so, with the two bottles in her hands and some mix tucked into her armpit, she kneeled down with a thump next to him.

"You need – Ha! Ha! – a pick-me-up," she laughed, and jabbed him with the vodka bottle till he rolled over. "Here, have some of this."

She let the mix fall, undid the vodka bottle, and gave it to him. Trying to drink while he was flat on his back made him gag, so he half sat up and set about sucking the vodka out.

"Do you want some mix?" she asked, waving it over his face, and when he sort of nodded, she uncapped it and tipped it over him. He roared with laughter, as if it was the funniest thing that had ever happened to him.

"Now I'm going to lick it off, Russell! Stay right where you are!"

She took a long drink out of the gin bottle. Some of it she swallowed, and the rest ran out of her mouth onto her blouse. Gasping and spluttering, she let the bottle slide out of her fingers and began licking his face. He could just about feel her do it. His head was revolving and nausea was setting in. When he shut his eyes it all got worse. She was licking his neck and ears when he suddenly dragged his eyes half-open.

"Mind out, Toni!" he managed. "I'm going to be sick!"

He did his best to haul himself away from her. As he did, his stomach emptied in heaves, and he slumped down with his face next to the vomit.

"Sorry," he mumbled into the carpet and, "Leave me alone, I'll be all right." But each time he closed his eyes, everything started spinning again, and he was retching up water before he finally blacked out.

Stone cold sober, Aubrey stood up and drove her toe into his side. He grunted, but that was all, and when she did it again, the same thing happened. She knelt down next to him.

"You stink, Russell Burney, CEO of Klemmsley Oil and Gas. You don't know me at all, but I know you as if you were made of glass. I know Sberbank is clearing your debts, I know Harvest Home will cause a tsunami, and I know who's put you up to it. I also know who's had a rethink about it. You don't have to know who that is, you're just a pawn. Pawns don't have knowledge, Russell, and they don't have willpower. They're moved around by others, and that's what's happening to you."

She brought her mouth near his ear. It was as if she was trying to talk directly into his subconscious.

"Your priority," she said, speaking slowly and insistently, "is to make sure the tsunami goes ahead as planned. But if anything should get in its way, you must not intervene. You have no willpower, Russell, you will step back and let it happen, even if it means abandoning the tsunami. That's what I most dearly want you to do – step back, let it happen, and abandon the tsunami."

She put the air conditioning on full to clear the air and shampooed the carpet. The empty bottles went into the green bin so he wouldn't know she'd been drinking water. His key was still in the lock of the drinks cupboard. Filled with the triumph of a job well done, she took it out, laid it on the mantelpiece, and locked the cupboard with the pick she'd opened it with before she'd phoned him – she'd had to be sure the right drinks were in there, including the warm champagne. She opted to leave him where he was. He'd be full of remorse in the morning, that was certain, but she wanted him aching and bilious as well. Just knowing his willpower had failed wouldn't be enough. Failure had to penetrate every cell in his body.

Five Beeches was easier to watch by night than by day because when the grounds were in darkness, the night watchers could move in closer. But this night they had nothing to report when they came off shift. No one had rung in or out, there'd been no visitors, and all the lights had been out by midnight. When the daytime watchers came on, they went to upper rooms in nearby houses. They weren't so good, but they had to do. The views were obstructed, and although the house owners were more interested in their civic duty than in a day rent, or so they said, there was always the chance someone would talk. As Saturday September 1st emerged from the night, Aubrey was up by seven, and a picture of her drawing the curtains duly went to Chelmsford. Burney came into the back garden towards eleven. He was wearing sunglasses, he moved slowly, and he was carrying a bowl. After ten minutes on a garden seat he went indoors again, and he didn't re-emerge till four, when Aubrey joined him carrying tea things for herself and a jug of iced water for him.

"He's drinking again," Snape said as the report and the pics came through.

"But she isn't," van Piet replied. "You'd think they'd both get drunk together."

"It doesn't always happen. Sometimes there's a control issue in there somewhere."

There was a pause, then van Piet said,

"I saw Cyril Burney last night. In private."

"And?"

"His vanity's been pricked, he's upset and he's angry. We'll draw on all those on September 22nd. When Sal and Gubby report back, we'll sort out precisely how."

Chapter 29

Parkland Zuka

Tilman despatched an Agusta AW 109 to collect Gulliver and Corbett. A roomy seven seater in Klemmsley red and white, it delivered them to Teesside with daylight to spare. Klemmsley Oil and Gas was on the north bank of the Tees, between a nuclear power station and a nature reserve. The Agusta landed on its heliport, and as soon as they were out, Tilman drove them to her freshly painted container-office.

Under functional LED ceiling lights, she clicked her electric kettle on and set out how she saw things over tea in mugs that didn't match.

"My information is, it's the VIP platform you're interested in. I'll show you where it is, and then we'll go there."

She went over to a large-scale map of Cockerel Field and the County Durham coastline. The map's edges were tatty, it had post-its stuck all over it and brass drawing pins through its four corners. Harvest Home was marked off in purple ink.

"We're in a place called Teesmouth right now," she said. "That's here. And out here's the platform you want. It's called Parkland Zuka. It's got fourteen support platforms, but Parkland Zuka's where all the fuss will be. Over here is Dassett Point. That's where Mr Cyril and his party will heave to till it's time to join us. Supply ships use dynamic positioning just like the rigs, so wherever you put them, that's where they stay. You'll see Parkland Zuka in daylight first, and then after dark. Is that OK?"

They said it was. She phoned through to the heliport.

"The Agusta's topped up and ready," she told them. "We can start right now."

When they were back on the heliport, she took them into a room headed 'Support Gear'. In a large metal cupboard were immersion suits in various sizes.

"You won't like these," she said. "We call them body bags. They're heavy and hot, but when you fly over water, you have to wear them. You'll see why once we're airborne."

They arc-ed wide to avoid the nature reserve, and the body bags made sense as soon as they left the coast. There was a lot of threatening water down there, and a North Sea headwind was banging straight into them. The rigs looked like postage stamps as they neared Harvest Home. Three miniature-looking supply ships were close by them, and two more were on their way back to shore. The helideck on Parkland Zuka seemed far too small, then it got bigger fast, and they landed with a lurch as the wind caught them from the side. The pilot kept the blades turning to keep them high as they clambered out, and a two-man helideck crew chained the wheels in place. When everyone was clear, the pilot stopped the blades, and they dropped to 45 degrees.

"Our deck crews do good work on our rigs," Tilman shouted above the wind. "Mr Cyril should let them get on with it."

"How do you mean?" Corbett asked.

"He only lets his personal crew near his helicopter. That includes chaining it fast out here. And when he refuels, the pilot or the co-pilot has to watch it happen. He doesn't trust anyone else."

They had to bend double to make progress, and Gulliver and Corbett both registered there was no safety rail round the helideck, which was 140 feet above the sea. No one could survive a drop like that. The drilling derrick – 160 feet of latticed steel – towered above them as they followed Tilman into the head of an enclosed metal staircase. She had her own cabin for when she was on the rig. She took them to it to shed their body bags and get organised.

"Put your Health and Safety coats on," she said, "and hold your hard hats on when we're outside. We've got a lot to get through before the light goes."

"Mr Cyril's helicopter crew," Gulliver put in. "Can we have their names?"

"Oscar Handley is his pilot and his co-pilot is Silas Wilmot. Plus Derek Quilter, his chauffeur. When they fly, he's the steward."

Tilman worked them hard, and by the time they went to the canteen, with daylight becoming deep night, they'd covered some 4000 square feet of steel, plus staircases, pipes, cranes, davits and drilling gear. The food was more filling than fine, but they were ready for it, and the tea was hot and strong. The crew all knew Tilman, but they kept themselves to themselves, as did the ringmaster, who'd been ordered to stay out of earshot. They were mostly in their forties or fifties. Years of long shifts in unforgiving weather were etched into their faces.

Gulliver and Corbett went through their photos, checked their clipboards, and kept their questions coming.

"Will there be any empty cabins on the night?" got the answer, "Between ten and twenty." And as they were pulling on their coats, Gulliver asked, "How could I get off this rig in a hurry?"

"Well, you can't jump, so you've got two choices. You could launch one of the lifeboats from the davits, but you'd need help, and it wouldn't get you very far. Or you could go by helicopter. That's it."

As Tilman had said to Snape, the rig by night was another world. Its lighting was harsh, and the gaps in between were in ominous shadow. Sky and sea were more sensed than seen, the other rigs were patches on an inky black background, and the ever-present supply ships were islands of artificial light that seemed permanently on the move. As Gulliver and Corbett went round, they made a lot more measurements than they'd done before. They also checked sightlines, hidey holes and doorways. They'd been talking to Snape, and they knew what they were looking for.

Finally they were on the drilling deck. The base of the derrick was forty feet square, with a lit up clearspace all round it. Behind the clearspace was mostly girders, but there were also storage places, a control bay, and several open staircases.

"This is where the VIPs will be," Tilman said. "We've got special lighting for Mr Cyril to jazz things up a bit, and all the chairs will have names on them. No one will make the mistake of sitting on his."

Before they left, Corbett asked whether there were any steps down the columns to the pontoons the rig floated on.

"Yes there are, but they're not for you and me, they're for when the rig's being serviced. There's no point going down them out here, there's only sea at the bottom."

While Gulliver and Corbett were in the Agusta en route from Chelmsford to Teesside, Dvorski was in Valkov's office drinking the latter's coffee and wondering why he'd been sent for. Valkov was looking concerned, but inwardly he was riding high. He knew Aubrey had got her story across to Shayler, now it was his turn again. He had to reinforce what he'd told Dvorski after Hallavy had disappeared, and then turn the screw tighter.

"As far as we know," he began, pressing his fingertips together, "no one's linked Russell Burney and Patrice yet, not in public anyway, so from our point of view Harvest Home is still on. But," and then, looking severe, he came to it, "we've heard a rumour someone may try to stop things at the last minute."

"What, out on the rig?" Dvorski exclaimed, genuinely surprised.

"Out on the rig. Just before Burney tells his Site Controller to go max, we think Fern Shayler, the Finance Director, will push in. She'll claim it's too dangerous to go on."

"You mean she knows about the tsunami?"

"Not at all. But she knows, as we all do, that new ventures are never completely safe, so she's been asking about on the quiet. Quite likely she's heard some gossip, and it's made her overreact."

"I still don't see why she should want to push in."

"Come, Oleg, CDB Global pays her large sums of money every month. She wants to keep the company safe and her monthly payments with it."

"I can't think who'll listen to her. What does she know about gas?"

"Cyril Burney will listen. He's trusted her for years and he hates Harvest Home. One word from her and he'll stop the whole business. That's why you're here now, drinking my coffee."

Dvorski shifted uneasily. He felt he was being manoeuvred into a corner.

"I'm sorry, Andrey Ivanovich," he fenced. "I don't follow you there."

"You can be startlingly dense when you choose, so I'll spell things out for you. Under no circumstances can Shayler be allowed to stop Harvest Home. It would be an immense loss for our country, and your career would be blown to smithereens. Not only would you be turfed out of the SVR – in disgrace, I might add – you'd be turfed out of Industry and Trade as well. You're middle-aged already, that's far too old to start again. If you got a job sweeping the streets of Vladivostock you'd be lucky. Most likely you'd end up behind bars. I've seen crimes against the state pinned on people for less. "

Dvorski was panicking. It was all too possible.

"What do you want me to do?" he pleaded, feeling his palms sweating. "Shall I go and see this Shayler?"

"Have you no brains at all? If her mind's made up, as we believe it to be, you'll simply put her on her guard. No, what you must do is this. You will be armed when you're on the rig with the other guests. If Shayler so much as looks like intervening, you must shoot her dead. You'll be all right, I promise. We've got it all worked out for you."

"But if I shoot Shayler, there'll be no tsunami anyway. Everything will come to a halt."

"Not so. Russell Burney will give the order regardless. You can rely on him absolutely. The word is, he's rock hard."

Dvorski still wasn't convinced, but Valkov was doing the driving.

"What shall I do for a gun?" Dvorski asked, doing his best to sound won round.

"We'll provide you with one. We thought a Walther P22 would do nicely. That 3·4 inch barrel has its attractions, and it might remind you of the Millers. The deceased Millers, I should say, since, alas, they're no longer with us. Unlike you, Oleg Aleksandrovich, and I expect you want to keep it that way."

"It's a natural wish. I want to serve my country for many years yet. But how will you get the gun to me?"

"You will find it in your flat, and it will be loaded. You will also find a loaded Smith and Wesson. You are to take it onto the rig as well. It's to protect you if you have to shoot Shayler."

"May I ask who I give it to?"

"The code word is Cotton. Listen out for it, and then you'll know."

Valkov was in no hurry to turn him out. He poured more coffee for both of them and gossiped about the secretary Dvorski had been fond of who, unfortunately, was not coming back to London. Then he moved on to the new Russia, the key role of the SVR, and how important it was to stay in favour. When Dvorski finally stepped out into Kensington Palace Gardens, he was shattered. He'd set Harvest Home up to show how loyal he was, and now this. He was furious with Shayler. He'd only met her once, at a function in CDB Tower when Dandy Torelli was still alive, and now the sow was fouling up everything he'd worked for. Well, she'd pay for that, one way or another, he'd see to that personally. When his anger subsided, he fastened onto the word 'we'. Valkov kept using it, but he never said who he meant by it. Dvorski drew his own conclusion – everyone was still his enemy, in Moscow as well as in London. That meant the tsunami was his only chance to find his way back into favour. Come what may, he had to make it happen.

At nine thirty-five that evening, Valkov played a recording of what he and Dvorski had said, and Zembarov, who'd touched down at Heathrow three hours earlier, liked what he heard. Valkov offered him a second glass of vodka, but he waved it away.

"I don't need alcohol," he said, his face like primeval stone. "Winning is enough, winning for the Motherland. If people get hurt, so be it. It's the state that counts, the individual is nothing at all."

Van Piet was playing Monopoly with Jackie when Ashell House told him Zembarov was in London. He'd learned a lot about the brooding hardliner since his father and then Garry had flagged him up. Obsessive, reactionary, and no good to Russia in a modern world, he cast a destructive shadow wherever he went. And now he was under two hours' drive from Gorris Hall. So where would his shadow fall this time? And what, van Piet wondered as he bought Pall Mall, would happen when it did?

Chapter 30

A Quarrel with Consequences

September began in a hurry. Snape combined with Kent Police to produce a twenty-strong armed force with Gulliver in charge; the Special Boat Service agreed a joint command between its Counter Terrorism Squadron and the SRO; and van Piet spent long hours in Ashell House making sure everyone knew what to do. Only Farrell was taking life easy – he was confined to the inquest reports. He knew he was being sidelined - the surveillance he didn't know about had been scaled down to match - but he didn't care. It freed him up to bask in Shayler's wealth, and Shayler couldn't get enough of him.

"I love you more than I could tell you if I lived to be a hundred," she murmured one lazy Sunday evening, the sky crimson from the setting sun. "You make me feel born again."

They were putting a dent in her Burgundy. The television was showing the *Leonid Golovin* entering the Channel, and a courtesy stop off Plymouth was being flagged up. But they weren't really watching, and the sound was on low. As they drank, Shayler mapped out their future. To her it was a future based on love, to Farrell it was one based on greed. Just thinking about it made him so content, she had no idea his thinking and hers weren't the same. Fondly she snuggled up to him and said,

"I want you to have a key to my house. If you think it's safe, that is. You're not out of the NCA yet."

"Why shouldn't it be safe? No one's more careful than me."

She took an electronic key out of her handbag.

"I've programmed it for the back door," she said. "You can keep parking round the back if I'm out. No one will see your car from the road then."

She showed him how it worked, then uncorked another bottle.

"Do you love me, Leo?" she asked hesitantly as she refilled the glasses. "Just a little, maybe? I know I'm old and skinny, but when I think of you, I feel all happy inside. And if I'm on my own – don't laugh – I start to cry."

He knew how he had to answer. She was the one with the money.

"If you knew how much I loved you, it would take your breath away," he told her, and gave her a long kiss to keep her quiet.

In Stanmore, things were less smooth. Russell Burney's drinking binge had shamed him so much, he'd begged Aubrey to keep him in line.

"I can't discipline myself like you," he explained. "I could once, but I don't seem to want to any more. I feel like a broken spring."

"If I help you, I help myself," she said, and ruffled his hair. "I'll say it again: I don't want to die before I have to. Neither should you."

She went out of her way to be strict and watched eagerly as, predictably, it ate into his nerves. More than anything else he wanted to open his drinks cupboard, it obsessed him all his waking hours, and guilt about murdering – especially about murdering his father – refused to go away. He tried working it off, but the long hours he spent in Klemmsley Marine simply made him more and more stressed. With all the pretending, he couldn't relax for a second, and finally he cracked. On Monday 17th September, two days after the first Harvest Home drillings had begun, he rang Shayler to ask whether he could come round after work. Quite by chance, Farrell had set out from The Wool-Staple that day to clear up some details with Trevor Hawley in Peterborough – again in his Morris Minor – and he didn't expect to be back till late; so she took a chance and said six forty-five. But he must be on time and he couldn't stay long. She had a life of her own to lead.

He was dead on time.

He'd phoned Aubrey to say Harvest Home had hit some snags, and could he trust her till he got back? She said he could, and he believed her, her will seemed stronger than his nowadays. But when she put the phone down, she wasn't happy. She had no idea he was riddled with guilt, she thought she'd sapped his willpower so much, he was losing interest in Harvest Home. That mustn't happen. He had to be there on the 22nd, one hundred percent fired up to make it happen, so she resolved to make a real effort to shore him up when he got home. It shouldn't be difficult. Fake love had worked so far. She'd turn it on again.

When he rang the doorbell at The Wool-Staple, Shayler saw straight away she had a problem. She let him garage his Morgan where Aubrey had garaged her Range Rover, and showed him into the sitting room. She'd already put the lights on, and as she went to make some tea, she automatically drew the curtains. She'd eaten some time before, and he said he wasn't hungry. She didn't insist.

She soon found out what was bothering him. Clutching his cup in both hands, he said,

"Just under three weeks ago when I sat in this room, you told me my father was going to sell Global. I told you about my debts, and you persuaded me to kill him. Fern, I can't go through with it. I'm not going to do it."

She didn't stop to think. Cyril's murder was her banker, and there was Leo to think of as well.

"You surprise me, Russell," she snapped, making no attempt to conceal her anger. "Tell me why not and be quick about it. I haven't got all night."

"It's wrong, that's why not. Cyril's a brutal man, he's trampled on me for as long as I can remember, but he's still my father. I couldn't live with myself if I killed him. It'd be one of the worst things a man could do."

"He's not trampling on you, he's killing you. That's why it's either you or him. I thought you understood that."

Her voice was going up, and so was his.

"I understand everything, there's nothing you have to explain to me. I'd convinced myself I should do it, I'd made all the arrangements but, er, something happened recently, and now I've had enough. All I want to do is put my head under a pillow and sob into the mattress."

A hundred miles away in Peterborough, Trevor Hawley, who had largely wound the site down, had had everything ready for Farrell to see. So even with over a hundred photos to sift through, Farrell was still able to get away early, and he was back in Sunningdale just after Burney had garaged his car. Looking forward to more of the good life, he pootled leisurely round the back, shut his car door quietly because he wanted to give Shayler a surprise, and let himself in with the key she'd given him. Her sitting room had a rear door for access to the back of the house. It was open a fraction, and through the crack Farrell heard everything after '... he's still my father.' Abruptly alarmed, he sat down silently outside the door. He didn't have to listen very hard. Things were getting loud fast.

"You do just that, you great baby!" Shayler yelled. "You stuff your head under a pillow and cry your eyes out! You can't stick to anything, can you? No wonder your father thinks you're trash! I think you're trash, and so does everyone else! You contribute nothing, absolutely nothing! You call yourself a CEO, but you're a parasite, that's all, a parasite and a drone! Useless runs through you like Blackpool through a stick of rock! Useless! Useless! Useless!"

She'd stood up to scold him better. When he didn't reply, she bent down to bring her inflamed face close to his, took a deep breath, and yelled at him again.

"You sat in this room and said you'd kill your father. I wanted it, I told you why, and you said you'd do it because it was in your interest, too. And now you want to cry off. You make me throw up, you pathetic little boy! Stand up and let me see if you've peed your pants! You've got your father's name, but that's where it ends. You're a Mummy's boy, that's all! A great big lala!"

The last bits were too much. He jumped to his feet and hurled his cup onto his saucer, sending the pieces flying.

"Don't you dare talk to me like that!" he shouted back. Then, more softly and shaking his head, "Please don't. You don't know what you're doing to me."

It went in one ear and out the other.

"What'll you do, drunk? Tell your father on me? You do that! But when you're out of a job without a penny piece, don't come crawling to me for help, because you won't get it!"

"I said 'Please don't', Fern!" he roared above her. "Please! Please! I don't know where I am. I thought you'd understand, and now this."

"I do understand, Russell, I understand very well! You want the pay-off, but you don't want to get your hands dirty! Well, think again, little boy, because you can't have it both ways! I never knew you were such a coward! All you have to do is go through with your master plan, and here you are, snivelling like a milkmaid!"

"I think it's *wrong*, that's why!" he shouted back.

That made her incandescent.

"Not that *again*!" she screamed. "Get it through your skull – you'll be broke! You know you're hopeless at everything, the only way you'll ever be rich is to sit where your father's sitting now! And how are you going to look after that fancy woman of yours? From what I hear, she drinks even more than you do!"

"Who told you that?"

"Your mother if you must know, so it must be true! You disgust me with your precious right and wrong! You're too broken-backed to take Cyril out, so you're coming goody-goody instead!"

She shrieked the last words and beat him on the chest with both fists. He tried to stop her, but all her insecurity was pouring out as rage.

"Get out of my house!" she shouted at fever pitch. She'd lost all thought of winning him over. "Get out right now! If you won't kill your father, I don't want you here ever again!"

There was a silence, then Farrell heard the other sitting room door slam, followed, more faintly, by the front door. Shayler opened the garage door for him without being asked, and then he was gone.

Farrell was at a loss what to think. He'd never asked why Shayler wanted his help, he'd assumed she was into some kind of power struggle at work, but now he knew – it was Cyril Burney's murder, and Shayler had to be sure nothing the police did would get in her way. He slipped out to his car and sat in the gathering night. If she saw him, he could always make an excuse – turning over Peterborough in his mind, something like that. As long as she didn't think he'd been in the house listening.

He didn't believe for a moment the murder was off, it obviously meant too much to both of them for that, but now he knew about it, could he go along with it? If he broke with Shayler, she'd ruin him, the blast he'd just witnessed told him that, so maybe he should turn a blind eye and keep enjoying her wealth. Why not? He'd already suppressed information, colluding was just the next rung on the ladder. What he definitely wouldn't do was pass what he'd heard on to Snape or van Piet: If old man Burney bought it, that was just too bad. He'd told Shayler no one was more careful than he was, and he believed it.

He allowed twenty minutes or so for the dust to settle, then he slammed the door of the Morris as if he'd just arrived and let himself in again, this time making a noise. Shayler heard him and came running through to kiss him. She'd cleared the room up, slipped into her denim suit and brushed her fading hair loose. She was angered and worried by Burney's about-face, and she could kick herself for letting him storm off like that, but she wasn't going to let any of that spoil things now Leo was back. She cooked him a meal and clung to him for the rest of the evening. On the way back from Peterborough he'd decided not to spend the night with her, but the way things had turned out had changed his mind. It would be the last time for the next little while though. If Snape found out he was feeling up a witness, he'd have him out of the police altogether, Lorrie or no Lorrie. He wasn't going to risk that. He'd leave in his own time, not before.

Russell Burney drove from Sunningdale to Stanmore in a mood blacker than midnight, but when Aubrey welcomed him home with an organised smile so apparently full of love, his emotions shifted wholesale yet again, and once more he was convinced he had to get rid of his father. It was the only way he could take care of Aubrey. So the next day, when Shayler was in a meeting with Cyril Burney, Russell was in Klemmsley Marine knocking on Marianne Halter's door.

"I want you to send an e-mail on your computer to Fern Shayler," he said. "It's about a very secret deal. Use the intranet and your personal code."

"But I'm far too insignificant," Halter protested. "She won't even begin to understand why it comes from me."

"Yes she will. If her secretary or someone sees my name and a deal in the same e-mail, you've got a leak waiting to happen. But if your name goes in instead, they'll think it's about Sellotape or something, and Miss Shayler will work out the rest. Now do as I say, please, and don't waste my time."

Halter's first rule was always keep in with the boss so, with Russell dictating, she typed, 'From Marianne Halter, Chief Marine Geologist, to Miss F. Shayler, Finance Director. Message reads: Second thoughts. Deal is on as agreed. – Marianne.' And when in CDB Tower Shayler finally emerged, fuming with anger, from Cyril Burney's meeting, she saw who it really came from straight away. And she couldn't have been gladder. Cyril had been intolerable – overbearing, patronising and, when the others had gone, unfeelingly clumsy.

"You're sawing off the bough you're sitting on," he'd said, meaning to pay her a compliment, "but you're doing it well, I have to say. That meeting would have taken twice as long if someone else had prepared it. I promised you something when I wind things up. Perhaps I can find a buyer for that posh house of yours. It'll be far too big for you once Global goes."

She stayed mousy and polite, it was her best defence. He wanted to be thanked, so she thanked him, he wanted some fresh water, so she fetched him some, and then she cleared away. When she got to Russell's e-mail, it swamped her with relief. She had to call Farrell, she wanted him to be part of her joy, even if she couldn't tell him where it came from. He read her message on his cryptophone and answered it from police HQ's car park. Something immense for both of them had happened, she said. Could he come over and be happy with her? He thought it was risky, but he messaged back yes, and tried to sound pleased about it. He'd come over for dinner.

He'd guessed what had happened, he still had his policeman's nous, and if he hadn't known what Shayler and Russell were planning, he'd have enjoyed himself even more once he got there. Shayler was a high class cook, she had a cellarful of wine and she was moving into sex in a big way. As she put it proudly, she was a class act now. But he stuck to his resolve not to spend the night there, and somewhat after midnight, after a careful drive from Sunningdale, he pulled into the yard behind his bed-sit. He locked his car and trudged up to the third floor, unaware he'd been followed. It was unwelcomingly dark as he stepped into the hallway. On one side were his kitchen and bathroom, on the other was his bed-sit, and after he'd switched the light on in it, he stood in the doorway staring contemptuously at the cheap chair and bed, the functional wallpaper, the fly-blown lamp shade and the aging television set. The contrast with Shayler's place couldn't be greater. Was this really all he was worth? If not, what should he do about it, knowing what he did? Run with the hare or hunt with the hounds? At odds with himself, he fetched some beer from the fridge and settled down to a *Daily Express* he'd bought in Peterborough. But he couldn't keep his mind on it.

In the end he dropped it on the floor and got ready for bed, still unclear what to do for the best. He felt he was on a very high wire. One slip, and he'd had it.

Chapter 31

Death by Fire

It was 22nd September at last. The morning was wet and blustery, but by lunchtime the sky had cleared and the wind had fallen away. The forecast said it would stay fine till early evening, when a band of rain, occasionally heavy, would move eastwards across southern England.

The SBS's Counter Terrorism Squadron, led by Lieutenant-Commander Ewen Gorse, had set itself up on RAF Leeming, a secluded jet fighter base forty-five miles south-west of Teesside. A large wooden hut from the Second World War had had its windows blacked out, its locks replaced, and an armed guard put round it. It was now Central Command. Gulliver's combined force – officially called Shrike – was also billeted at Leeming, and soon after daybreak Snape travelled up with van Piet in an Ashell House helicopter. Gorse, Gulliver, Snape and van Piet had hammered out a strategy between them. Amongst themselves and with a certain black irony, they called it Plan A. It was hazardous, and it had to work – there was no Plan B.

The busiest person on Teesside was Alice Tilman. She'd been ferrying electricians, lighting engineers, caterers, and all kinds of CDB-TV folk to and from Parkland Zuka virtually on demand. Then there were the remaining VIPs. Russell hadn't wanted anyone suspecting how stressed he was, so he'd clung to his 'big festive event' for as long as he could. But van Piet had got word to Tilman, she'd persuaded Russell small was better – for safety reasons, she'd been told to say – and

Klemmsley had hurried the cancellations out, likewise alleging safety reasons. Marianne Halter was in Russell's party. He was keeping her where he could see her, and Visual Data was firmly closed. The last thing he wanted was anyone looking at Dassett Point. Farrell was on Russell's list as well. He'd represent the police still working on Dandy Torelli's murder. As such, he'd be in uniform, with his Inspector's two pips on his epaulettes and the raised black band on the peak of his cap. It was a uniform he resented. He might have sold out to Shayler, but he was still convinced he deserved the pip, crown and silver band of a Chief Superintendent. Russell planned for his party to meet at Five Beeches, and one of Klemmsley's Sikorsky S-92s would take them all to Teesmouth. There'd be a gala dinner in the admin building, and then they'd be off to Parkland Zuka by supply ship and helicopter.

Cyril Burney, Enid and Quilter were travelling separately in Cyril's Executive S-92, a luxuriously modified Sikorsky. It was part of a mixed fleet kept for Global's top brass. The fleet was based on Battersea Heliport in London, and its livery – flamboyant blue and gold – made just the kind of statement Cyril liked. Oscar Handley and Silas Wilmot would fly to The Crofter's Hut and take everyone to the lab on Blackhall Rocks. There they would have their own gala dinner – the entire lab would be emptied for the occasion – and then be flown to Teesmouth on their way to Dassett Point.

In Wolvercote, some 240 miles to the south, it was Penderton's turn to clean the cottage while Bunting did the shopping in Oxford. Bunting wanted a new library book as well.

"We have to stay in this evening," Penderton reminded Bunting over lunch. "Conger says today's the big day, and we might yet get called on to help. If not, we must watch CDB-TV."

"I hadn't forgotten, Florence. We may be humble spear-carriers, but we always do our best. Now, since today's special, I think a special dinner is called for. I propose sweet chestnut and chorizo soup, roast leg of lamb, and apple Charlotte."

"Oh, Madge, how wonderful! And we'll drink champagne to our absent colleagues. Mike especially. He's been such a dear over the years."

"I think of him more as a friend than as a colleague. He's mended our cars more than once, and after the windows scare, he practically begged us to let him install a burglar alarm. That was your loss, of course. You'll never get a man in your bed with Mike's alarm keeping guard."

Penderton blushed and lowered her eyes.

"Madge, really!" she giggled, and put a hand to her mouth.

They had an afternoon nap, and then it was time to start cooking.

At 5.15 pm, when the aromas in the kitchen were gathering nicely, an Agusta 109 in blue and gold livery lifted off from Battersea Heliport and set course for Birmingham Airport, where it landed at 6.23 and refuelled. Its Operational Flight Plan – filed in Battersea before take-off – stated it was testing new night flying equipment. After Birmingham Airport, it would circle over the city, cruise south to Calbourne on the Isle of Wight, then swing north east back to Battersea. It had asked Birmingham for a take-off slot at or close to 7.00. It had been given 7.06.

At 6.40 pm Crane left his house in Witton. He was driving his Renault and wearing dark clothes. A combined Essex and SRO team, controlled from Ashell House, was keeping watch, and before he'd cleared Cannington Road he had a motorbike headlight in his mirror. It didn't surprise him, it was Saturday evening, and there was plenty of traffic about. But it wasn't long before the biker was talking fast into his microphone, because he thought Crane might be making for Sutton Park, a 2000 acre wilderness near Sutton Coldfield. The sun was almost gone, it would be dark and deserted in there, and Crane would see straight away if someone was following him. Unsure what to do, Ashell House contacted Leeming.

"If he goes in, peel off and abort the chase," Snape told the biker. "We'll handle it from here."

As he spoke, he glanced at Gorse and van Piet, and caught the vexation in their faces. Plan A was shaky enough. Now this was straddled across it.

While Snape's message was being put round, van Piet was talking to West Midlands Police.

"They're diverting a Traffic Police helicopter from the M6," he said when he'd finished. "It'll have good sight of the Park in under three minutes, and we'll get the infra-reds on a relay. A relief's taken off to stop it looking as if it's hanging about on purpose, and eight Armed Response Vehicles are being posted round the Park. That's all we can do for the moment. What happens next is up to Crane."

The biker had got it right. Crane pulled into Sutton Park and kept going till he came to a plain that was free of trees and water. It was dark and still as he switched the engine off, locked his car and stood waiting. He had a small rucksack on his back.

On Birmingham Airport, the Agusta lifted off on time. It looped west, then north, and in twelve minutes it was slanting down towards the plain. Crane flashed three times with a torch, the Agusta briefly lit up the ground, and as soon as it touched down, Crane ran towards it. The co-pilot let the door down to form a ramp, Crane pounded up it, and before the door was sealed, the Agusta was back in the air. In Leeming, Gorse put a Sea King Mk 7 up. It wasn't fast and it didn't have to be. Its function was airborne surveillance.

"If he comes this way, we'll know," Gorse said to Snape, who was handing the Armed Response Vehicles back to West Midlands Police. But it soon looked as if the Agusta was heading south, so the Mk 7 was called back to Leeming.

"Do I follow the Agusta?" the Traffic Police pilot asked Snape.

"Tell her no, Eddie," van Piet put in. "Get the relief to do it, it's safer. And definitely not too close."

While Snape was putting the change through, Gorse was talking to his HQ in Poole.

"I've got a Mk 7 flying north from base," he said as Snape flicked off his microphone. "If the Agusta doesn't divert, she'll pick it up somewhere off Swindon."

"What if it lands?" asked Snape.

"I've got a Mk 4 on standby in Poole. She's faster than the Mk 7, and she'll carry an assault team of eight – Alpha Attack we're calling them. I've also readied a Lynx for high-speed tailing. She's got her own four-man assault team, and we're calling them Lynx One. If the Agusta sticks to heading south, there's a stealth boat on full alert in Cowes. With 70 mph to draw on, she won't hang about."

He broke off as fresh tea and coffee were trolleyed round. They were needed. A heavy fug had built up in the hut, and a lot of people were talking at once. When van Piet spoke to Garry on the link with Ashell House, he had to turn the volume up so Snape and Gorse could hear what came back.

"Tom, you've got the Agusta's registration. What do you know about it?"

"It's part of the top persons fleet CDB Global keeps on Battersea Heliport. It left for Birmingham Airport at 5.15 this afternoon, refuelled, and took off again at 7.06. Its OFP says it'll fly back to Battersea via Calbourne on the Isle of Wight."

"Who commissioned the flight?"

"No one. The crew's testing night flying instruments, or so the OFP says. Apparently some of them have had to be replaced."

"So no one from outside got in touch to make this happen."

"Battersea said no when I asked. The crew organised the flight, and under 'Purpose' they've put 'Technical checks'. I've told Battersea not to ask any questions, and a couple of our people have gone over on motorbikes to underline that. Mr Benjamin sent them after I spoke to him."

Van Piet terminated the call. As he finished his tea, Snape said,

"It doesn't look as if Crane's going to be killed, Willem."

"No, they're going to pull him out, and my guess is, the plan's been on file for some while. Crane works for himself, so a fake job order would be all he'd need to tell him when and where. The Augusta crew could get a heads-up in the same sort of way, and no one would take any notice."

He broke off for a moment.

"I'm wondering about the Wolvercote pair," he went on. "Your people are handling that one. You'd better draft in some reinforcements."

"You think they'll be pulled out as well, do you?"

Snape was reaching for the phone as he spoke.

"If they're not killed off. We know from Ian they've been told to stay in their cottage."

"Why don't we blow the whistle on them? We've got enough against them."

"Can't be done, not at this late stage. What if they don't answer a pre-arranged phone call or something? It could wreck everything."

"It would keep them safe though. You said yourself someone might have a go at them."

"That's their problem before it's ours, Eddie. They've been keeping bad company, and bad company can always turn against you. They should know that for themselves."

The Agusta cruised steadily southwards and a relative lull set in. The gala dinners were winding on, Shrike was on Parkland Zuka, and CDB-TV was under orders not even to hint in its build-up that there was anything unusual on the rig. The trade-off was unrestricted coverage after the VIPs arrived. Van Piet had insisted on both parts without saying why. Cyril Burney had done the rest.

The Traffic Police helicopter had been sent back, and suddenly the Mk 7 was signalling the Agusta had left its OFP. Instead of making for Calbourne, it was sliding eastwards and losing speed. Was it arc-ing round to Southampton? That would bring it within forty miles of Poole. Gorse scrambled the Mk4 and the Lynx, and sent the Mk 4 towards the New Forest.

"Use your speed," he told the Lynx. "Get east of the Agusta without being seen. Then keep in contact with it."

The Agusta wasn't interested in Southampton. Staying east of Southampton Water, it was crawling towards the Solent and the Channel. From well west of Southampton Water, the MK7 was keeping parallel with it.

The *Leonid Golovin* was in the same area – it was anchored off Portsmouth in the Spithead strait – and there was something not right about it. Ships on goodwill visits are normally all lit up after dark, but the *Golovin*, apart from its navigation lights, only had its working lights on, and even they weren't very bright. So, once the Lynx had rounded the Agusta, Gorse told it to get as many night camera shots of the warship as it could. Meanwhile, van Piet brought in Kossler. He gave him the Agusta's registration and read him its position off one of Gorse's charts.

"Any chatter between the Russians and this machine?" he asked.

"I'll check."

It didn't take him long – the warship was monitored round the clock.

"Not a word."

"What about your sat pics? Can you see the decks?"

"I'll say yes. The lights are so dim, we're computer-enhancing."

"Slava-class cruisers carry just one helicopter. Is there one on the helideck?"

"Yes there is, it's moored in place. It looks as if they're getting ready to work on it. I'll give you a feed so you can see for yourself."

There was an encoding/decoding pause, then,

"We've got it and it's good."

Van Piet studied the feed with Gorse and Snape. Then it was back to helicopters that were airborne.

"The Agusta seems to have a rendezvous lined up," van Piet said. "Probably to drop Crane off. It's hovering on the edge of the mainland as if it's waiting for something."

"Like a pre-arranged time?" Gorse asked. "There's been no chatter, don't forget."

"Could be. Or making sure the *Golovin's* radar can see it."

"But it can't land on the *Golovin*, Willem. The helideck's totally blocked."

"The bad lighting's the give-away – hold on, I thought so! There, you can see why the *Golovin*'s so dark now!"

He switched the sat pics to a large HD screen, and on the side of the warship facing the small Isle of Wight town of Bembridge, the davits were lowering a black RIB into the water.

"I make it six on the saddle-seats and one steering," Gorse said as it moved off. "I've seen RIBs like this one before. They can do 50 mph if they have to."

He repositioned the Mk 7 so he could see the water between the *Golovin* and Bembridge better, sent the stealth boat out of Cowes at speed, and filtered the MK4 through the Saturday night air traffic into Isle of Wight air space. Then he went back to his charts. First he checked the currents, then the RIB's speed and rate of curve as it found its line. The rest was maritime maths and SBS charts of the Isle of Wight coastline.

"The Agusta," he said confidently, "will come down here."

He downloaded a file picture of an open stretch of grassland. It was two or three miles up from Bembridge's harbour and something under a mile inland. Along the edge nearest the sea was woodland with a footpath through it, then came the promenade that doubled as a sea wall, a sandy beach and the Channel. He contacted the Mk 4, gave it the story plus the grassland's co-ordinates, and told it to come in fast and low – 'low' meaning treetop height or less.

"I want Alpha Attack out and you gone before the Agusta gets near the place. Go now."

He switched directly to Alpha Attack.

"Hide in the woodland on landing and keep your target in sight till he makes his move. Further instructions to follow. Don't think about how you're getting out. We'll tell you when we know. One moment—"

He broke off as van Piet held a piece of paper in front of him.

"Use silenced weapons only," he read out, and added, using naval slang for the Mk 4, "Leave all submachine guns in the Junglie. That's an order."

The Mk 4 roared towards the grassland, its landing gear skimming the trees. It was pitch dark outside, the terrain raced past on the screens, and then it was shedding speed. Keeping its landing lights off, it hovered while Alpha Attack jumped out, then it was gone, staying low again till it was safe to gain height. Wearing night goggles, Alpha Attack fanned out into the trees and waited, but not for long. The Agusta had come round wide astern of the *Golovin*, passed over the RIB, and was landing on the grassland. Unlike the MK4, as Alpha Attack smugly noted, it put its landing lights on. As soon as it touched down, it dowsed them, the door came down and, looking greenish through Alpha Attack's night goggles, Crane scrambled out. He had night goggles on, too, the ones he'd worn in Matlock Bath, and in his right hand was a lethal-looking Ceska. The Agusta clattered away towards Calbourne, and behind and high above it was the Lynx. It shadowed the Agusta to Calbourne, and always keeping its distance, it landed ahead of it in Battersea. When the Agusta's crew entered the terminal, Lynx One quietly closed round them and eased them into a side room, where an SRO agent detained them under the Crown Warrant.

"They can send for their lawyers, but keep everything away from the media," van Piet had told the SRO man. "I don't want even a sniff of this reaching Teesside."

Team Leaders in the SBS aren't picked by rank, they're picked by ability, and Alpha Attack was led by Simon Luff, a corporal from the Royal Marines. He'd positioned himself near the beginning of the footpath. If he moved his head slightly, he could see Crane getting closer. He held his breath.

Crane was within a few feet of him as he passed. Cupping his hand over his radio, Luff called Gorse as soon as it was safe. The target was heading down the footpath.

"Stand by to follow," Luff heard. "Stop him reaching the RIB and take him alive if you can."

There was a pattering, rustling sound as they spoke – it was the band of rain and, as forecast, it was heavy. Luff was pleased about that – it would make it easier to move through the trees without being heard. It would also empty the promenade. He radioed Gorse's instructions on.

Crane didn't seem in any great hurry, and Luff kept him in sight without stepping onto the footpath. Occasionally he glimpsed one of his team deep in the trees, helping to keep Crane boxed in. Whoever reached the promenade first would watch him onto the beach till Luff caught up.

As predicted, the promenade was deserted when Luff reached it, and in the dim light it cast onto the beach, he saw Crane labouring towards the sea through the rain. The tide was three quarters out, so he had some way to go. Alpha Attack had dispersed along the promenade and Luff was well onto the beach when Crane stopped, took his torch out without putting his Ceska away, and looked out across the water. Luff stopped as well and tried to see what Crane was looking for. The rain was blurring his goggles, so all he saw at first was broken lights from out to sea. Then he saw the *Golovin's* RIB edging slowly in. Its navigation lights were out and the rain was killing the noise of its motors. Crane flashed it twice, and a single flash came back. It was the signal he wanted.

There wasn't much of a sea, the waves were little more than lapping onto the beach, and the RIB had a draught of under three feet. Wading out to it would be no problem, so Luff had to act straight away. He drew his SigSauer and ran across the sand towards Crane just as Crane stopped again, this time to put his torch back in his rucksack. As he half-turned, he saw he was being followed. Turning right round, he pointed his Ceska at Luff, who stopped and raised his hands.

"Keep your hands in the air," Crane called, "and drop your gun."

Luff let his pistol fall.

"Who are you?" Crane called again.

"Royal Navy. My orders are to prevent you leaving the country."

"There must be more than you. Where are the rest?"

"Along the promenade. They've got you in their sights right now."

"They won't fire, you're in the way. Stay where you are till I get on board, and don't try picking your gun up. I'll kill you if you do."

An eerie stand-off followed. Luff kept perfectly still, so did the rest of Alpha Attack, and step by step, Crane backed into the water. He could hear the RIB inching in as close as it could without grounding its propellers. He didn't dare look round, but he reckoned if he could get waist-deep, the Russians would take care of the rest. As long as the water was up to his ankles, he had no trouble, but as it got deeper, he had to keep stopping so as not to lose his balance, and when it was well up his thighs, he heard the motors' notes change. He didn't understand it, but he knew what it meant – the RIB was backing away. He had to risk turning his head, and as he did so, he was hit by a shaft of light so bright, it flooded his goggles and blinded him. It was the stealth boat. It had crept in from the north, and while the RIB's crew had been watching Crane, it had moved athwart its stern to block it in. Still reversing, the RIB tried to turn in the space it had left, but it couldn't make it, so it idled at an angle. Forcing an exit wasn't an option. Three marines had their side arms trained on Crane from the stealth boat's deck – they were silenced as well – and Luff saw his chance. Leaving his SigSauer where it was, he raced into the water and covered the last few yards half running, half floundering, as Crane was blinking his vision back. He thrust Crane off his feet and, grabbing handholds in his clothes, he forced him under water. On the beach, the rest of Alpha Attack closed in, a phalanx of shadows moving forwards to get into better shooting range. One of them added Luff's SigSauer to his own.

Crane fought desperately, but he couldn't cope with the comprehensively trained marine. Once he managed to seize Luff's throat, but his grip wasn't strong enough, and he crashed backwards into the sea as Luff broke his hold. Each time Crane went under, he came up weaker, till he simply couldn't fight any more. Totally exhausted, he stood in the streaming rain with his mouth wide open and his shoulders slumped forward, heaving air in and out as fast as he could. He'd lost his goggles, his eyes were stinging, and his Ceska was on the seabed somewhere. But even if he'd had it in his hand, he wouldn't have had the strength to use it.

Luff waded back to create some space.

"There are three weapons trained on you," he raised his voice to say through the rain. "Put your hands up now."

Crane did as he was told, then turned his head to look round again. The stealth boat's light was on reduced power, and he could see the Russians were watching him, but they were making no move to help him. They'd given him up.

"This way," Luff ordered. "Walk past me to the beach. I'll follow you."

When Crane reached the water's edge, his hands were manacled behind his back and he was guarded at gunpoint. Luff trod around in the sea and eventually found the Ceska. He got his SigSauer back as well. He had no idea what would happen next, but he could wait. He assumed the stealth boat had been talking to Gorse. When the captain came out on deck, it was to address the RIB's crew in fluent Russian with a faultless Home Counties accent.

"Gentlemen," he said. "Sometimes we get strange commands. You've been watched since you left the *Leonid Golovin.* You might be expecting to be detained, since you are clearly in breach of British law, but you are to reverse your RIB and return unhindered to your mothership. When I move my vessel, you can go. And put your lights on, please. These are busy waters."

Once the RIB had moved off, he called to Luff he'd be taking Alpha Attack and Crane back to Poole. He'd put a couple of inflatables out for them.

The Mk 7 had been streaming pictures nonstop, and in Leeming the hut burst into applause. Gorse was human and he liked it, but he felt more relief than triumph.

"We were lucky there," he exclaimed, emptying his cup. His tea had gone cold, but he didn't notice. "It was exactly what we wanted, Willem – contained, unseen and silent. But it didn't have to go like that. Crane could easily have taken Luff out."

"He'd have lost his human shield, but you're right, he could have. I hope you'll follow that up when this is over. Luff deserves it."

"Why didn't the Russians put up a fight?" asked Snape.

"Parkland Zuka's more important. They'll have been ordered not to create any kind of incident."

"But they left Crane to tell all."

"He won't, he's too brainwashed for that. He's the type."

As Crane had watched the RIB pull away, he'd accepted it as he accepted everything that came from Russia. He believed Russia was surrounded by enemies who had to be defeated if it was to achieve the greatness that was its due. That belief sealed his lips – if he couldn't hurt his captors, he wouldn't help them either. To him it was all a matter of loyalty. Bunting and Penderton would pay a heavy price for it.

The *Golovin*, too, maintained its silence, except that in amongst the routine signals between it and the Russian Embassy, a technical run-down mentioned 'salt corrosion' twice. It meant Crane had been taken. When the message reached Zembarov, who was sitting in Valkov's office, he showed no disappointment.

"Everything depends on Katya Danilovna now," he said.

He had no doubt she'd succeed and make everything right.

"You're confident, are you?" Valkov asked, stroking the old man's pride. "You're asking a lot of her. Some would say too much."

"She puts her country first. As you'll see, it pulls her through every time."

In Wolvercote, Bunting and Penderton had their special dinner, and they drank their toasts, especially to Mike, who was more a friend than a colleague. The rest of the evening they spent much as they usually did. Bunting took her new library book into the study, and Penderton stayed in the sitting room, crocheting and listening to Radio Three. They'd decided not to put their TV on early, they didn't like being waffled at, so they were still in separate rooms when their cottage caught fire at the calculated time of 10.50.

Their Russian handlers had always believed they were unsound. Unlike Crane, they were amateurs, and if they got caught, they'd give too much away. Crane, therefore, had got the assignment of making sure they could be silenced fast if they had to be. He knew Crime Prevention had rattled them, so it was easy to insist on the burglar alarm, especially as the police had made a big thing about having one put in. He gave them a router, installed the master unit in their cellar, and put an incendiary device in with it. Its timer could be pre-set remotely, and seconds before it went off, any doors and windows that weren't locked already would be locked automatically. It was housed in the same reinforced plastic box the master unit was in, and Crane – 'Such a dear!' – did all the servicing himself. The device wouldn't explode, but its starter heat would destroy anything near it, including the box it was in. An inferno was guaranteed.

Bunting and Penderton's time had come at last, so, following instructions, Crane set the timer for 10.50 before he left for Sutton Park. When it went off, the heatflash – nearly 4000°F – was into the floorboards under Penderton's chair within milliseconds. They were tinder dry and she didn't stand a chance. She and her chair crashed into the cellar, where she suffocated while she burned. Bunting was further away, but when she heard flames crackling, she wrenched the study door open, and the heat and smoke nearly got her right there. Panicking, she slammed the door to, but she had to get a window open or she was trapped. She ripped the curtains apart, grabbed one handle, then the other one, but neither would budge. Outside the door, the flames were roaring loudly, held back by the thickness of the oak it was made of. Realising the windows were locked, not jammed, she scrabbled wildly in a china box on the sill till she found the key. But it was useless, the locks were blocked electronically. In a frenzy, she beat on the panes with both fists, then she smashed the china box against one of them and finally, with tears of fright half-blinding her, she snatched up an upright chair and flailed at the glass with it. But it was shatterproof, as she'd serenely told van Piet. And the panes couldn't be prised out either. They were wedged in, again to defeat burglars.

Outside, Snape had a team of eight tightly ringing the cottage, with three more in cars nearby. When the fire engulfed the sitting room, the windows cracked and melted, feeding the flames with oxygen and sending them roaring upwards. The two officers at the front, joined by the two from the sitting room side, tried to break the front door in, but it wouldn't give, and then the heat beat them off. Still hoping, they raced round the back, where the other four were futilely trying to force the windows with their fingers. The electric wiring was burned out so there was no light inside, but they could hear Bunting beating on the glass, and when one of them shone his torch in, she looked frantic. The study door was still holding and the ceiling was non-inflammable, but the woodwork above it was burning fast and smoke was curling under the door. Every time Bunting breathed in, she choked, and now the study's floorboards had caught. Desperately, one of the officers scooped up a rock from the garden and pounded it against the glass. He might as well not have bothered.

"Get out of the way!"

It was a junior PC from one of the cars – Yasmin Hewett – and she had a crowbar in her hand. She drove it in hard between the bottom of the frame and the sill, and yanked at it with all her weight. But the frame didn't move and the crowbar came away. She tried again and the same thing happened. But when she tried a third time, the officer with the rock banged it in further before the rock split in two, and they both worked the crowbar as hard as they could. For a few long seconds it seemed as if they'd be frustrated yet again, then a gap opened up. They forced the crowbar in further, there was a snapping sound as the fixing screws came away, and they levered the whole frame out. There was no time to lose now with the air rushing in. A piece of ceiling had struck Bunting's head, she was unconscious on the floor, and the floorboards' flames were licking rapidly towards her. Despite the smoke and heat, Hewett clambered inside and heaved Bunting up to the sill, where two of her colleagues seized the older woman and dragged her out. Bunting was alive, but that was all. As Hewett was snatched to safety in turn, the rest of the ceiling came crashing down, the door burned through, and what was left of the floor became a sea of flames. Bunting's life had almost cost Hewett hers.

Manhandling Bunting by her shoulders and feet, the police staggered clear as the first of the emergency vehicles came clamouring in their direction. Orange-red flames were lancing into the night, the thatch was long gone, and as they watched, the roof timbers collapsed in a great shower of sparks. The neighbouring dwellings had their lights on, and frightened residents, many of them in dressing gowns and several clutching small children, had run out to see what was happening. The firefighters worked fast, but there was no saving the cottage, so they switched to protecting the adjacent buildings while Bunting was rushed to hospital. Three officers risked the garage's flickering roof to prise the door open, break into the Volkswagen, and wheel it away from the blaze, its alarm sounding and its lights flashing as if it was being stolen.

When Snape got the details from his team leader, he was convinced Bunting and Penderton had been got at, and he felt it was his fault. Van Piet, who shared Snape's conviction, didn't agree with the fault bit.

"You're wrong to blame yourself," he said to Snape. "When Bunting's up to it, maybe she'll tell us which of her friends set this one up and when. My guess is, it was well before we came on the scene, and if I'm right, we never had a chance."

It was all he had time for. The North Sea was where the big news was, so the Wolvercote blaze got crowded out. And, as both sides intended for their different reasons, the media missed Bembridge altogether. It had never happened and, therefore, it couldn't get in the way.

Chapter 32

Crisis Time

The dinner on Blackhall Rocks was like in a graveyard. The food and wines were top of the range, but with only five people eating in a virtually empty building, the atmosphere was deadly. It didn't help that Cyril Burney did most of the talking – and at one point walked out to take a call on his mobile. His health seemed to have gone down sharply, though he perked up a fraction when he boarded the Klemmsley Diamond, the supply ship that would take him to Dassett Point. It made the crossing under glittering stars, and when it reached the boreholes, its dynamic positioning locked it in place.

In parallel time, on a gentrified farm near Exmoor, Henry Seeler, who was home for the weekend, was sitting in the fortified barn he kept his hardware in. His wife was in the farmhouse finishing the ironing, and their three small children were asleep in the nursery. On an HD screen in front of him, a pulsating point of light was positioning itself in 2D. Seeler had no control over what he saw, he was watching whatever was fed to him. When the point of light halted, he was switched to four ROVs coming out of their cage with their lights full on. When one of them neared the borehole that once housed the regulator valve, the frame over it lit up and its cameras showed the ROV de-silt the top of the plug. Seeler had a wall clock over the screen. It was closing in on 10.25, and as the sweeper hand covered the last seconds, the screen split into quarters and four retrieval tools began their simultaneous descent. The timing was perfect. Seeler rubbed his hands and looked forward to the rest. Soon the point of light would go crazy.

That would show the ship was sinking and tell him he'd earned his fee. It was a lot higher than usual – 'special circumstances' cost special amounts. He could wait for his money if he had to, but he didn't let it happen often.

Russell Burney's dinner was, on the face of it, more cheerful. Six people in a smaller room made a difference, and Aubrey, who said she wanted to get to know them all, seemed to be talking to everyone at once. But below the surface the tensions were real. Russell's eyes were ringed, he dropped his fork twice, and when he covered up by saying Harvest Home was getting to him, "Me, too" went round the table.

Halter was the only one who could say it without crossing her fingers behind her back. Just by being there, Dvorski reminded Russell of the grip the Russians had on him. Killing his father and – it was almost self-destruction – killing his mother were about to become reality, and Farrell's uniform added fear to his guilt every time he looked in his direction. Then there was his sagging willpower. Shortly he'd be tested as he'd never been tested before, and he had no idea how he'd make out. Despite Valkov's threats, he might simply collapse and do nothing.

Dvorski and Shayler were also massively fearful. Dvorski was afraid Shayler would cost him his career, and Shayler needed to know Farrell was near her if she was to keep her nerve. Farrell, however, was fretting about one thing only – how to come out of this a winner.

When they finally left the admin building, they were wrapped up and shod for outdoors; but the night air still got to them as they boarded the Klemmsley Sapphire, the supply ship Tilman had put their way. Tilman was waiting on the gangway, she was going across with them. The helicopter crew who'd flown them from Five Beeches had had a meal laid on in the galley and were passing their time on the bridge. The refuelled S-92 was on the helideck in front of them.

"Can we have a look round? I've never been on one of these before," Aubrey asked Tilman as they left the Tees and the swell of the sea took over. She slipped on her leather shoulder bag and asked whether anyone else would like to come. Shayler hoped Farrell would say yes, it would give her a chance to be close to him, but guessing what she wanted, he said no. He was determined to keep his distance. Trying not to sound disappointed, Shayler said no as well. Russell, as host, felt obliged to stay with them, and that gave Halter her lead. Supply ships were part of her life, she said, glancing at her boss. So she'd rather stay in the warm this time, if that was all right.

"That leaves you, Mr Dvorski," Aubrey said, turning to look straight at him. "Please don't let me go on my own."

Dvorski really wanted to keep an eye on Shayler, but he didn't want to stand out either, so he said yes and eased himself into his hardshell. Aubrey gave him a peck on the cheek, Tilman found some life jackets and led them round the decks, explaining what everything was for.

"Can we go on the bridge?" Aubrey asked in her tinkling English. "I'm sure Mr Dvorski has seen it all before, but it would be an enormous treat for me."

Tilman laughed amiably. Aubrey had style.

"It's up to the captain," she answered. "I'll go and ask."

She disappeared up the steps and Aubrey switched to Russian.

"I'm Cotton, I repeat, Cotton," she whispered, adding spitefully, "and I'd know you anywhere with an ear like that. Grigory Viktorovich is in the Embassy, I thought you'd like to have that information. Now give me my Smith and Wesson. Quickly, stupid, before Tilman comes back."

He took it out of his hardshell.

"It's safed and loaded," he said, but she checked it herself before she put it in her shoulder bag.

'So Zembarov's in London,' he thought glumly.

He couldn't help it, the name weighed on him like lead. And then Aubrey speaking Russian and turning out to be Cotton. He'd been sure Cotton would be Russell, 'rock hard' Russell, as Valkov had called him. But he'd got something wrong again, and his confidence leaked some more.

"So who's telling you what to do? Valkov?" he asked, hoping it was. Irrationally, he felt Valkov might treat him better than Zembarov.

Malignancy suffused her face as if a mask had been peeled off.

"Don't you understand anything?" she sneered. "Valkov's a lackey. I work for Zembarov. He's the one with the power."

Tilman took them up to the bridge. Parkland Zuka was coming into view, as bright as a bonfire against the night sky. The other rigs were lit up, too, only not so brightly, and there was a cluster of vessels ahead that all resembled each other.

"They're fireboats," Tilman explained. "There's sixteen altogether, that's two rows of eight. When the Klemmsley Diamond approaches the rig, it'll pass between them while they shoot water into the air and shine their searchlights through it. It should be quite a show. They can shoot up to 400 feet high."

Finally it was time for them all to zip into body bags and climb into the S-92. Dvorski had to force himself inside, but once the door was shut he felt strangely relaxed: there was no going back now, he was committed, so he could stop fighting his nerves. When they landed on the helideck, Russell helped Aubrey out first, and the English rose smile she gave him was like balm on his raging distress. Shayler slipped back to be with Farrell, and they left the helideck last. As they all clustered at the head of the staircase to unzip their body bags, she secretly squeezed his arm.

"You're my strength, Leo," she whispered.

Smiling glassily, he stepped aside to let her through. That way he didn't have to reply.

The Klemmsley Sapphire had turned round, and the S-92 was readying up to fly back to it. On the next rig, in a sealed unit, GCHQ was monitoring all signals to and from Parkland Zuka, and on the far side, away from the lights, a supply ship covertly loaned to Gorse launched an RIB. When it was waterborne, a six-man strike force – code-name Gamma Attack – took their places on its saddle-seats. On Parkland

Zuka itself, Shrike were all in position, some in unlit corners, some in empty cabins. They were armed and all in radio contact. Russell hadn't wanted any police on the rig, but someone must have contacted Cyril, because word came through they had to be there – again in the interests of safety.

The focus of everything was the drilling deck. The drill was ready to go, all its crew needed was the word, and when it went, the drills on the other rigs would all go as well. At a safe distance from the derrick there were chairs for the guests. They were on thick carpeting under an awning, five in the front row for Cyril's party and six behind for Russell's. Each chair had a name card on it, and Aubrey read them all carefully. Drinks and a buffet had their own awning on the next side round, and the *son et lumière* people shared a third one with CDB-TV. The drilling crew was on the fourth side. They were in the open, sitting on steel benches and doing their best not to look as if they came from another planet. Filling in time, a TV presenter was explaining how gas was produced and drilled for. Next to him was an oversize clock with 11 o'clock marked in red. As Tilman led Russell's party to their places, close-focus shots showed them one by one, and their names and status were blended in. Van Piet, Snape and Gorse watched them in Leeming, Valkov and Zembarov watched them in the Embassy. All of them noticed the smiles looked very fixed.

The oversize clock was showing 10.35, the fireboats were on station, and a cameraman on the helideck was waiting for the Executive S-92. 10.45 was when it was due to arrive, but it could always be late, the presenter said several times. The North Sea was no man's friend, and Mr Cyril had ordered radio silence.

The minutes passed, the presenter talked on, and at 10.45 there was no show. Russell stared at the clock as if the Devil was waiting for his soul in it, but Shayler's eyes glistened and her hands clenched with joy as the time slipped away. Cyril Burney was dead! It was a new dawn breaking! 10.50 came and went and Russell, crazed by mental pictures of his mother and his father going under, was telling himself he'd never find the strength to order, 'Go max!' when three blasts on a foghorn sounded out of the dark and the lights of the Klemmsley Diamond all came on at once. Cyril had made it late out of vanity.

The Klemmsley Diamond's lights were the signal for two roaring, cascading walls of water and light from the fireboats. It was exactly as Russell had planned, even though he'd been sure it would never happen. Once the Klemmsley Diamond was through the guard of honour, the Executive S-92 lifted off and landed on the helideck. Tilman hurried to meet it, and as Handley and Wilmot did the securing, she unfolded the wheelchair she'd put up there ready to bring Cyril, along with the rest of his party, down to the drilling deck via a lift. There were no body bags to worry about – Cyril never used them.

A strange pause followed that seemed to have more than one layer. Cyril remained standing, but leaning very heavily on Quilter, till Handley and Wilmot had finished; and he wilted even more as Handley came towards him, slipping his protective gloves off. Confidentially Handley said he and Wilmot had better stay with the helicopter in case Cyril needed to be removed quickly, and Cyril, instead of resisting, agreed as if that was what he'd been wanting to hear.

"Have I done the right thing?" he asked Quilter as he slumped into the wheelchair and allowed Tilman to wheel him off the helideck.

"It's what I'd have done, Sir."

"Won't I look small, coming in with just you and Mrs Burney? There'll be two empty chairs now, don't forget."

"I shouldn't worry, Sir. I think you'll look determined."

When they reached the drilling deck, admiring introductions were made over the loudspeakers, then came a recorded fanfare, and Cyril – on his feet again but once more leaning heavily on Quilter – led his party to their seats, with a spotlight picking him out. Only three, not five, Aubrey noted with satisfaction – it was all going to plan. Gulliver, kitted up and armed like the rest of Shrike, noted the same thing from the deep shadow behind the buffet. She knew van Piet would have a TV on, but she radioed him softly anyway in case he had any updates. Coloured lights were weaving bright patterns round the drill, and when the fanfare finished, a military band, also recorded, played marches and ballads Cyril was known to be fond of. Keeping out of sight, Shrike was gradually closing in.

The helideck, now deserted except for the Executive S-92, topped one of the mighty columns that soared up from Parkland Zuka's pontoons. At the base of the next column and shrouded in darkness, Gamma Attack was silently accessing the maintenance steps.

Russell was horror-struck to see his father, it was like seeing the walking dead. But at the same time the pressure on his conscience lifted, so he was profoundly relieved as well. And dearest Enid, always caring and gentle, she was alive, too. Russell was so overwhelmed with emotion, he forgot everything else. He thrust his way past Quilter and, with his eyes brimming with tears, he embraced his father with a lifetime's frustrated love. Then he wrapped his mother in his arms, pressed his cheek against hers, and struggled for words that wouldn't come. But when he let her go and stepped away, cold reason struck back hard and quickly – there'd be no inheritance for him now, Global would be sold, and Valkov had him where he wanted him.

But remembering Valkov raised his hopes. Still believing Valkov wanted the tsunami, he also still believed Valkov might protect him if he did as Valkov wished. Valkov couldn't have known about Global being sold when they'd been in the Embassy basement together, he'd have said something for sure if he had. But maybe if he – Russell – went max as agreed, Valkov would go the extra mile for him out of gratitude when Global, having survived the tsunami and its aftermath, came onto the market. Russell's willpower wasn't up to going max, he was clear about that, but when he looked round for Tilman to give her the order, he had a substitute for willpower no one had reckoned with – sheer desperation. But before he could open his mouth, Shayler rushed between him and Tilman, exactly as Aubrey had primed her to do, except for one immense difference – Shayler wasn't acting rationally, she was completely out of control. When the Klemmsley Diamond had emerged from the night, her sense of betrayal had almost physically knocked her over. She could only explain things one way – Russell Burney had caved in after all and she was left with nothing. Nothing at all!!! And then she'd seen Russell actually embrace the father he'd said he'd murder. It was so buddy-buddy, so disregarding of her and her overwhelming needs, it made her go berserk.

"Don't you dare tell her to start that drill!" she yelled, her whole body heaving with fury. "I know all about you, Russell Burney! I told you your father was going to sell CDB Global, and you promised me faithfully – faithfully – you'd kill him before that happened, so you could inherit it and keep me in my job!"

"So that's why she's foaming at the mouth," Aubrey thought to herself cynically. "She's lost the lot, poor thing."

Aubrey felt easier now she knew that. Her big fear was not knowing something, because what she didn't know, she couldn't control.

Shayler looked round manically at Cyril Burney. She didn't care everyone was staring at her, and she was positively glad it was all being beamed world-wide. Destruction was the one thing she had left, and the bigger the audience, the better.

"You shouldn't be sitting there, you great bully!" she shrieked at him. "You should be dead! Do you hear me? Dead! Your own son was going to murder you! He hates you through and through, and so do I!"

"Fern, be quiet!" Cyril barked hoarsely. "You've said more than enough already!"

Quilter was holding him upright in his chair. Urgently he signalled towards the bar for some water so Burney could take one of his tablets. He looked as if he was going to pass out.

"No I will not be quiet!" Shayler shrieked back, as one of the waiters scurried over with the water. "I've been quiet all my life, thanks to you! But I won't be quiet any longer!"

She spaced out her last words to emphasise them, and by the time she got to the end, she was sobbing as much as shrieking. Pleadingly she looked at Farrell. The coloured lights were still playing, but no one was seeing them, the spotlight was gone, and the military band had been switched off. She was on her own.

"Help me, Leo," she begged, almost softly. "Please help me."

The stillness that followed seemed to last forever. She'd forgotten Aubrey might help her, but Aubrey didn't count anyway. It had to be Farrell.

"I don't see how I can, Miss Shayler," he answered stiffly. "And please don't use my first name. We've only ever met on police business."

Shayler went white and her eyes grew large. She'd never known such hurt, not even in her red-blotch days. Behind her a microphone on a boom craned forward.

"Get more of her face," the cameraman heard in his headphones, and he moved round a bit more.

"How can you say that, Leo?" she wept. "You've drunk my brandy, you've been in my bed, I've told you the most intimate things about myself, and you have a key to my house!" She wiped her eyes with the back of her hand and her tone softened further. "I fell in love with you, Leo, and I hoped you'd love me back. Now I can see you were only in it for yourself. Exactly like Mr Burney here," she lashed out, getting louder again. "All he's ever thought of is himself. But there's something he needs to know before I shut up and it's this. Harvest Home must not go ahead!"

It wouldn't do her any good to say why not, but she was determined to say it anyway. The red-mist urge to do damage – any damage, regardless of who it hurt or helped – had completely taken over. As she faced Cyril square on, she saw a movement on the edge of her vision, but she didn't follow it up. It was Dvorski tilting his chair towards Aubrey's. He was so worked up, he was gripping her wrist without realising it.

"I've got to shoot her before she says why not," he whispered. "Valkov said it'd all been worked out. Is that right?"

Aubrey tingled – success was just seconds away. This was what she and Valkov had lied for.

"Of course," she whispered back, unobtrusively freeing her wrist. "It came from Grigory Viktorovich. Shoot her now, the helicopter's waiting for you. So's your career."

So she knew about that as well.

"And Russell Burney will go ahead anyway? He'll keep the shooting and the drilling separate?"

"You can count on it. He's rock hard. Nothing will stop him, nothing at all."

Suddenly she became angry.

"What are you waiting for, misfit?" she hissed. "You've got diplomatic status. Do it now!"

He reached into his hardshell, unsafed the Walther using just one hand, and drew it out. He didn't notice Aubrey slip her hand into her shoulder bag. She was poised to shoot Dvorski as soon as he'd gunned down Shayler.

In the Russian Embassy Zembarov rubbed his blue-veined old man's hands. His moment of triumph had come, and he'd made sure Russian television would show it nationwide. When Dvorski shot Shayler, everyone in Russia, helped by well-briefed commentators, would see him as the kind of wild individualist Russia had to purge itself of, and when Aubrey shot Dvorski – the commentators would say 'executed' – she'd be a patriot doing a patriot's duty. On top of that, the Shayler woman would stop the tsunami – for her own reasons so far as Zembarov could see, but the outcome would be the same – and Russia would stay in the clear. Russell Burney, of course, would do nothing, Katya Danilovna had broken his will. Zembarov didn't know how desperate Russell was and why.

"It's all falling into place, Andrey Ivanovich," Zembarov said, and he allowed himself a rare smile of satisfaction. "All that remains now is for Katya Danilovna to rid us of Dvorski and make her heroic escape."

By this time, on Parkland Zuka, Shayler was hoarse.

"Harvest Home," she shouted, and her voice cracked with the strain, "is deadly dangerous. As soon as it goes max –"

"Fern, no, you mustn't! You can't do this to me! You don't know what you'll cost me!"

It was an anguished yell, and it came from Russell Burney. In his panic he didn't realise it was as good as a public confession. A voice in his head – it sounded weirdly like Toni's – kept saying, "Step back, let it happen," but in his desperation, he overrode it. Knocking over Handley's empty chair, he grabbed clumsily at Shayler as, still seated, Dvorski was raising his pistol. Corbett, who had edged behind Dvorski, grabbed Dvorski's arm, yanked him forward, and pinned him to the carpeting, while one of his colleagues whipped the Walther away and handcuffed him. At the same time, Russell was seized and handcuffed, while Shayler was bundled to safety behind the bar and handcuffed there. Beyond the lights, other Shrike personnel blocked the exits with well-practised efficiency. Finally Gulliver stepped out from behind the buffet, her ID held high in the air, and Aubrey stayed still, keeping her gun hidden till she could reason which of her contingency plans she should use, now her main plan had broken down.

A night-time breeze had sprung up, and salt air from the sea was blowing across Gulliver's face as she called out,

"This is a police operation! My name is Gulliver! No one moves till I say!"

Her pistol was firmly in its holster, and there was no way she could have drawn it quickly. It was as if she was sending some kind of message.

"Till *I* say, I think."

It was Aubrey. She was on her feet and pointing her gun at Cyril. She knew what to do now.

"On your feet, Derek," she ordered. "We're on our way."

It was a tense moment for Aubrey. She'd never met Quilter before, but she'd been told she could rely on him, and she was under orders to get him out. If he wasn't reliable, she was looking defeat in the face. Unhurriedly he stood up, put his hand in his coat pocket, and drew out a Beretta subcompact. It was a small gun, just 6·22 inches long, but as he moved next to Aubrey, he made sure everyone could see it. Cyril sat motionless, his arms hanging limply.

"If anyone tries anything, Cyril Burney dies first," Aubrey said loudly to Gulliver. "Release Russell Burney and Oleg Dvorski. They're coming with us."

Gulliver took her time, as if she was weighing up how to strike back. Then she ordered,

"Take their handcuffs off and let them go. Both of them. They're not worth a death."

Russell was totally confused, but he was thankful as well. Toni was looking after him after all, that showed how much she loved him. Dvorski, too, felt his confidence swilling back. Valkov had told the truth. It *had* all been worked out.

"I need a hostage," Aubrey continued. "Cyril Burney's no good, he's far too ill. I'll take one of your sort. You won't risk the life of one of your own."

She beckoned Farrell over and Quilter kept him covered.

"Stand that chair up and put Mr Dvorski's gun on it," she went on.

"Do it," Gulliver ordered.

Someone put the Walther down and Aubrey slipped it into her shoulder bag. Shrike were looking restless, but Gulliver signalled they were to stay where they were.

"We're going to the helideck now," Aubrey announced, "where, you might like to know, we're expected by arrangement. Miss Gulliver, your colleagues are not in the best frame of mind, so I'll say it for you. No one from the police and no one from the television is to follow us. If anyone does, Detective Inspector Farrell will be killed. And he won't be the only one."

Quilter started towards the exit from the drilling deck, prodding Farrell in front of him. Russell and Dvorski came next, while Aubrey covered their backs. No one seemed to be following them, and when they reached the helideck, it was deserted except for the helicopter. The chains were off its wheels, the entrance ramp was down and its rotor blades began to idle as soon as they came into view. The breeze was an outright wind here, and it tugged hard at their clothing. The deck itself, lit up by landing and perimeter lights, was wet, and the salt made it slippery. Aubrey moved up beside Quilter to hustle things along, and Farrell was thinking, if he could wreck their escape, he could yet salvage his career. Shayler would be easy to trash. He'd claim he was doing his own surveillance – that was why he'd been stringing her along. Everyone knew now she'd put Russell Burney up to murder. A little more proof, he'd say, and he'd have been reporting that fact himself. He really had been that close.

About two thirds of the way to the helicopter he suddenly spun round, snatched the Beretta out of Quilter's hand, and was fumbling for the small gun's trigger with his fat fingers when Aubrey, reacting faster, clubbed it out of his hand with her own gun. The Beretta hit the helideck and bounced away.

"Don't stop, don't stop!" she shouted to the others. "Run to the helicopter now!"

Farrell made a lunge at her, but she darted to one side, scrabbled up Quilter's Beretta with her left hand and ran off, with Farrell pounding behind her. She didn't want him to get close to the entrance ramp in case he carried on in, so she veered away towards the helideck's outer edge, keeping well clear of the tail rotor. He followed her, thinking he'd got her trapped, then she turned. He saw what was coming, tried to change direction, and slipped on the wet metal, just as she fired her Smith and Wesson. The bullet sped harmlessly past him but, he saw quickly, the second one might not. Labouring for breath, he dropped to his knees and held his hands in the air.

"I give up!" he shouted. "Please, please let me live!"

She had to get past him to get into the helicopter.

"Get out of my way then!" she shouted back.

He scrambled to his feet, and while he was racing towards the edge of the helideck, meaning to shelter behind one of the posts supporting the perimeter lights, she shot him in the back. She wanted to break his spine, but his stride was uneven, so the bullet shattered his shoulder blade. The pain was unbelievable, the force of the shot pitched him forwards, and his head struck the helideck hard. That and the agony from his shoulder disorientated him completely. Fighting for consciousness, he dragged himself in the direction he'd been running, his head swimming and his vision blurred. When his hand touched the post, he took hold of it and attempted to manoeuvre his body behind it, but the post was much nearer the edge than he'd thought. His nose was broken, making it difficult for him to breathe, blood was running into his mouth, and his awareness of things was so hazy, he didn't realise at once what was happening when one of his feet suddenly had nothing underneath it. Struggling to maintain some sense of himself, he managed to pull it in, but he was still desperate to take cover, since he thought Aubrey was going to shoot him again. So, struggling for breath, saturated with pain, and with the base of the post filling his whole field of vision, he tried again, and this time he moved too far. He slid over the edge, his hands couldn't take his bodyweight, and he fell the 140 feet into the sea. He died on impact just as Cyril's helicopter lifted off with Aubrey on board. At sea level, Gamma Attack heard the splash, and so did their supply ship captain. He checked back to Leeming.

"We can use lights to find out who or what it was," he radioed through to the RIB. "It seems we can't spoil anything now."

It didn't take them long. Farrell's uniformed body was pulled out of the water, photographed, and the pictures went to Leeming for positive identification. Gulliver, who'd reported the sound of both shots, was told what had happened.

"It's wrap-up time," Snape told her. "We'll get you back as soon as you're done."

Tilman made the first move. She'd been keeping well to one side. Now, following a nod from Gulliver, she walked over to the drilling crew and pressed her fist into the shoulder of each of them.

"Well done," she said. "You get a week's leave for this. You can go to your quarters now. I'll stand the other rigs down as well."

The drillers were volunteers and they'd been briefed in advance. Likewise the catering staff, the *son et lumière* people and the CDB-TV crew, who were still broadcasting, despite being kept off the helideck. The presenter was commentating off camera when Gulliver caught the producer's eye. He scribbled, 'Track Gulliver' on a piece of paper, showed it to the presenter and then to one of the cameramen and his sound assistant.

Gulliver sat down next to Cyril, who didn't look too ill to move now. They were waiting for transport off the rig, she told him, and as they talked, he laughed out loud.

"It was no hardship, I'm used to looking poorly," he said. "Looking well is my problem."

Gulliver laughed with him, then, to keep him in a good mood she added, "You'll allow me to say you've showed courage this evening, especially when Aubrey pointed her gun at you."

The smile left his face and his mouth trembled.

"My father was a brave man. It was a debt I owed him."

Hastily he excused himself, saying he'd get his own water for once, and Gulliver moved on to pass the time with Halter. Shrike were in the open now, with no trace of having been restless, and Corbett was listening politely to Enid. She was worried about her son, she said, as low-key as ever. Did he think Miss Aubrey might shoot him? At the same time she kept a watchful eye on Cyril as he made his way to the bar. When Gulliver walked round in front of her, she simply looked up with her meek smile. If she noticed the police ring tighten round her, she didn't show it.

"Raise your hands in the air, Mrs Burney," Gulliver said, just a little more loudly than necessary, and Corbett pointed his pistol at her. "You're under arrest for espionage and conspiracy to commit mass murder. Other charges may follow."

Then came the caution, and she was allowed to lower her hands to her knees.

"What nonsense you talk! If I had had anything to do with what we've just seen, that dreadful Miss Aubrey would have taken me with her. But, as you see, she didn't."

"I suspect that's because both of you expected you'd stay invisible, so you could continue your traitorous work. But, you see, some of my colleagues entered The Crofter's Hut earlier today – with your husband's permission, of course. They were following up the code name Alder. They searched your computer, and they now believe you are Alder. It seems you've been running quite a network, but when you run things, you have to keep records, and they've got yours. Now hold out your hands, please."

The handcuffs went on and Cyril, who'd been watching as if he'd known it was coming, told CDB-TV to round off the broadcast. They'd shown enough – Aubrey had fled and Enid was blown. It was a rout all round.

In London, Zembarov was seeing things differently.

"Dvorski's disgraced, that's the main thing," he said, sounding entirely upbeat, "and like Russell Burney, he's in our power. Katya Danilovna has made her heroic escape, and Harvest Home has victoriously been stopped in its tracks. It's been a good night's work, Andrey Ivanovich. Our country's been well served."

Gulliver was letting herself unwind. She realised she was thirsty, the salt from the sea air was doing it. Slowly she walked round to the bar for some soda water before it was packed away. En route she picked up Farrell's cap, he'd left it on his chair. Shayler was still sitting, under guard, in the space behind the bar. Gulliver offered her a drink, but, she added, she couldn't take her handcuffs off.

"Yes, thank you, I'd like some soda water like you," Shayler replied. "Don't worry, I'll manage somehow."

She held the glass with both hands and drank from it.

"That cap you're holding," she said as she handed her glass back. "It's Inspector Farrell's, isn't it? Do you know how he is?"

Gulliver hesitated, and then said he was dead.

"How did he die?"

"I can't tell you that."

Shayler looked painfully lonely.

"I expect it was one of the shots we heard. He was a bad man, Miss Gulliver, and I'm sure you'll say he let the police down. But I'm over fifty now, and for a brief time he made me happy. It's over now, of course. But I'm glad it happened."

Gulliver gave her a friendly smile, she saw no reason not to. But she couldn't feel sorry for her. She'd bought her happiness with the wrong kind of currency, and to Gulliver that meant one thing only: gaol for a good long while.

Chapter 33

Destination Russia

As Aubrey hustled into the Executive S-92, the co-pilot sealed the door from the cockpit and the pilot powered up for rapid take-off. There were only nine seats in the luxury cabin, they'd cost a mint to make and install, and it showed, as it was meant to. Quilter, Dvorski and Burney sat stiffly on one each, and Aubrey half-fell onto a fourth as the S-92 tilted into a tight rising turn.

"Where are you taking us, Toni?" Burney asked.

He was so bewildered, he hardly dared speak.

"I'm taking you all to Russia," she replied, making no effort to hide her contempt for him. "But first we'll land on a battle cruiser anchored off Portsmouth. You'll know it from the news you're so attached to, it's the *Leonid Golovin.* It's Russian territory, and once we're on it, it'll take us safely home."

"But you're not Russian. You come from Manchester; you told me when we were in the clinic together."

"I *am* Russian, and I'm proud of it. I'm in our Foreign Intelligence Service, just like your good friend Oleg Dvorski here, and I was under orders to stick close to you. I've never been to Manchester, I was never divorced, and I was never drunk. The gin went down the sink, and I made myself sick with syrup of ipecac. Only the urine was genuine – I peed myself and let it stay in my clothes."

"But I nursed you, Toni. And I was ready to do whatever, er, a certain person wanted to get money for you."

"Of course you were, that's why I kept getting myself into that dreadful state. I watched you very carefully after I moved in with you. I found out how committed you were to me, I even saw your eyes prickle. We had you, I knew it, and don't say 'a certain person', say 'Mr Valkov' straight out. I knew what had gone on in our Embassy basement almost as soon as you did, I got a message just before you came home with your pack of lies."

"They were meant for the best," he wanted to say, but he guessed she knew that anyway, so instead he said miserably,

"And now you're going to kill me, I suppose."

"No, you're more use to us alive. When we get to Russia, the state will take you over, and in return you will deny or twist everything the British and Americans accuse us of. We Russians never look right when we take to the media, but you will with your honest English face. We'll see to it."

"So we'll still be together?" he pleaded, puppy-like. "As if nothing had come between us?"

"Do you really not understand? You mean nothing to me, absolutely nothing. You're an assignment, that's all, and I'm glad – no, make that *very* glad – it's almost over."

The S-92 was veering violently. Instinctively Russell grabbed at his seat, but he was too upset to register he was doing it.

"What about Oleg?" he asked. "What's he got coming to him?"

"He'll find out soon enough."

"And Farrell? Where is he anyway?"

"On the helideck, I suppose, that's where I shot him. I don't think I killed him, he moved as I pulled the trigger. But he could have bled to death."

"What would you have done if he'd come on board?"

"Thrown him out once we'd got some height. Derek would have helped me, he's been told to help me. That's right, isn't it, Derek?"

Quilter gave her his obliging smile, and made as if to tug his forelock.

"Yes, Miss. He'd be gone by now. Gone and forgotten."

He wiped his hands as he spoke to show what he meant.

"You see, Russell?" she finished, holding tight herself. "Everything is as it should be. Now, I suggest you loosen your coat and put your seat belt on, just as Derek and I are going to do. You too, Oleg. Try to relax as well," she jeered in his face. "You're going back to where you come from. Be pleased about it."

Burney, like Dvorski, did as he was told, he had nothing left to resist with. He knew the Executive S-92 well, he'd been humiliated in it more times than he cared to remember, and when his eyes settled on a framed notice on the bulkhead stating, 'No one to enter the cockpit without permission – Cyril D. Burney', he could hear his father saying it out loud. Level with it on the cockpit door was a red flashing sign declaring, 'No admittance when sign lit'. On each table, and also let into the cabin walls, were matching screens headed 'Notices' in Gothic type. 'Sorry about the rough ride,' he read on them in more prosaic lettering. 'We're being pursued – Silas'. Another set of screens was headed 'Route' – again in Gothic type – but they were blank. The blinds had been dropped on take-off and locked. Aubrey, Burney, Dvorski and Quilter – they were all shut in together, and, Burney brooded, even Handley and Wilmot were traitors, just like Quilter. They had to be. So he had no one left he could trust. No one at all.

As Dvorski and Burney sank numbly into themselves, Aubrey undid her seatbelt and, struggling against the pitching and yawing, stumbled to the rear of the cabin to check the galley and toilet. She had her Smith and Wesson ready, but no one was hiding in them. Suddenly the helicopter plummeted fiercely, throwing her onto her knees and almost making her fire into the floor. As she scrambled up, a tone like the gong of a five-star hotel sounded through the roaring of the overstrained motors, and the 'Notices' screens showed, 'Miss Aubrey to the cockpit, please.' At the same time, the flashing sign went off. Precariously she made her way to the bulkhead door, used a convenient handhold to keep herself steady, and pressed the button next to it. When 'Enter' lit up, she turned the hand-crafted monogrammed door knob, went in, and closed the door behind her. She could see the cabin on an overhead screen in front of her. If anyone tried anything, she'd know about it.

It was much noisier in the cockpit than in the cabin, and since the only light source was the instruments, it was much darker as well. The co-pilot turned towards her and gestured her into the empty navigator's seat. If the co-pilot turned round and she leaned forward they could see each other. The pilot kept his eyes fixed in front of him.

"Put the radio helmet on," the co-pilot half-shouted. "Do your seat belt up as well. It'll get worse before it gets better."

'So you're Wilmot,' Aubrey thought. She could just make out the name on the breast pocket of his immaculately tailored blazer.

The helicopter fell away to starboard, then gradually clawed back altitude.

"That was close," came from the pilot, and almost immediately a metallic voice asked him to "squawk" a code number and "ident".

He leaned forward and turned the transmitter-responder off.

"That was air traffic control," the co-pilot explained. "They want us to identify ourselves. They've been harassing us since we took off, and they're not the only ones. Look above you."

The S-92's windscreen sloped from the nose. Aubrey leaned forward as far as she could, and as she craned her neck round, she saw a helicopter's underside strobe come on. She could scarcely believe it could be so close. And ahead of her was another one flashing ominously in the night. It was just descending into her line of vision.

"They're Lynxes," the co-pilot said as the S-92 plummeted again. "Mk 9As. There are three of them out there so far, and we think there'll be more. They can shoot us out of the sky any time they like, but what they're trying to do right now is force us down without making us crash. That's why we're tumbling so much, they keep catching us in their downdraught. It's only thanks to Oscar we haven't pancaked yet."

"What happens when we get to the *Golovin*?"

"We expect they'll try to block us off."

"Will it work?"

"We'll find out when we go at them. Excuse me a moment."

He scanned his radar screen.

"There's another Lynx out there, and it's coming at us fast. It'll probably buzz past our nose."

He turned away from her to look forward, and for a moment nothing happened. Then there was an immense roar, and the S-92 felt as if a giant hand had grabbed and shaken it. Without their seatbelts they'd have been thrown around like ping pong balls. Aubrey glanced up to see what was happening in the cabin. Dvorski and Burney looked transfixed like frightened rabbits. A superior sneer flickered across her face.

"I called you in to let you know how things are," the co-pilot went on. "We've been picked up early and we've got no chance at all of shaking off the Lynxes. That's the bad news. The good news is, we've got a strong tailwind. We should make it to the *Golovin* in under two hours, but I have to warn you, we'll be seriously put about till we get there."

"What's the alternative?"

"Surrender. We land somewhere and give ourselves up."

"That's not an option. We keep going."

As she spoke, the S-92 cut sharply to port to get into some air that was stable. Then it climbed hard.

"One more thing," the co-pilot said. "The *Golovin* doesn't want anyone carrying guns when we land. You can see why. They know Dvorski and Burney aren't here for the fun of it, and if there's a gun about, either of them might use it. It doesn't have to be theirs, they might just grab it from someone. Have they got any guns, do you know?"

"No, they haven't. I've got Dvorski's Walther and Derek's Beretta. Burney's never had one. I've got my own as well. It's a Smith and Wesson."

"You'd better hand them over. You can't use them in the cabin anyway. A shot through the hydraulics and we all go down."

Reluctantly she opened her shoulder bag and gave him the Smith and Wesson, the Walther and the Beretta, all safed. As he put them in a storage pocket, a Lynx took them close again and the S-92's pilot went to maximum speed as the Lynx spiralled away downwards. Another Lynx was flying overhead, and he wanted to shake it off, so as soon as he'd edged in front of it, he tilted the nose up and climbed ruthlessly. It was a collision course, it couldn't be anything else. At the last second, the Lynx arc-ed upwards almost vertically and temporarily yielded its patch of sky.

"It's going to be like this all the way," the co-pilot commented grimly. "You'd better go back to the others and tell them what I've told you. We'll put a route up so you'll know where we are. And keep your seat belts on, all of you. We don't want anyone breaking his neck."

Carefully Aubrey clambered back into the cabin. She felt naked without her gun, but what the co-pilot had said made sense. She'd almost shot into the floor herself. As she strapped herself in, the route came up. Their line was pretty much due south and their position was marked by a miniature blue-and-gold Executive S-92. Its progress seemed slow, but it was moving.

After a sequence of slews and climbs Dvorski undid his belt, scrabbled across to Aubrey, and strapped himself in again.

His scared rabbit look had got worse, and when he wasn't kneading his hands he was fingering his ear.

"What you said to Burney when he asked you," he said in Russian because Burney was listening. "About what would happen to me, I mean. Do you know what it'll be?"

"I don't make policy, I carry it out."

"I thought Grigory Viktorovich might have said something. You said you were working for him, not Valkov."

"Listen and understand, Oleg. You're a cowboy and we don't like cowboys, not these days. When you were running Torelli, we put up with you because there was something in it for us. When you got her tsunami book, same thing. But the minute the Millers got killed, things changed, and we decided to wipe you out, which is what we'd been wanting to do all along. But you had to die in disgrace – in disgrace in Russian eyes, that is – so you were set up to kill Shayler and put yourself in the wrong. I was going to kill you and purge Russia of your sort for good. You're the real enemy, you see. You're worse than the West."

"What about the tsunami? Burney was supposed to be rock hard."

"Don't make me laugh! Where he got that last push from is anyone's guess. We thought we'd shattered him."

Dvorski was ashen. Why hadn't he worked it out for himself? Beginning with Valkov making things easy for him.

"A very Russian way to die," he said bitterly. "A bullet in the back and disgrace by state television. The masses would have loved it."

"Just occasionally you catch on quickly. And it would have worked, too, if the British police hadn't got in the way."

"But if you'd shot me, you'd have been caught red-handed. You wouldn't have stood a chance."

"Wrong again, I'd have done exactly what I did do. The only difference would have been, you'd have been dead instead of sitting next to me. As it is, you're going back for a show trial, and I honestly can't wait till it happens."

There was no point in arguing, she was just Zembarov's parrot, so he lapsed back into silence. Then a detail crossed his mind.

"Did you know Russell Burney was going to kill his father? Was that part of your planning, too?"

"No, that was news. When he's working for us, we'll airbrush it out. It'll be easy enough. His parents are still alive, and Shayler came across as demented."

The flight was a never-ending nightmare. If they weren't tumbling they were climbing, spiralling or veering so hard, all they could do was try not to be sick. At one point all the cabin lights went out, and when the screens shut down as well, they were rocked and buffeted in total darkness. Once the lighting returned, Quilter and Aubrey recovered fast – they had something to look forward to. But Burney was the colour of tallow and Dvorski, who'd struggled back to his own seat, looked terminally ill.

Finally the miniature S-92 had almost reached the end of the route, and the 'Notices' screens lit up again.

'Destination ahead!' they read. 'We've got eight helicopters to get past, and we're going to call their bluff. When we touch down, don't try to open the outside door, I'll do it from the cockpit. And don't undo your seat belts till I tell you. It's tense out there. Silas.'

The nose dipped sharply. It was like being on a big dipper that had got out of control. The pressure built up in their heads, their eyes stared wide open, and their ears popped. Then the pressure switched to their feet as the S-92 looped upwards, stalled fleetingly, and plunged far too fast until, decelerating in the very last seconds, it touched down like a feather. When the rotors shut off, there was silence, and when the outside door swung down, bright lights shining directly onto the doorway stopped them seeing out.

"Stay where you are just a little longer," a voice said from the bulkhead doorway.

Instinctively they looked round.

"You're not Silas!" Burney exclaimed. "Who are you?"

The blazer might say 'Wilmot', but that was where it ended. And he was holding a SigSauer.

"I'm Royal Navy," he said. "So is the pilot. We – how shall I put it? – persuaded Silas and Oscar to let us take over while you were on the drilling deck, and I have to say, it was a nice little escape plan you were working to. They showed us how all the gadgets worked, then we locked them up in a couple of empty cabins where – surprise, surprise! – there were some spare clothes waiting for them so we could borrow theirs. As long as you and Mr Quilter didn't hear us or see us, we were safe. We didn't use the intercom and Miss Aubrey was the only one we let into the cockpit, because she'd never seen us before. We asked Silas and Oscar separately about that, and they had nothing to gain from lying, so we got the truth. Perhaps they were thinking how long their gaol sentences might be."

"Where are we then?" asked Quilter.

For the first time, he looked rattled.

The pilot answered that as he came through the same door. He had 'Handley' on his breast pocket and he also held a SigSauer.

"You're on an air force base called RAF Leeming," he said. "It's not far from Teesside, so we've been flying around a bit to make it last. The Lynxes were ours, of course, and they've landed here as well. The route we showed you was a little invention we'd brought with us. Someone on our side worked out where you were going and how, Silas and Oscar kindly confirmed that for us, and Miss Aubrey here repeated it just after we took off. Which reminds me ..."

He reached behind a lamp bracket in the cabin wall.

"It's a bug," he said, giving a pull to free the magnet. "Not tomorrow's technology, but they still have their uses. We recorded everything you said. We transmitted it live to Leeming as well, and a simultaneous translator took care of the Russian bits. I have to say, you've said some interesting things between you."

He nodded to the co-pilot who, shielding his eyes, went to the open doorway and beckoned. Half a dozen officers from

Shrike came in and fanned round the cabin. They were armed and ready for trouble. They were followed by Snape, who identified himself before formally arresting Burney, Quilter and, on an international warrant, Aubrey. Then they were handcuffed.

"I can't arrest you," Snape said to Dvorski, "since you have diplomatic status. But I'm detaining you under the Prevention of Terrorism Act. You'll stay with us like the others till we get things sorted out. I won't handcuff you unless you try something. Then I will."

"I've got three guns from them," the co-pilot told him. "A Beretta from Quilter, a Walther from Dvorski, and a Smith and Wesson from Aubrey. Aubrey's fingerprints are on the Smith and Wesson, plus mine. It may have been used to shoot Mr Farrell."

Snape nodded and looked round. They had their seat belts on, they had no weapons and, with the exception of Dvorski, they were handcuffed. Like stoats in a box, they were harmless at last.

"I'm not allowed to use your names in front of other people," Snape replied to the crew, "but I'll thank you anyway, since you've done a fine job. The rest is up to us. It starts right now."

Chapter 34

Russell Burney is Ground to Dust

The S-92 was cordoned off, an armed RAF police guard was mounted round it, and the prisoners were taken in separate vehicles to a compact residential block that was normally out of use. There was glinting new razor wire round it, the windows were freshly barred, and more armed RAF police, some flown in from other bases, were guarding it so Shrike could be stood down. The top floor rooms were for female prisoners, and Enid Burney and Shayler were already locked in. The rooms on the floor below were for male prisoners. Every lock in the building had been changed.

Russell Burney left the helicopter last. He'd wanted desperately to stay linked to Aubrey, but she'd been the first to go, and she hadn't even tried to look back. It was what he'd always dreaded – she'd left him behind for good. As he stepped out, the extra lighting shining onto the door was switched off, and the plunge into half-light made him feel so hopeless, he came to a sudden halt. It caught his escort out, and Snape, who was walking behind him, nearly bumped into him.

"What's up?" he asked in his kindly way. Russell seemed more like a boy than a man.

"When I first met Miss Aubrey, she told me, 'I don't want to die before I have to. Neither should you.' I still don't want to die, but I don't want to live either. I don't know what I do want any more."

Snape took his time.

"I was going to tell you something when we got to the car, but I'll tell it to you now," he said. "A colleague of mine has got some information for you. It's personal, and I don't think you'll like it, but it may help you get a bearing on things. You can see him now, if you want. Would you like to do that?"

In a defeated voice Burney said yes, he'd better know what it was. Snape put through a call, then told the driver he wanted the Camp Commander's office.

"Your father will be here as well," he said as they got out. "Do you want to change your mind?"

Russell stiffened; then, tonelessly, "No, I'm here now. I might as well go through with it."

"My colleague isn't a policeman, he's in a sister service, and he won't give you his name. Can you accept that?"

"Let's say I can't refuse. We'll let it mean the same thing."

The office was the only room in the block that was lit. It led off a corridor with a rubberised floor that smelled of cleaning fluid. All the curtains were drawn, and when van Piet answered the knock on the door, he asked the driver and the escort to wait outside. He'd pushed four easy chairs round a coffee table, and Cyril Burney was sitting in one of them. His eyes had deep shadows under them, and a glass of water stood ready on a side table. Snape and Russell took two of the other chairs, and after he'd locked the door, van Piet took the fourth. Cyril Burney was looking icily at the man who'd wanted him dead. It was a look Russell couldn't take, it shamed him too much, so he dropped his gaze. No one could hate him as much as he hated himself.

Van Piet didn't waste any time.

"I think you should know," he said to Russell, "that your mother has been arrested for espionage and conspiracy to commit mass murder. And I'll add, since you look at me in disbelief, that she's proud of what she's done and she's been talking to us freely. She's been a Russian agent for longer than you've been alive, and for much of this year she's been helping to turn you into a Russian marionette. She made you depend on Jocelyn Patrice, knowing he'd be killed when it would weaken you most. She also knew what Andrey Valkov was intending to do with you."

"How could she possibly have known that?"

"How could she not? They worked the whole thing out together, you see. She further knew Toni Aubrey would try to attach herself to you in the De Macey Clinic. She even advised on her appearance. She knew you'd had this craze for English roses, apparently you kept pictures of them hidden in a drawer. When Aubrey turned up looking exactly like one, she couldn't miss."

Russell's tallowy face went crimson at having his puberty unpacked like that. As for his mother, he couldn't take in what he was hearing. He'd called her a witch and he'd had bad dreams about her, but this was another league.

"My mother can't be a Russian agent," he insisted. "She won't even go to Poland."

"I wondered about that, so I asked her. Her line's always been, she was so badly treated –"

"She was raped. By someone called Patryk Konstantinov. She told me so herself. It's a family secret – or was, till now."

"But, unfortunately, one that was never worth keeping, since the plain fact is, she was never raped. She fell in love with Konstantinov when she was over there, and his parents used that to win her over to their way of thinking. When she came back to this country, she was tasked with founding a pro-Soviet cell. Later, it became pro-Russian, and she was overjoyed to do it."

"What happened to Konstantinov?"

"He's lived in Birmingham for a number of years. He became an electrician and called himself Mike Crane. One moment …"

Van Piet opened a wallet folder and laid out Crane's picture from his website. Cyril Burney was still saying nothing.

"This is what he looks like now," van Piet went on. "Do you know him at all?"

"No, I've never seen him before."

"Try this one then."

It was from Filipek's e-mail.

"No, it's a complete stranger."

"The next one is the same photo, but with the beard and some of the hair removed by a specialist colleague of mine."

Russell glanced at it at first, but then looked closely.

"It's been doctored!" he exclaimed. "What are you trying to pull?"

"It's not been doctored, Mr Burney, apart from what I said."

"Then why does it look like me?"

"Because you're looking at your natural father. It's Mike Crane when he was Patryk Konstantinov."

Russell fixed his gaze on Cyril.

"Is this true? That you're not my father?"

"It's as true as you wanted to murder me. I've always passed myself off as your father to avoid bad headlines, but you're no son of mine, and I'm pleased to say it out loud now. You'll never work for me again either. You're a failure, Russell, and you always will be. It's a good job you're going to prison. It won't show so much there."

"So I don't even own my surname. Russell *Burney*? Who's that? It's like wearing someone else's clothes. Did you know my mother was a foreign agent?"

"No, I didn't think she had the brains, and that was my mistake. Apparently she's been passing on Global's secrets for years. She pumped a lot of them out of Fern Shayler, and Shayler was too dense to catch on."

"Birmingham's not far from Ascot. Does my mother still see my – see this Konstantinov?"

"She's never stopped."

"When did you find out then?"

"When she became pregnant with you. She had to say something because I'm, well, I'm not able to father children, so she put a deal to me. Either she'd leave me and drag me through the media or, if I pretended to be your father and saw you both right money-wise, she'd play along and no one would be any the wiser."

"So the rape story was just a smoke screen."

"That's the size of it. She can say what she likes now, I'm rich enough to deal with it, and like you, she's heading for the slammer where she belongs. By the way, I hear some fool has bought your debts. Whoever it is, they'll never get their money back. I can't see you ever having enough, even if you sell the shirt off your back, and you won't get a penny piece from me. I'll leave my money to a cats' home first."

Russell didn't respond, he was beaten into the ground, and Cyril turned to van Piet, still fretting about Russell getting his debts bought up.

"Sberbank acted as middleman, that's what you said. Take it from me, they won't do it twice. They've made a lot of money through me, but they won't any more. I'll see to it personally."

He gestured contemptuously towards Russell while he tapped out one of his tablets.

"Tell him what's happened to his father. It'll do him good."

"He's under arrest for attempted murder, and as I see it, that's only the start. I can't tell you where he is, and you won't be allowed to contact him by phone. Not yet, anyway."

Russell raked his trampled emotions together.

"I'm not interested in him. If I saw him in the street I'd ignore him. You won't believe this," he said, turning to Cyril, "but more than anything else I want to touch you, to call you Dad, and feel you love me, father to son. It's what I've always wanted. And now I never can."

All that came back was silent contempt. Eventually Russell said to van Piet,

"I keep feeling I've lost everything, and then there's more. Can you tell me one last thing?"

"It depends what it is."

"Did my mother know Dandy was a spy?"

"Yes, she did. When Dandy was leaving ExxonMobil, Dvorski came up with a plan to pursue her here. He outlined it to a long-serving Kremlin man, who made sure your mother was brought into the loop. After that, every time Dandy leaked Klemmsley's secrets, your mother knew all about it."

Russell recalled the Sunday lunch in The Crofter's Hut. It was incredible, his mother hadn't given a single sign she knew anything. Then he reached back to something van Piet had said earlier.

"You said she made me depend on Patrice. How did she do it?"

"Dandy didn't want to spy for the Russians, which meant something could always go wrong, and your mother was convinced, if it did, you'd make it worse, because – in her words, not mine – you're such a helpless ninny. So she and the Kremlin decided to set up a rat trap – her words again – that could be closed on you if the need arose, and she said the rat catcher should be a stockbroker, since she knew you wanted to compete with your father. Patrice got the nod because he was already known to the Russians, and his first letter to you was your mother's idea. Things went well for a time, that made the whole thing credible, but after Dandy's murder, you had to be put under pressure. The rat trap's time had come, Patrice was expendable, and the rest you know."

So *that* was his dearest, loving Enid. She must have despised him as much as his father did.

"Did my mother know Fern Shayler wanted me –" He broke off and looked away from Cyril. "– wanted me to kill my father, as I still want to call him?"

"No. She got Shayler to leak the sale of Global to you to stoke up your insecurity. It never crossed her mind Shayler might draw conclusions of her own. Perhaps it should have."

Russell searched for a response but he couldn't find one, so he stood up.

"I'd like to go now," he said evenly. "I think I've reached bottom at last."

Snape called in the escort and left with Russell while van Piet put the images away. Like van Piet, Snape hoped an informal first contact would make a full confession easier later on. It was a professional calculation.

"Thanks for staying so late," van Piet said to Cyril when they had the room to themselves. "I'll drive you to your room when you're ready. Your luggage is waiting for you. We've had it fetched from Blackhall Rocks."

"I'm ready now."

"We'll go then."

He put the lights off, locked the door, and at Cyril Burney's faltering pace they walked down the corridor to the way out.

"Have you got any plans for the future?" van Piet asked as they drove off, more to be sociable than anything.

"I was going to sell my businesses and retire, but thanks to Shayler's big mouth, that's off, and it's no bad thing. I'm not going to retire; I can see I'm not made for it. I've got no family now and no friends, but there's always another deal to strike, another firm to buy up, and another billion to make. I'll settle for that till I go altogether."

When he pulled himself out of the car, a nurse from Leeming's sick bay was waiting for him. Van Piet had arranged that, too.

"I'll be in the room next to Mr Burney's," she told van Piet confidentially. "I'll give him a call stick, poor thing. I've got oxygen and stuff all ready, just in case. You have to feel sorry for him, don't you?"

Chapter 35

Fixes, Deals and Trade-Offs

Off England's southern edge, in the Spithead strait, the captain and the first officer of the *Leonid Golovin* had been watching CDB-TV on Russian television via satellite. They knew how long an Executive S-92 would take to get from Parkland Zuka to their battle cruiser, and their helicopter had been disassembled to clear the helideck. But when the ETA came round, there was no S-92. They waited another three quarters of an hour, then the first officer sent an apparently routine signal to the Embassy asking for a weather update. It included the word 'fog', and the bogus request was fast-forwarded straight up to Valkov's office, where Zembarov and Valkov were waiting for the *Golovin* to report. Valkov was trying not to let his tiredness show, but Zembarov, who sat immobile except for when he drank some tea, seemed beyond the reach of time.

"They haven't arrived," Zembarov said after he'd read the bogus request. "They must have been caught. We have to assume it, anyway."

"What will happen now?"

"The *Golovin* will re-assemble its helicopter and see its goodwill visit out as if nothing has happened. There's been no shooting, no chatter, it's completely uninvolved. Russell Burney will talk, of course, and so will Alder, but I think we can ride that out. These things are more political than legal once they reach a certain level, and I don't see either the British or the Americans wanting to fall out with us entirely. They want our market too much."

"You think we can do a deal?"

"If we scapegoat Dvorski we can, and it so happens Jethro Torelli's murder is being looked at again. Apparently someone has done some new sums."

"How can that help us with Dvorski? We're better off keeping him out of it, surely."

"Not if we handle things properly. It'll cost us another long-term friend but, as with Patrice, these things sometimes have to be."

Valkov was uneasy; he could yet be in the firing line himself.

"What about Alder?" he asked tentatively. "She's been arrested, we saw it happen. The British policewoman, Gulliver, she said they'd searched her computer and got into our network."

"Yes, it was set up for us to see and hear by someone who saw it coming. I interpret it as a signal – the British want to bargain, and they've got something to bargain with. You, by the way, are in a difficult position, because if they've searched Alder's computer, they'll have you in mind. We'll have to see what can be done about that."

Shortly after midday the same day, Zembarov left Heathrow for Moscow.

Eight days later, on Monday October 1st, a late-afternoon KLM Airbus took off from Moscow's Sheremetyevo Airport on the first leg of its flight to Dulles International Airport, Washington, where it would land close after midnight local time on Tuesday October 2nd. Travelling business class was a pudgy, pasty-faced man with a small package in his hand luggage that was addressed to the FBI. Both he and it had diplomatic protection, and the handover was in a closely guarded room at Dulles. After checks in FBI headquarters, the package was transferred to Special Agent Hermann Novitz at FBI Miami. A detailed briefing went with it.

The same Tuesday, at 11.05 am German time, a former Soviet spymaster landed in Berlin and took a taxi to the Hotel Adlon Kempinski near the Brandenburg Gate. A reporter from *Bild*, Germany's biggest and roughest mass-circulation newspaper, had a luncheon table waiting for him. A room was booked as well. They had a lot to talk about.

In Miranda Cove, Peter Busch was glad of the shade outside Nancy's Bar as he idly watched the boats and sipped his beer. He didn't miss Jethro Torelli, life was too good for that, though he sometimes missed lifts in his boat. The sun was shining, the sky was clear, and the air was the sort you wished you could bottle. He'd only had coffee for breakfast, so when he finished his beer, he reached for the menu card and picked out a lobster salad. A footfall behind him made him think someone was coming for his order, but when he turned round, he saw two FBI police in uniform and a man in his late thirties wearing a freshly pressed lightweight suit. His FBI card read 'Novitz' and Novitz didn't waste words. He told Busch he was under arrest for conspiracy to commit homicide and explained his rights. Then he told him they were going to FBI Miami, where his lawyer was waiting for him. They'd got her name from his temporary stay permit.

He was shown into an interrogation room with no windows. He and Novitz sat on opposite sides of a desk, and his lawyer sat next to him. The two FBI police had chairs by the wall.

"Does the name Jethro Torelli mean anything to you?" Novitz began. "A tiger shark killed him in Miranda Cove. You gave a witness statement at the time."

"I can't forget it, Mr Novitz. Professor Torelli was a close friend of mine. I miss him a lot."

"The Florida police thought the death was an NEF, but we now think it was provoked."

Busch was unfazed. He'd been a traitor for years. He reckoned he could bluff his way out of anything.

"Not by me. I don't know the first thing about sharks."

Novitz fetched a video from his briefcase. The labelling, which was in Russian, looked fresh.

"Do you recognise this, Mr Busch? It's some years older than the label someone's stuck on it."

It was the first chink in Busch's armour.

"No I don't. Why should I?"

"Let's play it anyway, shall we? It may bring things back. Foreign videos don't always play over here, but this one will. We made sure."

He put it on. Some flashes came first, then a somewhat younger-looking Busch was sitting in front of a plain curtain and saying, "Then I will tell them about Torelli and how to lure a tiger shark towards him." Novitz played that bit twice, then let the tape run its course.

"I guess you're surprised it turned up. We believe you were helping a Russian called Oleg Dvorski. Do you recall the name? It's written on the label here."

Busch knew then he'd been betrayed. He couldn't be sure who'd done it – Zembarov had used intermediaries all those years ago – but whoever it was wouldn't let him say he'd never heard Dvorski's name before. The label wasn't a label, it was a warning, and there'd be follow-up if he ignored it. Like being found dead in his cell.

"I recall the name, but that's all," he said, before his lawyer could stop him.

"We also believe Mr Dvorski recruited a couple called Miller. Their names are on the label as well. They came out from England, you told them what to do, and Professor Torelli lost his life. That makes it homicide, Mr Busch. Oleg Dvorski pulled the strings. You and the Millers did the rest."

Busch's lawyer got in quickly and told him not to say any more, so Novitz opened his laptop and went into *Bild* online. The top story was the spymaster's. *Bild*, predictably, had turned it into a high-decibel screech about Busch 'As Told By The Man Who Ran Him!' Novitz opened up some more German news sites. The story was whipping up a storm, and an international arrest warrant was out. Zembarov knew the Germans well. The spymaster had touched a raw nerve.

"We both read German," Novitz said. "As I see it, if you were back in Germany, you might just be afraid of being lynched. But you're not in Germany, you're over here, and because we got you first, we get first go at you. Your spying doesn't interest us, it's not us you sold down the river. The rap will be homicide, and we intend to make it stick."

It was late evening in London when the desk phone buzzed in van Piet's office. He took the call himself – he was expecting it – and he turned the volume up so Garry and Snape could listen in. It was from Novitz. He played the video into van Piet's desk computer, then he let them hear a tape of the questioning.

"It looks as if we've got Suspect X at last," van Piet said to Garry when Novitz terminated.

"So we can use this Busch to nail Dvorski, can we?" Snape exclaimed. "That would make my day!"

"I wouldn't bet on it, Eddie, we're in my domain now, not yours. How much hard evidence have you got against Dvorski? Evidence that will stand up in court."

Snape pressed his lips together.

"Virtually none," he had to admit. "It's all circumstantial. Millie's helped us with the Sanderson calls, but they only take us to the doors of the Millers' garage – we can't prove what they actually said to each other. That's why Busch is a breakthrough. He can make the link between Dvorski, the Millers, and Jethro Torelli."

"So you say, but try this. Busch spied loyally for Moscow for years and suddenly, just as he's being arrested in Florida, Moscow rats on him in Germany, knowing what the result will be. And why has it done that? Because traitors are serial liars, Busch was one of the best, and now it's all out in the open. So if Busch testifies against Dvorski in any court anywhere, no one will believe him, and where does that leave you? You've got no hard evidence against Dvorski, and Novitz won't get any either, not with the Millers dead and Dvorski not named in the video itself. The simple fact is, with Busch busted in advance, Dvorski won't have a case to answer, and that being so, Britain and America will make *no effort whatsoever* to have his diplomatic status lifted so he can stand trial in the West. That clears the way for the Russians to have him and that, Eddie, is what this song and dance is really all about. Dvorski's got more enemies than friends on his own side, Tom found that out, and once he's theirs ready-wrapped, they'll do as Aubrey said in the helicopter – they'll whip him off to Moscow and make him the all-purpose fall guy. It won't matter what he says or who he names – everyone will think he's lying to save his skin, and the buck will stop firmly with him. There's a well-oiled political fix going on between this country, America and Russia. I don't especially like it because it doesn't go higher than Dvorski, but Dvorski will certainly be nailed, and that meets us half way. If he isn't nailed, Valkov and Zembarov will get dragged in, and that's not going to happen. But take my word for it, Eddie, Dvorski's had it."

"Have you been involved in this fix?"

"I can't answer that, but you can see for yourself – everything points in the same direction."

"He drew a gun on Shayler, Willem, and a lot of people saw him do it."

"He didn't shoot her, though, and all three countries know it. The most we could do is expel him."

"So the Russians would get him anyway."

"They would."

"And his minder in the Russian Embassy?"

"Valkov? He'll be promoted back to Moscow. He's probably packing right now."

"What about Busch?"

"He said enough on the video to end up in a Florida gaol. And if he gets off somehow, the Germans are waiting for him. One way or another, he won't see freedom again."

Snape let that settle in his mind. Then,

"That still leaves Aubrey, Willem."

"The Russians are claiming Nicosia didn't handle things right when she applied for Cypriot citizenship, so she's still Russian really and can they have her back, please? That won't wash, so I expect she'll be tried here and sent home to serve her sentence. I don't think much of it will be behind bars somehow."

"That's fixed as well, is it?"

"Sorry, Eddie, but again I can't say. It's not especially nice, but it's how these things go in Shadowland."

"I can see now why Enid Burney – Alder – was arrested on TV with a soundman in her lap."

"Keep talking."

"Arresting Alder on TV told the Russians we'd blown her cell and its network, and we could do a lot more if we felt like it. So we bargained from strength, and now we've got a deal. Am I right?"

"You make a good case, Eddie. Let's say we got the best we could hope for."

It was time to call it a night. Van Piet locked up and walked with the other two through Ashell House to the car park in the extended basement. September 22nd seemed a long while ago. Shrike was disbanded, the Counter-Terrorism Squadron had melted back to Poole, Tilman was shutting down Harvest Home, and amongst others, England's top-security gaols had acquired Wilmot, Handley, the crew of the Agusta Crane had tried to escape in, and a driver/clerk in the Middlesex Mobile Library Service. Henry Seeler had been pulled in as well – Russell Burney had made the basic mistake of using someone he'd used before. Seeler's defence was that nothing had actually happened, but the police were arguing it was no thanks to him. So he, too, was being held till he had his day in court, and his lawyers were sounding out what it would bring him if he shopped not only Russell Burney but all his other clients.

"I hear John Lorrie's taking early retirement," Garry said as he put his card in the last of the inner doors. "I also hear he was less than keen to fall on his sword."

"I don't like to say it, but it's no bad thing," Snape commented. "He made a big mistake with Farrell. I wonder who pushed him towards the door."

"I did amongst others," van Piet said. "As soon as you told me what had happened, I urged Mr Benjamin to do everything he could to have him removed. He was a systemic weakness, he had to go. I'm sorry he's still got time to see out."

Snape, who had his own car, drove off for Chelmsford and Garry headed for Barnet. Idly van Piet watched the barriers come down, then he took the lift to the real top floor of Ashell House. Signals was busy – it always was – but he wasn't going in anyway. Instead, he walked to the emergency bed-sits and knocked on the third door. When it opened, Steve Hallavy was standing in the doorway. He stepped back to let van Piet in. He'd been told to wait up for him.

While Hallavy put the kettle on and topped up a 'Crown Property' biscuit barrel with Lincoln Creams, van Piet made himself comfortable in an armchair he'd come to know well since the end of August.

"Thanks for staying with us till everything's wound up," he said, as Hallavy poured the tea. "You can go home when you like now. I'll have your car released for you."

"I'm glad you talked me into coming here. It took a load off my mind being able to tell you everything."

He paused, and a shadow crossed his face.

"I haven't asked you this before, but I will now. I should have gone to the police the minute I found out about the tsunami, shouldn't I? But I didn't. Will I get done for that?"

"Since you ask me, I think you should get done, as you put it. But the Crown Prosecution Service thinks otherwise so no, you're a free man."

Hallavy's face lit up.

"So it was a trade-off, was it? I feed you with information, and the CPS lets me off the hook."

"That's some of it. But you'll still have to testify against Miss Shayler in court. There's been no trade-off with her. You'll hear all this officially within the next few days."

"So I did a wrong thing, but Fern takes the rap if I testify against her. I'll do it, of course," he added quickly. "I'll spill the lot out."

He helped himself to some biscuits.

"I ought to feel guilty, but I don't. All I ever wanted was a quiet life. Now I've got one, and Fern picks up the tab. I have to say I like it."

They drank their tea, Hallavy crunched contentedly, then van Piet said he had to be off. Before he left Ashell House, he phoned Célestine. He had some good news and he was on his way home, but she needn't wait up, it would keep till she'd had some sleep. But when he got back, he realised he shouldn't have said he was on his way home, because she was dozing on the settee in the downstairs living room. When she saw him, her tired face, as always, radiated love like a beacon. He made some cocoa, and as they sat holding hands, his mind drifted back over the last couple of months. Dandy Torelli, the Burneys, Shayler, Dvorski, the Millers, Aubrey, Zembarov – what a menagerie! He shook his head in disbelief.

"I've finished the assignment I've been on," he said, and he was wearily glad to say it. "We can start living again, Cissie. How are you fixed for, well, later today?"

"I'm not fixed at all. Everyone's at school."

Then he'd take the day off, he said, and they'd go out together, it was far too long since the last time. Aldeburgh Bay was always special in October, they'd take a picnic and let everything slide away. It would all come back soon enough. That was the way it was.

Meanwhile in Sofia, the capital of Bulgaria, an up-and-coming pimp named Penko Dimitrov was collecting the night's takings in his Toyota Avensis. There wasn't much traffic, so he took a chance in a one-way street and got blocked by a police patrol car. These things happen, and Dimitrov was reaching for his wallet as one of the officers approached, not knowing he was already too late. A right-hand-drive car in a country where everyone drives on the right just had to be investigated, and the patrol car's driver was already radioing in…

Chapter 36

Guests at Gorris Hall

November 5th – Bonfire Night – was permanently ringed in red in the van Piets' diaries, and van Piet did his best to be home for the celebrations. Célestine moved her horses out, the jumps and fencing were stored away, and the land between the Hall and the Blackwater was given over to a fireworks spectacular for the area's children's charities. Everyone was expected to help and everyone did, including the Garrys and the Snapes, who came every year, and Sal Gulliver, who was coming for the first time. The Garrys and Mrs Snape arrived mid-morning, but Snape and Gulliver weren't due till later. They'd gone to Buckingham Palace to see Yasmin Hewett awarded a Queen's Police Medal. Straight after, Gulliver was to receive a Royal Citation. When they finally reached Gorris Hall, they joined van Piet and Garry for a sixty-minute time-out.

"So how did it go?" van Piet asked, as they organised themselves in the kitchen/diner of the East Wing guest suite.

"It was wonderful!" Gulliver burst out, and clapped her hands for joy. "Yasmin Hewett's Mum and Dad were there, and so were mine, and they all looked so proud, I nearly lost it altogether. I'm sure my eyes were red when the Queen spoke to me, I couldn't help it! And Mr Snape, well, I could see him out of the corner of my eye, and he had this bright beaming look all over his face. Afterwards there were refreshments and photographs, and then we came here."

"I'm not surprised you looked the way you did," van Piet said to Snape. "You were the one who put their names forward."

Snape was caught off guard.

"It's no more than my job," he grunted. "Anyway, thanks for slotting in this time-out. Sal wants to go through the case we've been on, and if I'm honest, I want to as well."

Van Piet was warming up some pre-cooked beefburgers in a microwave. There was tea and coffee in flasks, and carrot cake on a serving plate. A basket of apples stood in the middle of the table, next to the mustard and the ketchup.

"Dvorski and Dandy were clearly master and slave," he said, as Snape set out the buns on paper plates, "and Dandy wanted out badly. Her father's photo told us that. Why Dandy was shot was anyone's guess at the time, but one thing stood out like a sore thumb – there was a shift to Russell Burney at that point. His finances collapsed, and he'd been made dependent on Patrice just as Patrice was snatched away. So, who might be behind it all, and what did they want?

"Dvorski was the stand-out candidate, but I couldn't see him acting on his own. When Eddie and I saw him in his flat, he spoke of being *transferred* to London, and the word stayed with me, because the Russians aren't free agents like us, there's always someone behind them with a plan in his hand. Later he spoke of being posted, by the way. Tom dug out Valkov for me, then Zembarov's name cropped up. But Zembarov didn't make sense, because he was an old-style Stalinist, whereas Dvorski had been a Yeltsin man. So were they really working in harmony now, and what would it mean if they weren't?"

"Could you get an idea what they wanted?" Gulliver asked.

"Only sort of. Dandy's doctorate was on mapping the Caribbean seabed, and we know from Bermuda Triangle lore there's loads of methane hydrate down there, plus it's highly dangerous. So, was Harvest Home a methane hydrate time bomb, and had Dandy told the Russians? If she had, they'd certainly want to get control of it, but how could they do it?

Well, one way was to have Dandy eliminated and turn Russell Burney into a yes man. It was a tempting thought."

"What about the Millers? Where did they come in?"

"Their big facts were these – they cased Saxley Castle with the help of the Wolvercote pair, Chris Miller made keys for the Hole of Death padlocks, and they abducted Patrice just when Burney needed his debts sold. Someone must have put them up to it, because Burney, Patrice and the Wolvercote pair were all strangers to them. Was it a Russian? Was it Dvorski? It could just be.

"Anyway, if the Millers were working for the Russians, they amounted to a safety buffer that vanished when they got themselves killed, and at that point the Russians did something so completely crazy, for me it was the breakthrough. You'll remember, Russell Burney told the police he was hoping for a deal with Gazprom. Well, the police thought the files were on the thin side, and when I went through them, I could see right off there weren't even the beginnings of a deal in them. Yet on August 27th, by which date both the Millers were dead and known to be so, the Russians finalised image rights from CDB-Media for the whole of their country, time zones and all, and the obvious question was: what on earth for? If they didn't know Harvest Home was a disaster waiting to happen, it made no sense, because if there was no deal with Gazprom, why should the entire nation be expected to watch a business event it had nothing to do with? And if they did know it was a disaster waiting to happen, why should the same entire nation be expected to cheer on something it could soon get the blame for, and quite likely the bill as well?

"In other words, what *were* the Russians being lined up to see, complete with Russian commentators, who'd be told what to say? Well, the Russians have a liking for show trials, so I thought Dvorski, the man whose face didn't fit, could be the star of the show. If the Millers' deaths had left him over-exposed, finishing him off on-screen would be one big coup for Zembarov. So, were the Russians going to trash Dvorski with Harvest Home and then somehow abort it before it did any damage? It seemed likely, and from our point of view it would come with a bonus. If we couldn't nail Dvorski, the Russians would do the job for us."

"Could you have worked all that out without Hallavy?" Snape asked.

"I think so. I'll say it again: the Russians gave the game away when they made sure of those image rights. All we had to do was trace out the implications. Hallavy was useful, there was no question of that, but he wasn't indispensable for that."

"How did you get on to him anyway? He wouldn't stand out in an empty room."

"He had Dandy's job, Dandy had been shot, and I couldn't rule out he might get shot as well. So while you were waiting for the Wavell interview, I was loitering near Klemmsley Marine with a piece of paper stuck to my dashboard telling me what kind of car he drove and what its registration was. I managed to shepherd him into a lay-by, and he came across as a thoroughly frightened man. He told me the disaster I'd been guessing at was a tsunami, and I didn't have to convince him he'd be safer with us than on his own in Chelmsford. We stopped off to let him pack a suitcase, write his letter to the police, and fetch his tsunami data out of his safe. Then we drove to Chelsea, and once he was holed up in Ashell House, he told all about Shayler."

"Did he know Russell Burney was going to murder his father?"

"No, and he didn't have to. Russell told Patrice he was going to ask for a rise, but he must have known his father would never wear it. So how else could he get rich quickly? The only way was by inheriting.

"But you can't inherit to a timetable unless you're prepared to murder to a timetable, and waiting at Dassett Point in the dark, which was all Russell's idea, struck me as so ominous, I nearly asked for the Klemmsley Diamond to heave to somewhere else. But when Hallavy told me first about the boreholes and then about Henry Seeler, manipulating a hack seemed a better idea, so I asked GCHQ to go into Seeler's stuff, see what was doing, and set up a double screen. Hallavy

– and I'll certainly thank him for this – knew where every camera, light, and sensor was, plus how the command software worked. With his input, we couldn't go wrong."

"Forgive my ignorance, but what's a double screen?" asked Gulliver.

"It's a GCHQ speciality. You switch your screen on expecting to see feeds from your hacker that your hacker will be seeing as well, but in the nano-seconds before the picture forms, GCHQ works out what it's going to be like and places a duplicate over it without anyone noticing. The hacker's commands are read as they come in and neutralised before they do any harm, but the duplicate screen shows your hacker and you what you're expecting to see. That's why Seeler thought he'd done a good job, but Cyril kept his feet dry. What happened after that was more your show than mine, Eddie, so do you want to take over?"

"It was Sal's show if it was anyone's, but I happened to notice all the key players were funnelling towards the same place at the same time, namely, Parkland Zuka, and Sal found out the only practical way off Parkland Zuka was by helicopter. So, we decided, why not let the villains show their hand and have a trouble-free escape, because once they were in the helicopter, we'd got them?"

Gulliver turned to van Piet.

"And you knew they'd head for the *Golovin*."

"They could expect to be chased, so they'd need somewhere safe to land, and there was nowhere within an S-92's range except the piece of Russian territory called *Leonid Golovin*. You make it sound harder than it was, Sal. When I think of you standing on Parkland Zuka with your ID in the air and your gun in its holster, I have to say, I had the easy bit."

Gulliver shook her head.

"No one was going to make trouble for themselves by shooting me if they could get away scot-free by leaving me alive. All I had to do was nudge them in that direction. If anyone showed courage, it was Cyril Burney. He had Aubrey's gun pointing at him, and he didn't flinch. How did you get him to play his part so well?"

"I saw him in London, and I told him something about his private life he thought no one knew. I also told him his son meant to drown him for his money, and Harvest Home would destroy CDB Global along with a great slice of Western Europe. The shock was so great, I thought he was going to die on me, but he's the sort who'd postpone his own last gasp to get his own back, so I briefed him with what I wanted, and he helped me all along the line. Just before he boarded his supply ship, I also called him to confirm his wife was a Russian agent, and Handley and Wilmot were on her computer. That fired him up even more."

Gulliver glanced at her watch. They were almost out of time.

"Is Enid still talking?" she asked. She had to know. She, after all, was the one who'd brought her to book.

"Oh, yes, she's the complete opposite of Crane in that respect. It seems her cell soon settled down as herself, Valkov and Crane, they found out whatever they could, and the mood of the times was on their side. The Cold War was on, of course, but my mother's told me more than once, you didn't count in this country if you weren't buying *Marxism Today* and quoting from *The Communist Manifesto*. That's how Bunting and Penderton were recruited. Their heads were full of Marx, they hadn't lived much, and when Valkov and his cronies went trawling for teachers by inviting them to the Embassy in bulk, they didn't take much finding. And they lived within driving distance of GCHQ as well. Enid recruited Quilter. He fancied himself as a worker intellectual, and she played up to it. His codename was Bracelet, by the way, and it's on all the right computers – it wasn't coincidence he was on the rig with a Beretta in his pocket. Handley and Wilmot were also fellow-travellers, and so was the Mobile Library man. Only the Agusta crew were bought, and the money came from the Embassy so Cyril wouldn't know about it.

"You'll notice all the people I've named are getting on, and Madge Bunting helped me with that one. She said she was growing old when I went to see her, and that made me wonder whether there wasn't a cell in place dating back to well before Dvorski arrived. And who else might be in it? Well, Farrell reported Enid brought Russell and the De Macey Clinic together, so did Enid know Aubrey was going to be planted on him there? Russell would never have gone there on his own, so the answer looked like yes. Then GCHQ turned up a sender called Alder. They traced Alder to The Crofter's Hut, Enid's computer was raided as soon as she was safely off to Teesside – to Cyril's great glee, I might add – and you, Sal, finished the job."

The sixty minutes were up. The weather had stayed dry, and the outside electric lighting was making the November darkness seem snug. Snape would be waitering in the refreshment marquee, where a mountainous tea was being prepared; Gulliver was in charge of the wheelchair trails; van Piet was down for drop-off duty; and Garry, who had stayed typically silent, was in charge of the Great Bonfire Draw. Whichever child got the lucky number could press the button and ignite the giant bonfire.

"Have you heard from MI6 about the *Golovin*?" van Piet asked him after Snape and Gulliver had separated off. He was starting the dishwasher, and Garry was giving the table a wipe.

"Yes I have. It meant disturbing some Kremlin sources they didn't want to, but it seems when Dandy Torelli's murder got the nod, the idea of the goodwill visit was dusted off in case anything went wrong at any point thereafter. To cut a long story short, when the *Golovin's* captain set course for the Channel, he had a bundle of sealed orders in his safe ranging from doing nothing to doing what we've seen. Some of these orders matched generic plans Crane already had, plus ones Aubrey brought with her from Russia, and everything was lined up in secret when the *Golovin* anchored off Plymouth. After that, code words in routine messages were enough. That's why there was no chatter."

"You said the goodwill visit was dusted off. What did you mean by that?"

"The goodwill visit was a portmanteau notion that had knocked around the Kremlin for years. The general idea was, if agents can't flee to Russia, why not bring Russia to them? In this case, the *Golovin* got the job of bringing the Motherland within reach of Aubrey for sure and of Crane if it could be done without a fuss. Nothing simpler."

"That's what made it clever. Thanks for finding that out, Tom. I guess it pretty much wraps things up."

"Well, yes and no, Sir. I noticed you didn't mention Mr Dobrynin to Mr Snape and Miss Gulliver."

"That's true. Would you like to tell me why?"

"I read recently, Mr Dobrynin was getting an award for services to education, and in a magazine my wife's dentist takes, there was something about a celebrity party in Hampstead. That doesn't sound like a hunted man's life to me – not hunted by our side, anyway – so it's tempting to think he's been turned. There's no doubt about it, an informant like him with Cyprus connections would be worth a lot to us."

"My thinking, too, Tom, and not just mine. From now on there'll be a shadow in his sunlit life, but it will come from his own side, not ours. You never can tell, he might be lucky. But I shouldn't want to be him if he gets found out."

That was it. Garry set off for the Organisers' Tent, and van Piet pulled on his orange top-coat. He'd call Jackie later. He missed her, but she was away at boarding school, no one was asking for special leave for her, and she wouldn't expect it either. He liked doing drop-off duty. He knew many of the children by name, along with their carers, helpers and parents. There were a lot of things he and Célestine couldn't do for them, they were both sadly aware of that. But if they could make them happy once in a way, they didn't see why they shouldn't.

Acknowledgements

I read about the historical North Sea tidal wave in the German news magazine *Der Spiegel.* The same magazine helped me with Conger's steganography, how to buy Cypriot citizenship, double screening, Glasgow University's super-magnification breakthrough, and the number of mobiles left in London cabs each year. *The Guardian* newspaper put me onto the body bags.

Betty Dodson gave me some prompts for Shayler's Secret. I consulted Rachel Swift's *Women's Pleasure* as well.

Twice I found myself wondering whether I was inventing, recalling, or both. My thanks, anyway, to *Blow Up* and *The Ipcress File* for two fine films that have stayed in the memory.

CB.